HER VOW TO BE HIS DESERT QUEEN

JACKIE ASHENDEN

PREGNANT AT THE PALACE ALTAR

LORRAINE HALL

MILLS & BOON

First published in Great Britain 2023
by Mills & Boon, an imprint of HarperCollins*Publishers* Ltd,
1 London Bridge Street, London, SE1 9GF

www.harpercollins.co.uk

HarperCollins*Publishers*, Macken House, 39/40 Mayor Street Upper, Dublin 1, D01 C9W8, Ireland

ISBN: 978-0-263-30683-5

06/23

HER VOW TO BE
HIS DESERT QUEEN

JACKIE ASHENDEN

MILLS & BOON

To my process.
Without whom I wouldn't have had to write the
beginning of this book three times.
Thanks for nothing!

CHAPTER ONE

Sidonie Sullivan stared, irritated, at the half-pint of lager and packet of pork scratchings sitting on the table in front of her.

'Happy birthday, Sid.' Derek, who was sitting in the booth seat opposite and who'd bought her both the half-pint and the pork scratchings, smiled. 'I know it's not much, but I've got dinner booked at Giovanni's and that's a bit special, don't you think?'

Sidonie smiled back, forcing away the slight twinge of impatience. 'Thanks, Derek. This is...lovely.'

It *was* lovely. Derek was an old school friend, and it was very nice of him to take her out for a birthday dinner, but he was part of a life she'd left behind five years ago when she'd moved to London. A life that didn't bear any resemblance to the life she had now, and one she didn't particularly want to return to.

She was only here in Blackchurch, the little Oxford-shire village she'd grown up in, to pay a visit to her aunt, and then she'd be returning to London the next day, and quite frankly she couldn't wait. Blackchurch was small and insular, and she'd never felt at home there. Plus, Aunt May had always been awful, and time hadn't made her any less so. It was more a duty visit than anything else, since May wasn't in good health and had no one else to check on her.

Not that Sidonie could afford time away from the children's charity she'd started five years earlier. The charity was getting bigger every day, providing opportunities for disadvantaged kids all over the country, and she had plans to take it to Europe too, then maybe the rest of the world. There was always so much to do.

So much so that she'd forgotten it was her birthday until Derek, on hearing she was back for a visit—the village telegraph was apparently very much alive and well—had knocked on her aunt's door and asked Sidonie out.

She hadn't wanted to go—she had emails to answer, a report to write, and a couple of phone calls to make—but Derek had been insistent, and Aunt May, who hadn't been all that thrilled to be visited anyway, had wanted to be left alone to 'watch her shows'. So Sidonie had reluctantly agreed. She couldn't recall the last time she or anyone else had actually celebrated her birthday—certainly her aunt never had—so it had been very nice of Derek to remember.

He *would have.*

The thought came out of nowhere, startling her. How strange for her to think of *him,* after all this time. Not that he was relevant at all right now. He'd left England five years ago and the only communication she'd had since then had been a terse email telling her it would be best if they didn't contact each other again.

So she hadn't. She'd put *him* firmly out of her mind that day, so why she was thinking about him now was anyone's guess.

She smiled determinedly at Derek because, while she wasn't attracted to him in the least, he was a nice man who'd wanted to do something lovely for her and she appreciated it.

'So, Sid,' Derek began.

But she never found out what he'd been going to say because at that moment the pub door banged open and in strode six powerful-looking men wearing black suits, sunglasses, and earpieces. One went straight to the bar to talk to the publican, while the others went systematically around the room getting people to their feet and herding them out of the door.

Sidonie frowned.

'What's going on?' Derek threw a puzzled look in the direction of the black-suited men. 'Is this a movie or something?'

Good question. The men seemed to be some kind of security team, though why on earth they'd be here, in this obscure English pub, she had no idea.

Then quite suddenly, all six of the black-suited men snapped to attention, one of them announcing something in a lyrical language that definitely wasn't English. The other five repeated it like a mantra and then another man strolled into the pub.

And Sidonie's whole world slowed down and stopped.

He was very, *very* tall, with the kind of wide shoulders and broad chest a Greek god would have been proud of, and he moved with all the grace of an apex predator. Which he most certainly was. His face was all sharp planes and angles, with the fierce beauty of a bird of prey, and his sharp black gaze missed nothing.

His dark, handmade suit was immaculate, his white cotton shirt serving only to highlight the burnished bronze of his skin, and he wore power and arrogance as if both had been tailor-made specifically for him.

There was nothing about him that was not beautiful.

In one hand he held a small but perfectly frosted chocolate cupcake with a candle in the centre and in the other a red balloon.

Sidonie felt as if her heart had stopped beating.

It was *him*. It was Khalil ibn Amir al Nazari. The man who'd once been her best friend in all the world. The man she'd fallen in love with and who'd walked away from her five years earlier, leaving her standing alone in a snowy street in London.

She hadn't seen him since.

She'd met him when they were both students at Oxford. He'd been one of the 'Wicked Princes', a group of three young royals infamous among the colleges of the university town. Galen Kouros, Prince of Kalithera. Augustine Solari, Prince of Isavere. And him. Khalil, heir to the throne of Al Da'ira, a small but very rich country near the Red Sea.

She hadn't paid much attention to the Wicked Princes—she was quiet and studious, and on a scholarship too, so she had no time for parties or any of the wild shenanigans they and their friends got up to.

Then one day, she'd been working at her part-time job stacking books in one of the college libraries, when a deep, dark male voice had peremptorily demanded her help, and when she'd turned around she'd found him standing there. Khalil, arrogant and so totally mesmerising she'd lost the power of speech. He'd repeated his question, even more arrogant and demanding than he'd been the first time, and she'd been so shocked and surprised that she'd laughed at him. Of course, then she'd felt terrible, and had apologised, but first he'd stared at her as if she was the most fascinating thing he'd ever seen. Then he'd told her that her apology wasn't necessary and that he should be the one apologising, since he'd been very rude.

That had been the start of their friendship, a strange meeting of opposites: the Prince and the scholarship girl. It shouldn't have worked. She'd been brought up by her working-class aunt, while he'd been brought up a prince. She was quiet and studious, while he was wild, going to all the parties with his friends, and barely attending lectures.

Yet they'd been drawn to each other and had become best friends, staying in contact even after they'd left university.

Or rather, they'd been best friends up until five years ago, when the disaster of that night in Soho had happened, and she'd said those things she should never have said, and he'd walked away from her. Then, a month later, she'd got that email from him telling her that he had no plans to return to England, and that it would better if she didn't contact him again. He hadn't given a reason why.

Not that he had to explain. She knew why.

He'd broken her heart that day, but she refused to let it be a mortal blow. Instead, she changed, armouring herself, guarding herself. Becoming a different person. A person who didn't give her heart so readily to someone who didn't want it.

She never thought she'd see him again, yet here he was, standing arrogantly in the middle of the pub like a god manifesting before his mortal worshippers, staring around until his black gaze finally settled on her.

All the breath left her lungs. There seemed to be no air anywhere in the room.

Derek started to say something but Khalil was already stalking towards them, the balloon bobbing with every step. It would have been amusing if the expression on his beautiful face hadn't been suddenly so utterly intent.

Her heart began to race. She was a rabbit caught in the headlights of a car, unable to move, unable to look away.

Five years since she'd seen him and he was still every bit the same mesmerising, utterly compelling man she remembered from their last meeting in London.

He'd been in England on a state visit, and they'd arranged to meet at a too-loud bar in Soho. That was when he'd broken the news to her that his father had died, and he had to return to Al Da'ira to take the throne. He wouldn't be back for some time, he'd said. Probably years. His country was in trouble, and he needed to be there to help it through the transition in ruler.

She understood. His father had been a terrible king and Khalil's presence was required for the nation's stability. But she'd also been upset at the thought of not seeing him for so long, and had had a couple more Cosmopolitans than she should have, making him promise all kinds of ridiculous things.

But it hadn't been until the time had come to say goodbye, as they'd stood outside the bar in the falling snow, that she'd made that terrible, costly mistake.

In a fit of wild emotion she'd told him she loved him, and as soon as the words were out of her mouth she knew she'd said the wrong thing. Because shock had flared in his dark eyes and then his beautiful face had shuttered, becoming as cold as the snow falling all around them.

He'd been gentle, prying her fingers from where they clutched at his coat, but he hadn't said a single thing in response.

He'd simply turned on his heel and walked away, leaving her standing there alone, her heart slowly shattering to pieces in her chest.

She'd cried all night into her pillow after he'd gone, castigating herself for ruining things between them, because she quite clearly had. He'd never given her any indication that he felt anything for her but friendship, so why she'd told him that she loved him she still couldn't understand. It had been the Cosmopolitans maybe, or the stupid promise she'd written on a serviette and made him sign. Or perhaps it had been simply that raw rush of emotion as she'd stood there looking up in his dark eyes and watching the snow settle in his black hair.

She should have known better than to say it out loud, though. Her aunt had always told her she was too needy and demanding, and it was obvious from Khalil's response to her that he thought so too. Which was confirmed a few weeks later when his email had arrived to tell her it would be easier on both of them if she didn't contact him again.

So she didn't. By that stage the charity she'd started up after leaving university was gathering steam and she'd moved to London, and it was easy to immerse herself in work. Easy to bury the remains of her broken heart and become someone else. Someone with purpose and determination and steel. A strong woman. A woman who didn't cry into her pillow all night because of some man. A woman who needed nothing and no one.

Now, though, despite all of that, her heartbeat was racing the way it always did whenever he was around, and she fought to find the steely determination that had helped her drive her charity to the top, meeting his dark gaze steadily.

It didn't matter that he was back five years after he'd broken her heart.

It didn't matter at all.

'Khalil,' she began, pleased with how level her voice sounded. 'What are—?'

'Get out,' Khalil interrupted. And there was no doubt about who he was talking to, because Derek was on his feet and through the door before Sidonie could get another word out.

Anger prickled over her skin.

So here he was, presumably for her, since there was no other reason for him to be in Blackchurch, having tracked her down after five years of silence. And the first words out of his mouth weren't 'I'm sorry, Sidonie, for walking away'. Or 'I'm sorry for telling you not to contact me again'. No, they were 'Get out' to the one man who'd actually had the decency to take her for a birthday treat.

She wanted to tell him how rude he was and how dared he come here and frighten away the first date she'd had in years? But that would make her sound angry with him. That would make her sound as if she cared, and she didn't.

She was over him. She'd been over him for years.

So she said nothing as he calmly slid into the booth, taking Derek's place as if the poor man hadn't ever been there. He deposited the cupcake on the table before holding the balloon out to her. 'Happy birthday, Sidonie,' he said in his dark, deep voice, as if he'd only been away a couple of days and not five years.

For a second she had no idea what response to make, her brain still trying to process the fact that he was here, in England, in this pub, let alone that he'd just wished her happy birthday as if they were still friends. Then, when the reality of his presence finally hit, despite all her assurances to herself, those hot, angry words filled her mouth anyway, and she had to swallow them down to stop them from coming out.

Shouting at him was pointless. It didn't matter that he'd broken off their friendship as if it had meant nothing. As if *she* meant nothing.

It didn't matter how he treated her; she didn't care. She was successful and happy and didn't need him any more.

Ignoring the anger that sat hot and burning in the pit of her stomach, she also forced down the betraying leap of joy that tightened around her heart. And gave him a cool, measuring look. 'Khalil. This is a surprise. I wasn't expecting to see you, obviously. But I was actually in the middle of a date.' Really, he should know he'd interrupted something. She hadn't been sitting around all these years just waiting for him.

Those dark, winged brows arrowed down. 'A date? With whom?'

It seemed some things hadn't changed. The Oxford colleges had had their fair share of arrogant people, but Khalil's arrogance was really something else. So far, so prince, she'd thought. Yet even his two friends, Galen and Augustine, who were also princes and whom she'd met very briefly a couple of times, weren't as arrogant as he was.

Then she'd found out that Al Da'ira was an absolute monarchy where the rulers were viewed as semi-divine, and their word was law. In that context his arrogance had made sense, though she hadn't put up with it. He'd liked that about her, or so he'd said. He liked that she treated him as an ordinary person, not a prince.

Except the man sitting opposite her now didn't look

like an ordinary person. He didn't look like the friend she remembered either, the intense, brooding young man he'd once been. He'd been like a stormy, dark sea, she'd often thought back then. Full of complex, dangerous currents, and yet when the sun shone through the water there was such lightness and aching beauty. His rare smiles. His compassion. His deeply hidden, wry sense of humour.

None of that was in evidence now, though. The lines of his face were hard and set and cold. He wasn't the sea any more. He was the rock that lay at the bottom of it.

'It was a birthday date,' she explained coolly. 'With Derek.'

'Derek?' Khalil glanced around. 'I see no Derek.'

'No. Because you just rudely ordered him out of the pub.'

'Him? He was in my way.' Khalil gestured insistently with the balloon. 'Take it.'

Her heart gave a tiny jolt that he'd remembered, but she'd told herself she wasn't going to let anything he did or said mean anything, so again she ignored it.

You want it to mean something, though.

No. No, she absolutely did not. She'd got rid of the last remaining feelings she had for him years ago. And if her heart ached and she felt breathless on seeing him now, it was only shock. Nothing more.

However, it seemed silly not to take the balloon, so she reached for it. Only to fight yet another jolt, this time physically as his fingers brushed hers and a familiar spark of electricity leapt between them.

She still remembered the first time she'd felt it, the night Khalil had thrown her a birthday party for her twenty-first. She'd never had a party before, because her aunt had never celebrated her birthday, still less a surprise party.

It had been the most wonderful night. She didn't have many friends, but he'd invited all of them, plus his own bigger, wilder crowd. There had been lots of music and laughter, and dancing. There had been balloons. There had been a cake. Everyone had sung her 'Happy Birthday', and she'd nearly cried because it had been so lovely.

Her first birthday party ever and it had been a huge success.

Much later that night, Khalil had pulled her into his arms and danced with her, and she'd become aware, all at once, of his warmth. The hard-muscled plane of his chest. His scent. She'd always thought of him as beautiful, dazzling even. But that was the night she'd realised she wanted him.

An echo of that old longing hit her now, making her hand jerk and the balloon bob violently in response. Luckily, he didn't seem to notice.

'Thank you,' she said, with what she hoped was some degree of calm. 'Both for the balloon and the cupcake. But really, you were inexcusably rude to Derek and I should go and make sure—'

'I will deal with it,' Khalil interrupted with the same arrogance she remembered from years ago. Or maybe not the same. There was a hard edge to it now that hadn't been there before.

He turned his head and instantly one of his men was there. He issued a curt command in the lyrical Arabic dialect of his home country, and the man darted away.

Sidonie frowned. 'What did you say to him?'

'I told him to go and find your Derek and pay him a suitable amount of money for the inconvenience of ending your date early.' Khalil smiled, his teeth flashing white against his bronzed skin, but his black eyes remained sharp as obsidian. 'Do not worry.'

That smile wasn't the same either. There was no warmth in it at all. A tiger's smile.

He is not the man you knew. Not any more.

'So, what are you doing here?' she asked in the most neutral voice possible, repressing the odd shiver that went through her. 'Apart from being terribly rude to a friend of mine, of course. I didn't know you were in the country.' She wasn't going to point out exactly how long it had been since he'd last contacted her, because naturally she hadn't been keeping track.

Khalil didn't reply. Instead, he frowned down at the cupcake. Then abruptly he held out his hand and one of the men in black suits sprang over and put a lighter in it. Khalil didn't look at him, proceeding to light the candle on her cupcake before holding his hand out again so the same man could take the lighter from it. Then he leaned back in the booth seat, powerful arms resting across the back of it, and fixed her with an intense stare.

'Blow,' he ordered.

Sidonie blinked. 'What?'

'The candle.' He didn't take his gaze from hers. 'Blow it out.'

Another shiver whispered over her skin as memories slowly filtered through her head. Of the way he'd used to look at her, the way he was doing now. Intense and focused, as if what she had to say was vital and he didn't want to miss a word.

He'd always had the ability to make her feel she was interesting and special, as if what she said was worth hearing, an addictive thing to the kid who'd lost her parents at eight and had to go and live with her father's cold and unemotional sister. Aunt May, who'd made it very clear to Sidonie that she was looking after her only as a duty to her brother. That Sidonie was an imposition she hadn't looked for and didn't want, but took anyway out of the goodness of her heart.

It's still addictive...

No, absolutely not. She wasn't going to fall into that trap again. She was a successful businesswoman with a charity dedicated to helping disadvantaged children, and she didn't need his or anyone else's validation, still less his. She'd graduated from Oxford with honours, had put all her drive and determination into making a difference to orphaned children's lives, and she wasn't lonely these days. She was secure and confident in herself, no matter how first her aunt and then Khalil's abandonment had made her feel otherwise.

Shoving her physical reaction to him away, Sidonie let out a silent breath and held his gaze. Back when they'd been friends, she'd never let him get away with his high-handed behaviour, and she certainly wasn't going to let him get away with it now.

She raised a brow. 'Only if you sing "Happy Birthday".'

'Very well,' he said and without hesitation began to sing, his deep voice making each and every word sound like an intimate caress. 'Happy birthday to you, happy birthday to you, happy birthday dear Sidonie, happy birthday to you.'

She shouldn't have told him to sing. There were too many memories associated with him singing her 'Happy Birthday'. Memories of the night he'd danced with her, and she didn't need those in her head.

'Now blow,' he ordered once he'd finished.

Arguing about blowing out a candle was ridiculous, and after all, it *was* her birthday, so she leaned forward and blew, watching as the flame flickered and went out.

Then she straightened. 'So, I guess I should be honoured that you—'

'You don't remember, do you?'

Sidonie blinked again, derailed by the unexpected question. 'Remember? Remember what?'

'How you told me that if you had not married by the time your thirtieth birthday came around, then you would marry me.'

A flush of heat swept through her, closely followed by a tide of ice, and all the cool demands she'd been going to make, such as what he was doing here and why, abruptly vanished from her head.

That night in Soho, that was what he was talking about. The night she didn't want to remember. Not the words that had come out of her mouth, that had driven him away, and definitely not the stained serviette she'd pulled out from under her cocktail glass and used to write down the most ridiculous promise. A promise she'd made him sign.

Heat worked its way up her throat, over her jaw and into her cheeks, and there was nothing she could do to stop it. The curse of being a redhead meant fine white skin that betrayed every single emotion. And, of course, he'd see it too. He missed nothing.

'It was on that last night in London,' Khalil went on smoothly, still watching her. Clearly, he had no problem with remembering it. 'My father had just died and we met for a drink in Soho. I told you I didn't know when I could come back for a visit, so you made me promise to return at least by the time you were thirty. You also promised that if you weren't married by then, you'd marry me.'

The heat felt like a fire now, burning her skin, the awful, awful memories of that night and how she'd humiliated herself so clear in her head. They'd talked of Al Da'ira and all the changes Khalil would make now he was King, changes he'd often discussed with her when they'd been at university. They'd both been passionate about wanting to make people's lives better, she already with plans for a charity, he with his plans for when he took the crown.

He'd told her that night that he would obviously need to marry at some stage and that was when she'd got it into her head that he could marry her. It had been the cocktails making her brave, the powerful feeling in her heart and the fact that he was leaving that had driven her to write it down as a promise. A vow.

It seemed so stupid now. So naïve. So...desperate. She wasn't that woman any longer and hadn't been for years.

So she ignored the blush burning in her cheeks and stared back into his dark eyes. 'Oh, right, yes. And wasn't there some kind of...?' She pretended to grasp for the memory. 'I wrote it down and made you sign something, didn't I?'

If he knew she was lying, he gave no sign. 'Indeed.' Reaching into the breast pocket of his suit jacket, he withdrew a dog-eared piece of paper. 'I think this is what you are talking about.' He laid the paper down gently beside the cupcake and unfolded it, his gaze somehow growing even sharper.

She couldn't help it—she glanced down at it. A stained serviette still with the slightly pink ring mark from her Cosmo, and her handwriting, untidy and rushed.

Khalil said nothing.

Half reluctant, half in the grip of a kind of horrified

fascination, she picked it up and yes, there it was, all her embarrassing need writ large in black ballpoint. And there, damningly, at the end, her own scrawled signature beside his, because she knew she'd never change her mind. Never in a million years...

She stared at the serviette for a long minute. Then she did what she always did whenever he did or said something preposterous.

She laughed.

Khalil waited patiently for Sidonie to stop laughing, watching her green eyes light up and her pale, creamy, freckle-dotted skin flush.

He remembered that laugh. Remembered the way it lit her up inside. Remembered how it had used to make him laugh too, which he'd always found curious, as he'd never had anything to laugh about.

It had been so long since he'd seen her. So long since he'd heard that laugh. So long since he'd laughed at anything himself. He'd almost forgotten how.

If he'd still been her friend, he would have laughed too. But he wasn't her friend, not any more, and so he only looked at her, drinking in the sight.

She was different. He'd been able to tell the moment he'd walked in.

Her fire-red hair was piled up on top of her head in her usual bun—he remembered her sticking a pen in it to hold it in place when they'd used to study together—but it wasn't messy the way he remembered it. It was neat and tidy, not a hair out of place. No stray curls falling down around her ears and the back of her neck, softening her lovely, heart-shaped face.

She wasn't in one of the colourful dresses she'd always worn either. Tonight she was in severe black trousers and a crisp white shirt, a black jacket folded neatly on the seat beside her.

She didn't smile at him, not the way she'd used to. Those green eyes of hers had been nothing but hostile ever since he'd sat down, and even the way she was laughing right now had an edge to it that held no amusement.

Are you surprised? After you ignored her for five years?

He hadn't ignored her. He'd cut her off completely. Which made coming back to England a gamble, but one he'd been willing to make.

Yet he'd been away a long time and, with the memory of their last meeting echoing in the space between them, this had never been going to be easy.

It had to be done, though.

He was here to hold her to her promise. She had to be his wife.

He'd wanted her even back when they'd been friends. Right from the first moment he saw her standing in the stacks in the college library, her red hair glowing in a shaft of dusty sunlight, her skin pale as porcelain, her eyes green as grass.

But an affair with her had never been on the cards. She'd been nothing but sunshine and warmth, while he'd been all darkness and doubt, and he hadn't wanted any part of his darkness to touch her. Friendship was all he could do and friends they were.

Until that night in Soho when she'd told him she loved him, and he knew he couldn't be friends with her any longer.

He'd been in shock that night, not expecting her confession. No one had ever said those words to him before, not one person, and to hear them from her...

Every part of him had wanted to take her in his arms and cover her mouth, kiss her senseless, tell her that he loved her too, that he didn't want to leave her. He never wanted to leave her.

Except his father had died and his country was in turmoil, and he'd *had* to leave. He had to take the throne he was heir to. He was responsible for protecting his people and it wasn't a duty he could walk away from.

So he'd walked away from her instead.

Love wasn't permitted for kings; he'd learned that from an early age. Emotion in general wasn't permitted. Kings had to make hard decisions, they had to do terrible things to protect people, and for him to make those decisions and do those terrible things he had to be hard too. Harder than stone.

It had been necessary to walk away from her. He couldn't be the man he'd been in England, Sidonie's friend. He couldn't be a man at all. He had to be a king. And so that was what he'd become.

He'd told her he wouldn't be coming back to England, and that she shouldn't contact him again, because he'd had to. It had been harsh, but he hadn't wanted her to live in hope he'd ever return her feelings, that he'd ever return, full stop.

It was always the sharpest cuts that healed the fastest.

He'd never thought he'd go back on that decision, either, not until the question of marriage and heirs had been brought up by his advisors. Not until he'd looked at the list of potential queens that had been suggested, and he'd seen they were all women with families who wanted position and influence in his court, perpetuating the cycle of intrigue and corruption once again.

He'd always intended to rule differently from his father, and his time in England with Sidonie had taught him about the power of laughter. Of happiness. Of hope. He wanted that for his people after the trauma of his father's reign, and, while he couldn't provide that laughter and happiness and hope himself, his queen could.

A queen like Sidonie.

He'd been toying with that idea while he'd looked over marriage contracts, which had then got him thinking about the promise Sidonie had written on that serviette. The one she'd made him sign.

It had come to him then, blindingly, that the answer had been staring him in the face all this time. The woman who'd taught him how to laugh, how to enjoy the simple pleasures in life, how to be an ordinary person, the woman who'd given him a taste of happiness... She could be his queen. She could bring all those precious qualities he'd once admired, her honesty and empathy, and warmth, to Al Da'ira. She could help him bring joy back to a country which had been crushed under the heel of a tyrant.

He'd hadn't wanted to contact her again. Taking his crown and cutting out the corruption that had been endemic in his court had turned him from mere stone into granite, and he wasn't the young man she remembered, the friend she'd once had. He'd wanted her to have only good memories of him.

But making the hard decisions was what was what being a king meant. It also meant living with the consequences so his people would have a better life. Balancing the needs of the few with the needs of the many. And the many needed Sidonie.

They needed her laughter. Her brightness. Her optimism and her empathy. Her ability to relate to people from all walks of life.

So he'd made the decision to hold her to the promise she'd written, and once he decided something, it happened. He never regretted and he never doubted. Certainty was strength in a king, another thing his mother had taught him long ago.

Sidonie would likely refuse, especially considering how he'd broken off their friendship, so he was going to have to convince her. He wouldn't accept a 'no'.

It would have been easier to do things the old way, the way of his ancestors from centuries past who simply put their chosen bride over the front of their horse and rode off with her. But, since he lived in the modern world and that was frowned upon, he'd have to go about getting her agreement instead.

Sidonie's laugh had wound down, and she was wiping her eyes, though he suspected that was for effect. 'I'm sorry, Khalil,' she said. 'For a minute there I thought you were serious.'

He did not smile. 'I am serious.'

'No, you're not.' All the laughter drained abruptly from her face. 'This is a joke.'

'You were not joking when you wrote it,' he pointed out.

'I was drunk when I wrote it.'

'You had had two Cosmopolitans and were mildly tipsy at best.'

He thought she might laugh again, one of her delightful, bubbling laughs, but she didn't. Instead her green eyes narrowed. 'You can't possibly expect to hold me to that.'

Interesting. She was…harder than he remembered. Sharper too. Not the passionate, warm woman he remembered. What had happened in the past five years to make her assume this…veneer? Because something had. Well, he'd find out. Once she was his wife, they'd have time to discuss it.

'I can,' he said flatly. 'And I will. You signed it. I'm sure I could even have my lawyers prove it is a legal contract that you are obliged to honour.' He didn't want to force the issue or hold a legal threat over her head, but the fact remained that he needed a queen. A royal marriage to give his people something joyful after all the years of his father's dark reign. And his queen had to be her.

Apart from what she herself would bring to the role, she also had no ties to his country, no family trying to gain influence, no political or business affiliations that would cause suspicion in the various factions in his court. She was an outsider with no previous history, which also made her someone most people would accept.

Sidonie's pretty features were almost hard. 'I have lawyers too, Khalil.'

He tilted his head, surveying her, noting the glitter in her eyes and the firm line of her soft mouth. Somehow she'd found steel. He wasn't sure he liked it. Where had the Sidonie he remembered gone? The Sidonie he'd been able to talk to about anything and mostly had, except for a couple of dark instances that he didn't want to remember himself, let alone talk about? The Sidonie who'd steadfastly ignored the fact that he was a prince? Who'd dragged him along to the movies and bought him popcorn. Who'd made him hold her shopping bags as if he was a servant while she tried on clothes. Who'd laughed at him when he'd told her he never carried a wallet because he always had someone to handle payments for him, and who'd then taught him how to use a debit card.

Back then he hadn't known why any of that had fascinated him so much. He'd only known she was beautiful and interesting, and that she seemed to like him. He'd never encountered that before. He'd had Augustine and Galen, of course, his friends and fellow princes, and they seemed to like him too. Yet in a way, Augustine and Galen and he had been forced together because they were all princes.

Sidonie, on the other hand, was nothing like him. She wasn't royal or rich, didn't come from nobility or money. She was friendly and warm, bright and sunny, while he'd been dark and scarred from the things he'd had to do to become heir. Despite that though, she'd seen something in him that had made her choose to be his friend.

That Sidonie would never have mentioned lawyers.

He should have paid more attention to what she'd been doing these last five years, but he'd cut off contact with her for a reason. He hadn't wanted to be distracted by the past. Not when he had the difficult politics of his nation to handle.

Not that there was any point thinking about that now.

'Then by all means engage them and we will fight this in the courts.' He held her gaze. 'I hope you have deep pockets.'

For some reason the flush that had crept through her cheeks deepened. 'You can't mean this. Five years ago you told me not to contact you, and yet suddenly you're here, shoving some ridiculous thing I wrote when I was drunk in my face, and demanding that I marry you? That's insane, Khalil.'

It probably was from her point of view. Still, he wasn't budging.

'It is not insane,' he said. 'I am in full possession of all my faculties, I assure you. There were reasons I told you not to contact me, but things have changed.'

'What things? Changed how?'

'Al Da'ira is more stable politically now, and I need a wife.'

'But I—'

'We can discuss that later. You made me a promise, Sidonie, and you will honour it.'

'And if I don't? What? You'll take me to court?'

Each word was spiked with something serrated, falling like an icy-edged little snowflake, cold against his skin, and Khalil felt something stir deep inside him.

He stilled, a ripple of shock arrowing down his spine.

It had been years since he'd felt that part of him stir. The hunger that had helped him win his crown, the old blood that ran in his veins, a poisonous gift from his father. After his coronation he'd buried that part of himself and he'd thought it had stayed buried.

Apparently not. Apparently all you need for it to wake is a challenge.

That may be, but he was done with challenges now. He was the King, he had nothing to prove, and certainly not where Sidonie was concerned. The cost was too high should that part of himself wake again. It had to stay frozen. It *had* to.

Khalil stared at her. He couldn't afford resistance. He needed a wife and heirs, and his people needed a queen untainted by the labyrinthine politics of his father's reign.

He could go back to the list of potential candidates his advisors had put forward and choose one of them. Or, if he wanted to find a woman from outside Al Da'ira, he'd no doubt find one—he'd never had any issues with finding women who wanted him.

But he didn't want just any woman. He wanted the woman who'd taught him what happiness had felt like, because if she could do that for him, then she could do it for his people.

'Yes,' he said coolly. 'That is what I said.'

She didn't flinch, another sign of the steel she'd somehow acquired. 'So, you're going to force me to marry you. Is that what you're saying?'

She is not the same Sidonie you knew.

No. But still, it had only been five years. She could not have changed *so* much in five years.

'It will not involve force.' He kept his voice level. 'You wanted to marry me, remember? If you had not found a husband by the time you were thirty, you would marry me—that is what you said. You were very, very definite.'

'But I wasn't—'

'You wrote that promise yourself,' he went on relentlessly. 'You insisted. Because you wanted me to hold you to it when the time came.'

She opened her mouth then shut it again, her gaze flickering. The flush in her pale cheeks had crept down her lovely white throat.

She remembered that night as well as he, about how they'd been talking of him taking the throne and what it would mean for his country. He'd mentioned that he'd have to marry at some stage, and that was when she'd said that if he couldn't find someone he liked, and she was still unmarried by thirty, he could marry her.

He'd thought it was a joke at first, but there had been something intense in her eyes as she'd said it. Then she'd pulled out her cocktail serviette and had written her promise to him, signing it and getting him to sign it too.

He'd wanted to tell her that she didn't need to make him sign some ridiculous promise. He would have married her right then and there. He knew how lonely her childhood had been and how much she'd wanted a family of her own. He knew all about the awful aunt who'd brought her up and resented every second of it.

But he was the heir to the throne of Al Da'ira, not the ordinary man he'd wished so passionately he could be in that moment. And he couldn't give her that future.

He'd loved those years in England with her, but they were never going to be anything more than an idyll. A brief moment of sunshine between storms.

He had a country to rule and a crown to wear, and the king he'd been brought up to be had nothing to do with the man he'd become in England. The two were incompatible. She deserved more anyway. He wasn't capable of giving her the kind of life she needed, and he didn't want to be Hades to her Persephone, dragging her down into his Underworld.

Yet because she was his friend, and he would have given her the moon if she'd asked for it, he'd signed her serviette. And he'd never thought he'd return to make good on his promise, yet the needs of his people outweighed all other concerns.

He had to convince her somehow.

'Well, I didn't mean it,' Sidonie said now, still cool. 'So you can take that ridiculous contract and—'

'Sidonie,' he interrupted, because he was tired of sitting in this sticky, musty English pub. They could have this argument later, in cleaner, nicer surroundings, when the shock of his sudden arrival had worn off. 'You must consider my proposal. I insist. Perhaps there is something you need from me that I could give you in return?'

'I don't need anything—'

'Think on it. In the meantime,' he gestured at the cupcake, 'eat your birthday cake and then we will leave.'

There were tiny green sparks in her eyes. 'Leave? What do you mean, leave?'

Khalil was normally a patient man. The heir to the throne wasn't permitted to marry until they'd been crowned, and he'd had to wait longer than most because his father had taken his time dying. Then, after his own coronation, he'd had to tidy up the mess Amir had left. It had all taken time. Too much time. He wasn't getting any younger and the business of heirs needed to be seen to now the political situation had been handled, and he didn't want to wait any more.

He'd expected some resistance when he'd arrived, but he'd thought that she'd at least be open to discussion, and it was irritating to get a flat 'no' immediately. However, her resistance wasn't insurmountable. There were ways he could make her more receptive to him. He hadn't, for example, explored the extent of their physical chemistry yet. He'd wanted to, but he'd never crossed that line with her, and not because she didn't want him, because she had. No, he'd decided it was better not to start something he couldn't finish, and so he'd kept his distance.

If she agreed to be his wife, there was no need for that now.

'I mean,' he said calmly, 'that we will leave England and return to Al Da'ira.'

Shock rippled across her face. 'Leave England? But you can't be...'

He didn't wait for her to finish. He didn't want her thinking too hard about this or arguing further. So he leaned forward, took the balloon from her fingers and held it out wordlessly. One of his security detail sprang to take it from his hand and then did the same when he picked the cupcake up and held that out too. When they were both taken care of he rose, stepped from the booth, and held out a hand. 'Come, *ya hayati*. We can have this discussion on the way to the helicopter.'

'The helicopter?' Her self-possession wavered and she stared at him as if she'd never seen him before in her entire life. And to be fair she probably hadn't. She'd only seen the man. She'd never seen the King.

A good thing, in that case. Better she saw him as he was now rather than thinking he was still the same man he'd once been.

He wasn't her friend any longer. He couldn't afford to be.

The King was merciless, pitiless. The King protected his country with his life and so he had to be harder than the rock his palace was carved out of. Harder than iron. Hard so the enemies of his country would shatter dashing themselves against him while he remained strong, a bulwark for his people.

To them *he* was the power and the glory, to be feared and obeyed. If not, there was the possibility that the unrest that had already cost his country so much would return, and he could not permit that. Not again.

But you don't want her to fear you. Fear wasn't supposed to be part of this.

No, and it wouldn't. If he had to take the time to convince her of the rightness of this marriage, then he would have to take the time. He wasn't his father. He wasn't.

'Yes, the helicopter,' he said. 'I have another birthday surprise for you.'

Except it was clear that she didn't want any more birthday surprises, because her beautiful green eyes turned sharp as broken glass, and her delectably soft-looking mouth firmed in a way that was most un-Sidonie-like.

'No,' she said flatly. 'I am not going anywhere with you.'

CHAPTER TWO

KHALIL REGARDED HER impassively for a couple of moments. Then, without a word, he turned on his heel and walked out of the door.

She was still staring after him, the anger that had been steadily building in response to his ridiculous demand knotting inside her, when two of his security detail approached her booth. They said nothing, merely stood to attention on either side of it, and it took her a full minute to realise that they were waiting for her.

For a second all she could do was sit there seething. Apparently, after presenting her with that ridiculous promise she could barely remember writing, let alone signing, he assumed she'd follow obediently. That she'd say yes and do whatever he wanted. Fly off in his stupid helicopter to Al Da'ira.

Perhaps the Sidonie of five years ago, desperately in love with a man so far out of her league he may as well have been on Pluto, would have done so. That Sidonie would have fallen gratefully into his arms and let him take her anywhere.

But she wasn't that Sidonie any more. Now she was busy and her life was full. She had friends and colleagues, and Mr Sparkle, her cat. She didn't need him.

The two men standing on either side of her booth didn't

move and it was clear they weren't going to leave until she did. She was very tempted to keep sitting there purely because Khalil expected her to follow him, but, since she didn't want to cause any trouble for his men—it wasn't their fault their king was an arrogant idiot—and giving Khalil a piece of her mind was far too attractive, she got to her feet and walked briskly out of the pub, the men beside the booth hurrying after her.

Outside there was quite a commotion.

The pub faced onto a large village green and sitting in the middle of the green was a sleek black helicopter. A crowd of small children was standing near by gazing in awe at it, and Sidonie found herself staring as Khalil strode straight over to them. He smiled and crouched down, digging into his pockets as he did so and bringing something out, handing whatever it was to the awestruck children. Then he said something and they all scattered like a flock of seagulls, whooping and shouting as they did so. All the while the black-clad security men gently ushered a few gawking adults away from the helicopter as the rotors began to spin.

She came to a stop, staring at him, watching the hard, sharp lines of his face soften as he spoke with the children. And, despite everything she'd told herself, her heart twisted behind her ribs. Just for a moment he'd looked like Khal, the man who'd once been her best friend. The man whose smiles had lit up her world and whose deep, soft laugh had made even the depths of winter feel like summer.

But as the children scattered the warmth left his expression and his features hardened. He rose to his full height and strode over to the helicopter. There, he finally paused and glanced in her direction, and she felt one of the security guys grab her elbow. Then, much to her shock, she found herself being ushered firmly towards the helicopter.

'Wait,' she said breathlessly, more startled than anything else. 'I said I didn't want to—'

But everything got lost beneath the noise of the rotors and then she momentarily lost the power of speech as the man holding her handed her over to Khalil, whose strong fingers closed around her elbow. Even through the light cotton of her shirt she could feel the warmth of his skin, his grip firm and assured, sending shivers through her.

It had been years since she'd been this close to him, years since he'd touched her, and she found herself unable to pull away as he guided her into the sleek machine with effortless strength, sitting her down in a seat of soft black leather. A headset was put on her and her seatbelt buckled. Then the door was being closed and he was beside her, speaking to the pilot in Arabic, then the whole thing shuddered before lifting off into the air.

What are you doing? You weren't supposed to be going anywhere with him, remember?

She stared at the seat in front of her, trying to get some oxygen into her suddenly starving lungs, and her brain, which had somehow disengaged the moment he'd taken her elbow, into gear again.

What was wrong with her? She *hadn't* wanted to go with him. What she'd been going to do was give him a piece of her mind then go to find Derek and continue with the date, not follow Khalil obediently. Yet…the moment he'd grasped her elbow she'd been like a kitten taken by the scruff of the neck, relaxing into his grip as if there was nowhere else she'd wanted to be.

And now it was too late to get away from him. They were in the air.

A bolt of something that wasn't quite fear shot through her, and not because she was afraid of where he was taking her, or even of him. No, she was afraid of what being close to him after all this time might do to her.

You can't let him hurt you...not again.

No, she couldn't. That email he'd sent her, cutting her off and dismissing their friendship as if it had never been, had devastated her, reminding her of the day she'd lost her parents with the sheer abruptness of it.

Of course, she knew why he'd sent it. She'd ruined their friendship by telling him she loved him. Her own fault, naturally. She'd always been too emotionally demanding, as her aunt had always said.

Except she'd thought he was different. He'd never made her feel emotionally needy or too demanding. Even when she'd forgotten herself at times and got angry with him, he'd simply let her say her piece and then discuss it with her. He'd never told her she was being ridiculous or threatened her with being left at an orphanage the way her aunt had.

Apparently, though, he hadn't been different that night, and now he was back as if he hadn't broken her heart, telling her things had changed, and he wanted to marry her, and she was just expected to accept it?

Was he actually out of his mind?

Anger simmered inside her once again, edging out that not-quite-fear, but she tried to ignore it. She didn't want him to know that he'd hurt her, because she didn't want him still to matter.

He does matter, though. You can't deny it. You wouldn't be so angry otherwise.

No. Her anger was just a reflex because she didn't like being ordered around. Once, he'd mattered to her more than anyone or anything in the entire world, but not now. She might still be attracted to him admittedly, but nothing more.

'I thought I said I *didn't* want to go anywhere with you,' she said coolly.

'You did say that.' His voice was calm, his posture relaxed as he leaned back in his seat. 'Yet you seemed to have no problem getting into the helicopter.'

The sun was going down, long streams of fading light glossing his black hair. She was conscious of his nearness, one powerful thigh almost touching hers, and she could smell his warm, spicy, familiar scent. Sandalwood and cloves, and the musky, masculine scent that was all his own.

He was so very beautiful...

She couldn't stop yet another shiver. No matter what she told herself about how he didn't matter any more, she was still as mesmerised by him now as she had been the first moment in the library when she'd heard that deep, dark voice of his behind her, asking a question. And she'd turned around to answer it...

As if he knew exactly what she was thinking, his hard mouth curved.

He looked exceptionally pleased with himself.

'Smugness doesn't suit you, Khalil,' she said, ignoring her simmering anger. 'Didn't you listen to me when I said no?'

He raised one winged brow. 'Were you forced at gunpoint? I do not think so.'

Well, even five years ago he hadn't been quite *this* confident.

Being a king did not suit him either, she decided.

'You should have asked me if I wanted to come,' she said. 'And you didn't.'

'You could have walked away at any time.' His gaze settled on her. 'And you didn't.'

She wanted to tell him he was wrong, that of course she could have walked away, but the words suddenly felt slippery and hard to grasp. Her whole world seemed to be consumed by that look in his eyes. It was so familiar, as if she was the only thing worth looking at in the entire universe. God, how she'd loved that. Loved it with her whole heart.

Those five years she'd spent as his friend had been the happiest of her life. She'd become someone new when she met him, someone brighter and more vivid, someone interesting, someone…extraordinary.

And you remember how it was when he left.

Oh, she did. It had felt as if she'd lost part of her soul. As if he'd taken all her passion and joy and optimism with him when he'd left, leaving her with only the worst parts of herself. The fear and the anger and the grief.

She'd been in a dark place after that, and it had only been sheer determination and the needs of her charity that had stopped her from succumbing to the pain and falling into the darkness. She wasn't going back there, not ever.

Turning away would be an admission of weakness, but she couldn't stand the intensity in his eyes, or the gravitational force of his physical charisma, so she glanced out of the window at the landscape unrolling beneath them instead, pretending it was an idle look, nothing more.

'You should have talked to me first.' She smoothed the fine black wool of her trousers.

'I did talk to you first.'

'That was not a discussion.'

There was no response, and she couldn't help glancing back, only to find that his dark, disturbing gaze hadn't moved. 'Do not be afraid, *ya hayati,*' he said, his voice softer and quieter. 'You know I will not hurt you.'

Too late for that, she wanted to say. But she didn't.

She smoothed the fabric of her trousers yet again, trying to find her equilibrium. 'Purely out of interest, why are you so set on marrying me? You must have more suitable candidates surely?'

Again, he was silent, his gaze just as enigmatic as it had been seconds earlier. 'I think now is not the time for that conversation. We will talk more about that when we get there.'

Briefly Sidonie considered arguing, but he'd always been a stubborn man and she suspected he'd be absolutely impossible now. Besides, getting emotional never helped anything—she'd learned that all too well. Her aunt had hated any what she termed 'fusses'. Best to keep her head as she had the moment he'd walked into the pub.

'And where is there?' she enquired. 'Surely we're not flying all the way to Al Da'ira in your helicopter?'

The intensity had died out of his eyes and he was now regarding her with a certain detached amusement. 'No. I have changed my mind. I am taking you out to dinner instead.'

Surprise rippled through her. 'Dinner?'

'We have not seen each other for some time and you have doubts. Therefore we need to talk and I did not want to talk in that pub. There are more pleasant places to discuss our marriage, so it is to one of them that we are going. Also, it is your birthday.'

'Our' marriage, he'd said. As if it was already a fore-

gone conclusion. As if she had no say in this whatsoever. It reminded her of the day her parents had died, after her aunt had collected her from school, told her the awful news, and had brought her back home, even though it wasn't her home any longer. May had instructed her to collect her things, because Sidonie would be coming to live with her. The look on her aunt's face as she'd said it had been pure resignation, and Sidonie had known then and there that her aunt hadn't wanted to be saddled with her. But, since May had been her only living relative, neither of them had had a choice.

'Keep carrying on like that and I'll drop you at the nearest orphanage,' May had told her once, when Sidonie had had a tantrum about something small. *'The only reason you're here at all is because I had a duty to your father. But don't think I can't change my mind.'*

Sidonie had never thought that. In fact, she'd lived in fear of it, making sure she wasn't demanding or bothersome. Being careful not to cause any 'fuss'. She toed the line, giving her aunt no reason to complain.

It had been hard, but then again, she'd been a child and hadn't had a choice about any of it. It was either her aunt or a foster home and she hadn't wanted that either.

The memory made anger gather into a tight, hot ball, shot through with jagged edges of hurt, but she calmly folded her hands over it, keeping it inside. 'And where is dinner?'

This time his smile touched his dark eyes briefly, a flash of his old warmth, and her heart gave a little quiver in her chest. 'I thought we'd have dinner in Paris.'

For the second time in an hour, Sidonie found herself blinking at him. Paris? He was taking her to Paris?

She fought to find her voice. 'In that case it's a pity I don't have my passport.'

'You do,' he said. 'I had my staff retrieve it. Your cat will also be taken care of.'

That hot ball squeezed tight inside her. 'But I have work—'

'I will contact your supervisor and inform them that you will not be there tomorrow,' Khalil interrupted smoothly. 'Do not worry.'

Shock at the sheer gall of the man stole her breath. He'd somehow found out where she lived and got her passport, had her cat taken care of, and now he thought he could ring her 'supervisor' and tell them she wouldn't be there. As if she were nothing more than a chess piece he could move around whenever he liked, with no thought to her feelings.

Something prickled at the backs of her eyes, but it surely couldn't be tears. She didn't cry about anything these days. It didn't matter that he was treating her as if she was a stranger he didn't particularly care about. Because she didn't care either.

She didn't care about him.

'I'm sure you didn't used to be this arrogant,' she said. 'What happened?'

His gaze glittered in the setting sun. 'I became a king, Sidonie.'

A creeping sense of dislocation hit her in that moment. He looked the same as she remembered, his face with all those beautifully carved planes and angles so familiar to her. The face of her once best friend. Yet there was a hardness to his strong jaw, a firmness to his mouth, a sharp intensity in his eyes.

He *was* a king. And it had changed him.

You aren't the same and neither is he.

That was true. She'd changed in the past five years, and she couldn't expect him to have stayed the same. Especially not since he'd been on the throne. The friend she remembered, who'd been puzzled by the existence of debit cards and then had been delighted when she'd shown him to use one, who'd been arrogant and yet had waited patiently outside a department-store changing room holding five shopping bags so she could try on clothes, who'd been intense and passionate about wanting to make the lives of his people better, encouraging her in her own dreams of starting a charity, had gone.

The man at her side looked iron-hard, and there was no passion at all in his dark, cold eyes. A stranger's eyes.

Perhaps she needed to start thinking of him like that now. As a stranger. It would certainly mean less hurt for her as well as helping her to keep her distance.

Khalil raised a brow. 'Lost for words? Surely not.'

She swallowed, her mouth suddenly dry. If she was going to think of him as a stranger then here she was, in a helicopter, being taken to Paris, essentially kidnapped by a man she didn't know. A man who was a king, who apparently had taken it into his head to marry her.

He wouldn't hurt her—not physically at least—and she wasn't afraid of him in that way. But she was afraid of being swept away from the life she'd built for herself. A successful life with important work and people who depended on and needed her. She didn't want to leave it. She couldn't leave it.

You will have to resist him.

The words whispered through her head, and she took a quick, silent breath, conscious of his intense stare. He was so very beautiful.

But no, resisting him was easy. All she had to do was think of how much it had hurt when he'd walked away and how she never wanted to open herself up to that level of pain again.

There. Easy.

'Not lost for words. I'm just considering what to say next, because you do understand that I have no supervisor, don't you?'

His expression remained impassive, but she thought she saw a flicker of surprise in his eyes, which sent an odd little ripple of satisfaction through her.

What had he thought she'd been doing these last five years? That she'd just be sitting around on her hands mourning him?

'Are you working for yourself, then?' he asked, the surprise gone as if it had never been.

'You must have forgotten the charity I started up,' she said acidly. 'Remember? We talked about it a few months before you left.'

'Yes,' he said expressionlessly. 'I remember.'

'Well, it's grown a lot since then and I have many people depending on me. If I'm not going to be back in London before tomorrow, I will need to make some calls.'

'I see.' The words sounded very neutral and yet she knew they were not. There were undertones in his voice, a thread of yet more surprise perhaps, or annoyance— she didn't know which.

The satisfaction that she'd knocked his seemingly unassailable confidence deepened. 'You didn't know, did you?' This time it was her turn to raise a brow. 'Perhaps you should have investigated that before you came back. Contrary to what you might think, I actually have a life of my own and it's a very successful one, thank you very much.'

Khalil's expression remained as impassive as ever. 'Clearly,' he said.

'In fact,' she went on, since she might as well, 'I bet there are many other things you don't know about me, Khalil.' She paused. 'Or should that be Your Majesty?'

Sparks glittered in his eyes just then, and she wasn't sure if it was the last rays of the setting sun catching them or something else, but it suddenly felt as if all the remaining air in the helicopter had been sucked out of it.

His gaze roamed over her face, studying her as if he'd never seen her before in his life, and she was once again suddenly and painfully aware of him. Of the lithe strength of his body and the pull of his trousers across his powerful thighs. Of his warmth. Of the bronze skin of his throat and the pulse that beat there, strong and steady.

The night of her birthday he'd pulled her into his arms for a dance. She'd never been that close to him before. She'd never been that close to any man before, let alone one so tall. He'd felt hard and hot, and her heart had been beating so fast. She hadn't known what it was she was feeling, at first. Then she'd understood...

Her heart was beating that fast now; she could hear it resounding in her head.

That hint of a smile curved one corner of his mouth again, as if he'd seen something that pleased him. 'I appreciate "Your Majesty",' he said, his voice almost on the edge of a purr. '"Sir" is also acceptable. My people, of course, call me a god, but that would be a step too far for you, I think.'

Sidonie's mouth had become even drier. She didn't need that memory in her head, not when it felt as if there was a fine current of electricity in the air around them, making her skin prickle and tighten.

He'd never looked at her this way before, with heat. He'd never given even the slightest hint that he was interested in her in that way. Yet that electricity was unmistakable, as was the look in his eyes...

She glanced away, flustered and hating herself for being flustered. She'd had very little experience with men. As a teenager she'd spent too much time trying to get good marks at school to allow time for crushes, and then, at Oxford, she'd met Khalil, and of course no other man would ever or could ever measure up to him. After he'd left England, and she'd decided she was going to put him behind her once and for all, she'd tried the dating scene. But was soon faced with the hard, cold reality that the men she'd met didn't interest her. So after a year or two of disappointment, Sidonie had decided she didn't want anything to do with them full stop.

Except now, sitting next to Khalil and not knowing what to say because of the way he was looking at her, to not even be able to hold his gaze... She was regretting that decision. It was ridiculous to be thirty and still a virgin, to be so inexperienced that her ex-best friend could fluster her with a mere look.

It gave him too much power and he was already far too powerful as it was.

So? Take some of it back.

Yes, but how? She would have to think more about it.

Sidonie looked down at her white shirt and brushed at an imaginary speck of lint to cover her fluster. 'They call you a god? Do people still believe the King is semi-divine, then? Surely not after your father.'

He shrugged. 'They decided he was too flawed to be divine. He was merely a man and should not be venerated.'

Sidonie knew about his country, because he'd talked

about it. It was fantastically rich due to its oil deposits and also had a very Byzantine political system where the King or Queen's word was absolute law, bolstered by the belief that, since an ordinary human being could never protect a nation, the ruler should be a god.

It had always sounded like a very interesting place, and she'd have loved to visit, but he'd warned her off travelling there. He hadn't wanted to show her Al Da'ira under his father's rule, because Amir had turned it into such a hotbed of corruption and nepotism. 'Come when I am King,' Khalil had said. 'I will show you the true heart of Al Da'ira then.'

She still remembered those conversations. About all the things Khalil would change when he was King. His passion had been so inspiring. But…where had that man gone?

He's a stranger, remember? You can't think of him as your friend any more.

'Then should I be prostrating myself in your presence?' She kept her voice light and casual. 'Make sure my face is pressed to the floor?'

'No need to prostrate yourself. Kneeling in my presence would be fine.' In the depths of his eyes, that ember of heat sparked again, and there was a wicked edge to that slight smile.

It shocked her, that heat. As did the sensual note in his voice. It was as if they were talking about something completely to different from what they were actually talking about.

Don't be stupid. He's flirting with you.

Sidonie took another breath, that sense of dislocation hitting her again, making her almost dizzy. Of course that was what he was doing. And it was strange because he'd never flirted with her before. He was arrogant, yes, but he could also be charming when he wanted to be, and she'd watched him make slaves of people with only one of his rare smiles. But he'd never turned that charm on her. She'd been pleased that he didn't, telling herself that it was because she didn't need charming. She was his friend, not a girlfriend. Except a secret part of her had always longed for him to flirt with her, look at her the way he was doing now, with heat.

Don't fall for him again. You can't afford to.

Shoving away the silly, quivering part of her, she met his gaze coolly. 'No one is kneeling, Khalil. Least of all me.'

If he found her lack of flirtatious response annoying, he gave no sign. 'Never say never, Sidonie,' he said, his voice giving nothing away. 'You should enjoy the view before the sun sets. We will talk more on this later.'

She didn't protest this time, and when he pulled his phone from his pocket and glanced down at it, indicating that he was done talking, she only felt relief. She needed a break to think about how she was going to handle this supposed dinner.

The rest of the short flight, Sidonie tried to pay attention to the view from the window, but her thoughts kept circling around this dinner they were going to have when they finally arrived, and what she was going to say to him if he kept on insisting that she marry him.

He'd mentioned something back in the pub in England, asking her to think about whether there was something she might need from him, but the only thing she could possibly need from him was his continued distance.

What about for the charity? He's a king. He could be useful.

Sidonie scowled out of the window. Unfortunately, yes, in that way he could be useful. She'd been looking for a patron to help boost the charity's profile, and having a royal one would be even better than the celebrities she'd been considering approaching.

He could give the charity a global reach, even beyond Europe if he agreed. And all for the small price of marrying him.

But think of how many children you could help.

It was true. And helping orphaned and disadvantaged children had been the whole reason she'd started it, having once been one of those children herself.

She thought about it the rest of the flight, until Paris was suddenly laid out beneath her, the Eiffel Tower in the distance, and then it vanished from her head.

She'd been to France once, on a school trip years ago, and all she could remember was that it had been cold and everyone had complained. But now it was here, glittering in the darkness as the helicopter swooped over the city before coming in to land on a large expanse of green lawn that appeared to be part of a private residence.

Despite herself, an excited little thrill shot through her.

Apart from that one school trip, she'd never been abroad, and certainly she hadn't while she'd been working on building up the charity. She'd been too busy to think of taking a holiday let alone where to take one. But if she'd had time, Paris would certainly have been top of her list. All those ancient churches and delicious food and rich history and culture…

You talked about it with him once, remember?

Another memory drifted through her head, of one night in her college rooms, where he'd joined her to study, and they'd talked about travel and the other places he'd been to, which had then evolved into a discussion about all the places she wanted to go, including Paris. Had he remembered that? Was that why they were here?

Again, if he'd done it five years earlier, she would have been thrilled. She was less so now, especially when he hadn't even asked if she wanted to go. Now, with his sudden reappearance in her life and this marriage demand, it felt…calculated almost.

The thought sat uncomfortably in her head as the helicopter door was pulled open and Khalil got out. He handed both his headset and Sidonie's to an aide, but when another aide approached he gave him a sharp look. The man bowed his head and dropped back as Khalil turned to her, holding out his arm.

'Come,' he said regally. 'I will escort you myself.'

There were people watching her and, since she didn't want to create a drama by protesting, she laid her fingers on his forearm, feeling warm wool and hard muscle, the power that he held contained within that magnificent body of his. It was rock-solid, that arm, and she had the sense, as she climbed awkwardly out of the machine, that she could lean her whole weight on it and it wouldn't move.

But she didn't want to think about how good he felt, so she forced the feeling away as he led her through an ornate and magnificent garden, towards an equally ornate and magnificent mansion, with stone balconies and huge windows. They went up some steps, stepping through the door into a grand hallway with a sweeping staircase and high ceilings. There were paintings on those ceilings, and glittering chandeliers hanging from them.

Khalil didn't pause as a whole army of servants surrounded them, merely continuing on straight through them as if they weren't there, guiding her up that sweeping staircase and down a long hallway. At the end of the hallway were some doors standing open onto a stone terrace.

The Eiffel Tower was squarely in front of them, taking up the whole sky, while on the terrace stood tubs of flowers and shrubs and small trees. There were candles everywhere. A small table covered with a white tablecloth stood in the middle of the terrace, and it had been set with silver cutlery and crystal glasses. In an ice bucket a bottle of champagne rested.

It was beautiful and achingly romantic. The perfect setting for an engagement.

If she'd been the old Sidonie, her heart would have burst from happiness. If she'd been the old Sidonie she would have said yes the moment he'd walked through the door.

But she wasn't the old Sidonie.

She was harder, more guarded, and that heart of hers had been broken.

He was the one who had broken it. And, while she was long over that now, she wasn't going to risk him breaking it again. Which was why her answer was always going to be 'no'.

CHAPTER THREE

KHALIL WATCHED SIDONIE'S beautiful green eyes widen, and he allowed himself a small measure of satisfaction at the flicker of awe on her face. But then, almost in the same moment, the awe was gone, her expression smoothing into that same cool mask he'd observed in the helicopter.

It annoyed him and at the same time intrigued him, he couldn't deny it. Sidonie had once been so open, never hiding anything from him. He'd always been able to tell what she was feeling and that was part of the reason he wanted her as his queen.

After the kind of childhood he'd had, brought up in his mother's house in the mountains and subject to the rigorous discipline that his mother had believed would turn him into a strong king, Sidonie's emotional honesty had seemed shocking to him at first. She'd seemed to be a relatively quiet and subdued person when they'd met, but he'd soon realised that her quietness had hidden a deeply passionate nature. She felt things deeply, the way he did, but they'd both been taught certain things about emotions, and it had taken some time to overcome those lessons and to trust each other.

Her aunt had taught her that her feelings were too demanding and needed to be controlled, while his mother had taught him that emotions were weaknesses, flaws to be exploited.

Gradually, as they'd become more open with each other, Sidonie had blossomed. She was so honest about her feelings with him, and he'd learned that there was nothing manipulative or fake about her. She always said what she meant, and he could always trust what she said.

Which was why that night in Soho, when she'd told him she loved him, had been so very hard. Because he'd known it was true. She *did* love him. She loved him and he was going to have to hurt her.

Perhaps that was why she was more guarded than she once had been, hiding behind that cool veneer of hers.

She was protecting herself because of him.

Regret twisted inside him, but he ignored it. Regret wasn't for kings. They made the decisions they did for the good of their country and they did not look back on them.

He studied her now, standing on the terrace in her tailored black trousers and plain white shirt, her red hair sleek in its little bun. Her lovely face betrayed nothing, her green eyes cool. So very self-possessed.

It made him want to know what she'd been doing these past five years. Certainly he'd made assumptions—her having a supervisor for example—that were clearly wrong, which was his own fault. He should have investigated how her charity was doing before he'd made the trip to England, but he hadn't because he'd thought... Well. He'd thought she'd still be the same as the woman he remembered. And she wasn't.

This little terrace scene he'd had his staff put together had been based on a conversation he'd had with her about Paris once, and he'd hoped it would sway her into agreeing to be his queen.

But maybe it wouldn't. Maybe she didn't care for Paris these days.

Sidonie's cool gaze met his. 'So, is this all for my benefit?'

'Yes.' There was no reason to deny it. 'Happy birthday, *ya hayati.*'

'If you think a nicely set table and an endearment will make me more likely to agree to marry you, you need to think again, Khalil.'

That poisonous part of him stirred yet again, responding to the challenge. And it *was* a challenge, whether she realised it or not. He forced it down. That part of himself could never be let out. It had to stay locked away. Not ever fully excised, because the day might come when his country needed it, and if that day came he'd have to embrace it.

Just as he'd had to embrace the battle of succession to determine his suitability to be heir. The battle was a ritualistic fight between the oldest children of each of the King's wives for the right to be the heir to the throne, a historical leftover from another time.

Khalil hadn't wanted to take part; he'd thought it medieval and outdated, but his mother had told him he couldn't afford not to.

'You have responsibilities, Khalil,' she'd said coldly when he'd voiced his reluctance. *'If you do not fight, then Yusuf will be named heir, and you know what he would do to this country should he become King. Protecting Al Da'ira is all that is important. What you want doesn't matter.'*

What he'd wanted never mattered. His father's blood ran too strong his veins, she'd told him, which made him more susceptible to the flaws of selfishness and vice than other people. He had to guard himself more strongly against them, never indulge his own needs. He had to learn how to place the greater good above them.

Well, he'd learned. He might have that old blood, but he didn't let it rule him. He couldn't. Not when the foundation of his kingship was *not* following in his father's footsteps.

'So, what would make you marry me?' he asked idly, since, although he had no intention of letting her walk away, everything would go much more smoothly if she wasn't actively fighting him.

'Nothing.' Her gaze was sharp. 'I don't want to marry anyone.' Before he could reply, she turned and moved across the terrace to stand at the stone parapet, her attention on the iconic shape of the Eiffel Tower in front of them. She was holding herself very stiffly, her back straight and her shoulders tense.

He studied her yet again, trying to puzzle out what she was thinking and what had happened to the woman he'd left behind five years earlier. Was she still there, hiding behind this woman's cool, smooth veneer?

He'd lost his ability to read her, that was the problem. Or rather, he'd never had to read her, because the Sidonie he remembered had always been open with him. But not this Sidonie. She was far more guarded. Though, judging from her rigid posture, he'd say she was still angry. *That was obvious.*

Yes, well, he would have to get her *not* to be angry with him, and that was going to be tricky. If he wanted her agreement to be his queen, he would have to find a way, which meant some convincing was in order.

Khalil studied the stiff line of her back for a moment, then stalked over to the ice bucket and picked up the champagne bottle. He popped the cork, poured some of the fizzy liquid into two flutes, and carried both over to where she stood.

'For you,' he said, holding out the glass.

She glanced at him, her expression still guarded. She smelled of apples and cinnamon, and another sweet scent he couldn't quite put his finger on, and it came almost as a shock that the scent was as familiar to him as his own name, despite the years. She'd changed, it was true, but she still smelled the same.

Desire stirred inside him, bright and sharp, which was another shock, since he'd thought he'd put that desire behind him.

Apparently not.

When he'd come to Oxford and become friends with Galen of Kalithera and Augustine of Isavere, his companion 'Wicked Princes' and two men who knew the unique demands of being an heir to the throne, they'd turned the university town upside down. There had been parties and wildness, and all kinds of beautiful women, and he'd indulged himself completely, using them to forget the terrible price he'd paid to be the heir, not to mention the doubt and the guilt that had followed him to England.

Yet no other woman had ever captured the unique combination of curvaceousness, sensuality and warmth that was Sidonie.

If he hadn't been a prince, if he'd been an ordinary student, he'd have seduced her in minutes back then. But the life of an ordinary student had never been his destiny. He'd been intended for the isolation of command, the cold logic of difficult decisions and heavy scales to balance. A man in control of a country couldn't be the same man who laughed in a pub or screamed at a football match or held a grieving friend on the anniversary of her parents' death.

Friendship was all he had to give and so he'd never crossed that line.

Yet for some reason now, standing close to her, with the achingly familiar scent of her winding around him, reminding him of things he'd purposefully forgotten, all those reasons seemed pointless now.

If she agreed, she would be his wife and heirs would need to be conceived. He could have her naked beneath him, and then he could put his mouth to her throat, finally taste her skin the way he'd always fantasised about, breathe in that delicious scent...

His body hardened and yet again he was conscious of deep surprise. Nothing happened unless he willed it, especially when it came to physical reactions, and for baser parts of himself to react to her without his control...

He realised she was studying him, so he ignored the grip of desire and met her gaze. 'Take the glass, Sidonie. I will not hold it for ever.'

She took the glass, and he observed that she didn't let her fingers brush his.

He raised his own glass. 'A toast,' he said. 'To your birthday.'

She looked at him a moment longer, then raised hers too, taking a small sip. 'So,' she said. 'What were you doing with those children in the village? You gave them something.'

Interesting that she should have noticed that.

'I gave them some money.' He took a sip of his own champagne. 'And then told them that the first person to find four totally round and smooth rocks and bring them to one of my men would receive another ten pounds.'

Her brow creased. 'Why?'

Did she think he wouldn't have thought about or noticed the attention his chopper had drawn when he'd landed it in the middle of the village green? Of course he had. Then again, she'd always thought he was too arrogant for his own good and she wasn't wrong. But kings had to be arrogant. Without confidence in themselves and their decisions, how could their people trust them? And without trust, how could they rule effectively? Confidence and certainty were strengths, and he was nothing if not strong.

His mother had made sure of that. Her methods had been...unorthodox, but he'd survived them. And his reign would be the better for them.

'I wanted to get them away from the helicopter, since we were about to take off.' He swirled the liquid in his glass. 'Also, I like children.'

The cool expression on her face rippled, betraying surprise. 'You do?'

Had she forgotten their discussions? About their dreams for the future? He'd never made any secret of the fact that he wanted to have a family one day. He had to. It was expected of him to secure the succession. Not that he'd ever have more than one wife, unlike his father. It was his father's greed that had caused all the problems after all, and outlawing polygamy had been one of Khalil's first acts as King.

'Yes,' he said. 'Do you not remember? I wanted a big family, as you did yourself. That is why you made me sign that piece of paper, after all.'

'I thought I made it clear—'

'I mean to marry you, Sidonie.' He let the steel of the King thread through his voice, so she would understand how serious he was. 'And I want it to be a marriage in every sense of the word.'

She said nothing. Then carefully put the champagne glass down on the stone of the parapet and turned to give him her full attention. 'Why?' she asked bluntly. 'It's been years since we've seen each other and even before you left you never displayed the slightest interest in me. Something's changed. What is it?'

He could only give her the truth. She expected—and deserved—nothing less. And he suspected that if he wanted her agreement, being honest with her was the only way to secure it.

'What changed?' he said after a moment. 'I became King. And I need a queen.'

'That's it? You need a queen and I randomly fit the bill somehow?'

'You are not random, Sidonie. I need a woman I can trust, and my people a queen they can look up to.'

She frowned. 'What do you mean, a queen they can look up to?'

'You know about my father's reign. You know what it did to my people.' They'd talked about it many times, all those long nights studying either in her rooms or in his. Drinking endless cups of coffee as he'd told her about his country and what his father had done to it. How his great-grandfather had reinstated polygamy so for decades the Kings of Al Da'ira had more than one wife, much to the disapproval of the rest of the world, including the neighbouring desert nations. His father had had four, and, like his father before him, had decreed that his children should battle for the crown as they had in centuries past. And so Khalil had grown up the only child of wife number three, and he'd had to fight his oldest half-sibling for the right to rule, the only one who'd been of the right age, and that had been Yusuf.

It had been a medieval childhood. A medieval and dangerous existence.

Sidonie had been shocked when he'd told her about that and the endless intrigues, assassination attempts, and corruption that his father actively encouraged. She'd asked him lots of questions and then they'd discussed how he'd bring change to his country, because they'd both agreed emphatically that change had to come.

And it had. He'd had to use force to quell the stubborn pockets of resistance who'd supported Yusuf, the sheer power of his will to lay down new laws. People had said he was too much like his father, that he was not divine, that he was only a man, and they couldn't follow a mere man.

But he'd shown them. He'd proved he wasn't his father, that he wasn't a mere man. He'd shown them that he was a king, and so they believed.

But now was not the time for more pressure. It was the time for peace and for that he needed her.

'Yes,' she said slowly. 'I remember. And you wanted to be different.'

'I have been different. But change was not easy, and my people have been...scarred.'

A look of concern flickered over her face, a glimpse of the empathic friend he remembered. 'Oh, I didn't know that. I'm sorry, Khalil. That must have been awful.'

Something inside him ached suddenly, a ghost of the longing he'd once felt for her, but he ignored it. He'd cut that feeling out of him long ago.

'It was,' he agreed. 'My people need some joy in their lives. They need hope and laughter. They need kindness and care.' He met her gaze. 'They do not need a king. What they need is a queen. What they need is you.'

Again, that cool veneer of hers rippled, betraying shock. 'Me? Why me?'

'Because you are all of those things, *ya hayati*. You are kind and compassionate. You are empathic and honest. You understand the value of laughter. In other words, you are exactly what my people need in a queen.'

Her green eyes were dark in the soft glow of the lights around them and she'd gone pale. She was looking at him as if he'd hurt her in some fashion. Then abruptly the expression vanished and she turned away, glancing at the Eiffel Tower once more.

Uncharacteristic impatience gathered inside him. He had no idea why she'd looked hurt, but had the appeal on behalf of his people not been enough?

'You taught me all of those things, Sidonie.' He tried to keep the impatience from his voice. 'You taught me what it was to have a friend and to be a friend in return. You taught me what it meant to be happy. Do you not understand? If you did that for me, you could do that for my people, too.'

Another moment or two passed and she didn't move.

Then slowly she looked back at him and her gaze was just as sharp as it had been across the table in that pub in England. 'This dinner is a nice gesture and I appreciate it. But there are many other women who have all the qualities you just listed. You don't need me in particular.'

'But I—'

'I too have people who depend on me,' she interrupted steadily. 'People who need me. And I can't just leave them because you decided I'm your perfect queen.'

'Sidonie—'

'No, Khalil.' There was steel in her green eyes now. 'I'm sorry. I'm not marrying you and that's final.'

Sidonie held herself very straight and made sure her voice was very firm. She didn't care if she interrupted him, even though from the way his dark eyes flared he'd obviously considered it rude. But that was too bad. If she let him take charge again, he'd bulldoze his way over all her objections the way he had back in the pub, and she'd find herself hauled off to Al Da'ira before she knew what was happening.

She couldn't allow that.

He'd been intense about changing his people's lives for the better back then, and she could see the same intensity now in the hard planes and angles of his face. In his eyes. And it had made her waver.

This mattered to him. This mattered to him very much.

But she couldn't say yes to him. She couldn't give up the life she'd built for herself and all the people who depended on her, all the children who needed the help her charity could give them, just because Khalil had commanded her to marry him.

Who says you need to give up all of that?

No, she didn't need that thought in her head. There would be no marriage and that was final. Because even apart from the charity and everything she'd built, she couldn't allow him back into her life, not again. Not when he'd left such devastation behind him the last time.

Khalil stood there so very tall and broad, the lights of the city falling on his compelling face. His gaze was fixed on hers, intensely focused, as if he was trying to see inside her head.

He was so close—too close. The scent of his aftershave

and the warmth of his body were doing things to her that she didn't like, making her want things she shouldn't. Things she thought she'd put behind her.

She should move away, but with that gaze of his on her, seeing everything, he'd notice and he'd know the reason. She didn't want to give away how his nearness affected her, so she stayed where she was.

'No?' His voice had deepened, become rougher. 'That is really your answer? I told you it was for my people's sake.'

'I realise that.' She tried to sound calm. She didn't want to give away the real reason, not given what that would reveal about her own feelings. 'But I don't know your people. And I don't know your country. And I...' She paused. 'It's been years, Khalil. I feel like I barely know you.'

'You do know me.'

'Do I? I knew my friend. I knew him very well, but you aren't him, are you?'

He hesitated a moment then shook his head. 'No. Not any more.'

Something she didn't understand glittered in his obsidian gaze just then, a hard edge that she was sure hadn't been there all those years ago. The hard edge she'd seen at the pub and in the helicopter.

Being King has taken its toll.

There was a strange tightness in her chest, because it was obvious now that yes, it had taken something from him. It had hardened him. Darkened him. He'd always had a darkness to him, even back at university, and she'd thought that maybe he still had some secrets he hadn't told her. Yet she hadn't pushed. If he'd wanted to tell her he would have, and she'd respected his choices.

But now…what had happened to her friend?

'Khalil,' she began, to say what she didn't know. But then he moved, putting his glass down on the parapet and taking a step closer to her. He raised a hand, and before she could draw breath he'd lifted it, cupping her cheek in one large, warm palm.

'But I still remember that man, Sidonie.' He looked down into her face, his expression fierce. 'I am not him now, but I still have his memories. He was your friend once and you were his. So, if you will not do it for my people, will you do it for him? For the sake of the friendship you once shared with him?'

She couldn't move. All the breath had left her body. Something inside her was trembling and no matter how hard she tried to ignore it, she couldn't. His fingertips lightly pressing against the side of her face burned like fire, and there was a familiar ache tightening inside her, right down between her thighs.

The glowing ember she'd seen in his eyes in that moment in the helicopter was back, lighting the darkness, turning his intensity into a force of nature that robbed her of all thought. He'd never turned it on her before, not like this…

She wanted desperately to tell him that man had also walked away from her and hurt her, to turn away so he wasn't touching her, but she couldn't bring herself to do it. It was as if she'd been waiting all her life for him to touch her like this, to cup her cheek in just this way and look down into her eyes as he was doing right now…

'I can make it worth your while, *ya hayati*.' His gaze searched her face, searing her as surely as the touch of his fingers. 'I know you still want me. I have seen it in your eyes.'

The humiliation she remembered from all those years ago crept through her. The words she'd said to him on the snowy street in Soho, and how his expression had closed up completely. How he'd turned away without a word and left her standing there alone.

That had been her last memory of him, watching him walk away while her heart had crumbled.

Her muscles tightened at the memory, but he gripped her a little harder, and murmured, 'No, Sidonie. Stay.'

'Why should I?' The words came out shaky and raw. 'You don't feel that way about me. I know you don't.'

'Do I not?' The glitter in his eyes became more intense and that was the only warning she got. The next second, he'd bent his head and his mouth was on hers.

The whole world stopped. It was as if a bolt of lightning had hit her, arrowing straight down her spine, rooting her to the spot.

Khalil was kissing her. Khalil was kissing *her*.

His fingers gripped her, pressing against her jaw, and she was tinder-dry grass, his mouth a flame, igniting her already smouldering desire and making it blaze into sudden, furious life.

A sigh of sheer relief escaped her, because she'd been waiting for this moment for ten years, hoping for it yet also knowing at the same time it would never come. Because he didn't feel that way about her. She'd told herself that so many times, and in the absence of any sign to the contrary she'd come to believe it.

Except apparently she'd been wrong all this time.

She was shaking as the reality of what was happening began to hit, and along with the relief came a dizzying wave of desire. All thought of pretending she wasn't affected by him, that she didn't still want him, vanished. The only thing that mattered was that she have more, get closer, because this was wasn't enough. It would *never* be enough.

Instinctively she lifted her hands, curling her fingers into the fine wool of his jacket, leaning into him. He was still, and for a terrible second she thought this would be that street in Soho all over again.

But then he moved again, pushing her up against the parapet and pinning her there with the hot length of his body. He was still cupping her cheek with one hand, and he shifted his thumb, pressing down on her bottom lip and opening her mouth to him, deepening the kiss.

Heat exploded between them, his tongue sweeping inside, devouring her as if she was a feast set before him and he was starving.

All conscious thought left her. There was only the press of his powerful body against hers, caging her against the stone. His hand slid from her jaw to the back of her head, cradling her as he kissed her harder, deeper.

Sometimes, alone in her college rooms at night, she'd allow herself to fantasise about what it would be like to kiss him or to have him kiss her, and she'd always thought it would be amazing. But the reality was better. Better than anything she could have possibly imagined.

This was what she'd been dreaming about for many years. His mouth on hers, kissing her as if he wanted her every bit as badly as she wanted him. And she *did* want him. She'd always wanted him and she probably always would.

What about your heart? You can't let him get this close...not again.

She wouldn't though. She knew how to protect herself. And anyway, this was just a kiss and she'd wanted a taste of him for so long. This was allowed, surely?

Her hands slid beneath his jacket, pressing against the white cotton of his shirt, feeling the iron-hard muscle and heat of his chest. He felt so good, warm and strong, and he smelled like heaven. Musk and sandalwood and exotic spices.

She'd missed him, she could admit that now. She'd missed him so much.

A helpless moan escaped her. She arched into him, the throb between her legs demanding, and, as if he knew exactly what she wanted, one hard thigh eased between hers, creating the most exquisite pressure.

She was a virgin. She'd never even been kissed before. But she knew what physical pleasure was and how to give it to herself, and yet the way he made her feel right now, even though he was barely touching her... It was more intense than anything she'd ever experienced. More intense than anything she could have imagined.

'Khal,' she whispered. 'Oh, please...'

His hand at the back of her head firmed and he kept her pinned against the parapet with his body. 'Come to Al Da'ira,' he murmured against her mouth. 'Give me two weeks. Two weeks to convince you to marry me. I will show you my country and my people. I will show you why I need you and only you.'

At first she barely heard him. Then gradually, through the haze of desire, the words penetrated.

He'd pulled back, lifting his mouth, his midnight gaze on hers. He didn't look away or try to hide the desire burning there. He let her see it.

It made her hot, made her heart flutter madly in her chest.

She could still feel his lips on hers, still taste his dark, heady flavour. And his body, rock-hard and tall and so broad… She'd never thought she'd have any of this. Never thought she'd have him look at her that way, have his kiss, have him want her.

'Two weeks?' She barely understood what she was saying herself, her voice husky, every part of her shaking.

'Yes, only two weeks.' He shifted, that hard thigh pressing insistently against her, right in the place she needed it most. His fingers pushed into her hair, tilting her head further back, and he lowered his mouth again, brushing it over hers. 'Only two weeks, *ya hayati*. You can stay in my palace, be waited on hand and foot, and I will give you everything it is in my power to give.'

Her senses reeled. 'Khal…'

'Please.' His voice warmed, became deeper, resonating with the part of her she'd always tried to keep closely guarded around him, and his lips moved over hers once again. 'Please, Sidonie.'

He'd never said 'please' to her before, never like this, with a note of demand and yet also with an echo of longing. As if he was desperate.

'I…'

'I will give you more of this.' His mouth explored lower, along her jawline. 'I will make you feel so very good.' He kissed a trail down her throat, his lips closing over her pulse. 'You have been waiting a long time for this, Sidonie. And so have I.'

He had? He'd been waiting, too?

The thought was there and then vanished, everything burning where he kissed her, as if he was scattering embers over her skin. Except instead of pain he left scorching pleasure, and all she could think was that she wanted more of it. Because he was right. She'd been waiting a long time for him and she was tired of it.

Why couldn't she have this? Have more of him? Two weeks of being in Al Da'ira, in his palace. Two weeks of being with him. She'd be careful, she wouldn't let herself get in too deep the way she had last time. And who knew, maybe it would even lay to rest a few ghosts?

He has to give you something too, though, and not just sex.

Yes. He could help with the charity, as she'd thought in the helicopter on the way here. He could be their royal patron, get them noticed, ensure they reached not just beyond the UK and into Europe, but globally too. There were so many orphaned children out there, children like her, children who needed help, and he could make a difference.

His mouth seared her tender throat, and she could feel the slight pressure of his tongue, the edge of his teeth. She closed her eyes, shivering in delight. 'You mentioned giving me something too,' she murmured. 'Something that I want, and I'm not talking about sex here.'

'I did.' His breath was warm against her skin. 'Name it.'

'You to lend your name to my charity. Be its patron. Help boost our profile.'

He answered without hesitation. 'I can do that.'

'Also, if I don't agree to marry you, I want to be free to leave. To go home.'

Another breath ghosted over her neck and then he commanded softly, 'Open your eyes.'

She did, automatically obeying him.

He'd lifted his head and was looking down at her, dark fire in his gaze. 'Yes, you will be free to leave. You have my word.'

Five years ago she would have trusted that word implicitly. But now… Well, he wasn't the same man she'd once known, he'd even admitted it himself. And she didn't know who this man was. She didn't know him at all.

An echo of grief made her throat close, grief for the friend who'd gone and left this man in his place. But grief wouldn't help. She had to be hard.

'Can I trust your word?' she made herself ask bluntly.

A flicker of something she couldn't decipher crossed his face and then was gone. 'You can. I swear to you on my crown.' His voice was flat and certain. 'And on the lives of my people.'

That meant something to him, she could tell. It was a vow.

'In that case,' she said, 'yes. I'll give you two weeks.'

CHAPTER FOUR

SIDONIE'S SKIN BENEATH his fingers was deliciously silky and warm, and Khalil didn't want to let her go. Her eyes had darkened into deep emerald and the pulse at the base of her throat, the pulse he'd just tasted, was racing.

He could hear his own blood roaring in his veins, desire like a giant heartbeat echoing inside him, and he could still taste her on his tongue, like summer, all honey and sunshine and sweetness.

He'd fantasised about how she'd taste many times, but the reality was better than any of his fantasies. He'd thought of kissing her many times, too, back when they'd been friends. Kissing her and more. But they'd remained just that, thoughts and fantasies. He'd kept his hands to himself no matter how difficult it had been.

Yet he hadn't been blind. He was an experienced man, and he knew when a woman wanted him. Sidonie had definitely wanted him back then and it seemed she still did, which was something he could use.

He hadn't wanted to. His mother's methods of using his emotions to teach him hard life lessons weren't ones he wanted to use on anyone else, let alone Sidonie. But he'd had to do something to get her agreement.

Putting his hand against her cheek had been calculated. He'd thought using her desire for him would aid his cause, but he hadn't expected the heat that had ignited inside him the moment he'd touched her.

He'd always wanted her, it was true, but his desire had felt like more than just want. It was as if the dam he kept between himself and his baser hungers had fractured, a dark and endless need welling up through the cracks, and he'd kissed her, pushed her up against that parapet before he'd fully understood what he was doing.

He had a longing not just for physical connection but also for her. For the woman he'd put out of his mind for so long that he'd thought she was gone for good. Except she hadn't gone. She was still there inside him, as was the ache of a loss he hadn't even realised he'd felt.

He hadn't been able to stop himself from deepening that kiss, from pushing her up against the parapet so he could feel her against him, her warmth settling into him. Easing the ache inside him. Her mouth beneath his had been so hot, like summer sun on his face after years of winter, and he'd had to force himself to remember what he was doing and what his goal was.

This wasn't about him and what he wanted.

This was about his country and his people, and no matter his pride. No matter that he'd never said please before in his life and certainly hadn't wanted to give her a two-week window in which to decide whether she wanted to marry him or not.

All that mattered was that she agreed.

So, he'd let her have it. Let her have his name for her charity too, because that was a small thing, and it wouldn't cost him anything, and it was clearly important to her. Two weeks wouldn't cost him either, would give her the illusion of choice at least, because at the end of that time he had no doubt at all that she'd marry him. He'd convince her. He'd use any and every weapon at his disposal if it meant she'd be his queen. His country demanded it.

Sensual pleasure would clearly be his weapon of choice, judging by the smoky green of her eyes, the delicate flush in her cheeks, and the way her full mouth had gone from firm to soft and pouty-looking.

Are you sure that is a good idea? Especially given your own response to her? You could become greedy, like Amir.

It was a concern, granted. Especially given his bloodline. But now he knew he was...susceptible, he'd be on his guard. He could control himself. His mother's lessons had been difficult, but he'd learned. And apart from all of that, he'd had five years of hardening himself into the King his people demanded. Of making sure the man he'd once been, the man full of doubts and flaws, was gone.

He could use their physical chemistry and not fall victim to it, he was certain.

She was staring up at him now from beneath her silky reddish lashes, and the temptation to kiss her again gripped him by the throat. But he mastered the urge. Instead he brushed his thumb over her mouth once more, relishing the give of her lower lip as he did so. 'Good. In that case, we leave tonight.'

Sidonie blinked. She was still pressed up against him, her fingers curled into the fabric of his jacket, and he was very, *very* conscious of the soft heat between her legs against his thigh and the press of her lush breasts against his chest.

You are hungry for her.

A physical hunger, nothing more. As a prince, after the nasty business of claiming his place in the succession was over, after his mother had died of the cancer that had taken hold of her, he'd let his desires run wild, let that poisonous blood have what it wanted, drowning the terrible doubt inside him about what he'd done. It had been before he'd met Sidonie and sex had been a good distraction.

But even then, his distractions had been calculated. His mastery over himself had never wavered, no matter how many women he took to his bed. And Sidonie, for all that she'd once meant to him, would be essentially just another woman.

Surprise crossed Sidonie's lovely face. 'Tonight? But… that's too soon.'

Khalil forced himself to release her jaw and step back, which took more effort than it should. 'I am afraid I need to be back in Al Da'ira as soon as possible.'

The surprise vanished, that cool veneer slowly sliding back into place, hiding the sensual, sweet woman she'd been not a moment earlier. The real Sidonie. The Sidonie he remembered.

He didn't like that veneer. He didn't like it at all. Well, shattering it completely wouldn't take long. He wouldn't need two weeks to make his Sidonie return to him.

'That's unacceptable, Khalil,' she said. 'I told you. I have a business to run and people counting on me. I can't just up and leave with no notice.'

Thwarted desire coiled inside him, hot and demanding, eroding his patience and his temper along with it. He wasn't a man who gave in to such frustrations, but he was tired of fighting her. He had to get home. Already he'd wasted too much time coming to Paris and preparing a birthday meal that he hadn't even needed in the end. He should have just kissed her back in the pub in England.

'You will have to.' He didn't bother to hide the curt note in his voice. 'I cannot afford any more time away.'

Anger sparked in her gaze. 'Well, neither can I. If you need to get back, why don't you go and I can join you in a few—?'

'No,' he interrupted with all the steel of the King he was. 'You will be accompanying me and that is final.' She had to be with him when he arrived; that was non-negotiable. The correct form had to be observed if Sidonie was to be accepted as his queen, and for that she had to arrive with him.

'Why? What's wrong with our arriving separately?'

She was standing far too close to him and he couldn't help but notice that his fingers had pulled some silky red curls from her bun. They drifted around her neck, drawing attention to her pale, creamy skin and the tender hollow of her throat. A couple of buttons on her shirt were undone too and it would only take a couple of flicks of his fingers to open it completely and expose her to his gaze...

Desire tightened inside him once more, coiling and knotting, encouraging him to forget his control and take her here, now. Make her his. But he ignored it. This was not the right time or the right place, and he would do nothing to jeopardise their eventual marriage. No matter how much his body was urging him otherwise.

'We have certain customs that I must adhere to,' he said, forcing away the heat inside him.

'What customs? I'm just a visitor, Khalil, and presumably you don't have to accompany every visitor to Al Da'ira.'

If they kept going down this road they would have another argument, and yet more time would be wasted. His boundaries would be pushed and his temper further eroded. He couldn't allow that, not when he was on edge already.

'This is not up for discussion,' he said flatly, done with the conversation. 'You may contact your people from the jet. Alternatively one of my staff will contact them on your behalf.'

It was clear she wasn't happy with that, because an angry flush had crept into her cheeks. 'I *run* the charity. You do remember that, don't you? I don't need "one of your staff" to contact my own employees.'

No, he hadn't remembered, and he should have, especially given all the discussions they'd had about her plans for starting a charity back in university. She'd been unsure of herself back then, but he'd encouraged her to follow her dreams. Because beneath that uncertainty she had drive and ambition, and he'd known she'd be brilliant at it.

He was annoyed with himself for forgetting, but his distance over the years had been deliberate, and there was no use regretting it. He'd made the decision to cut off all contact, and he couldn't go back and change it, even if he'd wanted to, which he didn't. He never second-guessed himself, never hesitated. Never let doubt undermine him. He couldn't afford to, not after Yusuf's death.

'Then you may contact them yourself,' he said. 'I do not care how you do it. But we *will* leave tonight regardless.'

Sidonie opened her mouth, but he carried on. 'One hour, Sidonie. Be ready.'

Then he strode past her and left her standing on the terrace staring after him.

CHAPTER FIVE

SIDONIE GROUND HER teeth with annoyance, watching Khalil's tall, broad figure disappear through the French doors.

She didn't like the man he'd become, not at all. He was insufferable.

'I knew my friend. I knew him very well, but you aren't him, are you?'

Her own words drifted back to her, as did his reply. *'No. Not any more.'*

That old grief pulsed inside her again, at the loss of the friend she'd once had. And it was clear that friend really had gone. But what she didn't understand was why.

What had happened to him? Why did Khalil feel he couldn't be him any more?

She turned away from staring at the door he'd just walked through, returning to the edge of the terrace and that view of Paris, trying to get a handle on the complicated mix of anger and loss that sat inside her.

He'd been so dismissive of her life and its requirements back in England. As if he hadn't sat with her all those nights in her rooms, going over her plans for the charity. Giving her advice and support, encouraging her. Believing in her.

Had he just…what? Forgotten about all of it? Forgotten

that this had been her dream, and that he'd been a huge part in helping her find the confidence to reach for it?

The Khalil she remembered would never have forgotten. He wouldn't have swept grandly back into her life as if he still occupied the same space in it after five years of silence, either. The Khalil she remembered would have talked to her, would have listened to her concerns, and if she'd said no he'd have accepted it.

But as she'd told herself so many times already, as he'd even admitted himself, he wasn't that Khalil.

Can you blame him for putting his people and his country first?

No, she couldn't. He'd often told her that was what being a king was all about, the needs of his nation put before everything and everyone else, including himself. She'd thought it had sounded far too black and white, and that surely a king had to see to his own needs at some time, otherwise how could he look after everyone else? He'd accepted that, but even then, it was clear he didn't really believe it.

It seemed he didn't believe it now.

He wasn't going to matter to you, remember?

True. So why she was thinking about all the changes in him, she had no idea.

She leaned her elbows on the parapet and let out a slow breath, conscious once again of the quick beat of her heart and how sensitive her mouth felt. She could still feel the pressure of his lips on hers, the taste of him making her hungry, making her forget what she'd told herself when he'd turned up only hours before. That she wasn't going to let herself be affected by him the way she had years ago. That she was a different person now, a *stronger* person, who didn't let her emotions run away with her.

Yet you're still dropping everything to go to Al Da'ira because he demanded it.

No, that wasn't quite true. She *had* agreed to go, but only after he'd said please and had agreed to be her charity's patron. And she was only going for two weeks. She hadn't agreed to his marriage demand, either. She *had* resisted him, and if she wasn't much mistaken she'd even got under his skin a little too.

Ahead of her the Eiffel Tower loomed, glittering in the night.

She stared unseeingly at it, thinking about the dark fire that had still been burning in his eyes after that kiss.

'You have been waiting a long time for this, Sidonie. And so have I...'

He'd been waiting, he'd said. Waiting a long time. Which seem to indicate that maybe he hadn't been as indifferent to her years ago as she'd thought.

A shiver went through her, a tight feeling settling in her chest. She shouldn't be thinking of that. It didn't matter what he'd felt for her back then, because he'd never done anything about it. She'd tried to cross that line and he'd rebuffed her, for whatever reason.

Only the present mattered now.

Still. Maybe you're not so powerless against him after all.

The thought glowed in her head. Whatever he'd felt in the past, he wanted her now and that *was* a power she had, a power she'd never used or even understood, since no one had ever particularly wanted her before, not like that. And, while she wasn't sure how she could use it quite yet, she still had it.

Thinking about it gave her a little thrill. Because how many times had she ached for him over the years? Dreaming of the day he'd finally see her as not just a friend, but also as a woman he wanted. Yet at the same time knowing that day would never come, because he would never see her that way. Why would he? When no one else ever had?

But that day *had* come. Now, finally, he saw her as a woman. Finally she could make him burn for her. Make him ache for her, long for her. Make him as desperate for her as she'd been for him. That would be fair, wouldn't it?

But can you? Or will you end up making yourself his slave once again?

Sidonie focused once more on the Eiffel Tower, all iron, hard metal to withstand the centuries.

Back when she'd been a kid she'd learned how to be quiet and undemanding, moulding herself into the perfect niece for her aunt, a good girl who never caused a fuss and never drew attention to herself.

Then she'd met Khalil, his intensity demanding something from her, something that living with Aunt May had forced her to keep down deep inside. An intensity of her own that she'd kept locked away, a passion and drive she hadn't known she'd had. He'd encouraged it, made it flourish. Being with him had felt as though she could breathe for the first time in her life. Then had come the mistake she'd made, his painful departure, and that email breaking off all contact. And the part of her that he'd unlocked, she'd had to put away again.

It had been a hard lesson to learn but she'd learned it. She'd never want anything from anyone, never open herself to anyone. She'd found the iron inside her, armour to protect herself. She visited her aunt when it suited her and only because May wasn't in good health these days, and besides, staying away would have meant May still had the power to hurt her and she didn't.

As for Khalil, well… He'd soon discover she wasn't as malleable as she'd once been, if he hadn't already.

'Miss Sullivan?'

Sidonie turned to find a woman in a black uniform standing behind her. 'Yes?'

'Your car to the airport is here. His Majesty also wishes to inform you that you will not need any luggage. He will see to anything you require personally.'

Behind the woman Sidonie could see other servants busily packing up the carefully set table and blowing out all the candles. Since she'd agreed to come with him, the birthday dinner clearly wasn't needed any more.

That gave her a slight stab of hurt, but she ignored it. The important thing was she'd got his agreement to help her charity and that mattered more than any silly birthday dinner. Anyway, she'd go to Al Da'ira and enjoy a pleasant two weeks' holiday, perhaps lose her virginity to him, lay those old ghosts, and then she'd come back to England and she'd *never* think of him again.

The trip from the private mansion to a private airfield just out of Paris, where Khalil's jet waited, wasn't long. She'd thought when she got into the car that he would be there too and was surprised when he wasn't. He wasn't on the tarmac when she reached the airfield, nor waiting by the sleek black jet with the gleaming gold tail livery.

She wondered if he was already inside, but after she'd climbed the stairs and stepped into the plane the series of small rooms she was led through were empty. The interior was all luxurious cream leather and gleaming dark wood, and the seat she was taken to was more a recliner than an aircraft seat, deep and enveloping her in comfort as soon as she sat down.

There was still no sign of him and she was beginning

to wonder what was going on, when she heard his deep voice coming from the jet's doors, towards the nose of the plane. He was speaking in his beautiful, melodic language, and despite herself her heartbeat sped up.

It was ridiculous. It hadn't even been an hour since he'd walked off the terrace and already she was excited at the thought of seeing him again. Not a good sign when she should be trying to ring Bethany, her personal assistant, to let her know she was having an unexpected break and to reschedule her meetings, plus check to make sure she didn't have any events planned for the next two weeks.

Except all she did was sit there, staring at the entrance of the little sitting area she was in, waiting for him to arrive.

But he didn't.

Even after the jet had taken off and they were at cruising altitude, he didn't show.

She made her calls, Bethany assuring her that a sudden two-week holiday was no problem at all, and in fact Sidonie probably needed it, so she wasn't to worry about anything.

Sidonie found it a little disconcerting that two weeks could pass without her being needed, but, since she was already in the air and flying to her destination, there wasn't much she could do about it but be glad it wasn't a problem.

She'd need to tell her team about his being on board to be patron, but she could do that once she had a formal agreement from him.

It was an overnight flight and, after dinner had been served and she'd eaten, a steward showed her to a bedroom that included a king-sized bed with luxurious white sheets for her to sleep in. She wondered if she should refuse on principle, but then decided that was silly. She was officially on holiday now and so why not avail herself of a bed in a private jet?

Khalil still hadn't appeared and she worried that she wasn't going to sleep while obsessing about him, but she must have been more tired than she thought, because she fell asleep as soon as her head hit the pillow.

She slept like the dead and the next thing she knew she was being woken by a stewardess, who told her that they were two hours out of Al Da'ira, and that she could avail herself of the bathroom facilities, which included a shower. His Majesty had also provided fresh clothes for her to wear. Because of course he had.

Sidonie stared at the dress that had been laid out on the small couch near the bed, the leaf-green silk contrasting vividly with the cream of the leather. It was beautiful, designed to wrap around her torso before flowing out into full, floaty skirts that dropped from her hips.

Her throat tightened, aching suddenly. She should be irritated at him for again arrogantly providing her with clothing that she had no doubt would fit perfectly, as would the lacy green silk bra and knickers that had also been provided. But she wasn't.

The lonely child she'd once been had never had anything bought for her. She'd had to wear clothes that were too small and shoes that were too tight, because her aunt hadn't noticed her growing. And even when Sidonie had told her that she couldn't fit into her clothes any more, her aunt had acted as if she was making a fuss over nothing. There had never been birthday presents. Never been Christmas presents. Only the bare minimum had been provided and she was expected to be grateful.

But this…this was not the bare minimum. This dress

was beautiful, in a colour she loved, and in her size. It had been bought specifically for her.

He thought of you. He remembered.

Her chest tightened as another memory drifted through her head. Of that twenty-first birthday party Khalil had arranged for her, and how she hadn't been expecting presents, since she never got anything, not for her birthday.

The party itself had been so wonderful and dancing with him more wonderful still, and she'd thought nothing could top it. Then, after everyone had gone, Khalil had given her a birthday present. It was a dainty necklace that consisted of a simple gold chain with a golden sun that sat in the hollow of her throat.

'Because you are sunshine, Sidonie,' he'd said. *'My sunshine.'*

She'd fallen in love with him in that moment. For the party he'd organised for her and the touching present he'd given her. She'd loved him for how he'd known what it would mean to her, and that she hadn't had to ask. Because her whole life up to that point had been having to ask for everything. And being afraid to.

Khalil had never made her feel afraid to ask. Not once.

And look what happened. Being cut dead on a snowy Soho street.

Oh, yes, she remembered. And the next day she'd thrown his necklace in the rubbish.

The memory was too painful, so she pushed it away, taking a shower instead and putting on the silky underwear and the beautiful dress. And indeed, when she looked at herself in the mirror, not only was it a perfect fit, but it also suited her. The colour accentuated her red hair and brought out the green in her eyes.

She debated briefly, putting her hair up into its usual

bun, but then decided that, since she was on holiday, she was going to leave it loose.

He might like it like that.

Yes. He might. And she could use that perhaps.

Satisfied with her appearance, Sidonie stepped out of the bedroom and went into the lounge area.

And stopped dead.

Khalil was sitting on one of the couches, his arms resting along the back, long, powerful legs stretched out in front of him and crossed at the ankles. He wore a black suit and a black shirt with a silk tie of many different shades of green.

Sidonie's heart leapt into her throat, her mouth going dry.

He was absolutely mesmerising.

And he was looking straight at her.

Khalil had been waiting for Sidonie to wake up for a good ten minutes and, while he'd tried for patience, this time he found each passing second a trial. He hadn't slept during the flight and he'd purposefully not visited her since they'd taken off either.

He'd had a lot of work to do and didn't want to waste time sleeping, and he'd also decided that the key to her agreeing to marrying him would be to keep her hungry for him and his presence.

You wouldn't have been able to sleep anyway. Not after that kiss.

Khalil ignored the thought. He'd never allowed his hungers to affect him in such a way and he wasn't going to start now.

Yet the moment Sidonie stepped out of the plane's

bedroom, glowing in the green silk gown he'd had made especially for her, all he was aware of was his hunger.

Green had always been his favourite colour on her. It made her skin seem pale as cream and drew emerald sparks from her eyes.

She'd used to wear a loose, silky green blouse almost exactly the same colour as the gown she wore now, and it had been his favourite. Once, when she'd invited him out to dinner at a restaurant one evening with some of her friends, she'd leaned across him to get something, and the fabric had brushed against his bare arm. He'd been transfixed. All he'd been able to think about was whether her skin would feel as soft and silky as her blouse, and how he wanted to find out.

She'd only been his friend for a couple of months at that stage, but that had been the first moment he'd realised he wanted her.

He could feel that want now, sparking in the air between them, along with an intense satisfaction that she'd put on the dress he'd bought for her and that she looked as beautiful in it as he'd thought she would.

No. She looked better. She was perfection. Exactly how he'd wanted her to look as he brought her back to his country as his bride. Bright and beautiful and all wrapped in green, like a spring morning. A sign of hope and a kinder, gentler change.

He didn't move for a second, taking her in.

A flush stained her lovely cheeks, but her gaze was cool. Clearly, the veneer was back in place. It didn't matter. Tonight he would shatter it once more, or at least put a few more cracks in it, and by the end of the two weeks she'd allowed, it would be gone completely. And his Sidonie would finally be what she'd always meant to be: his.

She is supposed to be for your country, not for you.

Well, of course. But he could have a small piece of her for himself. It was only physical hunger, and she would be his wife. Heirs had to be got somehow.

'Thank you for the dress, Khalil.' Her voice was as cool as her gaze. 'It's beautiful. But it's really more suitable for a ball than getting off a plane.'

'The arrival of my intended bride requires some ceremony.' He got to his feet, unable to stop staring at her and the way the gown wrapped around her, clinging to the generous curves of her breasts, waist and hips. 'And green is the colour of change.'

Her red brows drew together. 'But I'm not your intended bride. I told you that I was—'

'*You* have decided that you are not,' he interrupted gently. 'But *my* decision remains. You are the bride I have chosen and I will announce you as such.'

Her chin firmed, little sparks of anger glittering deep in her eyes. She was holding it back. He could see that now. Her veneer was not perfect. 'So what happens when I leave? After you've made such a big song and dance about me?'

He shrugged. 'Then you will leave.'

'But what will your people think? After you've told them that I'm going to be your queen?'

'I thought it did not matter,' he said silkily, 'because they are not your people.'

She reddened. 'No, but I don't want to be presented as something I'm not. It's a bit too much like lying for comfort.'

'If it makes you feel any better, I am not lying to my people. I truly believe that you will be my intended bride.'

'But I don't, Khalil. I don't believe that.'

The thing inside him, the predator, shifted. The way she challenged him excited him, the way it had always excited him. He was used to people doing whatever he said and certainly no one argued with him, and the fact that Sidonie was resisting him at every turn both annoyed and fascinated him.

She'd done the same back when they'd been friends, refusing to bow to his arrogance and always calling him out on it.

'You're being ridiculous, Khal,' she'd say, laughing. *'You're not a prince here, remember?'*

He wasn't, and he'd loved that, and that was why part of him had never wanted to leave England. Never wanted to leave her. The thought of returning to Al Da'ira to eventually take his crown, be a king, had seemed at times…unbearable.

She's dangerous. Remember that.

She had been back then, because back then there had been some softness in him. But that softness had gone. He'd cut it out of himself, along with that longing to stay in England with her. There was no longing now, and she was no longer a threat.

He shrugged. 'Then we will have an interesting two weeks, will we not?'

Something flashed in Sidonie's gaze, another challenge, and he felt that terrible part of him shift once again in response.

But he forced it back in its cage. He would not let it out. Not again.

'Come,' he said calmly. 'You need breakfast, and we land in an hour.'

She eyed him suspiciously but let herself be guided to a seat, and when breakfast was brought to them she ate with him. He'd already decided not to tell her about the custom of the Kings of Al Da'ira when it came to their brides, of carrying them into the new home they would share. The custom went back centuries, harking back to the days when the desert warriors went on raids to capture their wives, and, while Khalil was hell-bent on changing some of those customs, it wouldn't hurt to observe a few to ease the pain of too much change, too quickly.

She might not be happy with him carrying her, but the lack of sleep was catching up with him, and he was tired. He didn't want her to argue, not right now, and besides, a part of him wanted this very much. The part that had fantasised about a life that didn't involve his being a king. Where he was just a man and Sidonie was the woman he loved. Where he held her in his arms, nestled against his chest, and he carried her into the home they would share.

He would never be that man again, but he could indulge himself a little in that fantasy now, couldn't he? It didn't mean losing control of his baser appetites or admitting to any weaknesses. It was…merely appeasing old ghosts.

Anticipation gathered inside him as the breakfast was cleared away and the plane began its descent. Sidonie was gazing out of the window at the countryside unrolling beneath them, the vast mountains and wide deserts of his homeland. A stark and harsh land, but incredibly beautiful.

Once he'd stabilised the country, he had plans for a

big tourism push, to share Al Da'ira with the world. It was already a rich nation due to the oil, but his family's greedy hands had kept it for themselves, and so he'd also planned to redistribute that wealth amongst the wider populace. Once his people had food and good housing, they could then turn their attention to new business ventures such as tourism.

Survival mode was not good for anyone, as he knew all too well.

The plane descended then came in for a perfect landing on the private airstrip reserved for the royal family, and already he could see the usual entourage waiting to welcome their King back to his country.

That too involved a specific custom.

As his staff prepared to open the plane door, Khalil got to his feet, then reached out a hand to Sidonie, sitting opposite. She took it automatically and he could feel her stiffen as his fingers closed around her smaller ones, gathering them into his palm. Her eyes had gone wide, her luscious mouth opening.

No wonder. He could feel the electricity where their skin touched, a cascade of sparks igniting every nerve ending. Desire shifted and tightened, his body hardening in response, and he pulled her closer, looking down into her darkening green eyes and seeing his own desire mirrored back at him.

Tonight. He would do something about it tonight.

'What are you doing?' she asked huskily. 'I thought we were getting off the plane.'

'We are.' He let go of her hand, and before she had a chance to move away he picked her up and gathered her close against his chest. 'But as I said, there are certain customs I must follow.'

She'd gone rigid in his arms, her eyes widening. 'Khalil—'

'And one of those customs involves carrying my intended bride into the home we will share. My country is my home, therefore I will be carrying you from the plane to the car that will take us back to the palace.'

She glared at him, her body stiff. 'And as *I* said, I never agreed to be your intended bride.'

He tightened his grip, even though she hadn't moved, because she was warm and soft against his chest and he wanted to keep her there. 'Tell me you don't like being in my arms, Sidonie.' He stared down into her angry green eyes. 'Tell me you don't like being close to me. Make me believe it, and maybe I will let you walk to the car instead.'

Her mouth was a firm line, but then she looked away. 'You can have your custom.' A delicate pink flush stained her cheekbones. 'I don't want to offend your people.'

His satisfaction deepened. It wasn't about giving offence to his people, no matter what she said. She liked being in his arms, that was the truth.

'Of course not,' he murmured, turning towards the door. 'Though nothing you do could give offence.'

'I'm sure that's not true.'

He glanced down at her.

She was staring out of the open doorway of the plane, to the bright sun, the stark mountains, and the crowd of people standing on the tarmac ready to welcome them. There was a crease between her brows, her body tense where it rested against his, trepidation clear on her face.

'There is nothing you need to do,' he said, wanting to reassure her. 'You are here as my chosen one and as such you will be accepted without question.'

She glanced up at him and just like that the trepidation vanished, the cool veneer sliding once more back into place. 'And why is that? Because no one questions you?'

'Yes,' he said simply. 'The King has to be above question.'

Her mouth opened, no doubt to tell him something he didn't particularly want to hear, but it was time to exit the plane, and so he stepped through the doors and went down the stairs, Sidonie in his arms.

The most important members of his court were there, as he'd instructed them to be. They'd protested at his choice of potential queen, but he'd ignored them. He would have his way in this. He *would* change his country for the better.

He wouldn't let the death of Yusuf, the half-brother he'd defeated, have been for nothing.

Almost as one, the arrayed servants and members of his court dropped to their knees and prostrated themselves as he stepped off the stairs and onto the tarmac.

Sidonie's eyes went wide. 'I kind of didn't believe you when you told me that the Kings are semidivine here.'

'I take it you do now.' He strode through the crowd of servants and nobility, towards the long black limo that waited for them.

He didn't look at her, but he could feel her sharp gaze on him. 'Yes, I do,' she said. 'But what puzzles me is why you keep letting them believe that.'

They were nearing the car now, Al Da'ira's hot sun burning down on them even though it was still early in the morning.

'I do not let them believe anything,' he replied. 'My people make their own choices. However, their confidence in the crown was shaken by my father, and it is my job to give them back that confidence. Confidence that I am not the same as him.'

'But surely they can see that already?'

He glanced down, finding her clear green eyes staring back. 'They considered Amir just a man because he was so flawed. A king, on the other hand, must be without flaw. He must be more than a man, and so that is what I must be. It is a belief that will have to change some day and I will change it. But now is not the time. There are still too many scars left by my father.'

'I see.' Sidonie's voice was quiet, her gaze oddly searching. 'That's quite the standard you hold yourself to.'

For some reason the simple observation felt like a pressure against the piece of rock that was his heart. A pressure he had to ignore. It was a flaw that he thought he'd got rid of years ago.

They were at the car now and he paused as a servant leapt up from the tarmac to pull open the door, and then glanced down at the woman in his arms.

Her expression was difficult to interpret, but he was sure that the green sparks in her eyes weren't caused by anger now. She put a hand on his chest. 'Khalil.'

But whatever she was going to say, he didn't want to hear it. Didn't want to put any more pressure on that flaw. Besides, now wasn't the time for discussion. He had to be welcomed formally by his staff and then he would have a debrief from his advisors. That was likely to take a while, and if he didn't get to it now he wouldn't have time with her afterwards. And he wanted that time.

'Later,' he said. 'You will be going to the palace now.' He took a step to the open door of the limo and deposited her inside it.

'Wait.' Her fingers closed on his jacket, gripping tight, and that trepidation had crept back into her eyes again. 'You're not coming with me?'

The way she held on to him reminded him of too many things. Of that night in Soho, when she'd held on to his coat the way she was doing now, her green eyes full of painful hope. And he'd wanted more than anything for that beautiful mouth of hers to meet his and to hear the words no one had ever said to him before. *I love you.* And to say them back.

But he hadn't been able to then because he'd had a duty, and he still had that duty. Nothing had changed. He still was what he was, and those were words he could never say.

Love was not and never had been permitted to kings.

'I am not.' Gently he pulled her fingers from his jacket and because, after all, he couldn't help himself, he turned her palm up in his and bent to brush a kiss over it. 'But you will be well taken care of back at the palace and I will see you tonight.'

For a moment she just looked at him and he couldn't tell what she was thinking. Then she gave a nod, pulled her hand from his, and turned away.

CHAPTER SIX

SIDONIE STOOD BY the pool in the atrium that lay in the centre of what was the Queens' wing of Al Da'ira's royal palace.

The pool had been beautifully made with swirling patterns of blue, green, and gold tiles, its clear blue water full of glittering koi fish. There were water lilies here and there, the flowers open and filling the air with a delicate scent.

In the arcade surrounding the pool were shrubs in pots and at one end a fountain played. The light from the setting sun came through the glass that covered the atrium, painting the white marble floor with gold and red and pink.

It was beautiful.

In fact, the whole palace was beautiful, though she hadn't had a chance to explore it, not when most of her day since being transported from the airport to the palace had involved being introduced to the various staff members who'd be looking after her and then being shown around the Queens' wing.

That was beautiful too. It was a series of interconnected, white-tiled rooms with high, arched windows that gave magnificent views out over Al Da'ira's capital city, the mountains that surrounded it, as well as glimpses into private little courtyards full of fountains and orange trees.

There was a big, white-curtained bed piled high with pillows and a huge bathroom with a shower big enough for five people, as well as a vast bath carved from white marble veined with gold and set on a plinth. The rooms also contained a comfortable sitting room, a library, a small, private swimming pool with a waterfall at one end, and a gym with all the latest fitness machines. The palace staff member who had been assigned to her, a lovely woman in her late forties called Aisha, had also proudly showed her a study with everything she needed to work remotely, including a broadband connection, a desktop computer, and a sleek little laptop.

Everything was provided, including a wardrobe full of clothes and luxurious toiletries.

And tonight, Aisha had informed her, she'd be dining with His Majesty.

Sidonie swallowed, adjusting the neckline of the cocktail gown she was wearing. She'd wanted to stay in the green dress that she'd worn coming off the plane, but the moment she'd settled into her apartments Aisha had directed her to the wardrobe and had brought out the gown the King wanted her to wear for their dinner tonight.

It was in gold silk and floor-length, with a deep vee neckline that plunged between her breasts, almost to her navel, and long, flowing sleeves. The skirts were loose and flowing too. It would have been modest if not for that neckline.

She loved it. Gold wasn't a colour she had ever imagined wearing, but its rich tones made her skin gleam and her hair seem even redder, and that deep neckline... She wasn't able to wear a bra with it.

All that was missing, her brain reminded her helpfully, was the little gold necklace he'd given her for her twenty-first, the one she'd thrown away after he'd left her.

But there was no point thinking about that. The necklace was gone, part of the past she'd chosen to leave behind. And really, did she need it?

When she'd stepped out of the bedroom on the plane she'd seen blatant hunger leap in his eyes, and she'd felt fully the power of her sexuality. She'd once dreamed of him staring at her like that and he had, and it had been just as exhilarating, dizzying even, as she'd imagined. She'd wished she'd had more time to work out what she could do with it, but then there had been breakfast and they'd landed, and he'd pulled her into his arms and carried her from the plane.

She hadn't been entirely happy about that, because he hadn't warned her it would happen. Then he'd called her out on how much she liked being close to him and she hadn't been able to deny it.

He'd held her before, back when they'd been friends— that wasn't unusual. Hugs to greet one another and to say goodbye. Hugs of congratulation or commiseration. Hugs of comfort when the anniversary of her parents' death came around and she grieved the family she'd lost.

But the way he'd held her as they'd disembarked the plane had been different. He'd felt different. His chest had been broader and harder, his arms powerful and steady, and it hadn't been anything like those long-ago hugs. The intensity in his eyes as he'd looked down at her had stolen her breath. There had been a triumph of sorts in them, as if she was a prize he'd won, and yes, she'd liked it.

Being close to him had been as intoxicating as it had been in Paris, and she'd found herself staring up at the sharp, stern lines of his beautiful face. Lines that hadn't been there years ago, she was sure of it. The sight had made something inside her ache.

His expression was so hard, like granite, and all his court with their faces pressed to the tarmac.

'A king, on the other hand, must be without flaw. He must be more than a man, and so that is what I must be.'

Why did he think that? He'd mentioned his father as an example of flawed humanity, and she knew he was trying not to follow his example, but… Did he really think he had to be more than a man? And was it really for the sake of his people or for his own? As she'd told him, it was such a high standard to hold himself to.

'Miss Sullivan?'

Sidonie looked up from her contemplation of the fish pool, shoving away the ache that had somehow crept into her heart.

A servant in the black and gold of the palace livery was standing in the doorway to the atrium. He bowed. 'His Majesty requests the pleasure of your company. You are to follow me, please.'

It wasn't a request. It was an order. And if she hadn't been distracted by thinking of Khalil, she might have been annoyed by it. But she was distracted. She couldn't stop seeing the expression on his face as he'd carried her to the car. It had been so rigid. Then, as she'd gripped his jacket when she'd realised he wasn't coming with her, a sudden anxiety sitting in her gut, she'd seen that rigidity ripple, the look in his eyes softening almost imperceptibly. Then he'd kissed her hands.

The man you knew isn't gone. He's still in there somewhere.

Sidonie's heart ached a little more as she followed the

servant from the Queens' apartments and into the main palace wing. The marble floors were veined with gold and the walls were tiled in all kinds of patterns and in all kinds of colours, including glittering metallic silver and gold.

Did it matter if her friend was still there? Was that man still important to her? He'd been gone so long, and she'd changed so much. Did she really want to find him again? Connect with him again? After all her heart had suffered? Or was it easier only to deal with the stranger, the King he'd become?

She was only here for two weeks, after all, and she *would* leave at the end of it. And even if she did manage to find the friend she'd loved, what then?

You'd have married him. You wanted *to marry him.*

A shiver went through her. It was true, she had. That was why she'd insisted on that marriage promise. But now? She didn't know. Khalil her friend might still exist in Khalil the King, but did the old Sidonie still exist in her? And if she did, would she want to become her again? Let her heart get broken again?

You can't. You must protect yourself.

She did, yet… That ache inside her, that longing, was stronger now than it had ever been, even though she'd told herself she didn't feel it. The ache that told her she was a liar and that, while protecting herself was all well and good, it hadn't made her any happier.

Can you even remember the last time you were happy?

She tried not to think about that as they came to a stop outside a pair of massive gilded double doors. The King's wing of the palace. Ceremonial guards in black and gold uniforms were stationed outside and they regarded Sidonie without expression, allowing her and the servant to step through into the King's private apartments.

They were just as lushly tiled, though the furnishings were spare, perhaps to draw attention to the colours and swirling patterns of the tiles.

Eventually they stopped outside a simple door of dark wood. The man knocked once and then opened the door, gesturing to Sidonie to go inside.

Her heart gave a sudden hard beat, a fluttering feeling way down deep in her gut. A whisper of the old excitement that had used to grip her every time they met.

He still makes you feel like a love-sick teenager.

He did, oh, he did. And maybe she was a fool for still feeling this way so many years later, but she couldn't help it, just as she couldn't deny she felt it.

Taking a moment to steady herself, Sidonie then stepped through the doorway, the door closing softly behind her.

It was a small room and intimate, with more doors that stood open onto a perfect little courtyard. A fountain sat in the centre of the courtyard, filling the air with gentle music. The walls of the room were lined with bookshelves and on the floor were silken rugs in rich reds and deep blues. Low couches upholstered in pale linen stood grouped around an unlit fireplace and a low table in dark wood.

Khalil sat on one of the couches, reading something on a tablet, which he put down the moment the door opened.

He was dressed very simply, in a black robe embroidered with gold and loose black trousers. His chest was bare.

Her mouth dried completely.

She'd never seen him in anything but Western clothing, the jeans and T-shirt of a student, and then later a series of perfectly tailored, handmade suits. He'd been gorgeous in those, but dressed in the clothing of his country, with all that muscled bronze skin on show... God, he was stunning.

The sharp, predatory angles of his face seemed sharper somehow, his black eyes even blacker. He was every inch the regal, mesmerising, charismatic King.

Yet there was a part of her, a tiny, forgotten part, that felt a stab of disappointment. As if she'd wanted him to be someone else.

He rose as the door closed behind her, his intense gaze finding hers. 'Good evening, *ya hayati*. I hope you were well looked after today and that the accommodation is to your liking.'

Sidonie clasped her hands together in front of her, trying to keep her gaze from the broad expanse of his chest. Then she caught the gleam in his eyes as he watched her and realised suddenly that he'd done it on purpose. He was trying to tempt her, wasn't he? He was showing her what she could have if she married him.

You can't deny that you want it.

Oh, yes, she did. But sex wasn't enough of an inducement.

How would you know when you haven't had it?

'Yes,' she said, ignoring the voice in her head. 'The accommodation is perfect, actually. Though, I have to say, it's huge.'

'It would be. The Queens' wing was for queens, plural.'

Ah, yes, so it would. Khalil had told her that Amir had had four wives. He'd been the only child of wife number three and had been brought up in a house in the mountains, not at court.

'Your mother didn't live there, did she?' Sidonie asked, curious.

'No. She never wanted to. She preferred our house in the mountains.'

He'd told her of that house, with lots of gardens and trees, though his life there hadn't exactly been idyllic. There had been lots of rigorous schooling, he'd said, and physical training, and not much time for playing. No time for friends, either.

Hers had been the same, at least the school and friends part of it. Her aunt hadn't allowed her to have friends back because she hadn't wanted any 'shouting and screaming'. And Sidonie hadn't gone to other kids' houses because she hated asking her aunt to take her. Sometimes May would, but she always acted as if it were a huge imposition.

'Why?' Sidonie asked. 'Didn't she like living with the other wives?'

'She did not. She fell out of favour with my father anyway and he had her sent away.'

'Oh? Why was that?'

'She did not like the way he acted, and she was not afraid to tell him so. She also wanted to protect me.' Khalil's eyes gleamed. 'Do not worry, Sidonie. I will not be having more than one wife, I told you that.'

Sidonie had heard the horror stories of the battle of succession, a custom where the oldest children of each queen would fight a ritualistic battle for the right to be named heir. Long ago there had been assassination attempts on children and their mothers to take them out of the running, Khalil had told her, and that sometimes it still happened.

She knew Khalil had wanted to change that, since

his own battle had involved wounding his half-brother, Yusuf, badly enough that Yusuf had had to concede the crown. She'd been appalled when he'd told her about it, instantly afraid for him, and had wanted to ask more questions, but he'd changed the subject. And since it had been clearly a painful memory, she hadn't pushed him.

But…would he tell her now if she asked? Would it still be painful for him? Or was this all he was? This hard, cold king who looked as if he'd never known a moment's pain in all his life?

'What is it?' Khalil asked, his deep voice dark and smooth. 'You are looking at me very intently.'

And she answered without thought. 'I'm wondering what happened to my friend, Khalil.'

Sidonie stood there in the golden gown he'd chosen for her and she was every bit as beautiful in it as she'd been in the green dress she'd worn on the plane. She was glowing almost, the gold fabric making her look as if she'd been bathed in sunlight. Her red hair was in a simple, loose ponytail that hung over her shoulder and curled down over her chest, drawing attention to the deep neckline and the shadowed curves of her breasts.

He'd been looking forward to this moment all day. The moment when he'd finally be alone with her and he could start the business of convincing her to say yes to his marriage proposal.

He'd prepared and his preparations were thorough.

A special meal would be brought here, to his favourite room, which he often used when he needed some time alone, along with some of Al Da'ira's finest wines. And while they ate, he'd talk to her about all the benefits of being his wife. Then after that he'd continue with the seduction he'd initiated back in Paris, demonstrate those benefits physically.

In fact, he was thinking that maybe he'd seduce her first, before the dinner. He was finding it difficult to pay attention to what she was saying, too distracted by the sight of her.

'Your friend?' he asked impatiently. 'I told you. He is gone.'

'Why?'

'Because he was not the man to rule this country.'

A crease deepened between her brows. 'I don't understand. I thought he'd have made an excellent king.'

The pressure in his chest, the one that had gripped him that morning as he'd put her in the car, intensified. Why was she talking about this? Their friendship had been precious, a long golden summer in the middle of a harsh winter, but it was gone now. It was over, and the man he'd once been had gone along with it, and that man wasn't coming back.

'He was not strong enough,' Khalil said. 'I told you; a king must be more than a man.' Gesturing at the couch, he went on, 'Come and sit with me, *ya hayati*. I will pour you a glass of wine and you can tell me about your charity while we wait for our meal.'

She gave him a considering look and he thought she might not let it go, but then she came over to the couch and sat down, the neckline of her golden gown shifting, giving him the most intriguing glimpse of the shadowed valley between her breasts. It was obvious that she was not wearing a bra.

His heartbeat accelerated, sudden and intense desire gripping him. It would be so easy to seduce her right here on the couch, to have her naked and beneath him, to be inside her. It wouldn't take him long. She wanted him. The way she kept looking very pointedly everywhere except at his chest told its own story and that was as he'd hoped.

You are too impatient.

Yes, that was true. But he'd waited a long time to have her. And no matter what he thought about the man he'd been, that man's memories still filled his head.

Of Sidonie looking up at him the night he'd given her that necklace for her twenty-first. A sun because she'd been sunshine to him. There had been tears in her eyes along with a bright, painful emotion that had caught him by the throat. She'd looked at him as if he'd given her the moon and all the stars, and he'd wanted to kiss her right then and there. Wanted to tell her that he meant it, that she was the only sun in his sky. Because after Yusuf's death, he'd been able to see nothing but darkness.

Except he hadn't kissed her, and he hadn't told her, because he couldn't back then. He hadn't wanted to start something he wouldn't be able to finish.

But things were different now. She wasn't his sun any more—he didn't need sunshine to survive these days—but she was still every bit as beautiful, every bit as desirable as she'd been back then. And now he could kiss her. Now he could do more than that, and he wanted to. He *wanted* to.

She was fussing with her dress, pulling at the neckline, and, since he was still standing, he found his gaze settling on the curves of her breasts and the pale, creamy skin revealed by the fabric.

Her gaze lifted to his suddenly and he didn't look away. Didn't make any attempt to pretend he had been looking anywhere else but at her and the beauty of her body.

A flush rose into her cheeks, but she didn't look away either. Her eyes darkened as the space between them became full of a crackling tension, all the aching years of desire and the pull of a longing he'd deliberately cut out of his heart.

Are you sure it isn't still there?

No, of course it wasn't. The longing he felt now was only physical.

'Why did you go?' she asked abruptly. 'Why did you walk away from me that night?'

It was the very last question he'd expected and the very last question he wanted to answer. Though he should have known she'd ask at some point. And he had to tell her. She had to understand what he was now. Who he was now.

'I had to.' His voice was rougher than he wanted it to be. 'I was always going to leave, Sidonie. I had a country to rule. Al Da'ira was my responsibility, and I could not walk away from it.'

'But I told you I loved you, Khalil. And you just…left.'

The pressure inside him climbed. He knew he'd been abrupt, knew that his sudden dismissal of her had hurt her, but it was either that or drag her into his arms, which would have been equally hurtful.

'Yes,' he said. 'What you told me was a shock and I did not…know how to deal with it.'

Her expression was painful in its honesty. 'Was me loving you so very bad?'

'No, of course not.' The tight feeling in his chest made him ache. 'But… I could not love you in return, Sidonie, though I very much wanted to. All I could do was walk away.'

There was a kind of anguish in her eyes that felt like a knife to his heart, and some part of him was disturbed by it and the pressure inside him. She shouldn't still have the power to affect him like this. She shouldn't.

'And that email?' There was pain in her voice. 'Did you really have to tell me not to contact you again?'

There was pain inside him too now, seeking the flaw in the stone, trying to crack him apart. But he was harder than that these days. Far too hard. He had tempered himself in the fire his mother had built for him, to protect him, and now nothing could get through. Not even her.

'Yes.' He held her gaze, letting her see who he was now. What he would always be. 'I sent you that email because the friend I was to you, the friend you remembered... I could no longer be him. And I thought it was better that you forget me.'

Her green eyes darkened still further, becoming the colour of deep jungle forests, full of shadows. 'I don't understand, Khalil. You know, I wasn't asking you to love me back. I just wanted to tell you how I felt. And I get that it was a shock. But dismissing five years of close friendship because...what? You didn't want to be my friend any more? That I don't get at all.'

The ache in his chest twisted. He didn't know why he still felt it, why it was still there after all these years when it shouldn't be. Memories, yes, he could do nothing about those, but that ache, that longing, that *feeling*...

Feelings were not allowed. They never had been. His mother had taught him that and he'd learned those lessons well.

'It was not that I did not want to, Sidonie,' he said flatly. 'I could not. Love, friendship...they are not allowed for a king. Yes, I could have remained in contact. I could have continued to visit England. But I was not the man you remembered, and I thought... I thought that would hurt you.'

Her gaze flickered, her expression closing up and becoming for once unreadable. 'I should never have told you that, should I? Never have said I loved you. That was my mistake.'

A brief flare of remembered agony went through him once again, at the memory of the painful hope in her eyes that night, and the pressure of his own terrible longing. A longing for a life that would never be his. A life with her.

He crushed the memory. Pain was another flaw he had cut out of his life. 'It was not a mistake,' he said roughly. 'But it was why I sent that email, yes. I thought a clean break would be easier.'

She stared at him. 'Easier for who? For me or for yourself?'

'Sidonie…' he began.

But she suddenly got to her feet and put out a hand, her palm landing on his bare chest, a starburst of heat crackling over his skin. He lost his breath, every muscle he had gathering tight.

'I didn't just lose a friend, Khalil,' she said, looking up at him, searching his face. 'Don't you understand? That night you broke my heart.'

Pain twisted inside him, the flex of an agony he shouldn't feel. Hurting her had never been the goal, but of course he'd hurt her. She'd told him she loved him, she'd revealed her heart to him, a heart that had been trodden on and walked over for years by her aunt, and he'd just…walked away.

You cannot let that matter. You did what you had to do.

He had. The decision to leave her, to cut her off, had been the hardest of his life, but that was what he'd been brought up to do: to make the hard decisions. To make them so people like her didn't have to.

He did not regret that decision. He'd had to make it for both of their sakes. But...it was obvious that the wound he'd caused had been deeper than he'd thought. And it hadn't healed. He could see by the pain in her eyes.

Apologies were the sign of a weak ruler, his mother had always said. A king made his decisions and he stood by them. He didn't doubt and he certainly never admitted to his mistakes.

But this had hurt her, and he wanted to make it up to her, to make it right, and there was only one way he knew how to do that. Words got in the way, and he was tired of talking, so he put his hand over hers where it rested on his chest and then he pulled her into his arms.

CHAPTER SEVEN

SIDONIE HADN'T WANTED to admit to him how he'd hurt her. She'd sworn she wasn't going to allow him to get to under her skin the way he'd done years ago, because to admit to that pain was to admit that he still mattered to her, even now.

Except he did matter. The loss of the man who'd once been the most important person in her life mattered. She couldn't deny it, and as he'd stood there, telling her that man was gone, that friendship couldn't matter to a king, she hadn't been able to hold back.

She wanted him to know what his walking away from her, his cutting her off had done, that he'd broken her heart. And maybe it had been a mistake to reveal that to him, but she couldn't keep hiding her hurt, not any more. It was too hard.

The problem is you, no matter what he said. You should never have told him you loved him.

She shouldn't have, not after the lessons she'd learned in her aunt's house. When to ask for anything or to reveal any feeling at all, even her joy, was an unwanted intrusion. But that night in Soho, she'd wanted him to know. He'd signed her marriage promise and she'd thought... She'd thought he'd felt the same way. A mistake.

He'd told her it hadn't been, that he'd been trying to

protect her because he'd had to go back to being a king, that he couldn't be her friend any longer, and she still didn't understand why. None of what he said about flaws and having to be more than a man made any sense.

But maybe that didn't matter right now.

It was all in the past and he was right here, his ink-black eyes looking down into hers, the hand at her back holding her firmly against him, making her aware of all the leashed power and strength contained in that muscled chest and ridged stomach, those powerful thighs…

She was aching deep inside, all the longing in her broken heart spilling out of her.

'I know, *ya hayati,*' he murmured and then raised both hands and cupped her face between them. Her heart was beating so loud she could barely hear him. 'And I will make it up to you, I promise.'

Then he tilted her head back and covered her mouth with his.

She sighed, intense relief sweeping through her. Despite her anger and sense of hurt, she'd been hoping for this moment, longing for it. And, while she'd had great plans of not letting her emotions get in the way once again, she couldn't remember what those plans were or even why she wanted to do that in the first place.

What was important now was that his mouth was on hers and he was kissing her, and all she wanted to do was melt into that kiss. To glory in it then give back to him all the pleasure that he was giving her.

She leaned into him and he angled her head back further, kissing her deeper, hungrier, and this time she began to kiss him back, tentative at first and then, as he made a soft growling sound in the back of his throat, with more confidence. He tasted so good, hot and rich and dark, like the very best chocolate and the finest brandy all rolled into one. She couldn't get enough.

His teeth sank into her bottom lip, giving her a nip that sent white-hot sparks of sensation along every single nerve ending, making her shudder in his arms. And then he was easing her down and onto the couch, his hands moving from her jaw to the neckline of her dress, pushing the golden fabric off her shoulders. The neckline was wide and loose anyway, so it didn't take much doing, and then she was sitting on the couch, bare to the waist.

The realisation sent a hot shock through her, but then he was bending over her, his mouth still on hers, her head resting on the back of the couch, kissing her senseless as his fingers brushed down the side of her neck to her collarbones, stroking gently. Then moving further down, delicately tracing the curve of one bare breast, touching her as if she was made of glass and had to be handled with care.

Her nipples tightened and she shivered, part of her reeling that this was actually happening, that she was half naked and he was touching her, while another part wanted more and harder and right now, because she was going to go up in flames and she didn't want to just yet... not quite yet.

She had waited for him for so long. She couldn't bear to wait any more.

'Khal...' she whispered against his mouth, arching into his hand. 'Khal, please...'

But he only gentled the kiss, turning it into a slow, deep exploration, at the same time as his fingers kept on brushing over her curves, learning her, stroking her skin as if he couldn't get enough of the feel of it.

She shuddered, her breath coming faster, ripples of delight forming wherever his fingers touched and moving outward, increasing that dragging, aching pressure that was concentrated between her thighs.

He circled one nipple lazily, tracing small circles around and around, teasing her, making her shudder and twist on the cushions, and then, just when she thought she was going to go mad, his thumb brushed over the tip of her breast, sending an arrow of such intense pleasure through her that she gasped aloud. Then he did it again, and again, and she gasped a second time, reaching for his hand to guide it where she wanted it.

'No.' His lips brushed hers as he moved his thumb back and forth over her nipple. 'Keep still for me, *ya hayati*. I will give you what you want, but I am going to savour this first. I am going to savour you.'

'But I… I…don't mind,' she said breathlessly. 'I want—'

'I know what you want.' His voice was very deep and very certain. 'But I have waited years for you and so I am going to take my time. You deserve nothing less.'

Years. He'd been waiting years.

Her heart squeezed tight in her chest. There were so many things she wanted to say that right now she didn't care about what she deserved, she only wanted him to end this exquisite torment, but it was clear that nothing she could do was going to stop him.

So she let her hand fall away and kept still as he kissed her long and deep and lazy, his hand stroking one breast and then the other, making her pant and arch, the pressure between her thighs becoming almost unbearable.

The way he touched her made her ache, made her feel vulnerable, made her remember all those fleeting moments of contact over the years. The gentle hand on her arm, the touch on her shoulder. The warmth of his arms as he'd pulled her in for that dance the night of her birthday. No one had ever held her the way he had. No one had ever touched her the way he did. No one had ever touched her full stop. Not since her parents had died. Her aunt hadn't hugged her, or kissed her, had never even laid a hand on her shoulder for comfort, not even at her parents' funeral. She hadn't realised how starved for touch she'd been until now.

Until Khalil's stroking her, caressing her as if she was a work of art he needed to be careful with. A precious work of art.

Had she ever felt precious to anyone? No, she didn't think she had, but she felt it now. She felt precious to him.

He put one knee on the cushion beside her, his powerful body leaning further over her, his mouth moving down her neck to the hollow of her throat and lingering, tasting the frantic beat of her pulse. His palm was hot against one breast and he squeezed it gently, making her shudder, then he slid it down further, beneath the gold fabric of her dress, over her stomach.

Sidonie went utterly still, every part of her trembling as his fingers slid lower. She let her thighs fall open, desperate for him to touch her there, and he finally did, pushing beneath the waistband of the lacy knickers she wore and brushing over the slick folds of her sex.

She cried out, lifting her hips into his hand, wanting more, but he only stroked her lazily, his fingers sliding and exploring everywhere except the place where she needed it most. His mouth lingered at her throat and then moved lower, tasting the curve of one breast. Then his tongue traced a burning circle around her nipple, his fingers between her thighs mirroring the movement, again and again, until she was whispering his name, barely conscious of what she was saying.

Then right when she thought she couldn't bear another second, the heat of his mouth closed over her aching nipple at the same time as his fingers moved between her thighs, brushing over the most sensitive part of her, and the pressure inside her burst apart like a firework, the most intense, unbearable, incredible pleasure flooding through her.

She gave a helpless cry of ecstasy, shaking and shaking and unable to stop, until she thought she might come apart at the seams. But then he was on the couch beside her, pulling her into his lap, his arms warm and strong around her, holding her, keeping her together as the aftershocks passed.

She lay against him, her head on his shoulder, relaxed and heavy and sated, unable to move and not wanting to either.

He was very still and gradually she became conscious that, though the beat of his heart was strong and steady, all his muscles were tense. She could feel the hard press of his arousal and it made her flush with heat. That was because of her, wasn't it? She'd aroused him, she'd made him hard. That was all her.

She shifted her head on his shoulder and looked up at him. He was staring back, his eyes sharp as shattered obsidian, a deep, hot glitter in them.

'Khal,' she said huskily. 'Do you need—?'

'No.' There was an unfamiliar, rough edge to his voice. 'That was for you and only for you. You do not have to reciprocate.'

'But you're hard.'

He lifted one eyebrow. 'So? I am quite able to manage myself, believe me.'

She swallowed, searching his face, something inside her falling away. And the question came out before she could stop herself. 'Is it me?'

He frowned. 'What do you mean?'

'You're hard but you don't want me to touch you. You don't want me to give you pleasure.' Her chest felt tight, an echo of his rejection from so long ago resounding through her. 'Is there something the matter with me? Is that why you don't—?'

Khalil laid a finger across her mouth, silencing her, a burning look in his eyes. 'There is nothing wrong with you, Sidonie. *Nothing.* Why would you say that?'

She shook his finger away, her heart beating far too fast. Protecting herself was instinctive these days, but there was no protecting herself from him. She understood that now. 'Why wouldn't I think that? All I got from Aunt May was how much of a burden I was and how grateful I should be for every little thing she gave me. She made me ask for everything, and I always felt so needy and desperate when I did. And then...' Her throat was tight, and she had to swallow past the lump in it. 'When you walked away from me that night, I thought I'd frightened you away. I thought that Aunt May was right about me. I *was* too needy and desperate. I was just...wrong somehow.'

The words hung in the air between them, and she wished abruptly that she could take them back. She'd been too honest and that left her vulnerable.

She shivered, but didn't look away, even though part of her was dreading his response. She wouldn't be a coward.

His gaze was full of darkness, but something bright glowed at the heart of it, a flame that burned hot and strong. 'It is a good thing your aunt is in England. If she was here, I would have had her imprisoned.' A note of ferocity vibrated in his voice. 'And I would have had myself thrown into a cell with her.'

Sidonie took a shaky breath. 'The problem isn't you. The problem is—'

'The problem is that your aunt stifled and starved you,' he interrupted harshly. 'She hurt you. The way she brought you up was a crime, and the fact that despite that you remain such a warm, bright light is a testament to your strength and your courage.'

She blinked, staring at him, her heart squeezing tighter and tighter.

'And I did not help,' he went on. 'I did not think about how leaving you would affect you. I knew cutting you off completely would hurt you, but I thought that you would heal.' His arms around her tightened, the look in his eyes abruptly intensifying. 'You asked me whether it was easier for you or for myself, and the truth is... The truth is that it was for myself. Because I did not want to leave you, *ya hayati*. I wanted to stay with you. I wanted to give you the family you wanted and be at your side. I wanted to marry you. But my country needed me. I could not have that longing in my heart and still be a king.'

'Khalil,' she whispered, her throat tight and sore.

'No, I have not finished. You wondered where your friend is? He died, Sidonie. Leaving you hurt him, and because I could not have that pain and be the king my country needed me to be, I had to destroy him.'

Her heart was now a hot, sharp ball in her chest, full of jagged edges. He was telling the truth, she could hear it in the intense note in his voice, in that flame in his eyes. It made her throat close with bittersweet anguish, and an old, remembered grief.

The look on his face that night as she'd told him she

loved him, his expression becoming hard and cold and set. A stranger's face.

This man's face. The King's face.

But inside he hadn't been hard and cold. He hadn't wanted to go. He'd wanted to stay with her.

There were tears in her eyes now; she couldn't stop them. And she didn't know what to say. He'd told her that the friend she knew was gone, that he'd destroyed him. But part of her didn't believe that. Because if that was true, why had he told her all of this? Why had he come back to England? Why had he been so insistent on marrying her?

Oh, he'd had many reasons and they all sounded good, but... His mouth on hers had been so hot and hungry, and she'd been able to taste his need. His desperation.

He'd brought her here for a reason, and maybe he wasn't fully aware of what the real reason was, but she knew.

He'd brought her here to save him.

She lifted her hand and touched his face. 'I don't think he's dead, Khal. I think he's still here. And I think he needs me.'

Sidonie's pretty face was flushed and those fascinating emerald-green eyes of hers held a softness he remembered. It was painful, that softness, reminding him of too many things he didn't want to recall.

But he didn't want to let her go, no matter how painful or otherwise it was to have her there.

Giving her pleasure had tested both his control and his patience to the limit. She had blushed so beautifully, had whispered his name so huskily, and her skin had felt like satin and had tasted as sweet as he'd thought it would—

no, it had tasted better. Made him hungry for more, to have her naked with nothing between them.

But this wasn't about him and what he wanted. This was about her and wanting to give her pleasure to make up for all the years of pain, and he had. He just hadn't expected her to turn around and want to give him the same back again.

You should have. She was never one just to take.

Of course she wasn't. But he'd needed time to get himself under control. He'd felt too close to the edge, and she called that old poisonous blood to the surface far too easily.

Except then she'd taken his refusal as a rejection and there had been pain in her eyes. Pain in her voice as she'd talked about her aunt. And some part of him hadn't been able to let that go.

He should have known it would all lead back to Aunt May and her emotionally barren upbringing, and he just couldn't let her believe that there was something needy and desperate about her. As if those things were wrong, which they weren't. Sidonie had lost her parents too young and had been brought up by someone who'd withheld the love and affection she should have had.

That didn't make her needy and desperate. It made her hungry because she'd been starved.

Knowing that meant he couldn't hold back the truth about what had happened all those years ago. She should know how desperately he'd wanted to stay with her and how leaving her had caused him pain. Because it had. And how he'd had to cut away that part of himself. A king could not be broken. A king was strength enduring and there could be no flaws, no jagged pieces of a shattered friendship piercing his heart.

There were no flaws in him now, so he wasn't sure why her soft words sent a jolt of electricity down his spine. She was wrong, of course. The dead part of him was gone.

He took her hand from his cheekbone, kissed her fingertips. 'If he were still alive, *ya hayati*, he would. But he is not. Come, we did not have our dinner in Paris, and I do not want to deny you the birthday feast I promised.'

Yet she didn't move, her red hair over his shoulder as she looked up at him, her gaze glinting green from beneath long, auburn lashes. 'I don't think you brought me here for your country, Khal,' she murmured. 'I think you told yourself that and I think you believe that. But that's not really the reason, is it?'

He stilled. That gaze of hers, it seemed to see inside him. The way it had years ago. She'd always seen deeper than other people. Everyone at Oxford had thought his arrogance had been a pride thing—even Galen and Augustine. But only she had understood that it had been a self-protective thing, to keep people at a distance. He'd never told her why, had only said that Yusuf had been injured in the succession battle, because he couldn't bear to tell her the truth, that he'd killed him. He couldn't tell her either, about the shadow Yusuf's death had cast over his life, or about the doubts that had plagued him. Doubts the heir to the throne should never have had.

He hadn't wanted to tarnish her light with his darkness.

He couldn't even bear to do it now.

She's right, though, you did bring her here for you.

No. She was here for his people, his court. For his country. He wanted to marry her for them, not for himself. He wanted her, it was true, but that was a purely physical want. A man had needs certainly, but he wasn't a man, not any more. He was a king.

'There is no deeper reason, Sidonie,' he said, an edge creeping into his voice. 'What I told you about being the queen my people need is true.'

'Maybe. But why care about me, then?' She pulled her hand from his and touched his cheek again, her fingers light and cool against his skin. 'Why give me these beautiful dresses and prepare dinners for me? Why give me two weeks? Why agree to be the patron of my charity? Why bother to discuss this with me at all?'

Everything in him tightened. 'Because I wanted your agreement. I did not want to demand or use force. Those are my father's tactics, and I will not use them.'

'No, Khal.' Her hand dropped to his chest, her fingers trailing over his skin, stroking him. 'You can tell yourself those things, but I don't think they're true.' Her gaze was so clear, so direct. 'I think I'm here because my friend needs me and I'm the only one who can save him.'

'I have told you, that is not—'

But this time it was her turn to silence him with a gentle finger across his mouth. 'You don't have to be a king with me, Khalil. You never did. Just as you were never a prince all those years ago.' She lifted the finger then dropped her hand over the front of his trousers, tracing his rapidly hardening length through the fabric. 'You were just a man back then, just my friend. And you can be that now, don't you see? You don't have to be anything more than who you already are with me.'

His whole body felt tight, the heat inside him building. And he wanted to stop her, because his body, after all, was only a man's and it was tired of constant control. It wanted her. It had been waiting for her for ten years and it didn't want to wait any more.

Yet what she was saying couldn't be. That man had

known happiness, had known love, but it wasn't something that was possible for a king. A king was a surgeon, cutting out anything that might make his country sick, and sometimes that was healthy tissue. He needed steady hands for it, and a cold, clear, analytical brain. He couldn't afford to be at the mercy of either his body or his heart.

Except he could feel need inside him, that desperate, terrible longing he thought he'd excised so long ago. The longing for her. For her hands and her mouth, and the beautiful body he'd fantasised about and wanted so badly. For her heat to chase away the dark.

He could have that at least, couldn't he? It was only physical, and after all, he was going to need heirs at some point. No, she hadn't agreed yet to marry him, but perhaps if he gave her what she wanted now, she might.

He could remember what it was like to be that man for her. Not pretend—he had no need to fake anything with her—but he could try to be at least a little like that man again. He couldn't be him totally, but maybe with her alone he could.

He'd just have to make sure when he was away from her to be the King he had to be.

Her hand pressed against him, the heat of her palm seeping through the light cotton of his trousers. The breath hissed in his throat, a spike of pure pleasure lancing through him.

Her eyes had darkened, and so he put his own hand over hers and held it against him, the light pressure almost agonising.

Her fingers squeezed lightly.

'Sidonie…' Her name came out half a groan, half a growl.

She moved closer, her scent all around him, her warmth seductive as a siren's song, making him acutely aware of every second of those ten years of longing.

'I want you, Khalil,' she said huskily, the honesty that was at the core of her laid bare. 'I want to give you pleasure.' Her eyes had darkened still further, like shadowed forests. 'Teach me. Teach me how to make you feel good. Please…' The way she said the words, the plea in her voice…

Desire burned hot in his blood, the way she was touching him making it difficult to think. Not that there was any thinking needed. Not when he'd already made his decision.

Khalil pulled her hand away and lay back on the couch cushions with her on top of him, her soft warmth against his chest. She was very flushed, the slightest hint of challenge in her eyes. A shudder of heat coursed down his spine, his heartbeat accelerating.

'You wanted to touch me,' he said roughly. 'So touch me like this.' And he took her hand and drew it down over his stomach, to the waistband of his trousers, then beneath the loose linen fabric and under the cotton of his underwear, to where he was hard and ready for her.

Her eyes widened, her mouth opening slightly as he curled her fingers around him. A sigh escaped her.

'Yes,' he growled, the pressure of her hand sweet agony. 'Stroke me, Sidonie.'

So she did. Hesitantly at first, then with growing confidence, her gaze on his, watching his reaction to her touch.

It was incredibly erotic. But he wanted to taste her so he reached out and slid a hand behind the back of her head, pulling her mouth down on his, kissing her hungrily.

Sidonie moaned and kissed him back, her hand moving, doing what he told her to and stroking him.

The intensity of the pleasure was impossible to contain. Every nerve-ending he had was alight from the touch of her hand and the taste of her mouth. He'd waited years for her touch. Years and years. Had once wanted it more than life itself.

He had it now and it was going to destroy him.

Well, he would let it. Because in this moment, she was right. He didn't have to be a king. Right now, with her, he could be a man, take all the pleasure and passion she was giving him and drown himself in it.

So for the first time in his life, Khalil didn't think. He didn't reflect or pause to examine the implications. He acted on instinct, driven by desire and desperation, and a need deeper than words.

He shifted, pulling her hand away from him and turning her over onto her back, settling himself between her thighs. Then he bent and kissed her again, hungrier than he'd ever been in his entire life. 'I have to have you, Sidonie,' he said in a voice he didn't recognise as his own. 'I have to have you, *now*.'

CHAPTER EIGHT

THE WORDS WERE rough gravel and velvet and the heat in them nearly set her alight. He was a hot, heavy weight on her, pressing her into the couch cushions, and she loved it. She loved the feel of him pinning her there, holding her down, reducing her world to the softness of the cushions beneath her, and the hardness of the man on top of her.

'Yes,' she whispered, her hands sliding up his chest, pushing the robe he was wearing off his powerful shoulders, wanting to keep on touching him because the feel of his skin, velvety smooth and so hot, was like a drug she couldn't get enough of. 'Oh, yes. *Please.*'

She thought she'd got through to him and that some part of him had heard her. He'd resisted her telling him the man was still a part of him, his body taut with negation, but something in him had surrendered to her.

Now it was her turn to surrender to him.

It was as if something had been unleashed inside him, because his mouth was on hers again and he was kissing her deeply, with all the intensity that was part of him. And Sidonie felt herself go up in flames.

There was nothing in the entire world except the heat of his mouth and his skin beneath her fingers, the wild, intoxicating taste of him and his hands pulling at her dress, easing it up, getting it out of the way. Then he tugged at her underwear, the flimsy lace of her knickers tearing and coming away so she was naked from the waist down.

He freed himself from his loose trousers and underwear, and then he was right there, between her thighs, pushing inside her. She gasped, feeling herself stretch around him. It burned, but she was so ready for him that the burning sensation stopped almost as soon as it had begun. There was no pain as he pushed deeper, only an intense feeling of fullness that had her shifting and squirming beneath him, trying to find some space for herself, because it felt as if he took up every part of her.

Then he slid one hand behind her right knee, lifting her leg up and over his hip, opening her up so he could ease deeper, making her gasp aloud, shuddering as the sense of fullness became more intense.

'Sidonie,' he murmured, his deep voice rough and full of heat. 'My Sidonie...' He looked down at her, his gaze black and velvety and all-encompassing. 'You are mine, *ya hayati*.' The fierce, possessive note in the words thrilled her down to the bone. 'You know it. You feel it.'

He began to move inside her, flexing his hips in a deep thrust in before a slow, delicious slide out, turning the sensation from an uncomfortable fullness to an insistent, aching pleasure that tore a moan from her throat.

She couldn't look away, pinned to the couch as much by the look in his eyes as by the thrust of his hips, and soon she was moving with him, watching the same pleasure she felt burning in her light the darkness of his eyes.

She did feel it. Because this was what he'd always given her, the release of the passion inside her, all the deep feelings living with her aunt had stifled.

Yet it hadn't been her aunt stifling her these past five years. It had been herself. She'd protected her heart, saved it from pain, and yet as he moved inside her, the pleasure intensifying, she knew she'd lost something.

Something he was giving back to her, right here in this moment.

His name escaped like a prayer as ecstasy began to overtake her, and her nails dug into his shoulders because it was too much and yet not enough.

He'd always been giving her things. Birthday presents and parties. The rare treasure of his smile. The gift of his anger at those who hurt her, and the most important thing of all: acceptance.

He'd accepted the wild part of her, the passionate part. The part she'd locked away for years after her aunt had crushed it and he'd given her the key to unlock it again. And he'd gloried in it as much as she had.

'Don't stop.' The words fell helplessly from her, and she let them. Just as she let him see what he was doing to her. 'Please, Khal. Please don't stop.'

He didn't say anything, but his gaze flared and he moved faster, harder. He slid one hand behind her head, holding her still, and then he bent and covered her mouth once again in a kiss so hot it felt like a brand against her skin.

Her heart swelled inside her, pushing painfully against her ribs.

He still gloried in that part of her. She'd pushed back at him, but he hadn't taken her 'no' for an answer. He hadn't let her push him away. And now she was here with him above her, inside her, all around her, wanting her, demanding her passion...

She couldn't hold herself back any longer.

She surrendered, losing herself to the pleasure he was giving her, the pleasure they were creating together, building like a bonfire, adding more tinder until it was a roaring conflagration, blazing into the night.

Then just before the orgasm hit her, catapulting her into the stratosphere, she knew with a bone-deep certainty that, whatever she'd told herself about leaving in two weeks, it was lie.

She'd come back with him because she wanted him. Because she'd wanted *this*. She'd always wanted it. And she'd never stopped wanting, not deep down in the depths of her heart.

Because she'd loved him then and she loved him now. She'd never stopped loving him.

The knowledge was intrinsic and cell-deep, then it was lost in the storm as the pleasure overwhelmed her. And all she was aware of was the hard thrust of Khalil's hips and then his deep voice growling her name as it took him, too.

For a time afterwards there was stillness and silence, broken only by the sound of their breathing, rough and ragged. He didn't move, his body a heavy weight that she was in no hurry to escape. In fact, she never wanted to escape it.

And you don't have to. Not if you marry him.

The thought made tears start in her eyes and her throat close. She couldn't tell herself now she didn't want this with her whole heart.

She still loved him. Of course she'd marry him. He'd said something about kings not being permitted love, but what did that matter? If she was his wife, he'd never be able to walk away from her again.

He shifted, easing his weight from her, lifting his head, and looking down at her. His gaze, normally as unreadable as a shard of obsidian, was full of emotional currents and she stared back, trying to read him.

'What is it?' she asked, lifting a hand to his face, hungry for the feel of his skin.

'I did not intend to take you like an animal on the couch,' he said after a moment. 'It was not supposed to happen like that.'

She smiled. 'But I like you being an animal.'

He didn't smile back, a fierce gleam in his eyes. 'You were a virgin. Do not think I did not notice.'

Oh, that. She'd forgotten about that. She was glad she'd waited for him, though. Not that she'd waited, she knew now. It was either him or no one.

'Does it matter?' she asked.

'I would not have been so...demanding if I had known.'

She let her fingertips brush over the sharp line of his jaw, the light prickle of his stubble against her skin. 'I want you to be demanding. In fact, I demand that you be demanding.'

Something in his face relaxed, and for the first time since he'd come back into her life the dark shadows in his gaze lightened. 'Did you wait for me, *ya hayati*?'

'Of course.' There was no reason to hide the truth from him. 'You said I was yours, and I am. Just as you've always been mine.'

He turned his face into her hand, his mouth brushing her palm. 'In that case, I cannot help but notice that you have given yourself to me.'

'Yes? And?'

His gaze shifted, turning hot. 'That means I am your husband already in everything but name.'

A hot, electric feeling pulsed through her. He'd always been intense, but this was intensity on a whole other level. Certainty blazed in his eyes, along with a possessiveness he'd never turned on her before. It made every part of her ache. Her aunt had never cared about her. Her aunt had never wanted her. But Khalil… He was looking at her as if he'd been searching half his life for her, and was now determined not to let her out of his sight.

'Hmm,' she murmured, tracing the line of his lower lip, deciding he could bear a little teasing. 'Are you wanting to renegotiate the two weeks you gave me?'

'No.' He nipped at her fingertips, an unfamiliar wickedness now in his gaze. 'I am wanting to dispense with it completely.'

Her heart turned over in her chest. The look on his face, intense and yet with a slight playfulness, reminded her of the old Khal. Of him when he wanted his way and would try and convince her with humour.

He's still in there. He's still him.

'A new agreement, then?' She kept her tone light while her heart thudded hard in her ears.

'A new agreement,' he confirmed. 'You belong in my bed and at my side, *ya hayati*. You always have. And I do not think you want to wait two weeks to decide. I think you already know what you want now.'

She did. But he could work for it. 'Oh? I do?'

'Yes.' The edge of his teeth grazed her fingertips again, making her shiver. 'You want to be my wife.'

He was so arrogant she wanted to laugh, the way she had years ago. 'And I suppose you're going to insist, are you?' She was smiling; she couldn't help herself.

'I am.' Abruptly, the playfulness died out of his eyes, leaving behind only intensity. 'I told you that my country needed you, Sidonie. And they do. But…you were right. I need you, too. And… I want this. I want you.' He paused. 'I do not beg for anything. But I will beg for you if you require it.'

Her heart squeezed tight. He would. She could see it in his eyes.

She wanted to tell him right there and then that he didn't need to, that she'd marry him because she loved him, but those were words she couldn't say quite yet. They'd driven him away the last time and she wasn't sure what he'd think of them now.

'Love, friendship...they are not allowed for a king.'

Well, she could wait. Perhaps later, as his wife, she could convince him otherwise.

'That,' she said, 'is the most romantic proposal I've ever heard.'

He shifted, his body once more settling on hers, pinning her. His hard mouth curved, and she could see amusement in his eyes. 'It is not a proposal. It is an order.'

She laughed, lifting her hands to take his beautiful face between them. You don't have to order me to be your wife, Khal.'

'Sidonie, I—'

'Yes, I will marry you. Yes, I will be your queen.'

A blaze of heat and triumph lit his eyes. 'Then I will—'

'On one condition.'

His gaze narrowed. 'What condition?'

It was something she'd thought of just now, because of course being his wife would have implications for her charity. Excellent implications.

'You are still to be the patron of my charity. And I will not be giving it up, understand? In fact, being your queen will open up a lot of opportunities for us. So, you'll have to provide me with everything I need to run it remotely. Plus, I'll need to visit England regularly in order to keep an eye on things.'

This time his smile was slow and utterly heart-melting,

easing the tense lines of his face, lighting up the darkness in his eyes. A smile of pleasure and such warmth that her heart tightened in recognition.

It was him. It was her Khal.

'You drive a hard bargain, *ya hayati.* But yes, I think I can accommodate those conditions. But I, too, have some of my own.'

She stroked the line of his jaw, loving the velvety feel of his skin. 'Oh?'

Khalil gripped her wrists gently. 'I need you in my bed. Every night from now on.'

Sidonie pretended to think about it for, oh, half a second. 'Okay. Yes. I want that too.'

'Good. In that case we will be married tomorrow.'

An electric shock arrowed down her spine. 'Tomorrow?'

Khalil eased her hands away, pressing them down on either side of her head. 'Yes, my Sidonie. Tomorrow. I have already waited five years and I am tired of it.'

She didn't resist, conscious that beneath her shock there was also excitement and a gathering anticipation. 'But isn't that too soon to organise anything?'

'No. Not if I will it. I am the King.' He gave her the most ridiculously smug look she'd ever seen. 'In a month we will have a grand celebration of our marriage and you will be formally crowned, but my people have already observed me carrying you from the plane. They know you are my intended. Some may be unhappy with the speed and wish for more ceremony, but once you are legally my wife there will be no disagreements or protests. I will make sure of it.'

He was so certain, so absolutely sure of himself. Sometimes that certainty of his drove her crazy and sometimes it was the most reassuring thing in the entire world.

She found it reassuring now.

'Okay,' she said huskily. 'Then tomorrow it is.'

The intense, possessive look was back in his eyes. 'And now, *ya hayati,* I suggest we start practising for our wedding night.'

'Good,' she said happily. 'I thought you'd never ask.' Then she lifted her head and kissed his beautiful mouth and lost herself for the rest of the night.

Much later, after the remains of a very late dinner had been cleared away and Sidonie was where she should have been years ago, fast asleep in his bed, Khalil stepped out of the French doors and into his private courtyard.

He felt too energised to sleep, as if something that had been wrong for many years was now suddenly right, that pressure inside him abruptly lifted.

Finally, after so long, she would be his wife.

He hadn't realised, not fully, what making love to her would mean to him. Or perhaps some part of him had known, but he hadn't wanted to admit it to himself.

The moment he'd pushed inside her and felt her around him, holding him tight, and he'd stared down into her green eyes, seeing her...seeing *her,* all sunshine and sweetness and warmth. And she'd looked back, her face so beautifully flushed, the pleasure they'd created between them glowing in her eyes...

Perhaps she'd been right, he'd thought. That he *had* brought her here for him, to save some part of him he'd thought lost for ever. It felt wrong to think it though, because that was an indulgence, something his father might have done. Putting his own selfish greed before the needs of his nation.

Yet finally being inside her there on the couch...it had

felt so right. As if that had been where he'd always meant to end up, as if she was his destiny somehow. The rush of possessiveness that had then followed had shocked him, and he hadn't been able to hold it back.

He couldn't let her go. He couldn't. Yes, she was for his country, but having a wife he wanted would be good for him. A wife he trusted. A wife he'd enjoy getting heirs with.

A wife who knows you, deep down.

Yes, she knew him. Knew parts of him, the man he'd been certainly. But she didn't know everything. She didn't know what he'd had to do to make himself strong, the lessons his mother had taught him to protect him.

Hard lessons.

He couldn't tell her about them, though. She didn't need to hear how painful they'd been. It was his own pain, and he would be the caretaker of it.

But the most important thing was that she'd agreed to be his wife. Now she would help him change his kingdom for the better. She would help him rebuild what his father had broken. And he would help her in turn with her charity. He'd rip out the substandard office in the Queens' wing and install the fastest internet connection he could, ensure that she had all the technology she needed. Perhaps he'd even buy her a royal jet of her own so she could come and go to England as she pleased.

They'd discussed it over dinner and then she'd filled him in on the progress she'd made over the past five years. He'd been so impressed. Her charity work was amazing, and she had such vision. Such drive. She'd always had that, even back in university.

Satisfaction filled him. She was going to make the most remarkable Queen.

Tomorrow couldn't come soon enough.

At that moment his phone buzzed and he took it out of his pocket, glancing down at the screen, then hitting the answer button. 'Galen.'

'Khal. You left me a message. Is this about our meeting next month in Al Da'ira?'

Every month, or whenever their schedules allowed it, he, Galen, and Augustine would get together to renew their friendship and to allow themselves time to be just men, not kings. Also to remember old times, when they'd been the 'Wicked Princes' back at Oxford, causing mayhem in their respective colleges and breaking hearts everywhere.

One of the three would usually host their get-togethers and it was Khalil's turn next month. He'd already decided ages ago that the timing would be perfect to host an engagement ball just like the one Galen had had for his beautiful wife, Solace. His friends already knew of Sidonie—they'd teased him good-naturedly back at university about their friendship—but Khalil had made sure to keep her away from them, since both Galen and Augustine had been unrepentant playboys and Sidonie was nothing if not lovely. Galen, however, was now happily married, though Augustine had remained the same unrepentant playboy as he'd been all those years ago.

However, now it would not be an engagement ball.

'Yes,' he said. 'I wish to throw a celebration for my marriage while you and Augustine are here, and I could use your advice.'

There was a long silence down the other end of the phone and then a strange choking sound.

Khalil stared at the fountain in his courtyard and frowned. 'Galen? Are you still there?'

'Yes.' His friend sounded slightly strangled. 'A celebration for your marriage? When did this happen?'

'It has not happened. Not yet. I am getting married tomorrow.'

Galen coughed. 'You've been keeping that quiet.'

'Keeping what quiet?'

'The fact that you even had a fiancée.'

'You did not need to know,' he said, since it was the truth.

'You are, as ever, an enigma, Khal.' Galen sounded amused. 'So are you going to tell me who the lucky woman is, or do I have to guess?'

'You remember Sidonie? My friend at Oxford? Her.'

There was another long silence and then Galen laughed. 'Oh, yes, I remember. Very quiet and studious. Pretty, though, which was why you kept us away from her, I seem to recall.'

Khalil scowled as a wave of possessive annoyance filled him. 'I fail to see what is amusing about it.'

'Nothing is amusing,' Galen said soothingly. 'It's only that you were quite certain about the fact that she was only a friend.'

'She is only a friend. But she will also be my wife. The two are not mutually exclusive.'

'I see.' Galen's tone was very neutral. 'So you are not in love with her, then?'

Electricity prickled through him. Perhaps he *had* been in love with her back then, not that he'd ever told his friends about it. She'd certainly loved him. But love, along with all the rest of those very human emotions, was forbidden to a king and so he'd cut it out of his life.

He certainly wasn't in love with her any more.

'This has nothing to do with love, Galen,' he said

curtly. 'I chose her because she is just what my court and my country needs. I will explain when you get here.'

Again, there was a silence.

Galen had changed since he'd met his wife, Solace, becoming much more relaxed and open. He ruled with a lighter touch than he once had and Khalil was sure it had something to do with his beautiful wife.

He was in love, he'd told Khalil and Augustine when they'd commented on his good mood, and, while Khalil had been pleased for him, love wasn't anything he could allow himself.

'I look forward to it,' Galen said, still sounding suspiciously neutral. 'So tell me, what kind of celebration are you thinking?'

Khalil gave him a few thoughts, and five minutes later the call ended with Galen promising to get his events team—which was far better than Khalil's own—in contact with some of Khalil's staff so they could start planning.

After that, Khalil pulled up Augustine's number because his other friend needed to know and he should hear it from Khalil personally.

'Khal,' Augustine answered in his rich, melted-honey voice. 'It's been a while. How are things at home?'

Unlike Khalil's own reign, Augustine's had been calm and relatively untroubled. His father had been a good king, and Augustine looked to be carrying on the tradition. He'd mentioned once to Galen and Khalil that he'd been thinking of abdicating, though he refused to tell them why. But he hadn't abdicated yet, and Khalil was starting to wonder if it was all just a bluff.

'Fine,' Khalil said. 'I assume you're coming next month?'

'But of course.' Augustine sounded amused for some reason. Then again, Augustine always sounded as if he was enjoying some kind of private joke that no one else was privy to. 'Wild horses couldn't keep me away.'

'Good. Because I will be throwing a ball to celebrate my marriage.'

'Your marriage?' Augustine sounded surprised, as well he might. 'When did this happen? Has Galen been putting ideas into your head?'

'It will be happening tomorrow,' Khalil said. 'And no, it is not Galen. It is merely time. My country needs a queen and I need heirs.'

'Ah, heirs,' Augustine drawled. 'That old chestnut. Well, better you than me. So, do I know your fiancée? Or perhaps a better question: is she someone I've slept with? Could be awkward if so.'

It was a joke and Khalil treated it the way he treated all Augustine's jokes. He ignored it. 'It is Sidonie. Do you remember her? We were friends years ago at Oxford.'

'Her? Really?' More surprise echoed in his friend's voice.

And Khalil found he had the same response to Augustine that he'd had to Galen. 'Why is that so surprising?' he enquired, his tone dangerously soft.

'Only because I thought you'd have claimed her years ago.'

You should have. Instead, you broke her heart and left her for five years.

That ache, that flaw in what could surely not be his heart, throbbed.

He ignored it. 'And I was not going to,' he said stiffly. 'My situation has changed, however.'

'Has it? You took your time.'

A lecture from Sidonie was one thing. A lecture from Augustine was quite another.

'I did not ask for—'

'Or did she refuse you?'

Khalil's jaw went tight with unexpected temper. He didn't want to get into the particulars of what had happened with Sidonie, especially given how poorly he'd treated her. 'The ball will be—'

'Oh, so she did,' Augustine interrupted a second time, more amusement in his voice. 'What happened? Were you not convincing enough?'

'She has not refused.' Khalil held on to his temper but only just. 'She has accepted my proposal.'

'Just as well,' Augustine said. 'I was just going to suggest taking her to bed. She'll be begging for your ring by morning.'

'Why do women like you?' Khalil asked acidly. 'I cannot understand it.'

Augustine laughed, unoffended. 'My reputation is somewhat intriguing, I believe. And I live up to it. So tell me, is it love, Khal? Did you catch that nonsense from Galen?'

Again that electricity passed through him, as if the word was a badly earthed wire that he kept putting his hand on.

He didn't want to keep thinking about it.

'No,' he said flatly.

But doesn't she deserve to be loved?

Of course she did. She did more than anyone else he'd ever known. Except he couldn't give her that love. He never would.

'Thank God for that,' Augustine said. 'At least one of us is keeping his head. Well, I shall look forward to seeing her again.'

After he'd finished the call, Khalil took a couple of steps into the warm night of the courtyard, the fountain in the middle playing its gentle music. He had a million other things he wanted to think about, yet he couldn't stop thinking about Sidonie and the question of love.

It was true, he *had* loved her. He'd come to Oxford a dark and tormented man, and she'd truly been the sunshine in his life. Giving him back hope and the kind of happiness he'd only ever known as a very young boy, and maybe not even then.

She'd been his first love. Yet he'd never been able to forget that eventually he'd have to give her up. That he'd have to cut his heart out of his chest and sacrifice it for the good of his country. And indeed, that was what he'd done.

He could not love her again. Love—any of those warmer, softer emotions—was not allowed for kings, and especially not for a son of Amir.

Amir hadn't been the divine being his people had wanted. He'd been a petty, flawed man, and if Khalil wanted to be better, to be stronger than Amir, he had to be more than that. Being a true king of Al Da'ira meant not falling prey to the same greed that had tainted his father. The need for more wealth, more power, more physical indulgence.

His mother had told him it would always be harder for him than for other people because of that poisonous blood, so he had to be more careful. But he hadn't been careful in England. With Sidonie he'd always wanted more. More of her laughter, more of her empathy, more of her warmth. More of *her*.

He'd been greedy. That was the truth of why he'd had to leave her in the end.

And that was why love could never be a part of their relationship, no matter that she deserved it. He had to guard himself. He couldn't love her and be a king—the two were mutually exclusive for someone like him. Nor could he give up his country for her, not when he'd fought to the death for the right to rule. That would negate everything he'd done.

Khalil put his hands on the edge of the fountain and leaned on them, staring down into the water, unseeing.

A king wasn't supposed to care about individuals, only the wellbeing of his country as a whole, but he couldn't deny that he did care about Sidonie.

He cared that she'd lost her parents so young and had been brought up by her sorry excuse for an aunt. He cared that he'd broken her heart all those years ago, and that heart of hers was still broken even now.

He wanted her to be happy, here with him.

It was dangerous, that caring. It was a flaw.

'Things are different for kings,' his mother had told him as she'd handed him the knife. *'They have to do hard things. They cannot be soft or uncertain, and they cannot let their emotions rule them. Especially you, Khalil. You have your father's blood and so you must be extra-careful.'*

He hadn't wanted that knife. He'd cried as she'd forced it into his hand, loathing the heavy weight of it in his palm, knowing even then what she wanted him to do. But his tears had made no impact. She'd been relentless, nodding to the servant to bring Dusk, his half-grown chocolate Labrador, into the room. The dog had started to get sick a week earlier, and even though the vet had done all he could to save him, it was clear that Dusk wasn't going to get better.

'You know what you need to do, Khalil,' his mother had said. *'Dusk will die in agony if you do not do this. And it must be you. He is your dog, and you are responsible for him. You cannot ask another person to do something you lack the courage to do yourself. Because a king is*

not a coward. They must make difficult decisions and do the things other people cannot.'

He'd known his mother was right, that Dusk was in pain, and that this was a mercy. The dog was his, and asking someone else to grant that mercy because he was too afraid to do it himself was a coward's way out. And he wasn't a coward.

So he'd put his dog down. He'd forced himself to watch the life drain out of the animal's eyes and he'd felt as if he'd killed part of himself. But he'd learned a lesson that day and it wasn't just about making hard decisions and taking responsibility. It was also about how much love hurt.

Love had also been part of the decision he'd made later, to fight for the crown, and to take Yusuf's life, because he loved his country.

'You did the right thing', his mother had said after the fight, when Yusuf's body had been taken away. *'If you had not killed him, he would have killed you. And even if you had beaten him and let him live, he would have drawn sympathy. His supporters would have torn this country apart.'* Her expression had been like iron, the kind of iron she'd shaped in him. *'You were a surgeon, Khalil. He was a cancer that had to be cut out so our country could live. Do not spare him a single moment's thought.'*

But he'd spared him more than a single moment's thought. Because even though intellectually he'd known Yusuf had been planning to take the crown whether he won the battle for succession or not, and had been fomenting an insurrection that would have torn Al Da'ira apart, he'd never been able to quite suppress the doubt that had consumed him afterwards.

The battle was not supposed to end in death. It was

supposed to end when one participant yielded, thereby accepting defeat. So when Yusuf had pulled out the knife he'd had hidden in the middle of their fight, making it clear that yielding was not an option, and that he meant to kill him, Khalil had not been expecting it. And it was only in that moment that the full horror of it had descended upon him: only one of them was going to make it out of the battle alive. And it could not be Yusuf. His country could not afford for it to be Yusuf. Which meant it had to be him.

He'd not felt like a surgeon then, or even the heir to the throne.

He'd felt like a killer.

The memories made something shudder and shift inside him, so he shoved them away. That was in the past and he couldn't change what had happened.

The most important thing was Sidonie and her happiness, and she needed to be happy for the sake of his people and for his country. He couldn't give her love, but perhaps he could give her that happiness. It was his responsibility after all.

Determination settled inside him.

He turned from the fountain and strode back inside to his bedroom. There, he went over to the huge, canopied bed where Sidonie was curled, fast asleep, and he got in, gathering her warm, sweet, naked body close.

She gave a little sigh and snuggled into him, her red hair spilling over his chest.

He tightened his arms around her.

Yes, he would make her happy. He would. If it was the very last thing that he did.

CHAPTER NINE

SIDONIE STOOD IN the deserted throne room of Khalil's palace, a thousand butterflies fluttering in her stomach.

When she'd woken this morning, Khalil hadn't been there, but Aisha had. The woman had delivered a raft of instructions on the day's schedule, and then she'd had breakfast brought to the King's apartments so that Sidonie could eat.

Sidonie hadn't felt much like eating—she'd been far too nervous—but she'd forced something down. Then Aisha had escorted her back to the Queens' apartments, where she was pounced upon by a fleet of servants who dressed her in a simple, unadorned gown of white silk that flowed like water over her curves and then out behind her in a long train.

She'd had no idea how he'd managed to find a gown that fitted her so perfectly on such short notice, but he had. And it was beautiful. Then they laid a veil over her face and hair, of white silk lace embroidered with tiny, glittering diamonds, and she loved that too.

Khalil clearly wasn't wasting any time, because then she was escorted through the echoing palace corridors that seemed to get grander and grander, until she was shown into a huge, ornately tiled room, its roof supported by many elegant columns.

The sun shone down through a hole in the roof in the very centre of the room, making the tiles glitter and bathing everything in light.

Sidonie was guided to that shaft of light and now she stood there, feeling as if she was standing in a waterfall of sunlight, waiting to be married. To Khalil.

Are you sure this is what you really want? He's not your Khalil, you know that.

No, but she wasn't his Sidonie either. They weren't the people they'd once been—five years apart and heartbreak had seen to that.

But what did that matter? She loved him, that was the constant, and as his wife she'd have the time to rebuild the relationship they'd once had. And anyway, she was stronger now than she'd been back then, and more certain. More than a match for the King he was.

What about love, though? What kind of marriage would you have without that?

But they did have love. Her love.

Will that ever be enough?

The thought brought memories, dim now after so long, but still there. Of her parents, her mother's warm hugs and her father tossing her in the air and making her laugh. They'd loved her. They'd loved her so much. And she'd ached for them after they'd died, ached for those moments of affection and tenderness, and she'd spent years hoping for the same from her aunt. But her aunt hadn't loved her and there had been no tenderness or affection from her, none at all.

Khalil might not love her, but he wanted her, and he cared about her, and he gave her pleasure. His touches set her on fire. He could give her affection and tenderness, too; it wasn't that he didn't.

It was enough.

Are you sure about that?

But the thought slid away as a tall figure strode through the gloom of the throne room, then stepped into the shaft of sunlight with her, bathing him in glory. And for a second she could understand why his court laid themselves on the floor and pressed their faces to the ground whenever he passed. Because in this moment he truly seemed divine.

There was a lump in her throat as she looked at him, and she had to blink back her tears.

He wore white, as she did—white shirt, loose white trousers and a white robe over his broad shoulders, heavily embroidered with gold thread. It glittered in the sunlight, a spectacular contrast to the smooth bronze of his skin and the inky blackness of his hair and eyes. And those eyes were fixed on her, a burning flame glowing in the darkness.

He didn't speak, merely raised his hand to her, and she walked towards him, drawn helplessly, reaching for his hand. His fingers wound through hers, warm and strong, and the nervous fluttering inside her settled.

This was right. This was what she'd wanted. What she'd always wanted. He didn't question it, so why should she? And, while she had no idea what this marriage would bring, she'd be strong enough to deal with it.

Are you sure? After all those years of letting your aunt walk all over you, hoping for a scrap of affection that she was never going to give? After he walked away from you and broke your heart?

Well, once they were married, he couldn't walk away, could he? She wouldn't let him.

Sidonie held tight to Khalil's hand as a priest appeared

in the sunlight too, and then there was no more time for thinking as the ceremony began.

It was short and sweet and she said her vows in a steady voice, mirroring Khalil's deep tones of certainty as he said his. Then he pushed a narrow band of white gold studded with diamonds onto her finger and she did the same for him—his ring was simpler, with a single diamond in the centre.

Then the priest pronounced them husband and wife, and Khalil stepped towards her and with careful hands lifted her veil. There was a triumph in his eyes that stole her breath. Then he bent and kissed her, a hard, intense kiss. A claiming.

She was trembling as he lifted his head and turned to the priest, nodding and murmuring a word of thanks. The priest glided away, leaving her finally alone with her new husband in an echoing throne room.

It was done. Finally, he was hers and she was his.

Her gaze met his and she could see the satisfaction in it. He felt this rightness too, didn't he?

But you're just his trophy. His prize. His queen. You're not really his wife.

In those years where they'd been friends, she'd indulged herself in fantasies about marrying him. About their wedding day and his ring on her finger, and what their wedding night would be like. And in every one of those fantasies it had been love she'd seen in his eyes, not triumph. He'd told her he loved her, too. Saying the words in his deep, dark voice.

An icy thread of doubt curled through her, that perhaps loving him wasn't enough after all, that she needed more than that, but she shoved it away.

It was too late for doubts. They were married.

'I hope you did not mind the lack of ceremony,' Khalil said, reaching for her hand once again and closing his fingers around it. 'I did not want any witnesses other than the priest. This was just for you and me.'

'No,' she murmured, her voice not quite steady. 'I didn't mind at all. But...why the throne room?'

'It is customary. All royalty in Al Da'ira are married in the throne room.' He frowned at her. 'Your fingers are cold. Are you okay?'

The satisfaction in his expression had been replaced by concern, and it made her heart ache. He *did* care about her. He did. She wasn't just a prize he'd won.

'Just nerves,' she said, forcing a smile.

His gaze narrowed slightly as if he didn't believe her. But he didn't say anything else, merely tightening his grip as he walked towards the doors, drawing her along with him. 'No need to be nervous, *ya hayati*. I have something special planned.'

His hand was warm, so she concentrated on that, and not on the uncertainty that had gathered in her stomach. 'What something special?'

He glanced at her, his eyes dark as obsidian, and he flashed her a brief smile, a smile she remembered from years ago, so rare and yet so full of warmth that her heart turned over in her chest, banishing the doubt. 'You'll see.'

Yes, she could do this. Loving him would be enough. She didn't need him to love her in return. And who knew? Maybe one day he would, and everything would be fine.

She followed him as he strode into the ornate hallway just outside the throne room, palace guards falling into step with them.

They went up a great, sweeping staircase and then down a few more corridors, before coming out onto a large terrace that, given the helicopter sitting in the middle of it, must have been a helipad.

Guards were everywhere, flanking her and Khalil as he went straight to the machine and opened the door for her. 'Another helicopter ride, Khal?' She gave him a look from underneath her lashes. 'Let's hope there is actually dinner at the end of this one.'

Much to her surprise he laughed, the sound deep and warm and incredibly sexy. 'Oh, there will be many things at the end of this one, *ya hayati*. Dinner being the least of them.'

Five minutes later they were in the air, leaving behind the royal palace and Al Da'ira's capital city, and in another ten they were soaring above a starkly beautiful mountain range. Then, almost before Sidonie was ready, they were descending towards what looked like a small palace that stood on a mountain plateau, surrounded by a series of terraces and balconies.

Her heart kicked inside her chest. She'd never been here before, but she was certain she knew this place. It looked familiar to her in some way.

They landed on a helipad beside the little palace. It was cooler up in the mountains, a fresh but pleasant breeze lifting her veil as Khalil helped her out of the helicopter.

Royal servants were kneeling on the ground, their faces pressed to the stone as Khalil led Sidonie to the palace's doors.

'Khal,' she murmured, deciding that, since she was going to be Queen, she may as well start straight away. 'We could make a small change right now, couldn't we? They don't need to prostrate themselves.'

'They do not have to,' he murmured back. 'I told you that. Their beliefs require it.'

So he'd told her, yet she still didn't like it. 'But you're not a god. And if all of this is to build confidence in the throne after Amir, you have been ruling for five years. Surely they know you're not your father by now.'

He stared at her a moment, his expression unreadable. Then he glanced at the servants. 'You do not have to give me formal obeisance,' he said. 'That will not be required in future.'

Slowly the servants stirred then got to their feet, looking at Khalil cautiously.

'But, Majesty,' one old man said, 'you must have acknowledgement.'

Khalil frowned. 'Do you think that I am Amir? That I need this level of acknowledgment? That I demand it?' There was no heat in his voice. It was a simple question.

The man eyed him. 'No, Majesty. You are not him in any way. But we wish to honour you.'

There was another silence. Khalil's expression was oddly still. 'You can continue to serve me willingly,' he said at last. 'That is all the honour I need.'

A flicker of something that looked like respect passed across the old man's face. Then he bowed deeply. 'Your will, Majesty.'

Khalil inclined his head in acknowledgement but didn't say anything else. He reached for her hand, though, as they approached the palace doors, and he squeezed it gently. He'd liked what she'd said. He'd liked it a lot.

There was still hope for him.

The palace was made of white stone that gleamed against the black rock of the mountains, set off by the small, yet beautiful gardens that surrounded it. There were also colonnades and courtyards and airy arcades, the silence broken only by the sound of fountains playing.

It was absolutely beautiful.

'What is this place?' she asked as Khalil led her inside. 'It's gorgeous.'

'It was my mother's palace,' he said. 'I grew up here.'

So that was why it was familiar. He'd told her how his mother had been fiercely protective, yet very strict with him. And he'd had a harsh childhood.

Why would he want to come here?

She wanted to ask him, but then more servants approached and Khalil was murmuring instructions. Then he led her from the entrance hall and straight out through an atrium courtyard shaded with orange trees, with a small fountain and arched colonnade. He pulled open another door into a shady interior hall and up some stairs. Then he stopped before a simple wooden door and pushed it open, stepping into a large room. The walls were simply tiled in white and light blue, the floor of pale wood. High, arched windows gave a magnificent view of the mountains.

Though it wasn't the mountains that Sidonie noticed, not when the huge, canopied bed piled high with white cushions took up most of the room.

Khalil shut the door behind them, then shrugged off his white robe, leaving it to lie carelessly over a nearby chair. Then he looked at her and there was fire in his black eyes, and it blazed.

'Come here, wife,' he murmured, his voice getting darker and deeper.

Excitement gripped her, goosebumps rising on her skin, her heartbeat getting faster. So that was what he was impatient for. She should have known.

Not that she wasn't impatient too, even after the night before, when he'd kissed, tasted, and explored every inch of her body, before showing her how to do the same for him.

She wanted him. She wanted to finally claim him as her husband every bit as much as he wanted to claim her.

Slowly she walked over to where he stood, so tall and broad and beautiful in his white wedding clothing, then stopped in front of him. 'What can I do for you, my husband?'

A smile curved his beautiful mouth, a wicked smile that looked far too good on him. 'We have another custom in Al Da'ira. When a couple marry, on their wedding night the new wife undresses her husband so she may worship him.'

She had to smile. 'Sounds like a custom you've only just made up right now.'

He laughed, the sound so sexy she almost shivered. 'You are far too clear-sighted, Sidonie al Nazari. You see right through me.'

She stepped forward and lifted her hands to the buttons on his shirt, beginning to undo them, the sound of her new name settling something inside her. 'If I saw right through you, Your Majesty, I would know why you brought me here.' She glanced up at him. 'This place doesn't have happy memories for you, I know it doesn't. So why did you choose it for our honeymoon?'

Khalil was already so hard all he could think about was having his new wife's hands on him as quickly as possible. Everything had taken far longer than he'd either hoped or wanted, even though logically it had all happened as fast as it could.

Also, he'd wanted some degree of ceremony, because he knew Sidonie would like it. Hence the throne-room wedding in the shaft of sunlight, and the priest. Then coming here for their honeymoon...

He hadn't expected her to ask about it, though in retrospect he should have. He'd talked to her many times about his childhood here, though not about Dusk.

He tensed slightly despite himself. 'I wanted somewhere out of the way, where I could spend days with you without anyone else around.'

Lies. You shouldn't have brought her here if you didn't want to revisit the past.

Except he wasn't going to revisit the past, or at least he wasn't going to right now, not when he had other, more pleasant things he wanted to do.

Sidonie was looking up at him, puzzled almost. Her fingers were in the process of undoing a button on his shirt with maddening slowness, fingertips brushing his bare chest and winding his impatience even tighter, making him want to tear her hands away and take her right there on the floor.

But he didn't want their wedding night to start with such a loss of control. That would hardly set a good precedent. He wanted something slower and more sensual to mark the occasion.

It was difficult, though, to hang on to his patience when she was standing so close and he could smell her delicious scent, feel the seductive warmth of her body. She was so lovely in her white wedding gown, with her red hair loose and covered by the white veil, the diamonds sewn into it glittering like a scattering of raindrops.

How he'd always imagined her as his bride. His to claim. And even though he'd already done so, every instinct he had was urging him to do it again.

'I hope you do not want me to answer that now,' he said. 'Not when we have more important things to do.'

'Why not now?' She looked down at what she was

doing, slowly undoing another button. 'You obviously brought us here for a reason.'

He gritted his teeth, his muscles tensing as she brushed his chest yet again, igniting fire along all his nerve-endings. 'Let me rephrase,' he said tightly. '*I* do not want to answer that question right now.'

'We have all night, Khal.' She undid the button and looked up at him again, her gaze searching. 'Or is there something you don't want to tell me?'

Telling her shouldn't matter. The things he'd done he'd done for the good of his nation. But this was their wedding night. It was hardly the time or the place for such confessions.

She should know. She should know what kind of man she married.

Tension coiled through him, though he didn't know why. She'd married a king, that was what he was, that was what he'd become. And he wasn't ashamed of what he'd had to do to be that king.

She must have sensed his tension because she frowned. 'There is something, isn't there? What is it?'

You doubt. Even now.

Once, he had. But he certainly didn't now. His doubt was a flaw he'd cut out of himself the night he'd walked away from Sidonie, along with the pain of leaving her, and the longing. Because Al Da'ira needed a strong king, a king without flaws, and so that was what he'd become.

Yusuf had been a sickness he'd had to cut out, a mercy he'd had to give, the same mercy he'd given Dusk.

Perhaps he should tell her after all. That way she would know exactly where she stood.

Her hands dropped. 'I don't have to—'

'Did I ask you to stop?' This wasn't going to be a

pleasant conversation, but he wasn't going to let it ruin his wedding night. 'Keep doing what you were doing.'

She searched his face for a moment and then nodded, lifting her hands to push his shirt from his shoulders.

Cool air moved over his skin, but for some reason it didn't soothe him. Every part of him was tense. She stepped in closer and it was all he could do not to put his hands on her hips and pull against him. But touching her while he told her about all the...unpleasantness seemed wrong, so he kept them still.

'You know about the battle of succession. About the fight between the oldest children of my father's four wives.'

Sidonie's stroking fingers paused. 'Yes, I remember you telling me.'

'My grandfather changed it so that the fight was more ritualistic and no longer to the death.' He held her gaze. 'Again, I did not tell you to stop.'

She flushed then lifted her hands again, running the tips of her fingers along his collarbones. 'Yes, you told me about the fight, too. How your half-brother was injured.'

'He was not injured,' Khalil said flatly. 'Just before the fight, my mother had intelligence that Yusuf intended to kill me. He wanted the crown, and he was going to take it. He'd been planning insurrection and already had an army of followers waiting for his call.'

Sidonie's face paled, her eyes widening, and that tension inside him made him feel as if he was made of iron. He didn't understand why. His decision had been correct, the only one he could have made.

'He had brought a knife with him, so my mother secretly passed a knife to me so I would not be unarmed.' He remembered the weight of that knife too. 'It was important that I win the battle. Yusuf was…too much like my father. He took pleasure in cruelty, and he wanted power. It would have been a disaster if he'd won the succession.'

Sidonie had gone white. 'Khalil…'

'Yusuf was not as good a fighter as I was,' he went on, making the words hard and cold, just as he himself was. 'Though he tried very hard to kill me.'

Her gaze darkened. 'But he didn't kill you. And obviously you won, since you're King.'

'I did win. But there was a cost.' The word 'cost' sounded ugly to him, as if a life had a monetary value. 'Only one of us was going to come out of that fight alive and I made the decision that it would be me.'

Sidonie stared up at him for a long moment, her gaze searching, and for once in his life he couldn't tell what she was thinking.

His heart was beating far too fast, all his muscles tense. He wished she hadn't had to hear this. He wished he hadn't had to tell her the truth. Everything about it had been dark and ugly, and he hadn't wanted her to know, because he hadn't wanted her to see him differently back then. He'd loved the way she saw him as just an ordinary person. But ordinary people didn't kill other people for their country's sake, not if they weren't soldiers.

'I killed him, Sidonie,' he went on, so there could be no doubt. 'I did it for my country. I had to. But that does not make what I did any less terrible.'

She contemplated him for a moment, then slowly she leaned into him and pressed a kiss to his throat, her lips warm and soft. 'I'm so sorry,' she breathed. 'I'm so sorry you had to make that decision.'

Her kiss should have relaxed him, should have made

him burn with desire, and yet every muscle was rigid. Sorry. She was sorry. He didn't know what to do with that.

'You do not need to be sorry.' His voice was somehow rougher than it should have been and his grip on her hands had tightened. 'It was the correct decision.'

'This was before you came to Oxford, wasn't it?'

'Yes. I was eighteen.'

Sidonie's face was full of a terrible sympathy. 'You were so full of shadows back then. I used to wonder what haunted you, but you never talked about it, and I didn't want to push.'

'It did haunt me,' he said. 'But it does not now.'

Yet her gaze was very steady, looking at him as if she could see things he couldn't. 'Yes,' she said slowly. 'Yes, I think it still does.'

Shock went through him like a lightning strike, shaking something inside him. 'Why would you say that?'

'Because I can see it in your eyes.' Her green gaze held his, that sympathy still shining there. 'You didn't want to tell me, did you? You wanted me to keep on believing that Yusuf had only been injured.'

'I did not want to tell you because—'

'You brought me here, Khal. You wanted me to know your past. And you wanted me to know, because no matter how you deny it, it does haunt you.'

Another shock hit him, harder this time. 'That is not true.'

'Isn't it?' Sidonie pulled one hand from his grip and touched his face gently. 'You don't have to pretend. I've known you for ten years and besides, I'm your wife. You can be strong for your people, but you don't have to be strong with me.'

For some reason her touch hurt, shaking that thing

inside him, the lump of rock that he'd turned his heart into. That rock he'd *had* to turn his heart into because he couldn't allow it to be anything other than stone.

He gripped her wrist, wanting to pull her fingers from his cheek and yet for some reason not being able to. 'A king cannot afford doubts,' he said harshly. 'A king cannot be haunted by anything.'

Yet you still have those doubts. You didn't want to take his life, just as you didn't want to take the life of your dog.

She didn't speak, just looked at him, her gaze full of a tenderness that stopped his breath.

'Kings have to make difficult decisions,' he heard himself say, the urge to explain himself too strong to ignore. 'They have to do terrible things in order to protect people. They need to be strong and certain, and they cannot second-guess themselves. I made the decision I had to make and I took action. So no, it does not haunt me.'

There was a strange sheen in Sidonie's eyes. 'Then why are you so tense? You're holding my wrist so tightly.'

Another icy wave washed over him. He forced his fingers to open, to let her go, even though every part of him felt as if he was desperate for the touch of her skin.

You are hurting her. You are always hurting her.

He took a step back from her, putting some distance between them, forcing away the strange desperation and trying to master himself. His heart was too loud in his head, and he couldn't bear the look in her eyes.

You should not have married her. She undermines everything you were taught.

No, that wasn't true. Marrying her had been the right decision. It was all those old feelings she brought back that was the issue. The feelings he thought he'd cut away years ago and somehow hadn't.

It wasn't her fault. It was his. It was his father's poison-ous blood in his veins, the greed and selfishness threat-ening to overtake him. He had to be stronger than it, he had to be.

The pressure was back in his chest, as if that lump of stone was getting heavier and heavier, an aching weight that felt as if it would crush the air from his lungs.

It was doubt, that weight. Doubt that he had made the right decision in marrying her. Doubt that he'd done the right thing in even bringing her here.

You will never make her happy. Never.

She hadn't wanted to be here, yet he'd forced her. He'd essentially kidnapped her then seduced her into staying and marrying him. And he'd told himself over and over again that it was for his country, just as he'd told himself over and over again that Yusuf's death had been for his country, too. That he'd had to die. Just as Dusk had to die.

But that wasn't true, was it? Those were lies he'd told himself. Because if he'd truly thought that Yusuf had had to die, he wouldn't still have these doubts. The same doubts that had consumed him after Dusk's death, that perhaps it hadn't been a mercy after all. Perhaps it had been his own suffering he'd wanted to ease, not his dog's.

Perhaps all of it had been for himself.

You are just the same as Amir.

Sidonie's lovely face was full of concern, though she didn't come any closer. 'What is it, Khal?' she asked softly. 'You look upset. Please, let me help you.'

'I am not upset,' he forced out, his voice sounding as if it was coming from far away. 'But I understand if you cannot now go through with this wedding night.'

'Why would I not want to go through with it?'

'You don't care that I killed a man?' He didn't understand why she was looking at him as if it didn't matter and he didn't understand why it even mattered to him. 'You don't see me any differently?'

'No. You didn't do it for no reason, Khal. You were defending yourself. And you did what you thought was the right thing for your country and your people.' Slowly she walked towards him, closing the distance between them. 'And you didn't want to do it, did you?'

He felt rooted to the spot, unable to move as she came closer, and then she was there, raising her hands and placing her palms on his bare chest, her skin warm against his. Making the stone around his heart crack, letting all that poisonous doubt seep out. 'No,' he heard himself say hoarsely. 'I did not. But there should be no reason to doubt. It was the right thing to do. The only decision to make.'

'You were very young, Khal. And you took a life you didn't want to take. Anyone would be affected by that. Anyone would be haunted.'

He looked down into her eyes. 'That was not the only life I took.'

Shock flickered in her eyes. 'What?'

Another decision he'd had to make. Another decision he couldn't doubt and yet…there seemed to be nothing but doubt in him now.

'My mother's job was to bring me up strong in order to be a good king. But she was always afraid that my father's blood ran too hot in me. She believed that strength lay in being hard, and cold, and certain. That emotion clouded thinking, made a man weak. I had a dog and he got very sick, and there was nothing that could be done to save him. So, my mother decided he would be a good lesson for me. She gave me a knife and told me that if

I wanted to be a strong king, to be responsible for others, I had to learn how to make difficult decisions. And that I could not ask another to do what I was too afraid to do myself.'

A horrified expression had crossed Sidonie's face, the sheen back in her eyes. Tears. They were tears. 'Oh, Khal... Did she make you put him down yourself?'

She knows the truth of you now. You did not have to make that decision and yet you did. You have horrified her.

The weight in his heart, the doubt, became even heavier, crushing the life out of him.

'Yes,' he said hoarsely, unable to stop himself. 'Dusk was sick. It was a mercy.'

'But you don't believe that, do you?'

He couldn't keep it all inside. 'Mercy should not hurt, yet it was the most painful thing I have ever done. And I could not help thinking that I did it to ease my own suffering, not my dog's.'

A tear escaped, running down her cheek, and he thought she would pull away from him, and he didn't know what he would have done if she had. But she didn't. Instead she lifted her hands to take his face between her palms, and it shocked him so much that she should want to touch him after what he'd told her that he couldn't move. 'Oh, Khal,' she said huskily. 'Of course it was painful. You loved your dog. He was sick and you were only a child. You shouldn't have been made to do that.'

He lifted his hands to hers, wanting to pull them away and yet wanting at the same time to keep them exactly where they were. 'My mother's intentions were good. She wanted to make me strong because she believed I would make the best King. That I would save Al Da'ira from my father. But I was also my father's son, and she did not want me to turn into him.'

Sidonie didn't say anything then, merely rising on her toes and brushing her mouth against his, silencing him once again. 'You're not him,' she said against his lips. 'You're just not, Khal, and you never were. Your people think so too. Remember what that old man said to you just before? He didn't think you were Amir, so why torture yourself with this?'

He gripped her tightly, his heart beating faster, harder, the doubt inside him eating away at his foundations, weakening him. 'Because Amir was a flawed man. A greedy and selfish man. Everything he did was for himself. So how am I any different? What if I took Yusuf's life because I wanted the way clear to be King? What if I took Dusk's because I hated to see him suffer and did not want to deal with it any more?'

Her hands gripped his face, holding him tightly, her green gaze on his, suddenly fierce. 'You *are* different, Khal. You have *always* been different. You're protective and generous, and you care about people so much. You don't want what's best for you. You want what's best for your people. But your problem, my darling husband, is that you're too rigid. Your standards for yourself are so high. And I think you're trying to be this strong, semi-divine king because you're too afraid to be a man.'

'That is not true. I am—'

'It is true. Doubts are normal. Doubts make you human. And you're a wonderful, special human. A good man, a kind man. Yusuf, your dog…they were things you did because you felt you had to, but those things don't change who you are inside.' She let him go and put her palms back on his chest, pressing down. 'Your heart is still the same. You're the kindest man I've ever known, the kindest person.' Yet more tears were escaping and were running down her cheek even as the warmth of her palms seeped into him, easing the jagged ache inside him. 'And you're a good king. You held your country together through all those years of unrest, and you want what's best for it. You want what's best for your people.'

'A good king would not doubt himself.'

'No.' Sidonie gave him a smile through her tears. 'Doubt makes the best kings, you idiot. Don't you know that? It shows he cares, and you have to care, Khal. That's why you're different from your father and you always will be. It's because you care about other people, not because you don't.'

He stared at her, smiling at him despite those tears on her cheeks, feeling a kind of slow-dawning shock. He didn't know about all the other things she'd said about him, but what she'd said about doubt...resonated. He'd been taught that certainty was strength, and so he'd pushed away his doubts, crushed them, cut them out so there was nothing left in him but the strength he needed to rule.

He'd never thought that perhaps a king might need that doubt. He'd never thought that a king should care. His mother had told him that it was a weakness, not a strength, and yet... Perhaps Sidonie was right. His mother's intentions had been good, but she'd been rigid in her way. Her father hadn't treated her well and she had come to hate him in the end.

After all, his father really hadn't cared about his people or his country, and look what had happened to Al Da'ira.

He wanted to be a better king than that, he always had, but what if that meant admitting that he was just as full of doubt as the next person?

This is how she will change things. By changing you.

That fractured stone around his heart shifted again, making him ache for something he couldn't name. An ache that puzzled him when what he truly wanted was already standing right in front of him.

All he knew was that the tension that had gripped him wasn't there any more, and now all he could think about was her. He wanted his new wife and he wanted her now.

He took one of her hands in his and lifted it to his mouth, gently biting the tip of it and making her eyes go very wide. 'You are always wise, *ya hayati*. And I will have to think about what you have said. But…it is our wedding night, and, since you have not left me as I thought you would, I would like very much for you to continue the job you started.'

CHAPTER TEN

THE GENTLE NIP on her finger had sent a shockwave of sensation through her, and she was very conscious, all of a sudden, that he was shirtless, the wide, muscled expanse of his bronzed chest right in front of her.

Her husband.

He was so much more complicated than she'd ever guessed. She'd thought he'd told her everything about himself and yet he'd been holding on to those secrets. Those terrible, painful secrets. Secrets that had hurt him so badly.

It made her heart ache.

'I know,' she said softly. 'But I wish you had told me those things years ago. You didn't need to torture yourself for so long with them.'

'I did not want to tell you. I thought you would see me differently if I did. And I...could not have borne that back then.'

She blinked back the tears that kept filling her eyes. 'I would never have seen you differently. Not even back then.' And she wouldn't have. Because she'd told him the truth. Granting mercy to his sick dog was an act of kindness, though naturally it would haunt him. And as for Yusuf... No wonder he'd been tortured by that too.

He wasn't a killer. He'd just been forced into a situation that required him to defend himself, and that had had consequences.

It would be terrible if he *hadn't* doubted.

Khalil shook his head. 'You were everything bright, everything beautiful back then, Sidonie. You were the only happiness I'd ever known. I did not want to risk losing that for anything.'

Her throat ached and she wanted to tell him right then and there that he wouldn't have lost it, because she'd loved him then and she loved him still.

But this was already painful enough without bringing love into it.

What she wanted was to give him comfort, help him in any way she could, and she knew the best way to do that. He'd been waiting long enough.

'And you won't lose it now either,' she said quietly, dropping her hands to the buttons on his trousers, and she held his gaze as she undid those one by one, watching the flames start to ignite his sharp black eyes.

'You want me to worship you, husband?' She pulled open his fly. 'Then let me worship you.'

She went to her knees in front of him, dealt with his shoes first, then eased his trousers down, along with his underwear. He stepped out of the fabric and kicked it aside, standing before her completely naked, a sculpture of the perfect man cast in bronze.

Sidonie's mouth dried. He had shown her what to do for him the previous night, but this was their wedding night and she wanted to worship him as he should be worshipped, show him how much he meant to her, that nothing of what he'd told her changed the way she felt about him.

She put her hands on his powerful thighs, but then he

reached down, taking her chin in a firm grip and tilting her head back so she could look at him.

His gaze was dark and very serious. 'You still want this? Even after what I told you?'

She could see the doubt in his eyes, but while he might doubt himself, she didn't. She knew who he was deep down. She'd spent ten years knowing him. And she knew his worth.

'Nothing's changed, Khal,' she said, putting the strength of her conviction into each word. 'For ten years you made me feel as if I wasn't just a lonely, unwanted orphan. You made me feel as if I was more, as if I was special.' The flame in his eyes glittered and his grip on her chin tightened. He looked as if he was going to say something more, but she pulled away gently. 'So now you need to be quiet and let me make you feel special too.' Then she pressed her lips to his stomach and began to work her way down.

The breath hissed out of him and when she reached to take the long, thick length of his sex in her hand, he muttered a low curse. And when she put her mouth on him and tasted him, worshipped him, he slid his fingers into her hair, the veil sliding off it and onto the floor, and held her tight.

He was a man full of doubt, but she wanted him to know that it didn't matter to her. That he was her husband and when she'd agreed to be his wife, when she'd married him, it was because he was that man. That friend. Not some kind of semi-divine king.

So she put the strength of her conviction into the way she stroked and tasted and explored him, until finally he groaned and pulled her to her feet. 'I need to be inside you,' he growled. 'Now.' Then he tore the gown from her body, along with her underwear, and picked her up and put her on the bed. And he followed her down, spreading her thighs with his strong hands and without hesitation thrusting deep inside her.

She gasped as pleasure bloomed like a flower, and she closed her legs around his waist, reaching for him to bring him close. His mouth came down on hers and then they were moving together, fast and desperate, clinging to each other as the storm broke around them and washed them away.

In the aftermath, lying beneath his hot, hard body, her arms around him, trembling like a leaf and feeling the aftershocks shake him too, Sidonie knew deep in her heart that she'd made the right decision in marrying him.

The thought of leaving him was unfathomable. It had broken her the first time he'd walked away from her and she wasn't going to let it happen again.

She loved him with a fierce, true love. And those doubts she'd had before?

She didn't feel them now. So what if she was his prize, his trophy? So what if he never talked about love or gave it to her?

Her love was enough for both of them, she knew it down to her bones.

Finally, Khalil moved, pressing his mouth to her throat and beginning to kiss his way down her body. It was clear he didn't want to talk any more and that was okay with her. She didn't want to talk either. Her realisation could wait, and besides, there had been enough revelations for one day. They could afford some time to relax and simply enjoy each other.

So she lay back and let her new husband do what he wanted with her.

As it turned out, it was exactly what she wanted too.

* * *

Khalil came to the wide French doors that opened out onto a shady terrace, stopped, then leaned on the doorframe.

Sidonie was lying on a low outdoor sofa piled high with pillows, dressed only in a loose robe of green silk. She had a book beside her, but it was clear she wasn't reading it because she looked to be fast asleep.

No wonder. He'd been keeping her up very late at night and waking her early in the morning. A hunger had set in inside him and he couldn't get enough of her. It was bordering on obsession and normally he wouldn't have permitted it, but, since she was his wife and this was their honeymoon, he allowed it.

Eventually it would wear off, he assumed, then they could settle into their marriage.

It had been three days since their wedding and he knew that soon he was going to have to get back to the palace and resume the task of ruling his country, but he wanted a few more days alone with his wife.

He shifted against the doorframe, watching a breeze lift the edge of Sidonie's robe, exposing a pale expanse of thigh, and his body responded with predictable speed. But he didn't move, content to stand there for a few minutes longer, watching her.

He couldn't stop thinking about what she'd said to him on their wedding night, about how he was a good king and that doubt would only make him better. He still wasn't sure about that—his mother's teachings would take a while to unlearn—but what he was sure about was that she was wise, his Sidonie. So very perceptive.

She knew now the worst parts of him, and she hadn't turned away. She'd only looked up at him with those beautiful green eyes of hers and told him that those things didn't change the person he was inside. That he was a good man.

She also called you rigid and afraid to be a man.

That was true, and maybe she was right. But he had to be rigid. And it wasn't fear, it was necessity. He couldn't be the King he needed to be otherwise.

But maybe he could be a man with her. He could try at least.

Sidonie stirred on the couch, and he pushed himself away from the doorframe, moving over to where she lay, that heavy, aching feeling in his chest getting stronger. It was there all the time now and he still didn't know what it was. But only being near her eased it. Yes, he needed her, and he probably always would.

Carefully, he sat on the couch beside her and brushed a strand of red hair off her cheek, tucking it behind her ear. She smiled and her eyes opened. 'Hmm. I was having the loveliest dream and now I'm awake I realise it wasn't a dream at all. Because here you are.'

The heavy ache in his chest was getting painful now.

He ignored it, smiling back at her. 'Keep dreaming, *ya hayati*. I will make it even more pleasant for you.'

She gave a soft laugh and turned over onto her back, the silk robe shifting and clinging in the most delectable places. He was growing even harder, especially when she gave a sexy, sensual little stretch, her back arching. 'Again, Khal?'

He reached down and traced the curve of one full breast with light fingertips. 'Do you object?'

'Of course not.' The look she gave him from underneath her lashes was smouldering. 'I might even have to insist.'

It was his turn to laugh then, because she was beautiful and he loved it when she flirted with him, and the expression on her face softened. The glow in her eyes became somehow more intense and the smile that curved her mouth took on a warmth that nearly stopped his heart.

'I love you, Khalil ibn Amir al Nazari,' she said quietly. 'I love you so much.'

She had said those words to him once before, years ago on a snowy street in Soho. And the effect they'd had then was the same as it was now, the words cutting through him like a sword through silk, opening him up.

And they should not have done. He had hardened himself thoroughly since that night. He was different. He'd changed. He shouldn't have felt as if all his insides were spilling out, pain gripping him.

Your fault. You should have talked to her about this. You should have told her that marrying her had nothing to do with love, and that love was something you couldn't allow.

He felt cold. They should have had that discussion. But she'd distracted him with sex the night before, and then he'd been so impatient to marry her he hadn't had time for yet more talking. And last night, there had been all those painful confessions and afterwards, when she'd touched him, all he'd wanted was the warmth of her body and the comfort only she could give.

You have been selfish. Greedy. Like Amir.

Yes, he had been.

'I have been meaning to have that discussion with you,' he said flatly, the knowledge sitting in his gut like a stone. 'Love is not part of this marriage, Sidonie. It will never be part of it.'

The look on her face didn't change despite his tone, her gaze very steady. Not at all the same as five years earlier, when there had been only fearful hope in her eyes. 'Why not?' she asked.

The cold inside him deepened, though he tried to force it away. 'Because I do not want it.'

'I see. Because why? Love is not permitted for kings?'

It was impossible to read the expression on her face.

'It is not.' He tried to keep his voice even.

'I didn't say you had to love me,' she said. 'I only said that I love you.'

'No.' He hadn't even realised he'd pushed himself off the couch until he found himself standing a few paces away, staring at her, as if he wanted to put some distance between them. 'We should have talked about this, and I am sorry that I did not. But no, there can be no love between us.'

Sidonie was sitting up now, the green robe gathered around her, red hair falling in a pretty waterfall over her shoulders. She was still looking at him with the same terrible certainty. 'Why? What is so very threatening about the fact that I love you? Tell me what's going through your head.'

'Why do you think?' His voice was hoarse. 'Because I do not love you back, Sidonie.'

She lifted a shoulder as if it wasn't a big deal. 'So? I didn't ask for you to love me. That's not why I said it.'

'Then why did you say it?' The words came out sharp, full of edges, like razor wire, and he was breathing very fast. 'Five years ago, you said it to me, and I broke your heart. That is what you told me... I walked away from you then because I could not give you what you wanted. And nothing has changed, Sidonie. I still cannot.'

He couldn't. There were already cracks in the stone around his heart, the doubt inside him deepening. He could not love her back because love was a weakness that undermined his strength. And he was supposed to make her happy, that was what he'd promised himself.

No. That's a lie you told yourself. This hasn't got anything to do with what kings are and aren't permitted. You want to love her, but love makes you do such terrible things.

He'd loved his country, so he'd killed Yusuf. He'd loved Dusk, so he'd killed him too. And all those years ago, he'd once loved Sidonie. And he'd walked away from her, dealing her a mortal blow.

There was a weight around his heart, crushing him, suffocating him.

'It doesn't matter,' Sidonie said. 'It doesn't matter that nothing's changed. I told you because even kings need someone who loves them.' Her red brows drew together. 'Why is that so bad?'

She didn't understand. Which meant he would have to tell her. 'Because I do not love you,' he repeated. 'And I *never* will, Sidonie. *Never.* I am too much like my father. I have his blood in me.'

He wouldn't do it again. He couldn't. The blood inside him was too strong and his hunger for Sidonie was too intense. He had to keep his emotional distance, he *had* to. He didn't know what would happen if he didn't.

Sidonie pushed herself off the couch and crossed the space between them, the green robe flowing around her, making her look the goddess of spring that he'd hoped to give his people. And the terrible, crushing ache in his chest squeezed tighter.

'You're not listening,' she said calmly, coming up to him and putting her hands on his chest, smoothing the black cotton of the robe he wore. 'It doesn't matter.'

He couldn't bear for her to touch him, it felt too painful. So he took her wrists in his hands and pulled her fingers away from him. 'It may not matter to you, but it matters to me.'

Still she didn't look upset. 'Why?'

He didn't want to spell it out to her, but it seemed as if he was going to have to. 'You lost your parents, Sidonie. You lost the two people who cared about you most in the world, and you were raised instead by that awful aunt of yours.' He looked down into her eyes. 'Tell me that you don't want to be loved. Tell me that you don't need it like you need air to breathe. Tell me and make me believe it.'

Finally, her gaze flickered. 'I don't. You're what's important to me.'

She was lying to herself, but that didn't matter. He already had his answer. 'But I should not be. What you want matters, *ya hayati.* You should not be putting what you need second all the time. You do not deserve it.'

She didn't try to pull her hands away and she didn't try to touch him again. 'It seems to me that I should be the one who gets to decide what I deserve, not you. Just like I get to decide what's important and what's not. Yes, I lost my parents. Yes, my aunt was awful. But then I met a wonderful man who became my friend, and he showed me what I deserved, and I decided that what I deserved was him.'

'I broke your heart,' he said desperately. 'That is what you said.'

'You did,' she said. 'But you won't do again. I know you won't.'

'How? How do you know that? You know nothing of the man I have become, nothing about the sacrifices I have made for my country. What is to say that one day I will not sacrifice you too?'

'Of course I know about your sacrifices,' she shot back. 'You told me about them, remember? And don't tell me I don't know you. I've known you for ten years and, while we've both changed, we're still who we were deep down inside. I told you last night what kind of man you are, the kind of man you've always been, so yes, I know you. And you'd never break my heart, not again.'

He tightened his grip, pulling her against him. 'But am I not doing it now? Telling you I can never love you while you pour all your love into me? You giving me everything while I give you nothing in return? How is that not breaking your heart into pieces?'

She went pale. 'But given time I can—'

'Did time work with your aunt?' It was a low blow but he had to make her see. 'Did that ever change her?'

Her lovely green eyes glittered. 'You are not my aunt.'

He dropped her wrists and stood there, rigidly, covering up the fractures in the stone around his heart, holding on to what he knew to be true, to the certainty, that *this* was the right decision to make. The only decision. And not for himself, but for her. 'No, I am not. And I will not be her. I will not hold you to me when I cannot give you what you need to be happy. And I want you to be happy, Sidonie. I want you to be free to choose for yourself, to have someone who will love you the way you deserve to be loved.'

Her chin lifted, her back straight and proud. 'But I have chosen. And I choose you.'

Every part of him was tense. 'Then you have chosen poorly.'

And before she could say anything else, he turned and stalked back to the house.

CHAPTER ELEVEN

SIDONIE WATCHED KHALIL stride away from her, feeling her heart fracture into a million tiny pieces.

It was happening again. She'd told him the truth and he'd walked away the way he had five years earlier.

Your own fault. You should never have told him you loved him.

It had been a risk, she'd known that. But when he'd smiled at her, looking like the man he'd been years before, she hadn't been able to stop herself.

He was her husband and she loved him, and she wanted him to know that. After the truths of the night before, she'd thought he deserved to know that nothing had changed her feelings for him, and that nothing ever would. She loved him unreservedly, accepting him for everything he was, the way he'd accepted her, and she couldn't bear for him to think that somehow he was unworthy of it, or didn't deserve it after the things he'd done.

She didn't know what she expected, but she hadn't thought history would repeat itself.

'So that's it?' She didn't raise her voice. She didn't need to. He would hear. 'I tell you that I love you and your answer is to walk away? This is so five years ago, Khalil.'

He stopped dead right before the French doors, his back to her, his black robe swirling around him.

'If you want my happiness so badly, explain to me how that is going to fill me with joy?' she went on, since he didn't look as if he was going to. 'You did this last time too, making me feel as if this was all my fault somehow.'

'No, that is not...' His deep voice sounded ragged, and she very much wanted to cross the distance and put her arms around him, but she wasn't going to. Not this time. 'That is not what I am saying.'

'So, if I had never told you everything would be fine?' Anger was filling her now, the anger she'd never let herself truly feel years ago, an anger that she'd fought down and pushed away, hidden under the milder layers of irritation and annoyance. The anger that her aunt had never allowed her. The anger she should have given him five years ago and hadn't. 'That our marriage would be full of bliss if only I hadn't mentioned the L word?'

He was silent, his back rigid, his wide shoulders tense. Then he turned around, and her breath caught. The expression on his beautiful face wasn't impenetrable or hard to read now, no, she could read every line. He looked as if he was in agony. 'Sidonie, that is not what I am—'

'*No*,' she shouted suddenly. 'No, *you're* the one who's not listening to *me*.' Then, before she could stop herself, she stormed up to him, stopping inches away from him as he stared at her with tortured dark eyes. 'I can't believe you'd tell me all those lies about how you can't love me, and you want me to be happy, only to walk away from me *again*.' She stared fiercely back, letting him see her anger. 'You're a coward, Khalil. That's the real issue. It's not that you can't love me or that kings aren't permitted love. It's that you won't love me. Because you are afraid.'

'It is *not* fear.'

'Then what is it?' she demanded. 'What is so very bad about loving me, Khalil?'

He looked as if he was going to come apart at the slightest touch, anguish bleeding out of him. He took a step so they were almost touching. 'Because you broke me.' His voice was ragged and hoarse. 'Because you broke my heart, too. I loved you, but I could not have you. And I cannot… I *will* not…let myself be broken again.'

It was the truth; she could see it in his eyes. She could feel it in her own heart, the shattering pain that had torn them apart all those years ago.

Leaving her *had* broken him, and he was protecting himself now, just as she had.

If she'd been the woman she'd been five years earlier, she'd have softened. She'd have put her arms around him and told him that it was okay, he could protect himself. She didn't need to be loved back and being married to him was enough.

But it wasn't enough. She understood that now and he'd made her see it.

She couldn't spend the years of her marriage pouring her soul into a man who was too afraid to love her in return. Because she knew what would happen if she did. She'd lived it already with her aunt.

She'd become smaller, quieter. She'd push her own thoughts and feelings and wants and needs right down. She'd become weaker. A faded, washed-out version of the woman she was now.

The woman she'd become because of this man.

She didn't want to lose that woman. That woman was strong and passionate and brave. That woman had learned to ask for what she wanted, and if she was going to hold on to her she couldn't give in now.

Because deep down she knew, in her heart, that Khalil wanted her. That he needed her. And she thought that maybe he loved her too, but that was something he'd have to choose himself.

She'd stopped protecting herself and had stepped into her truth. Now it was his turn.

It was a risk to do this, to insist, but she had to do it.

For both their sakes.

'Then leave.' She took a step back. 'Go on, run away, Khalil. You're so very good at doing that, after all. If you're not brave enough to bear loving me and having me love you in return, then you're not the man I thought you were.'

He stood there, staring at her, his black eyes burning in his proud, sharp features.

But she wasn't going to wait for him to walk away from her, not this time.

So it was she who strode past him, and went into the house without a backward glance.

Khalil didn't want to stay while she was there. So he ordered a helicopter to be brought, and when it arrived he got on it.

He couldn't bear to be near her. Couldn't bear her fierce determination to love him. Or the way she'd flung that accusation straight in his face: *you're a coward.*

It wasn't fear that drove him away, couldn't she see that? He had to protect himself. Walking away from her the last time had broken him so utterly that he'd had to destroy the person he'd been just to survive.

And he had to survive. For his nation and his crown. If not then everything he'd ever done—Dusk, Yusuf—would have been for nothing.

He couldn't allow that to happen to him again. He couldn't.

The helicopter finally landed and he got out, dismissing his servants and striding for his apartments. He needed time to think about what to do next, because for the first time in his life he didn't know. He had no idea.

There, he tried to involve himself in work, but he couldn't concentrate. None of the decisions he had to make seemed right and he doubted every one. He doubted everything, including himself.

She'd told him doubt would make him a better king, but he didn't see how, not when he couldn't make any decisions. It seemed impossible.

He poured himself a neat vodka, a taste he'd developed over the past couple of years, and threw it down, relishing the burn. Hoping for some clarity, even though he knew drinking wasn't going to give him the kind of clarity he wanted.

Sure enough, after a couple of hours, he found himself sitting on the couch where he'd first taken Sidonie, the heavy, aching feeling sitting there like an elephant sitting on his chest. Making it hard to breathe, making it hard to even think.

His phone went off and he grabbed at it, staring down at the screen, wanting it to be Sidonie for some reason. But it wasn't. It was Galen.

He didn't want to answer it, but he did anyway. 'What?' he demanded gracelessly.

'Hmm,' Galen said. 'You sound like you're in a good mood.'

'Did you want something, Galen?'

'It's about your marriage celebration ball... I was thinking—'

'There will be no celebration,' Khalil cut him off tersely. 'I have decided it is a bad idea.'

There was a silence down the other end of the phone.

'Any particular reason?' Galen asked, his tone neutral.

And Khalil didn't know why he said what he said next. Perhaps it was because Galen had been through this and he knew what it was to have a woman love him. And he'd found it difficult, too. 'I do not know what to do,' Khalil said bleakly. 'She loves me, Galen. She told me so. But I cannot make her happy and she deserves it. She deserves it more than anyone I have ever met.'

There was another long silence. Then Galen said, 'You married her, didn't you?'

'Yes.'

'And do you love her?'

'I cannot.' He took a breath, the memory of what he'd flung at her in desperation resounding in his head. 'I... loved her before. But I could not have her and I...'

'You what?'

He could feel it inside him again, that pain. The same pain that had torn him when he'd had to put Dusk down. The same doubt and grief that had fractured him after Yusuf. 'It broke me,' he said starkly.

'Ah,' Galen said. 'I am familiar with that kind of break.'

Khalil shut his eyes, Sidonie in her green gown right there in front of him. Blazing with all that beautiful fury and passion. Telling him he was a coward and how dared he walk away from her a second time?

How could you? How could you break her heart again?

'She called me a coward,' he heard himself say. 'She called me a coward and walked away from me. And she was right. I barely survived losing her the first time. I do not think I could go through it again.'

'I know,' Galen said, no amusement in his tone now. 'It's hard. But ask yourself what you want, what you *really* want. And whether that's more important to you than anything else in your life.'

Khalil let out a breath. 'More important than my crown?'

'Yes,' Galen said without hesitation. 'A crown is just a thing. Someone else can wear it. And you don't cease to exist just because you're not a king. But will you cease to exist without her?'

Khalil stared at the wall, the words echoing inside him, resonating like a note with a tuning fork.

What did he want? What did he really, truly want? More than anything else in his life?

You know what you want. You've known it all along. And she was right. You went to England for her and you married her. You brought her back to your mother's house and you told her your secrets. And it's not for your country. It's not for your crown. It's not even for your own gratification. You brought her back because you lived without her for five years and you can't live like that any longer.

The truth of the thought hit him like lightning. Like a bullet from a gun. Shattering the stone around his heart, setting him free.

He loved her. He'd always loved her. He'd loved her for every second of those five years and that was why it had broken him, why he'd retreated so rigidly into the strictures of his kingship.

He'd loved her and he'd thought he couldn't have her, and the pain had torn him apart. The only way he'd been able to cope had been to tell himself he didn't feel it. To cut out his heart and get rid of it.

Galen was still talking. 'It's not easy, as I think I said to Augustine when I realised I was in love with Solace. Facing up to my fear was one of the hardest things I've ever done in my life, but I did. Because without Solace I was nothing and I knew it.' There was a pause and then he added quietly, 'It's worth it, Khal. Believe me, it's worth every second of pain.'

Yet he'd already had too much pain and so had his Sidonie.

She was more important to him than anything in his life. More important than his crown and more important than his country. Without them he would still exist.

But he couldn't exist without her. And if she was brave enough to love him, then he had to be brave enough to love her back.

'Galen,' he said roughly, 'I think I have just made a terrible mistake.'

'Thought you might say that,' Galen murmured. 'Then you'd better fix it, hadn't you?'

'Yes,' Khalil said and dropped the phone.

He didn't even waste time ending the call.

It was dark, but Sidonie sat still on the terrace, even as the wind became colder, the stars wheeling in the night sky above her head. She was thinking of plans and discarding them, trying to decide what to do about Khalil.

She didn't know whether he'd come back, and she was on the point of deciding that she would just go to him, when she heard the sound of a helicopter overhead. Returning. And her heart squeezed tight in her chest.

Then five minutes later a man strode onto the terrace, still in the robes he'd worn when he'd left that morning, and he came over to where she sat. And before she could say anything, he knelt at her feet and looked up at her.

'My queen,' he said roughly. 'Will you forgive me?'

She was trembling all of a sudden. 'For what?'

'For leaving you. For walking away from you again.' His face was stripped bare of any of his usual guards and there was nothing but naked desire and a burning, fierce need that lit his eyes like stars. 'For being a coward. Because you were right. I was afraid. The way I left you in London hurt so much. It tore me apart. And that is what I have been afraid of ever since. I never wanted my heart to be so at risk again. But…another good friend of mine asked me what I wanted more than anything else. What was more important to me than even my crown.' He reached for her hand and held it gently in his, her wedding ring glittering in the starlight. 'And I realised that it is you, Sidonie al Nazari. Without my crown, I am just another man. But without you, I am nothing. I have only been half-alive these past five years, barely existing, and I am tired of it. I loved you back then, and I told myself many times that I could not possibly love you now. But I was wrong. I love you, *ya hayati*. My life. You were my sunshine back then and you still are. You always will be.'

She didn't mean to cry and yet a tear escaped, running down her cheek. 'I didn't want to walk away from you, Khal. I didn't. But I wanted you to choose for yourself.'

In the darkness he smiled, and took her other hand, turning both of them up. 'You are so very wise.' Then he kissed one palm and then the other. 'And so, I have chosen. It is you, my beautiful Sidonie. You are my life, my heart. You are my soul. And until death and beyond I am yours.'

There were more tears on her cheeks—she couldn't

stop them, joy lighting up inside her. 'Now, that's a romantic proposal,' she said huskily, and then, since she couldn't stand it any more, she pulled her hands away and tugged him to his feet. 'Kiss me, you idiot.'

He laughed softly. 'Perhaps is it I who needs to teach you some romance.' Then he pulled her into his arms, and his mouth was on hers, and her whole world turned to flame.

He'd once been her friend...now he was a king and her husband, and they would have a family. They would bring healing to this country, *their* country.

They would bring healing to each other.

It was the happy ending she'd always longed for, yet never quite dreamed would be hers, and now it was. And all because of a vow she'd written on a stained serviette, one night in a bar in Soho.

Once, she'd thought that getting him to sign it had been the stupidest thing she'd ever done.

Now she knew it was the best decision she'd ever made.

EPILOGUE

KHALIL LOOKED OVER the crowded ballroom to see if he could spot his beautiful wife.

Everyone was here for his marriage celebration ball and his staff had outdone themselves. Sidonie had insisted it be in the throne room because that was where they had been married and also because the tiles were beautiful. He'd agreed, and so now his throne room was full of light and music and people laughing. Exactly as he'd hoped when he'd first come to get Sidonie from England a month earlier.

She had taken to being his queen like a duck to water, helping him to organise the redistribution of wealth to his populace, drawing on her charity and management experience in order for the whole process to run smoothly. And it did.

Her charity, too, was making waves in Europe, helping disadvantaged children everywhere, and soon they would be launching it in the States, with a fundraising ball planned in New York at Christmas.

Managing her new role as Queen with her charity commitments was a big job, but Sidonie was an excellent manager of both her own time and other people's, far better than he was. Already she had every single person in his court eating out of her hand.

Galen and Solace had a little crowd of people around them, while Augustine kept checking his watch and looking irritated. Apparently he was waiting for Freddie, his personal assistant. She'd got delayed in London by something and wouldn't be back until much later.

Cool fingers suddenly gripped his.

Khalil frowned and turned, only to find Sidonie's green eyes looking back at him.

She was magnificent tonight in the green gown she'd had especially designed, an off-the-shoulder number that laid bare her pale shoulders and with sweeping silken skirts. And gleaming in the hollow of her throat was the delicate little golden sunburst necklace he'd presented to her just before the ball had started, in reminder of a very private, very personal memory they shared. She'd cried and he'd kissed away her tears.

His breath caught at her loveliness.

'What is it?' he asked.

But she only smiled mysteriously and pulled at his hand, drawing him over behind one of the pillars, where it was quieter.

'What, *ya hayati*?' Sudden concern tightened inside him. 'Are you well?'

Sidonie's smile was radiant. 'I'm well. I'm very well.' Then she closed the space between them, put her hands on his chest and rose up on her toes. 'I'm also very pregnant,' she whispered in his ear.

He didn't know what it was that went through him, a lightning strike of emotion that rooted him to the spot. And then, as her lips brushed his ear, he understood.

Happiness. It was happiness.

'Sidonie,' he whispered back. 'My sunshine. You make me so very happy.'

He'd thought his heart was made of stone until she'd taught him his mistake.

It wasn't made of stone.

It was made of love.

There was no doubt at all in his mind.

* * * * *

PREGNANT AT THE PALACE ALTAR

LORRAINE HALL

MILLS & BOON

For Soraya.
Thank you for your boundless enthusiasm.

CHAPTER ONE

As far as King Diamandis Agonas was concerned, royal weddings were a royal pain. His only comfort in being involved in the planning of this one was that it was not his own wedding.

That would be a disaster.

But being the king while his sister—the long-lost princess who'd only been returned to them earlier this year—got married was proving more challenging than he would have preferred.

In any other circumstances, he would have labeled the whole affair a debacle. First, Zandra and her betrothed had run off to Athens to get married months ago and then the announcement of her pregnancy had brought about the need to move up the date of the royal wedding ceremony, and Diamandis had found himself uncharacteristically bending over backward for his sister.

He blamed it on the fact he'd considered her dead for nearly twenty years. What man wouldn't want to make up for lost time? What king wouldn't want to give his sister, the princess, all she desired, and all that was befitting a Kalyvan princess?

He eyed her now, moving around his office. She was not a *sitter*, this woman. Not the placid, obedient princess she might have been if she'd grown up in the palace. If their family had not been murdered in a bloody attempt at a political coup twenty years ago.

Instead, the monarchy had managed to withstand the attack

and Diamandis had been proclaimed king in the wake of his parents' and brothers' deaths.

Zandra, with the help of a servant boy, had somehow escaped, lost her memory in the process, and grown up on the streets of Athens as an orphan. That same servant boy—Lysias Balaskas, who was now a billionaire and Zandra's husband—had returned her to Kalyva earlier this year.

So Zandra was home where she belonged. She was his sister, proven by DNA tests, and yet it was like his sister was two different people to him: the toddler he'd known for the first four years of her life, and now this woman, whom he didn't understand and couldn't begin to make sense of. So open and sweet, with a backbone that was giving him a headache.

Yet she was his sister—he knew this elementally—and he loved her.

No matter how she puzzled, irritated and defied him.

Because her eyes were the same—whether she was the four-year-old poking him in the throat, or this woman saying things that nearly knocked him off his feet.

"When I was in Athens, you'll never guess who I saw." Luckily, she did not pause and make him guess. "Katerina."

Diamandis did not stiffen. He did not allow himself to be caught off guard by *anything* anymore. Or so he told himself. His former assistant had caught him off guard more times than he cared to count.

He did not allow his mind to conjure up images of her. She had fled in the middle of the night, leaving only a note, and so she was as good as dead to him.

At least that was what he told himself whenever the memory of her popped up. He tried to convince himself this was simply because she was the best assistant he'd ever had and every attempt at replacement had failed dismally.

He did not allow himself to think of *that night*. In *this* office. The exquisite perfection of her and all that could not be.

Ever.

"What does this have to do with the wedding preparations?" Diamandis asked, stiffly.

His curtness did not deter Zandra, but then very few things did. "It doesn't, but I think I may have solved your mystery of why she up and left."

"Oh?" Diamandis had his own suspicions, but they were ones he would never share with his sister. Or anyone.

"I saw her in the baby store. With a belly bigger than mine."

Diamandis did not move. He did not hear whatever Zandra said next. Everything was simply a buzzing in his ears.

A belly bigger than mine.

"I suppose that's why she left," Zandra said after she'd rambled on about something. "Heaven knows I wouldn't want to be growing a human while suffering under *your* beck and call."

"What?"

Zandra slid her hand over her rounded belly as if that was the answer.

It *couldn't* be the answer.

"It is odd, though," Zandra said, tapping her chin as if deep in thought.

"What is?" Diamandis said between gritted teeth, beyond irritated that his frustration was leaking through when *nothing* about Katerina Floros mattered to him. *Nothing.* Not why she'd left or what state she was currently in.

She had left. The end.

"She didn't seem to want to see me, so I didn't approach her and ask. Of course every pregnancy and woman is different, or so I've read, but she seemed to be even farther along than *me.* Considering how you had her working practically around the clock, I'm not sure how she found the time to become pregnant while working for you." Then all the casual indifference turned sharp, her dark gaze pinning his. "I don't suppose *you* had anything to do with it."

"With what?"

She rolled her eyes. "Please tell me you're not the deadbeat father of her baby, Diamandis."

Diamandis straightened and stared down at his sister. "I am the king of Kalyva."

"So?"

She really was the most impossible creature. He did not understand why Lysias didn't...*do* something about her.

Or why you, the king and her brother, don't.

But that was neither here nor there. "I am *not* a deadbeat. Nor the father of Katerina's child. She left in the dark of night all those months ago and I have not seen her since."

"Yes, six months ago. About the time she likely found out she was pregnant. It just seems likely that the two events are connected."

"I assure you *I* had nothing to do with whatever predicament she finds herself in."

Zandra shrugged, her hands resting over her own rounded belly. Diamandis refused to let his imagination create a version of Katerina in that state.

He was a *king*. If the regrettable night of passion had led to a child, his efficient assistant would have informed him and requested compensation. They would have dealt with the problem at hand. There would have been no cause to run away.

To do so would be foolish and shortsighted, and Katerina had never been any of those things, even in the aftermath of their one...*hiccup.*

He preferred to refer to it as that.

"I have much to do, Zandra. Was there anything else you wished to discuss?"

She eyed him carefully, and he did not know what his sister was searching for, or whether she found it. She moved forward, brushing a kiss across his cheek. "Nothing else, Diamandis. I will see you at dinner." Then she departed.

Diamandis stood exactly where he was. He told himself that this information changed nothing. He would go on about his day as planned.

He pressed the button on his desk that would alert his assistant that his presence was required.

While he waited, Diamandis stood staring blindly out the window. It was impossible. He was sure it was impossible.

But unfortunately, Zandra was correct. Katerina's life as his assistant *had* been demanding. When would she have had time to go off and engage in some affair? He would have heard about it, known about it.

So there was only one course of action now, no matter how impossible this all seemed.

When his new assistant *finally* appeared, Diamandis didn't look at him. He simply said, "I will be flying to Athens. Make the arrangements. Immediately."

"The brave, courageous prince stood between the princess and the dangerous dragon, and with one mighty swipe he saved the princess from certain death!"

Katerina Floros *hated* this story, but the children in her classroom loved it. The illustration of the prince slaying the dragon was just gruesome enough to be titillating for the four-year-old set, the tale of a prince and princess and a dragon just imaginative enough to fill many of them with the typical childhood awe.

Any awe Katerina might have had at royalty and glittering dresses and fearsome princes had long since fallen prey to disillusionment. Instead, she felt sorry for the dragon. *He* likely had been minding his own business, doing his job, only to have the prince swoop in and ruin everything.

The children made excited conversation about the illustration, as per usual, and then Katerina hurried them through their end-of-day routines. Parents began to arrive to pick up their children after long days at work.

It was hard for Katerina to believe she would be one of them soon—rushing about, working and parenting. She liked to believe she'd be the flawless, unbothered mother with big smiles and hugs. She had a bad feeling she'd be the harried one, bustling around, begging for the children to *please* move along faster because they had places to be. But that was still a little way off…though it was getting ever closer.

Once all the children had been picked up, and most of the staff had gone, Katerina collected her things. Her boss—the director of the childcare center and Katerina's personal savior—joined her.

"Won't be long for you now." Fifi gave her stomach a little pat. Katerina *hated* people touching her belly, but Fifi had been a godsend for giving her a job and time off to attend doctor's appointments, and Katerina didn't have it in her to ask her not to do that.

They walked outside together into a cloudy evening, offering small talk and then goodbyes. In her head, Katerina was praying her little junker of a car would start. When it did, she offered a little thank-you to the universe and then drove home.

She parked on the street in front of her apartment complex in a questionable neighborhood on the outskirts of Athens. It was not a palace. It wasn't even the glittering beach bungalow she'd grown up in on the island nation of Kalyva. It was, in fact, a hovel, at best. But it was *her* hovel, which she paid for with money *she* earned. Because she *refused* to follow in her mother's footsteps any more than she already had.

She'd make her own way. She'd love her child, and if that meant struggling for money in the beginning, so be it. There would be love—and that was better than secrets and money.

Katerina would make it work. She always did.

There was a crowd a way down the street, and though Katerina was curious, she kept her head down and walked into her building. Nothing good came from gathered crowds— this she knew.

So she walked up the stairs, cursing her third-story apartment as she did every evening when her stomach felt particularly heavy and her feet positively ached. She was starving, exhausted, and couldn't wait to eat dinner in the bathtub as had become an indulgent ritual every night after work.

She unlocked the door, stepped inside and froze. There was a strange scent in the air. Something very…masculine. Her heart seized there in her chest and she reached for the door behind her with one hand. In the other, she held her keys in between her fingers, ready to defend herself in whatever way she could.

But even as she did so she knew there was no defense against this.

He was here. In her apartment. On her raggedy, sunken couch cushion. She had done everything to make her place cozy and cheerful, but in the shadow of *him* it seemed dim, dirty. Shameful.

The king of Kalyva sat on her couch. Her former boss. *And more.*

Her hands slowly dropped from their fighter's stance to her stomach, as if she could hide that fact from him. She had a lie ready. She'd hold on to that lie with all she had, and yet…

The sight of him still stole her breath. It seemed time away had stripped her of all those old tricks she'd once employed in order not to react outwardly to the man.

The king.

She could still hear herself breathlessly call him "my king" that one stupid night she'd forgotten every promise she'd ever made to herself. All because this man had kissed her.

All because she was a *fool*. The fool her mother had always told her she'd be when a handsome, powerful man took what he wanted—and *you* wanted.

She should have known he'd be here. She'd thought she'd managed to hide from Princess Zandra in the baby store the other day, but she should have known. Should have known the princess was kind enough to have pretended not to see her as Katerina had clearly not wanted to be seen.

But not kind enough to keep it to herself.

Diamandis unfolded himself, the height and breadth of him seeming to block out the sad light of the fluorescent fixture behind him. His dark hair was cut in the same ruthless style it always was, his dark brows and eyes as severe as ever. His muscular frame was enhanced by one of his requisite black suits. She knew he thought it practical and that it made him look intimidating to all who would oppose him, but it was little more than repressed mourning, because he had never dealt with any of the tragedies that had befallen him.

She knew this all too well, and it was a large part of why she'd run the moment she'd found herself pregnant. Diamandis did not deal with anything that did not suit the narrative he had created for his life—and she could not even hate him for that after the way he'd lost his family and had somehow kept his kingdom from crumbling. At *fourteen*.

She hadn't trusted herself to be strong in the face of him, and she would have needed an immense amount of strength. He had spent *years* telling everyone who would listen that, if he had the choice, he'd never marry, never have children. So this little *lapse* would not fit into his plans.

And *she* would pay the price.

A price she knew intimately. And she had no wish to pass any of that on to her children the way her own mother had done.

So Katerina had left. Disappeared. *Run*. Determined to handle all of this on her own. She had always been on her own, even when at the whims of her mother, so it had seemed the only course of action. She'd been certain he wouldn't think twice about her disappearance.

He'd forget *all* about her, and never, ever know. Or care.

She was saving them both, really.

But now he was here. Now he likely knew. And what power did she have against a king?

You will have to find some, Katerina. She held her hands more tightly around her stomach.

"Has it really been so long that you've forgotten protocol, Ms. Floros?" he said, and she recognized that cool, detached tone and the way he said her formal name with those clipped vowels. It hid a fury most people never guessed at. But she knew.

She knew all too well.

He studied her, encased in all that ice he wielded so well. "You are supposed to curtsy in the presence of your king."

CHAPTER TWO

SHE DID NOT CURTSY. Diamandis did not know if this was some act of defiance—which he did not understand—or whether in her state she would struggle to make such a movement. He seemed to remember his mother walking about the castle when heavy with child, complaining bitterly about her size, her discomfort, then, upon seeing him, flash a smile and bring him into a hug he was far too old for and tell him it was always worth it.

He did not care for memories of his mother, and he could admit that this soured his already less than controlled disposition.

"What are you doing here, Diamandis?"

He raised an eyebrow at the cheek of her using his first name without any honorific. But she didn't wither. She'd always been an effective and efficient assistant, capable of hiding in the shadows and also capable of standing up to him when it was necessary.

But today she'd picked the wrong moment to stand up to him.

"An interesting question. I imagine you have some ideas."

She rested her hand on her belly, which was round and lush. The moment he'd seen her his hands had itched to reach out and feel the swell of it under the loose, gauzy fabric she wore. Her dark, curly hair was pulled back, but quite a few strands had fallen out and wisped around her face. She wore no makeup and did not resemble the slim, efficient assistant he'd once known.

Which seemed to change his body's reaction to her not at all. She had long been a problem. A temptation. He'd convinced himself he was immune, that he was *better* than his baser urges, because his entire life was pledged in service to his kingdom. There was no room for his wants.

That night had been a failure in so many ways, but he'd at the very least convinced himself he'd exorcised such foolish lust.

Even when he could still taste her. Even when her "my king" still echoed in his head.

He curled his hand into a fist, needing something to remind him of his purpose. He must not touch her. He needed to determine if she was pregnant with *his* child, because clearly she was indeed pregnant.

He did not want a wife, a queen. He did not want children. Finding Zandra might have fulfilled him on a personal level, but it had also taken a great weight off his shoulders. He did not have to worry about heirs.

He knew what it was to be the heir. It was why he was still alive.

No matter how much time he'd spent wishing he'd been the one murdered.

"My sister comes home from a shopping trip to Athens with news that my former assistant, who ran away in the dead of night, is gallivanting about Athens, pregnant. More pregnant even than my sister herself, which seemed odd timing to Zandra, since she did not think you'd have had time to become so when you were working for me."

"The princess does have a curious, inquisitive mind," Katerina returned. Her tone was cool. Her hands were still, but her eyes…

Her alluring green eyes had always told another story than

the masks she wore so beautifully. He hadn't always wanted to uncover that story. Had actively avoided seeing beneath her composed demeanor.

Except for that one night.

"You know why I am here, Katerina."

"I do not, Diamandis. While I can understand why you might be under the impression that our one...*encounter* might have caused my current situation, that my entire life in Kalyva was spent being a slave to you, you are mistaken. I had my own life, and I lived it. Now I am happily living it in Athens with my husband, who happens to be the father of this child."

He was surprised—not by the information, but by the blatant lie. Did she really think he hadn't looked into her life over the past six months on his way here? "So. You've married?"

"Yes."

Diamandis took a moment to try and decide whether she thought him *stupid*, or whether she was just very, very desperate. He did not understand desperation, did not understand this place or her, so surely she thought him stupid.

Some people thought worse of him than that, he supposed. Still, it grated. Particularly as she'd been privy to much information few other royal staff members were. "I am supposed to believe this ludicrous story? You forget that I knew your every move, and still do."

She sniffed. "Impossible."

"I am the king, Katerina."

"You are *a* king, Diamandis. One of many that exist in this big world."

She had often been forthright with him in her position as his assistant—but she had known her place. She had been adept at using the appropriate tone. Usually. This was not forthright and it was not measured.

This was defiance. He looked around the hovel she had tried to make into a home, and he could not understand this game. "There is not one shred of evidence that a man lives here. There is no record of a marriage, and as we stand here and discuss it, no dutiful husband returns to make you dinner."

"He works nights," she returned with a sniff, still standing there by the door as if she might make a break for it.

Surely she knew there was no escape now?

"Does he? Then show me, Katerina. Prove this union to me."

She stood there, her arm curved around her belly as though she held the weight of it in her hands. She said nothing.

Which was answer enough. "Ah, you cannot." He shook his head. "You will return to Kalyva with me at once. If you continue to insist I am not the father, I am afraid a test must be done."

"Why?" she demanded, something in her slumping, and Diamandis did not like watching how that fierce light of defiance seemed to dim. He had always admired her backbone. Her strength. She had never been afraid of him, even when he had wanted her to be.

"What do you mean *why*? We were together and reckless. I am sure you remember."

She lifted her chin and looked at some point on the grimy wall behind him. "Not really," she said loftily.

But the telltale flush that spread across her cheeks told another story, and it aroused him, when he could not afford such a distraction.

Ever again.

There was a child. His child. And he had to fix this problem before it became unfixable. "You lie, Katerina."

She slumped again, leaning back against the door. She looked tired and her eyes were growing wet when her gaze met his again.

"You do not want children, Diamandis. You have always been very clear on your stance on that. Why take me back to

Kalyva? Why run tests? You do not want this, even if you are the father."

"Is this why you ran?" He knew it must be, in part. Or she would have run the night after they were together, not a few weeks later.

She did not answer. She just looked at him with a hopeless kind of expression that had his insides twisting into hard knots. He supposed it was some kind of guilt, though he could not see how he had done anything wrong.

She had not told him. *She* had not given him an opportunity to have a say in the matter. She'd simply fled. She did not get to make him feel guilty now.

"I could have you arrested. I could have you taken, forcefully, back to Kalyva."

"I'm sure you could."

She sounded so tired. She had likely worked all day at the daycare center that sent her monthly paychecks. She had walked up three flights of stairs all to rest her head in this cramped, uncomfortable space, and she would still refuse to return to Kalyva? Where she would be taken care of, regardless of his wants when it came to children?

She made *no* sense.

Still, while he *could* have her arrested under Kalyva law thanks to a treaty with the Greek government, he much preferred a peaceful capitulation. "I am a fair man, Katerina. It does not have to be all about me."

She snorted. "Since when?"

He ignored this derision. "What is it you desire? Surely not this sad little apartment, and a job that underpays and no doubt underappreciates you? Surely not a life in Athens when you could come home and—"

"And what? Be the butt of every joke? Be fodder for gossip? Watch my child grow to be whispered about and called the king's *bastard*." The fight, the fire was back in her eyes and in her posture. She radiated an anger he had not anticipated. "No, Diamandis. I will not sentence any of us to such a fate. Maybe this life is not as nice and fine as the one you are used to, but it is respectable. It will allow my chi—"

"*Our* child."

She stopped at that. As if her words had dried up and she had nothing more to say. He struggled to find his own.

Our *child*. His child. An heir.

"I have no wish to return to Kalyva to gossip and cruelty," Katerina said on little more than a whisper. "You do not wish to have a wife or a child. Let us leave it at that, Diamandis. I will ask you for nothing if you stay away from me. Surely this is fair to both of us."

"I am afraid this will not do, Katerina. You will return to Kalyva, and you will begin preparations."

"Preparations for *what*?"

"For our wedding, of course."

Katerina was certain she was dreaming. There was no other possible explanation for this. Only it wasn't a dream. It was a nightmare.

Perhaps when she'd worked for him she had sometimes allowed her fantasies to wander perilously close to *caring*—at least when it came to the man he was underneath the crown and the trauma responses—but she had always known a happy ending was not on the cards. That he had found her attractive had been shocking enough, and she had not dealt with that realization wisely.

So she had to deal with these events wisely. Because it wasn't about her. It was about…

Our child.

He had said ours, and her heart… Oh, it was traitorous.

"I cannot marry you, Diamandis."

"Getting married solves all of your concerns."

"Hardly. The pit vipers in your court will still deem this pregnancy illegitimate. Conceived out of wedlock. A stain on the monarchy." She couldn't bear it. Would not allow it.

If she had to run away again, she would. Farther this time. She could go to England or America or anywhere Diamandis couldn't reach her.

"We will concoct a story. Lysias and Zandra had an unsanctioned Athens wedding, why not us?"

"Diamandis, you are the *king*." It felt a bit like going back in time, back to when she had been his assistant, and in a way, his conscience. Because he tended to listen to his old, stuffy, aristocratic advisers, but when she'd voiced concern, when she'd reminded him that tradition had its place but the world was also changing, sometimes he'd listened.

"And due to some health issues, we needed to conduct ourselves secretly," he continued, as if she hadn't spoken at all. Another reminder of the past. "The pregnancy complicated your health, so you remained in Athens under a doctor's care while I returned to Kalyva. It was imperative we did not let the public in on such events so you could recuperate in peace. We could not be married in their eyes until you were well enough."

"Who will believe this?" And why was she even entertaining such an absurd possibility? She would not marry him. She would not...

"Everyone. Because I will make certain it becomes the truth."

Katerina knew he believed this. He might even be able to make it work by sheer force of will. That was the power of Diamandis. It was hard and it was implacable. He had been forced to build himself up into such a man after everything that had happened when he'd been little more than a boy.

She couldn't start thinking about *that*, though, or she might soften as she so often had as his assistant. "I am still as common as common comes, and you cannot make that different.

You cannot change the narrative around you marrying your former assistant."

"Lysias was a servant boy. They have taken to him well enough."

"Oh, the billionaire who saved the princess's life? Shocking that they would be supportive of the princess marrying such a man."

She saw impatience simmer behind his eyes and yet he stayed perfectly still. "You are giving this too much thought."

"And you are not giving it enough."

These were lines they had said to each other often when she'd been in his employ—but in the reverse. She had always wanted him to...loosen up. Katerina had often seen ways he might make himself more human to his subjects. *She* had once been the one to accuse him of thinking too much.

And he had always accused her of not thinking of the *implications*.

How on earth had their positions switched? How had she ended up *here*?

"You will be an effective queen, Katerina."

"I have no desire to be queen." No desire to be *effective* for him again. A tool to be trotted out when he saw fit and nothing more.

"And we have proven that we are compatible. In and out of the bedroom."

"What bedroom, Diamandis?" she said tiredly, because they had hardly had some grand love affair. They'd had a night of foolishly shared grief. On his desk. In his office.

She could not travel back to that night in her mind or she would remember too many things that were best lost to time.

"Ah, so you do remember."

She sighed. She was too tired for this ridiculous conversation. For this. For him. To fight her own reaction to him as he stalked over to her and stood above her, glaring down at her with that dark gaze that at one time she'd known how to *pretend* didn't affect her.

"I said no," she said, trying to sound firm. Like she had in the old days when she'd stood up to him. "I will not go back. I will not marry you. The answer is *no*."

"It was not a question, Katerina. Your king has commanded you, and so you will obey." He waited a beat, but she could not control her fast breaths enough to speak in that pause.

"Would you like me to help you pack?" he asked with that condescending I-am-the-king smile that had made her angry even when she'd been his assistant.

"You haven't packed a bag once in your life, Diamandis."

"And you have excellent skills in that department," he offered.

The worst part was that she had no doubt he thought that was a compliment. He thought he was being kind. And that broke apart what little control she was holding on to.

Because he had all the money and power in this situation, and she did not understand why he would use it for this purpose. She was giving him what he wanted—a chance to be free of the children he did not want. She was giving them both what they wanted by getting out and keeping the secret to her grave. So she could not understand this or him.

"Why, Diamandis?" she asked, eyes filling with tears. "You do not want me. You do not want children. I have given you an out. Why won't you take it?"

His expression was grim, his eyes flat. She recognized this side of him. The way he disassociated and focused only on his duty—never on what he actually wanted. "If I let you go, if I pretend this never happened, there is no guarantee that you will not change your mind. No guarantee that the child should not come of age and find out and cause an uproar. We must be married and make the child legitimate. There is no alternative if that child is mine."

It hurt, because perhaps deep down, a part of her had wished that his showing up here meant he'd changed his mind, or that perhaps he cared for her in some small way.

But no. It was about duty. Potential scandal. It was about protecting his crown at any and all costs.

She could not win in this, but she could at least wipe that superior look off his face.

"If the *children* are yours, you mean."

"Excuse me?"

"It is not *a* child, Diamandis. It is children. We are having twins."

CHAPTER THREE

DIAMANDIS FELT AS though that word echoed around in his head as a sort of cymbal crash. Over and over. *Twins, twins, twins.*

Two babies. Two children. And Katerina.

"You look a little pale," Katerina said with a thinly veiled smirk. "Perhaps you should sit down."

He swallowed and straightened his shoulders. It was a surprise, yes, but hardly the blow she wanted it to be. Diamandis had been through too much to be knocked fully off course by this.

Twins.

He did not clear his throat, though it felt clogged and tight. He was still able to speak clearly and forcefully, at least in his own head. "If there is anything you need from this…place, I suggest you collect it."

"Are you going to sic your guards on me if I do not?" she returned.

"Of course not, *glyko mou*. I will carry you myself." And then he smiled, because he would carry her if he had to.

He'd do whatever he had to do. He was the king and had been since he was fourteen. Since he'd had to order the blood of his loved ones to be cleaned from their bedroom floors. Since he'd realized after that first dark year that some of his advisers had, in fact, acted in their own best interests—not the kingdom's or his.

So nothing deterred him anymore. Nothing got in his way. He had his father's legacy to uphold. He could not be beloved as King Youkilis had been—too many mistakes had already been made—but he could keep his country safe and prosperous. He could make certain his behavior was above reproach so no one ever had reason to believe him less than his father's dutiful son and heir.

Katerina had been a mistake. He could blame it on the emotional upheaval of finding out Zandra was alive, or he could take responsibility for his actions.

Diamandis always took responsibility. So, though he had no desire for a queen or family, she would become his. There was no question. The child—*children*—she carried were his. There were no other possible outcomes.

What he wanted or did not want had never signified before. They would not now.

"Do you need a countdown, Katerina?"

She held his gaze for what felt like hours. He saw the myriad greens that leaned toward blue and gray in different lights; the elegant curve of her neck; the soft, honeyed skin over which he'd once run his hands.

It still echoed within him. Between them...the way she had fallen apart in his arms as though she had yearned for him exactly as he had yearned for her since that very first meeting.

He was not alone in this torturous want, he knew, simply by the color rising on her cheeks. He wished that were some kind of comfort.

"I cannot understand your reluctance."

"Reluctance?" She groaned in disgust. "You are delusional. This is not reluctance. It is refusal."

"We will be married, Katerina, and while you seem to view that as some kind of tragedy, I assure you that you will want for nothing, as queen."

"Except a warm, loving home and privacy," she returned.

He had once had that warm, loving home. His childhood was nothing but memories of his parents' love, his family's devotion. But these things did not matter, regardless of how good they might feel. These things were as fragile as glass and could be taken away by any person's whims.

So, no, he did not plan to fill his home with *love*.

Twins, twins, twins.

"You get along quite well with my sister. I'm sure the two of you can forge some kind of friendship as you enter motherhood together. You may fill your part of the palace with as much warmth and love as you so wish."

This did not wipe the frown off her face. The downward curve only settled deeper, when it was a good and kind point, all in all.

"Do you recall what I said to you when your plan was to throw Lysias in a dungeon the minute he stepped on Kalyva soil?"

Diamandis did not care to think about the days that had led up to learning Zandra was indeed his long-lost sister. At the time, Diamandis had been certain his former best friend had returned to Kalyva with an imposter, meant to hurt Diamandis. Now, months later, he felt justified in *most* of his treatment of Lysias, who had not returned with Zandra out of the goodness of his heart, but with revenge on his mind. But somehow love had changed that for Lysias, though Diamandis did not know why any man who'd been through what they had could be felled by *love*. In the end, Lysias had fallen for Zandra and given up on revenge.

Now, somehow, they were a family…as Zandra kept reminding him, no matter how much Diamandis withdrew into himself.

He looked at Katerina, knowing she would now have to be part of it all, knowing it would be harder—but even more necessary—to withdraw from her.

His duty was to Kalyva, and Kalyva alone. So he had heeded her advice at the time and not thrown Lysias in the dungeons.

"You said it would be seen as the action of a cruel, lifeless robot, which I was not," he returned stiffly, because she had been right about the situation and that fact still burned. He wished *cruel, lifeless robot* was more within his reach than his conscience ever let it be.

"I was wrong," Katerina said, looking at him with an anger he'd never seen there in her eyes. "You *are* a cruel, lifeless robot. I don't want anything or anyone to ever hurt my children. I know you will. This alone proves it."

She had never been afraid to stand up to him in the years she'd worked for him, but she'd also never stabbed such a dagger into his heart. "I do not hurt people, Ms. Floros. As king, it is my job to protect them."

As his family had not been protected. And now, somehow, he had family once again. The one thing he did not want. For he would never be worthy of it.

"You speak of violence, Diamandis, but it doesn't take a bloody coup or an attack to hurt people. You can hurt them by not listening to them. By ignoring their needs. You can hurt them by—"

"This is your last chance," he said, struggling with the temper he knew was one of his worst traits. He'd learned to control it over the years, but it was a constant battle, particularly when someone was being so unreasonable—someone he had once respected before she'd betrayed him.

"My last chance for what?" she returned tartly.

"A civil, voluntary arrangement. If you do not come with me now, you will lose your job, this apartment, and the chance to have anything else. When those children are born, they will be taken from you. I will make certain of it. This is not my wish, but if you twist my arm, I will make it happen. They are the heirs." *God help them.* "They are mine. This is the *only* course of action."

Her breathing became ragged, but she did not fall apart. She did not beg his forgiveness or jump to act. She simply stared at him with hatred in her beautiful eyes.

He hated that a black, oily emotion roiled through him— one he refused to examine. "I will be in the car. You have fifteen minutes to make your choice." And with that he strode out of the apartment.

He had done the right thing. For his kingdom. For his legacy.

Whatever came next was Katerina's choice, and he would not feel guilt over that.

He refused to.

Katerina stood stock-still and in place for long ticking minutes after Diamandis exited. She could scarcely catch a breath. She couldn't think.

He had threatened everything. He had left her with some choice but it was no choice at all. Because he was a king, and she was a no one.

The only way to be someone, darling, is to align yourself to the right man.

Oh, how her mother would love this. Marrying a king. She'd likely crawl out of the woodwork and Katerina would have to deal with her, too.

How could this have all come crashing down so quickly? All because of a chance meeting at a baby store. If she'd stayed in her lane—poking around secondhand shops—she never would have seen the princess. Diamandis would have never known.

She wanted to wallow in the what-ifs, spend time self-flagellating over her mistakes, but Diamandis had given her fifteen minutes, and as much as she might have enjoyed thwarting him, she knew him. She had been his personal assistant for too long not to understand at least in part how his mind worked and what had shaped him to think that way.

He did not want a queen or children, but he would suffer through anything he didn't want if he could avoid a scandal that might put a stain on the throne. He considered this his duty to his long-dead parents, and that was a duty he viewed as sacred.

So, yes, he would not be above getting her removed from her job, her apartment. He would not balk at taking her children from her, because in his mind there was only one right way: to have control over his heirs, and, for the sake of his royal subjects, the respectability of being married to their mother.

He had truly given her no choice, and if she faltered or hesitated, she would pay the price. She'd have to wait until they were back in Kalyva to wallow in her poor choices.

From *that* night on.

She went to her room and packed a few things, but she'd taken very little with her when she'd fled the palace and Kalyva. She'd bought even less since building a life in Athens. Still, she packed the few things she'd bought for the baby, her maternity clothes and toiletries. She gave her apartment one last look.

She could not say she'd enjoyed her time here. It had felt necessary, not fun or independent. But it had been *hers*.

And now nothing would be.

She was tired and hungry. Weak and devastated. If she forced herself to look on the bright side, a stay in the palace would mean a comfortable bed and good food and someone else taking care of the details for a little bit.

Maybe once she rested, she'd have a clearer head and be able to come up with a way to get around Diamandis's will. She had talked him out of things before. She only needed time to talk him out of things again.

She turned away from the life she'd built and walked down

the stairs to the sidewalk. The commotion earlier must have been over the sleek car on the street, but it had since been cleared. The driver stood outside the car, as no doubt Diamandis would not risk being seen. He was not well known outside of Kalyva, but Greece was close enough that you never knew when someone might recognize you from old news stories about murdered royals.

The driver opened the door for her as she approached. "Christos," she greeted with a small smile. Clearly Diamandis did not know that his driver-slash-bodyguard and his partner had been the ones to help her get off Kalyva without detection. "So good to see you again."

He bobbed his head. "And you, Ms. Floros."

She turned to the car and looked to the spacious back seat where Diamandis sat.

"If your ridiculous story is not believed by all and sundry, I will take my children and run and you will never, *ever* find me. I will not tolerate whispers, gossip, or ridicule for my children."

"Nor will I, Katerina."

She knew that was true to an extent, but she also knew he didn't fully understand how people could twist things. How whispers could follow you, ruin you. Which brought her to her second condition.

"If my mother appears in any context, you will refuse to let her anywhere near me."

Diamandis raised an eyebrow, and she knew this would give him reason to poke into the matter. Of course, he must know a little about her mother from the extensive background check he'd run before he'd hired her, but he likely thought himself above and immune to Ghavriella Floros's machinations.

Katerina wasn't so sure.

"As you wish," he replied, unbothered. "Get inside the car, Katerina. There is much to do."

Katerina gave one last backward glance at her apartment.

At her life in Athens. No matter what happened next, she knew she would not be able to come back here. The door was closing on this chapter of her life.

But so many doors had closed on her—some by her choosing but most by someone else's. She knew how to do this. She knew how to start over. She knew how to fight, and she would always, *always* fight for her children.

So she slid inside the car, not yet resigned to being a queen but determined to make the best choices for her children.

CHAPTER FOUR

IT WAS QUITE late by the time they returned to Kalyva and the palace. Katerina had slept most of the way, groggily moving from car to boat before falling asleep once more.

Diamandis should have been making arrangements or working, but instead he'd found himself watching her, monitoring the slow rise and fall of her breathing, cataloging every change in her now that she was pregnant.

And realizing how much he'd observed her before without fully realizing that was what he'd been doing all the years she'd worked for him. He certainly did not know or care what Tomás's eyelashes looked like against his cheek, or how exhaustion might look on any of his assistants' faces.

Except Katerina's. As it had after long weeks around special events and committee meetings. As it did now.

When the boat docked at his private royal pier, he briefly considered staying right here until she woke up on her own. She needed a bed, though. Comfort. And likely a meal. There was no way she'd been taking appropriate care of herself if she'd been working and walking up and down those apartment stairs every day.

He fought off the anger, icing it away into its compartment. There were things he could control and things he couldn't. The past was one of the few things that fell into the *couldn't* category.

The future, and how she was taken care of, was well within

his control, and that was all that could matter. He eyed the swell of her stomach. Children. *His* children. For a moment, he had the foreign impulse to reach out and smooth his hand over where his children grew inside her.

He ignored it.

"Katerina."

Her eyes fluttered open, and for a split second she smiled, but she must have quickly remembered everything, because it died as she straightened and her expression went fully blank. "Ah. We're here," she said flatly.

"Yes, you are home."

Her lips firmed, but she did not argue with him. She allowed him to help her to her feet. They were ushered to the royal car and then driven up the hill to the palace.

Home. With its white walls and spires, tall on the hill that looked down over his island nation. The stars were out tonight, the moon bouncing against the softly crashing surf and the white of the palace, making it glow in the darkness.

Sometimes, late at night like this, he could almost understand why people believed in fairy tales.

Then he remembered his mother's screams.

Katerina said nothing as they drove, which was not unusual exactly. Part of why she'd been such an excellent assistant had been her ability to sit comfortably in silence and stillness without needing to make small talk.

So why it bothered him now, he could not begin to guess. And since he couldn't, he chose to ignore it.

It was the dead of night, and he helped her out of the car at his personal entrance to the castle. He had instructed his staff to take the night off as it was still best to keep everything as under the radar as possible. Only Christos, his driver and head bodyguard, knew about Katerina's return so far.

He wanted to keep it that way for as long as possible. He helped Katerina out of the car and inside. The hallways were lit dimly, as they often were when no one was about, so he took her hand.

"I am sure you are quite hungry. Why don't we go to my private dining room? I will have a meal brought up."

She removed her hand from his and stopped abruptly, turning to face him with raised chin and stubborn brows.

"I think I am too tired. I'm sure you can have a tray sent up to my room, and since I know all the rooms in the palace, you needn't show me where, only tell me."

He opened his mouth to argue, but something about the sharp look in her eyes told him she was *hoping* he would argue. That arguing would fall right into whatever plans she was no doubt already formulating.

Katerina was extraordinarily intelligent and savvy. It was why he'd hired her, and why he'd come to rely on her so.

Still, he would not be so easily maneuvered. He did not argue. He smiled pleasantly. "Why, the queen's bedchamber, of course."

Her mouth dropped open, and this was quite gratifying, if nothing else today had been.

He took her hand once more, and no doubt her shock at his statement kept her from jerking away. He held her gaze as he lifted her hand and brushed his lips across her knuckles.

She let out a shaky breath. Perhaps *two* things were gratifying, because she was not immune to him, and while immunity would be best for both of them, he got a perverse thrill out of her reaction all the same.

"I will have a tray of food sent up at once. I know what you like after all." In concerning detail. He dropped her hand and turned on a heel. If he stayed, he would be tempted.

And it would not do to be tempted.

Just yet. After all, if they were to be married, it would not be quite so necessary to endeavor to keep his hands to himself.

They were bound forever now, and why not take the simple pleasures of that when they were pleasurable indeed?

It was too easy to remember that night. The way a simple kiss had turned into a heat that had consumed him. *That* had been a mistake, but it no longer needed to be.

They were to be married.

He had to push those thoughts away as he strode to the kitchens looking for Mrs. Markis, who had been the head of the kitchens since he'd been a boy. He found her already up and serving Zandra in the small dining area that was meant for staff.

"What are you doing up and *here*?" he demanded of his sister.

She raised an eyebrow. "I could ask you the same." But she shrugged. "I am hungry and I did not wish to wake Lysias. I was going to make myself some tea and a snack, but Mrs. Markis insisted on handling it."

"I did not expect you back this evening, Your Majesty," Mrs. Markis said with a curtsy. "I'll make up a plate for you at once."

"A tray, Mrs. Markis, to take back to my rooms, if you would be so kind. And ensure there are no olives on it, if you would."

She nodded and moved quickly back to the kitchen.

"You love olives," Zandra said, staring at him speculatively.

Diamandis did not justify this comment with a response.

"Where did you disappear to for most of the day, brother?" She smiled at him innocently.

Like she already knew.

He narrowed his eyes. "What do you know?"

"I suppose Lysias heard some whispers that you'd taken a surprise trip to Athens. No one could quite fathom why you would do such a thing." Zandra took a bite of cookie and smiled at him. "Except me, of course."

"Perhaps I simply went to Athens to obtain your wedding present."

She shook her head. "You went to see her, and you went to find the truth. So?"

There was no point wasting time. Zandra had her suspicions and by tomorrow he had to have everything perfectly in place. He would have to work around the clock. "Katerina and I will be married quickly."

"How quickly?"

"As soon as everything is in place. She is very concerned about image and gossip, so we will have to concoct a bit of a story. You're one of the few people who know the truth, Zandra. I'll need you to go along with it."

While his sister was often irreverent, her gaze was serious as she nodded. "What's the story?"

He explained the fake Athens marriage that he would make real. The health issues he would invent. As long as there was a paper trail, no one could prove him wrong.

"Ask Lysias to help you. He's excellent at all those illegal things."

Diamandis scowled. He did not care for *illegal* methods, but he had no doubt Zandra was right. "Very well," he said through gritted teeth, though it added another person who knew the truth. But if there were two people he had learned to trust since he'd taken the crown, it was Zandra and Lysias.

And Katerina.

Zandra finished her cookie and studied him. "You know, if you need to do it quickly… What if you just…took *our* wedding?"

"What do you mean?"

"Lysias and I have no use for some fancy affair—that was *your* insistence. I'm quite happy with the Athenian elopement. So you and Katerina could take our places at the royal wedding. You can say it was the plan all along, and that you were simply waiting for Katerina to be well enough to deal with the responsibilities and attention before you told everyone it was to be *your* wedding. It lends credence."

Diamandis watched Zandra sip her tea as she expressly did not meet his gaze. He wasn't surprised that she did not want the pomp and circumstance of a royal wedding. She had not grown up with it all and was still getting used to the ceremony of being royal.

But what did puzzle him was that she was helping him. "I am surprised you are supporting me in this."

"If I confess that part of why I can't sleep is because of the preparations for this wedding, because my nerves over this grand ceremony keep me awake every night, would you understand better?"

"Is this true? Why didn't you tell me?"

"It would not have changed your mind, and I want to have *some* respect for tradition even though I remember so little. But it has become a larger burden than I anticipated, and I would not be sad at all if you and Katerina took our place." Then her face scrunched up into a frown. "Why would you be surprised at my support?"

He'd walked right into that one. "I am quite tired. I'll go and fetch the tray from Mrs. Markis. Do keep this quiet for the time being until everything is in place."

"Diamandis. She *wants* to marry you, doesn't she?"

He did not look at his sister. "I am sure she came to the same conclusion I did. That this is what's best for everyone involved."

"Anóitos," Zandra said under her breath. "You are not forcing this poor woman to marry you."

"I gave her a choice."

"Oh, I'm sure it was a *great* choice." She muttered a few more choice words for him as she got to her feet and began to pace.

"She is pregnant with my children," Diamandis said, having

no idea why he was defending himself when he was king, and he did not need anyone's support. Everyone had to do what he demanded. "What else am I to do?"

Zandra's hands rose to her own belly bump. "Children... plural?"

Twins. Twins. Twins. He cleared his throat. "Yes. Twins, apparently."

"Like Achilleas and Rafail?"

Diamandis could not confirm this immediately. His throat had grown too tight. Sometimes the things Zandra couldn't remember hit him sideways. Like their brothers.

Sometimes he heard their screams in his sleep, and she did not even remember having met them.

"Yes, like Achilleas and Rafail," he managed roughly.

"I wish..." But she did not voice her wish. She had no need to. He knew she wished she could remember, but sometimes Diamandis felt it was best she did not. She could study the history books, learn the names and faces of her family, but she did not have to live with the bloody reminders of what had happened to them.

She crossed the room and wrapped her arms around him, as if such gestures of affection could ever become commonplace or comfortable. "Take our wedding then." She pulled back and looked up at him. "But maybe don't think of it as royal business and something to be done for the crown, but an opportunity."

"An opportunity for what?"

"For happiness, Diamandis. For love and family."

But Diamandis knew what love did to a family.

It ended it with blood.

Katerina awoke slowly, cuddling deeper into the softness around her. She was half-convinced it was a dream and she'd wake up in her uncomfortable apartment and find that her alarm hadn't gone off that morning.

But she was too warm, too content to worry about that and search for her phone to find out what time it was. She could be late...just this once.

Then there was a...smell. She could not identify it, but she knew. She remembered. She was not in her apartment. She was not living *her* life.

She was a prisoner to the Agonas throne once more. She opened her eyes and stared at the gilt ceiling above her. Because she was in the queen's bedroom, no less.

You will be an effective queen.

Of course she would. As far as she could tell, being the queen was little more than being Diamandis's assistant in public rather than private. She'd been an *excellent* assistant in private, so why would the promotion to public figurehead change that?

Such a promotion. She rolled her eyes here in the privacy of the room where no one would see, then she pushed herself up onto her hands. She was supposed to be more clearheaded today. Ready to problem-solve.

Ready to plan her escape. Again.

But her gaze landed on a tray next to the bed—where she'd left the remains of her dinner last night. At some point when she'd been asleep it had been taken away and replaced with one full of pastries and juices.

She tried very hard not to be happy or excited. It was just *food*, just a *bed*, and the price was her whole life. So she shouldn't enjoy a decadent *bougatsa*, her favorite. She should protest, or something.

But her stomach rumbled, and this had been the best sleep she'd gotten in months. At the end of the day, none of this was ideal, but she was seven months pregnant with twins and someone had made her two meals in a row and she had slept on a bed that felt like being carried away in clouds.

Would it really hurt to enjoy this for a few days while she formulated a plan? She would have to get around Diamandis somehow, but that didn't mean she had to be miserable in the process.

A door opened—she heard it squeak—but the door to the bedroom remained resolutely shut. Which was when she turned her head and saw there was *another* door. A *connecting* door.

As Diamandis strode into her room with no knock, no request to enter, she realized their bedchambers must adjoin.

She scowled deeply. No, she could not stay here and enjoy the amenities for a few days. She needed to find a way out of this now, before she was doomed to spend the rest of her life fending off whispers.

Her mother.

And this pang for a man she would never, ever reach.

"Good morning," Diamandis greeted. He frowned at the tray. "Why haven't you eaten? Is the selection not to your liking? I thought *bougatsa* was your favorite."

Something inside of her fluttered that he might know that. Why would he know that?

It hardly mattered when she had to somehow thwart him and his grand royal plans.

"The selection is just fine. Send my compliments to Mrs. Markis. Or are we still acting secretly? Am I allowed to leave my room?"

"You are the one desperate for secrecy, Katerina," he returned in his stiff manner.

"Only as much as you, Diamandis. Certainly not more than you want to avoid any reason for someone to suggest you might have disappointed your father."

She did not often stoop to mentioning his parents. He got that cold look on his face that she knew hid pain. So much pain. He did not speak of the *before* times, but it had been clear in her years of working for him that the stories about how devoted the royals were to each other were true, not just fodder to make subjects happy and content that they were led by nice people.

The Agonas family had been a close one, before the coup that had ended most of their lives.

"You have no idea how hard I tried to disappoint my father when he was alive, Katerina. It would be my great pleasure to disappoint him now, if it meant he was here with us. But he is not."

And those words made Katerina feel very, *very* small. As was clearly his intent.

"Everything will be in place by this evening," he said. He stood there, hands behind his back in what she had always called his *proclamation stance*. "We will make an announcement to the press and ask for privacy for a few more days before you are introduced. On Friday. The wedding will be the following week."

Week. *Week.* "Week."

"Yes. It is already settled."

"But it is not. First of all, I have refused to marry you. Second of all, Diamandis, you have no idea what you're getting yourself into marrying a commoner. People accept Lysias marrying your sister because he made himself into a billionaire, because his parents—servants though they might have been— were named martyrs for the Kalyvan cause. I am a bastard commoner. My father's identity is unknown." Sometimes she wasn't even sure her mother knew it. "And my mother... Surely you have looked into my family, Diamandis. If not today, then before you hired me. You have to know that my blood will never be considered fit for royalty."

He stood there and his face betrayed nothing. "I do not wish to speak ill of your mother. It is of no matter."

Of no matter? Katerina did not know how any living man could be so stubborn. She got out of bed, unable to sit still while he stood above her like some kind of...

Well, king.

She was shorter than him, so he was still looking down at her, but at least she felt like she had an almost equally powerful position by standing up to him.

The bed was safely between them. She needed that safety or she might—

No, she could not give in to him again, not when she had so much to lose. She could not let this flutter turn into the twirling, desperate hold of need.

She had learned her lesson. She could not forget it.

"Then allow me to speak ill of her for you because it *does* matter. She is a gold digger. A narcissist. And I have been as far beneath her notice as possible since I flat-out refused to sneak her into any of your events so she could mix and mingle with what few men of power she hasn't yet slept with or attempted to."

"I do not see what this has to do with you."

"How can you *not* see? You are a king."

"Yes," he agreed, taking a few steps toward the end of the bed. "And as king, it is quite easy for me to keep your mother as far out of your life as you wish."

What might her life have been if *anyone* had been able to keep Ghavriella Floros as far away from her life as she wished.

But Katerina could not change the past. Or who her mother was. She could only focus on extricating herself from this mess before it was announced. Before she was married.

Before you give in. Again.

"If you had gone to your council before any of this had happened and proposed me as your future queen, not one of them would have given you their support."

He lifted a shoulder as he came around to her side of the

bed. She was now trapped, between bed and wall. "I would never seek the council's approval for my future wife. *I* am the one who has to live with her." His gaze moved over her then, and she saw all the things she should ignore. Should fight.

Interest.

Desire.

Need.

She did not understand how, when she felt as unwieldly as an elephant, this kind of heat could bloom within her. How she could burn at all for a man—let alone *this* man, who infuriated her beyond reason. Whom she had run from, because he could be far too cold when he wanted to be.

But she could imagine it all too clearly. His hands, his mouth. The way he had made her feel that night—as though she was lit up from within. How she had shattered, beautifully. There had been no coldness then. Only heat. Only them.

She could not fall for this again. It was a lie. A trick. A temptation meant to ruin them both, maybe. And she didn't wish that for either of them. She couldn't risk it for her children.

You are already pregnant. What more harm can be done?

She blinked at that unbidden thought. And when she lifted her gaze from Diamandis's mouth to his eyes, she felt as though he'd read her thoughts. Down to that one.

It was as though they were tied by that thought, brought increasingly closer against their wills. Some magnetic pull that would ruin them both.

And she struggled to care. Just like that night.

"Katerina," he said, and she must have misheard the gravel in his voice because he kept talking about his plans. "The plans are in motion. You will be my wife and Kalyva's queen." He moved forward and took her hands in his. "Trust me. I will take care of all your many concerns."

She hated that she did trust him. That for all these years she had gotten to know the man under the armor and had come to care for that man. But how she felt didn't matter. It couldn't. Not when she had two children to consider.

"The royal doctor will check you out today to make certain you are healthy and well enough to deal with crowds and wedding preparations. We will not do anything to risk your health or the children's. I am led to understand that twin pregnancies can be difficult."

"My doctor also cautioned me in regard to that, but so far I have had a very routine pregnancy," she said, knowing she should pull her hands away. Knowing she should put more distance between them.

But he was closer somehow. Toe to toe, his head bent toward hers so that when he spoke, his breath danced across her cheek. She wanted to lean. She wanted to forget everything— this was his power, and no matter how she knew he would use it against her, no matter how strong she was, *this* was the thing she could not best, could not escape, could not survive.

"This is excellent news."

"Why?" she asked breathlessly. Stupidly. What was she doing here? Surely he wasn't going to—

But his mouth crashed to hers, exactly as it had done that night—fierce, cunning, and confident that she would not resist.

Because she could not. She was powerless in the face of him, in the face of the heat that erupted between them when they got too close. Even knowing it was wrong and she would regret it, her body simply insisted she give in, as if it cared not at all what her mind told it.

So she did. She gave in, held on, kissed him back with all the passion that had not died inside of her though she had tried desperately to quash it—both before and after.

She fell into the maddening heat all over again. No matter the many costs.

CHAPTER FIVE

LUST WAS LIKE some kind of wildfire in Diamandis's mind, turning every rational, important thought to ash. When Katerina had been his assistant, when he'd felt such a loss of control coming over him, he'd been able to order her away, to excuse himself.

Except that one time. When it hadn't been work, but…disaster.

That one time, which had haunted him every night since. He'd controlled himself because there was only ruin if he didn't. Because she knew too much…and those who knew that much had only betrayed him.

When he'd come into her room this morning, he'd tried to remind himself of the inevitable betrayal, the inevitable end and loss—all the ways he could not trust what he felt, because the crown came first. All the ways she should never trust him because, deep down, he was not what he seemed.

But she'd been sitting in the bed, hair rumpled, cheeks flushed from the warmth of the blankets and pillows piled around her. He'd seen the swell of her belly where their children grew and it had given new fangs to old feelings he thought he'd vanquished.

Then she'd gotten out of bed, wearing an oversize T-shirt that barely skimmed her thighs and was most certainly not fit for the queen she would soon be. Her feet were bare, her hair a sleep-tangled maze of curls. He had never seen her in such a state.

He'd tried, valiantly—if he did say so himself—to resist. But she was like a magnet. She was like air, and he had forgotten how to breathe.

There was no choice but to kiss her. No choice but to devour her mouth as he once had. But this time his hands moved over her round belly, marveling at what he had had a hand in creating.

She was carrying his children. She would be his wife—no matter how many objections she tried to throw at him. The plans were in motion; *everything* was in motion. It was a risk to form this union, but letting her go would be a bigger one.

So why shouldn't this be his reward?

Particularly when she met his kiss with all the passion she had shown him that night, as though she too had been fighting to hold herself back from this.

This. A need like no other. And for those first few weeks after, he'd been able to convince himself that he had solved the problem by giving in that night. That by tasting her, by being inside her, he knew what it was and could then resist it. A known enemy was always better than a mysterious threat.

But he knew, here in this moment of heat and passion and desire, that it had not been his impressive control or some vanquished feeling that had kept him from kissing her again.

It had been *fear* that had meant he'd kept his hands to himself in those weeks afterward. Fear that nothing else could ever match *this*, and it was best never to know it again. Fear that she'd seen too much, and now held too much power over him. She might be a good person, but he was not, and if he fell into forgetting that, too much was at stake.

But Katerina was inextricably linked to him now. There was no turning back or sending her away. He would have to find a way to win when she was in his orbit because she would be Kalyva's queen. *His* queen.

Something strange roared inside of him—too many emotions that if he named would become unwieldy. Dangerous.

So he pushed his thoughts away and focused on the taste of her. The way she moaned as his hands slid under the ridiculous T-shirt she wore, to find warm skin, soft and supple. Her rounded belly, her delectable breasts, nipples pebbled tight and wanting just for him.

"Diamandis."

His name on her lips, her breathless sighs, and the way she gave in to him after spending so much time fighting with him… She was a curse, and he reveled in it.

He pulled the T-shirt off her, revealing her beautiful body. She fumbled with the buttons of his shirt as his fingers dove into her tangled hair. As he drowned in the pleasure of her mouth once more. As she rid him of his shirt, her own hands touring his body as though he were her long-lost lover, returned from the unknown. As if she were desperate for someone she'd once lost.

But he had not been lost. She'd *left*.

That might have broken through the thick sexual haze, maybe, but she ripped her mouth from his.

"Diamandis. This… We… I'm too…big." But this was not a refusal. Not a *no*. It was merely…foolish self-doubt, when she was nothing short of perfect. She was the only woman who had ever tested him, ever bested him.

"You are a goddess," he murmured, lowering himself from her mouth to the round glory of her breasts, her stomach, and lower still.

She sank onto the bed and he got to his knees to worship her, spreading her out on the bed behind them, drinking deep until she was shaking and saying his name, over and over in breathless desire.

But he wanted more than his name. More than her hands

in his hair and the taste of her a drug he'd never survive. He had had her once and had convinced himself it was enough.

But he hadn't looked twice at another woman since and had not allowed himself to ask why that might be. Why she was not interchangeable with any other woman who might share his bed. Why he missed her voice crisply correcting him on something or another.

Or moaning out his name.

He stood and she looked up at him, flushed and dazed and so wholly perfect in every way. "But...how..."

He did not care *how*, only that he was inside her. He got onto the bed with her, then maneuvered her on top of him, naked and wanton, while he still wore his pants, though she'd disposed of his shirt.

She fumbled with the button on his slacks but did not make it to the zipper because he needed something from her first. He did not seek to understand why. He just wanted it, so he would demand it.

He was the king.

The whys did not matter.

He clamped his hands over her wrists before she could succeed in unzipping his pants. "Say it."

Misty green eyes met his. "Say what?" she returned, breathless and flushed.

"You know what I want to hear, Katerina."

She swallowed. She was straddling him, needy for him, and yet there was hesitation in her eyes. Not over the act, no. She wanted him as desperately as he wanted her. And he was so lost he might capitulate without getting what he desired.

Impossible.

"Please," she said, so quietly he almost didn't hear it. "My king."

He freed himself from his pants, not waiting for her to do it. Not waiting for her to sheath herself on him. The position, the place did not matter—the need was the same and all-encompassing. He took control and moved inside her, enjoying the exquisite, inexorable fit.

She was his perfection. She was meant for this and for him. He could not give her or himself everything, but he would give them this.

His hands slid up her thighs, to rest at her hips. He guided her in the rhythm he wanted, needed. Her head fell back as she lost herself in the pleasure of their bodies meeting.

She sobbed his name as she shattered around him, over and over again, her hair tumbling around her shoulders, her skin flushed with exertion and pleasure. She was art, and everything centered on her. Even as his blood roared in his ears, as the spiking flame of need threatened to explode, he waited. He moved, he absorbed, and he *waited* for that one thing he desired.

"My king," she rasped once more, sending him over the edge with her.

Katerina did not know what had come over her, but this was not a new feeling. She'd felt the same that night months ago, in the aftermath of reckless pleasure—she did not know who that woman was. It was a stranger who'd taken over her body, who had enjoyed a man she knew would never give her what she wanted.

She should hate that stranger who was so weak, but she felt too good. Warm and sated. Comfortable and content. A future did not matter in the present of satisfied need. Oh, this was very bad. Because Diamandis no doubt saw this as a win, but…

Well, she'd won too. If only temporarily.

She turned her head to look at him, expecting to see the same sort of reaction she'd seen on him in his office—a slow, dawning horror at his loss of control, a stiff, detached mask as he withdrew, which made it very clear what a mistake they'd made.

But he did not look stiff in the here and now. He did not

move to straighten his clothes or make a careful, dignified retreat.

He lounged there in her bed, looking quite content, arms thrown back behind his head, showcasing all that muscle she'd just enjoyed. But it wasn't the sleek lines, the rangy body, the way every masculine part of him made her heart beat triple-time. It was the expression on his face.

She could not call anything about Diamandis soft, but there was a relaxed air to him that went deeper than just sexual satisfaction. He looked...content.

Her heart ached. When had she ever seen him enjoy any sliver of contentment? It was very rare. She could count the times on one hand, and those moments never lasted more than a few seconds because he felt he was under constant scrutiny, and any hint at enjoyment sent the *wrong* message.

She still remembered the first time he'd truly smiled in her presence. She had been frustrated with another one of his diatribes on tradition and propriety. She had picked up a dark, shriveled pebble from the grounds and handed it to him.

Here. I think you lost your soul.

He had looked at the rock, and then his mouth had curved. For a moment, true humor had danced there.

This was the problem with Diamandis. Even as he was taking over her life, threatening everything she wanted for her children, she found herself incapable of ruining this moment. She was glad he seemed content. A joke about his black soul was one of the few things that had ever made him laugh in her presence. It was clear that reality and Diamandis's many responsibilities and duties would crash down upon them soon enough.

"I have much to do," he said, his voice a shade rough, his tone more philosophical than determined to make any movement or action.

"Then you should do it," Katerina said agreeably.

But they both lay there, maybe an inch of space between them, not touching.

This was her fate. She saw it so starkly. She could have pieces of him and she could control certain aspects of him, but there would always be this invisible line between them. And if it was between him and her, it would exist between him and their children as well.

Could she bear it? Could she ask her as of yet unborn children to bear it too?

"You may choose your own staff as you see fit once the announcement is made," he said, switching to business so easily she hated that she'd given him an ounce of contentment. "I trust you know everyone currently on staff except your replacement. You may choose from the current pool, or I can bring in applicants as you wish."

"I'm sure the current pool is sufficient, though I would be very interested in meeting my replacement." She watched him then, wondering whether he would ever look at her, or would simply stare at the gilt ceiling until he rolled off the bed, tucked himself away, and left her alone.

"He is...not as good as you," Diamandis said carefully. "But then, you left very big shoes to fill."

It was a compliment that should not make her happy, and yet it did. She had taken pride in her work, in making herself indispensable. *In proving your mother wrong.*

Ugh.

She pulled the blanket tightly around her. The thought of her mother was a stark reminder that she was, at her core, not any better. She was a slave to her wants and damn the consequences.

She heard a rustle of movement, felt the mattress dip then pop back. Diamandis was getting up. He was leaving.

And what the hell was she supposed to do now? Run? Try to convince him, yet again, that marriage wasn't possible and that he should let her go? She knew how it worked, even if not how this specific thing worked. The wheels of his plans were already in motion, and nothing would stop them.

"I think we should put off any announcements, Diamandis," she said, sounding stronger than she felt. "I am not convinced this is the correct course of action."

He shrugged. "I am."

He spoke as if that was it. As if that was all that mattered.

Oh, how she wished she had the energy to punch him. "I know what it is to grow up in a house devoid of love and warmth, Diamandis. I may not have grown up in the castle, but I had quite a few luxuries. It did not make up for my mother's cruelty."

"There is a big space between love and cruelty, Katerina. I will not be cruel to you or our children. I will never love anyone, but that does not mean we cannot share a mutual sort of respect for one another."

It hurt. Far more than it should considering she knew this man, maybe better than he knew himself. "Is that what we're calling it?" she returned, incapable of keeping the acid out of her tone.

His mouth firmed. "It does not have to be a mistake, Katerina. It could simply be life. Is it really so much worse than scratching by, alone and destitute in a hovel in Athens?"

"You're such a snob, Diamandis. Just because it wasn't a castle doesn't mean I was destitute."

"I may not have experienced it myself, but I am well acquainted with what poverty looks like, and how hard people have to work to survive it. I cannot understand why you'd choose to struggle like that when you could have this." He waved his hand as if to encompass the palace.

And the thing was, she didn't fully understand it, either. Which sacrifice was better for her children? She couldn't seem to come to a conclusion that settled her. No conclusion was the right one. No choice gave them everything.

"Zandra didn't go running back to the streets of Athens just because she didn't like some elements of royalty."

"I am not your sister. You cannot *save* me from a life I have chosen with my own free will." *I would choose you*, she realized. And it hurt, because she knew he would never choose her.

Only Kalyva.

And yet, he was not *totally* wrong, was he? If they could somehow avoid the whispers that had tormented her in her childhood, then this would be quite the life for her children. The best of everything. Was her pride more important than that?

She didn't know. She just didn't know.

But Diamandis certainly thought he did. "We shall see." And then he left.

Without looking back.

CHAPTER SIX

DIAMANDIS SPENT THE remainder of the morning hard at work. There was much to do and he'd spent over an hour...not working.

He was going through with the announcement. And if there was a strange tug of discomfort deep in his gut, he ignored it. Because there was nothing to be guilty about. He was doing what was right.

No, he could not promise Katerina some fairy-tale love and warmth. He knew all too well where that led, and he would protect his children. Loving them would only leave him open to the sorts of things that had been his father's downfall. His most trusted adviser had made this clear to Diamandis on the very day of his parents' deaths: that if his father had not been blinded by love, he would have seen through the cracks in the kingdom. He would have been able to stop the coup before it had started.

Love was a death sentence.

But he could promise Katerina everything else she could possibly want, and he firmly believed in what he'd said to her this morning. There was space between love and cruelty, where his secrets could remain in the dark—where they belonged. It was a space where love did not threaten everything. He could exist in the middle. And would, as he had all these years.

He entered the dining room a few minutes later than usual

and frowned when only Lysias and Zandra were present. "Where is Katerina?"

Zandra's eyebrows rose. "Are we supposed to know? I thought you had her locked up in a dungeon so no one would know she was here."

"My assistant was supposed to notify you both of today's change of plans. We have put the announcement in motion. After dinner, the four of us will address the council and explain the change in wedding participants."

His sister and brother-in-law exchanged glances. "I haven't seen Tomás today," Zandra finally said, somewhat reluctantly. "But perhaps he left word and it didn't make it to us."

Diamandis's temper flared. He'd gone through three assistants since Katerina had left, each more useless than the last. "I wish I could continue to give him the benefit of the doubt."

"Well, he's afraid of you, Diamandis. Hard to blame him for that."

"So hiding from me and not doing his work will fix the problem?"

"He's young," Zandra said, but it was clear she was enjoying defending Tomás, not because she thought he warranted defending, but because she liked to frustrate her older brother.

"He's useless. Messages never went astray when Katerina was my assistant," Diamandis muttered, wondering how long he would last before he went and hunted her down himself.

"Should I point out that Ms. Floros is no longer his assistant, or would you like to?" Lysias said to his wife.

Diamandis scowled at them both, but he did not have a rejoinder because the door was opened and Katerina stepped inside.

She curtsied, and he knew the symbol of deference was more habit than actual deference, at least toward him. "Your Majesty. Your Highness. Mr. Balaskas. Or have you conferred a title on your brother-in-law as I suggested many months ago?" She smiled sweetly up at him.

The smile was exactly the one she used to bestow upon him regularly, once upon a time, when she'd been his assistant, suggesting things she thought he should have already done. He did not understand what twisted inside of him, only that he wished they were alone so he did not have to keep his hands to himself.

She was dressed for dinner in a plain black dress that hugged the glorious swell of her bump. He had to force himself to look away so he did not picture what it might look like if he peeled the dress away.

"You are late."

"I did not know I was allowed to leave my prison until just recently. Luckily a maid was available to help me dress as I also discovered that my bag with all my things in it had been confiscated."

"It is best if you look fit to be queen when around the palace. Your old clothes were *not* that."

"Perhaps we should leave you two to quarrel over dinner without us?" Zandra suggested, her glass hiding her face—though Diamandis had no doubt she was hiding a smile behind it.

"That will not be necessary," Diamandis replied stiffly. He moved to the chair next to him and pulled it out for Katerina before the waiting staff member could.

Katerina hesitated, though he couldn't imagine why. But she sat without saying anything. Diamandis took his own seat, royal protocol not necessary at a family meal.

Family. After years of it just being Diamandis, the past few months had been an adjustment. There was his sister, and Lysias, who had once been as close as a brother to him before...

Everything had been destroyed that night, and he had never thought there would be any recourse. But Zandra and Lysias...

And now Katerina. Who was to be his wife. The mother of his children. Family, in all those ways he'd promised he'd never have.

But life changed on you, this he knew quite intimately. He was rolling with the punches, as one must. As a *king* must.

"How are you feeling, Katerina?" Zandra asked as the staff began to serve dinner.

"Well enough. I am very fortunate that I've had such an uneventful pregnancy. Twins can often be complicated."

"It's hard to imagine that soon enough we will have *three* children running about the palace." Zandra smiled broadly. "I don't remember much of my childhood here, but I remember the feeling of being glad I had so many other children to play with, even if I was much younger. I can't wait for…"

Diamandis tuned her out. Because *he* remembered. In color. He could hear his brothers' voices even now. They had loved to play pranks on him—the angrier he got, the more hilarious they had found it.

Their laughter haunted his dreams. As did every cruel word he'd ever uttered to them, thinking himself better—older, more mature, the *heir*. A person with real responsibilities, while they got to *play*.

He could remember Zandra as a little girl. Their mother had given her too much freedom, in Diamandis's estimation. The girl had always followed him about, and when he'd return her to the children's wing or tell her that he was busy with important things, she would poke him in the throat.

Hard.

He remembered, too well, taking all of them for granted. Their love, their existence. He assumed Zandra could only bear it because she remembered so little.

And none of the aftermath.

Wasn't she lucky?

"Diamandis?"

It was Katerina, looking at him like he'd never wanted her to: with a sympathetic kind of understanding, when there was nothing to understand.

Everyone but Zandra had been murdered. The end.

"We will approach the committee as a unit," he said, not worried about whatever conversation they'd been having that he hadn't been paying attention to. They were eating together to discuss business. "They will no doubt have some questions and concerns, but we will assuage them all." He gestured to Lysias. "Thanks to Lysias, we already have an Athenian marriage certificate, dated late last year."

"I assure you, no one would ever question the validity," Lysias said, smiling broadly at Katerina. "It's amazing what money can buy."

Diamandis endeavored to keep the conversation to subjects like the council and what would happen next, but Zandra somehow kept bringing up children and families. Diamandis forced himself to eat, though everything tasted like ash in his mouth.

He would not think about these things. He would no longer engage in these dinners. This was about the crown, not *family*.

When he was certain Katerina and Zandra had eaten their fill, he signaled the staff to begin taking things away.

"Is everyone finished? We must head down to the throne room. The council should be assembling as we speak." He did not look at Katerina as he offered her his arm.

This wasn't about her, or about their children, or about his sister, and most of all not about his childhood.

It was about the throne. It was about lines of succession and making sure nothing tarnished what his father had left him any more than he already had.

When Diamandis held out his hand for her, Katerina only hesitated for a moment before she took it.

It was now or never. If she went along with him to this council meeting, it was all over.

Are you really going through with this?

He led her into the hallway and toward the throne room without question, without hesitation. In his mind, it was already done. That alone should make her balk.

She watched him as he kept his gaze straight ahead, jaw clenched tight as it often was before he faced the council.

She knew she did not have to be by his side—as future queen or former assistant. *She* had the choice here, but...

Her choice had already been made when she came to dinner. It had been the doctor's visit earlier that had swayed her. Not the royal doctor she'd expected, whom she'd always found a bit aloof, but a woman, maybe in her forties, who had brought along a specialist who was well acquainted with multiple births and high-risk pregnancies.

They had gone over not just where she was at now—heartbeats and everything healthy and as they should be—but what was still to come. How they would care for her and her babies in labor and delivery and address any complications that could come up.

Katerina would never be able to afford such care on her own, and the risks with twins were higher. By leaving the palace, by refusing to be Diamandis's queen, she was risking *all* of their lives.

Or perhaps you really just want to be his queen.

She closed her eyes as Diamandis led her up the aisle of the grand ballroom. The council liked to have their meetings here and hear their voices bounce loudly against the high vaulted ceilings back to their own ears. They liked to look up at the king on his gold, jeweled throne and fancy themselves important for serving him.

Katerina had always thought it a foolish exercise in grandiose wealth and self-importance, and now she was being led up to sit on a throne. The queen's throne.

Instead of standing in the shadows as she'd once done.

There was no turning back if she did this. No escaping. Once their marriage was announced to the council, it was over.

She'd gone to dinner. She hadn't attempted to talk Diamandis out of his plan. Part of her understood how stupid this was, and yet...

She could not turn her back on all that the kingdom would offer her children, and so she had made her decision. The doctor had warmly informed her that everything was good and she would be by her side through the remainder of the pregnancy as well as after, and so Katerina had decided that she would do this. For the opportunities it would give her children.

Diamandis might not love them, but *she* would be all the love their children needed. She would shield them from every rumor, every whisper. She was not her mother and so she would put her children above herself.

Always.

And none of those decisions revolved around Diamandis. Not really. She couldn't control him. She couldn't change his mind or make him want to be a loving father.

She watched him as he took his seat on the king's throne and gestured for her to take the queen's.

She would never reach him. But that did not mean she could not make something positive out of this...strange situation. Make *many* positives. Just as she had when she was his assistant.

She could live without his love. She'd lived without her mother's. She'd survived and somehow managed to be a rather decent human being, she liked to think.

So she sat. In the queen's chair. In *her* chair. She could apply herself to being queen and mother just as she had to being an essential assistant.

That will not make him love you.

She frowned at the insidious thought, and luckily she had no time to really think it over as the council approached and took their seats at the table situated in front of the thrones.

Lysias joined them at the table as though he was now a member of the council—and this was new, as were a few of the faces. This was, after all, not the first council meeting to which Katerina had been privy. While there were often parts of the meeting she and other staff were asked to withdraw from so delicate conversations could be had in private and away from the untrustworthy help, she had been Diamandis's right hand man in many meetings.

She didn't like them. She found most of the men on Diamandis's council far too stuffy, traditional and cruel. More often than not, she left said meetings complaining to Diamandis and urging him to consider a council purge.

He had refused, of course. It had taken Lysias producing evidence proving that a few of the members had been planning to betray Diamandis all those months ago to bring in these new faces.

Katerina had her doubts that this new group would be any better, considering two of the men she'd long hated the most were still on it. But Diamandis must have listened to her at least a little, because some of the new faces were younger. Two were even women.

"Council members, thank you for agreeing to meet on such short notice," Diamandis said. "We have come in front of you this evening to announce a few changes to the royal wedding."

One of the men she didn't like—who was closest to Diamandis, much to her eternal consternation—Marias Remis, turned to Lysias. "Did this really necessitate a meeting?"

Lysias did not respond. He merely pointed to Diamandis.

"It will not be Princess Zandra and Mr. Balaskas's wedding

next week. I know that is what we had led you to believe, but this was a ruse to keep my wife safe and healthy."

"Your...?"

Murmurs amongst the council members sounded like a dull buzz to Katerina, and it reminded her of how often she had been the reason for the buzz of gossip—or rather, her mother had been the reason. Katerina had dealt with the fallout.

"Some of you will remember Ms. Floros," Diamandis continued over the buzz that had Katerina curling her hands around the arms of the chair to keep herself from running out of the ballroom. "Unfortunately, she has been plagued by some ill health. This is why she stepped down as my assistant. Though we wanted to marry, we knew Katerina was not strong enough yet to withstand the rigors of a royal wedding and all that goes with it, so we were married in Athens."

"Athens!" someone said, as if Diamandis had claimed they'd been married on Mars.

"This is incredibly unorthodox, Your Majesty," Marias said disapprovingly.

"It is, and I think you all know how much I regret any behavior that could be so described. However, Katerina's health made keeping this under wraps incredibly important. I could hardly ask her to carry the weight of the kingdom when she was in such a state. But she is much improved, and the doctors have assured us that the pregnancy is coming along quite well. We wanted to ensure, Katerina's health withstanding, that we could have an official, traditional wedding before the twins are born."

There was a moment of quiet, short-lived. Marias stood and spoke as if he was speaking for everyone.

"Your Majesty, this is impossible. And seems incredibly far-fetched."

Diamandis stood abruptly, and the whole table not only quieted but stilled. Even the pompous Marias did not dare speak when Diamandis looked down at him in clear censure.

"Regardless of how it might seem to you, this is the truth, and I would think long and hard before you question it again."

Marias bowed his head. "Yes, Your Majesty."

Diamandis sat once more. "We knew we wouldn't be able to plan it quickly enough, so we began preparations with the ruse of using the princess and her husband as the bride and groom. Surely you can understand that our subterfuge was necessary in order to protect Katerina's health."

He sounded so…calculated, Katerina thought. And she knew that was what the council required. It was how he always spoke to them. They always had more arguments when Diamandis showed any emotions—usually frustration.

He knew how to play them, and she knew that they did not like this. It wasn't just the open questions, the little comments about *unorthodox* and *tradition* and *your parents*. It was the way they looked at her.

Like she was gum to be scraped off Diamandis's shoe. She raised her chin in response. She had spent her whole life fielding looks like that.

And you wanted to escape them, remember?

It was an impossible choice. The best doctors, the best chance for health and survival versus the way these men looked at her and how they would likely look at her children.

But her children would have *love*. If not their father's, then their mother's.

And Katerina would make certain that was all that mattered.

CHAPTER SEVEN

THE MEETING WAS INTERMINABLE. The questions, the pearl-clutching so over the top that Diamandis's head throbbed with poorly leashed anger.

He had not expected his council, aside from Lysias, to take all of this information well, but he hadn't anticipated that so many of his council members would make so little attempt to veil their distaste for a *commoner*—something many of them were themselves, having only risen in rank by their wealth and position on this council.

Katerina had warned him, and he had not listened. It would not be the first time. She had a better sense of people than he did—a fact that had always irked.

And now, it will make her an excellent queen.

He let that thought be a kind of balm. Perhaps he had not chosen this. Perhaps his plan had been to never wed and instead to pass along the throne to Zandra or her children. This would have been a decent enough plan.

But having an effective queen to act as his partner, rather than simply waiting to die, was perhaps a better option. Perhaps.

"I am not sure how the people will react to this, Your Majesty," Marias said. Again.

Next to him, Katerina sighed. Loudly. Diamandis gave her a censuring look, but she did not temper her response. Instead, she leaned forward.

"May I address the council?"

Diamandis was surprised by the request but nodded. This was an interesting turn of events. Though she had been present at many a council meeting before, she'd never spoken at one.

She got to her feet and surveyed the table of people below. "Marias," she said, when she probably should have called him "Mr. Remis." "It is interesting to me that you are suddenly worried about what the people will think, when I've heard you, more than once, insist that the throne is more important than the opinion of its subjects."

"This is *about* the throne," Marias returned. "And who should sit upon it."

"And why should I not, Marias? What's done is done. Diamandis and I are married—regardless of Kalyvan ceremony. As you can see, I am quite pregnant. With twins. What would the people think, on the other hand, if Diamandis discarded me and my children?"

Marias puffed out his chest. "That is hardly what I'm suggesting."

"Then what *are* you suggesting?" she returned, as though she genuinely wanted to hear an answer to that. As though she was waiting with bated breath for him to explain himself.

She was beautiful. Diamandis had never considered what it might be like to have a partner in this. Zandra had slowly begun to take on some responsibilities as a working royal, but she didn't yet feel comfortable dealing with the politics of things, though she was studying hard to prepare herself. She was just so behind, so out of step, after having lived twenty years on her own and having little to no memory of Kalyva.

But Katerina didn't need to study. As his former assistant she was abreast of everything, except maybe what little had changed in the past few months. She had always been keen, savvy, and clearheaded.

She had always been an effective tool to utilize…and now she would be more than that. She would be a partner.

Could his biggest mistake actually work out in his favor? It was hard to imagine. But Marias was standing there, open-mouthed, as if desperate to say something but incapable of coming up with the words.

Diamandis stood. "Katerina is right. What's done is done. This was not a meeting to open the floor to opposition. It was a meeting to inform you of what has already taken place and of what will be taking place shortly. If you cannot agree, then I will gladly take letters of resignation."

Marias sat, unmoving. No one else said anything. Satisfied, Diamandis held out his hand to Katerina and led her out of the room, followed by Lysias and Zandra.

"Bravo, Katerina," Zandra said, coming forward to link her arm with Katerina's free one. "Honestly, why do we have this ridiculous committee?"

"Are you calling me ridiculous?" Lysias asked his wife, teasingly.

"The council is tradition," Diamandis said firmly before Zandra and Lysias bantered more—a situation that always reminded him of his parents. "Besides, a king making proclamations without listening to anyone else is a dangerous precedent to set. They will all have roles to play in the ceremony now that it is my wedding instead of yours."

He stopped. "Tomorrow will be a long day as we work on changing the wedding preparations. Katerina, I will walk you back to your rooms. Lysias, Zandra, I bid you good night." He gave them a quick nod, then led Katerina away and toward the king and queen's quarters.

He opened the door that led into her sitting room for her. He followed her inside, not sure what his purpose was.

Are you not?

She played with the bracelet she wore, crossing to the big glass door that would take her outside to the balcony. She did not go out, just looked at the night outside.

"You were magnificent," Diamandis said, standing behind her, admiring what the moonlight did to her olive skin.

"I was tired. I should have handled it more diplomatically. That's why I was a better assistant than speaker."

"It was just what was needed. A strong queen is a good symbol for our people." He reached out and stroked his finger down the elegant curve of her neck.

But she stiffened, turning to face him and holding out a hand as if to ward him off. He looked down at it, then raised an eyebrow at her. Her green eyes were direct, everything about her...cool.

"I have come to a decision," she said very firmly.

"Oh?" he returned.

"You have made your position quite clear. Respect but not love, and I can live with this."

Her words confused him because he thought that had long since been decided. "Wonderful."

"However, you will not share my bed, nor I yours. We will go back to the way our relationship was—but with more equality, of course. We will be business partners—in the ruling of Kalyva, in the raising of our children—but we will not blur the lines with anything else."

He kept himself very still and did not let the response clawing within him take root. She could make whatever decisions she wished. He was not the kind of man who forced a woman to do his bidding.

But that didn't mean he had to *like* what decision she'd come to. Or how it would prove...difficult. "I suppose you expect me to find my pleasures elsewhere?" he returned coldly.

She blinked. Clearly she had not thought of *that*. He took some grim satisfaction in the frown that caused a crease to form on her forehead.

"I do not think that kind of behavior would befit a king," she said stiffly. Stiff was usually *his* reaction.

"On the contrary. It has been the kind of behavior that has befitted many a king. Not my father, of course, but he loved his wife and she him." Their love had caused a softness, indeed the very blind spot that had ended too many lives.

Something passed over her face then, a kind of shuttering in her eyes that he had seen before but had never understood. And he didn't understand it now, but he felt something twist inside of him in response all the same. *Guilt*, a voice whispered, but he pushed it away. Especially since the voice sounded like his long-dead mother.

"If it is not for love, then we should go about it as business," she said firmly. "If you need to seek pleasures elsewhere... I suppose that is your business. But it won't be mine."

There was nothing to say to that. Nothing to do about it. She was probably right. This was best. A business partnership, nothing more. Just as he'd always wanted.

He left her, knowing he had won a victory, but the expected satisfaction didn't follow. Because no matter what he knew to be the case, it felt like she had come out on top.

Katerina did not sleep well. She wished she could lay the blame on pregnancy, or even on Diamandis himself, but it was her own weakness. If she were stronger, she wouldn't have given in to him.

Twice.

If she hadn't been at his mercy, if she hadn't felt all they could create between them, it wouldn't feel like such a mistake to resist him now.

The thought of him with another woman made her want to retch. She was trying to be philosophical about it. Mature and worldly. Because this was *not* a romantic marriage. It was a protective one. A *business* one.

So he could do...whatever he wanted. With whomever he wanted. She would not be her mother throwing very public fits when half the time *she* had been the other woman. Like with the principal when Katerina was thirteen.

And the fit had been in the middle of her lunch hour at school.

Well, you won't be doing that. So.

So. Maybe she would be uncomfortable. Maybe she would hate it, and maybe she would even feel like throwing a very public fit.

But she wouldn't. Because her life wasn't about Diamandis. It was about her children. It would always be about her children.

She told herself this, over and over again, as she got ready for breakfast. She would be meeting with some of the staff after the meal to determine who might be her own assistant. She had two people in mind with whom she'd worked, though it was still hard to fathom relinquishing control of her life to an assistant when doing the work had always been her job.

Maybe, once she'd had the babies and recovered, she could phase out having an assistant. But for now, she needed help. Especially with the royal wedding next week.

She didn't mind the idea of the spectacle. She was used to hiding in the shadows, so being in the spotlight would be new, but she'd spent the past few years watching how Diamandis handled it, and she'd often had to instruct rooms full of people how to behave according to royal protocol. She wasn't afraid of crowds or attention.

But once it was announced, once the wedding had happened, not only would her every move be scrutinized, but so would Diamandis's.

What would be whispered about her when he was seen gallivanting about with other women?

Maybe she didn't want breakfast after all. Maybe a walk would be better. But just as she was about to pass the dining room entrance and head toward the back of the castle where she could take a walk, she heard Zandra call her name.

Katerina turned to see Zandra a ways behind her. Katerina stopped and Zandra met her at the dining room entrance.

"Are you coming to eat?" Zandra asked pleasantly.

Katerina thought about denying it, but instead she smiled. "Yes."

"Excellent. I cannot eat enough to satisfy this child." She patted her little belly bump. "So I eat an early breakfast by myself, then a second breakfast with Lysias and Diamandis once they're done with their manly grunting."

"Lysias joins Diamandis for his workouts?" Katerina asked with some surprise as they walked into the dining room and took seats at a table already set with platters of food. Just a few months ago, Diamandis had insisted his morning physical activity be a completely solitary endeavor. Even his guards were only allowed to stand outside or watch from afar.

He had been quite adamant about it.

"Yes, it's become quite the thing. Oh, Diamandis was a bit stuffy about it at first, but I'm determined to see them friends again. Did you know that? That they were boyhood friends?"

Katerina smiled as Zandra began to fill two plates without even asking what Katerina wanted. It was the kind of familiar gesture for which their relationship didn't really have any foundation, but Katerina appreciated Zandra for just accepting her and treating her like part of the family, with no questions or concerns.

No snooty words, like the council last night.

"I did know that," Katerina returned, deciding to pour tea for both of them while Zandra handled the food. "Or surmised it, I suppose. Diamandis never came out and said it directly."

"No, he doesn't do that much, does he?"

Katerina felt the familiar twist of empathy for the man. No matter how angry she was, no matter how determined she was to forge a business partnership with him rather than any kind of friendship or romance, he brought out a reaction in her that drew her back to him.

"It is...very hard to read him at times," Katerina said carefully. It was an odd line to tightrope. She did not wish to speak ill of him to anyone, nor did she want to say something that might offend Zandra, but part of her hoped for a friend with whom she could be honest.

Zandra nodded, taking a bite of her breakfast sausage and chewing thoughtfully. "I suppose it served him well in the aftermath of the coup."

"I suppose."

"I know he still harbors regret for...well, for many things I don't know. I still don't fully remember what happened to me that night." Zandra studied the piece of sausage on her fork and frowned. "Diamandis has not filled me in, and I have not asked. I suppose I should be more curious, but I think I'd rather not know. I'd rather focus on my future." She smiled then, patting her stomach with her free hand.

Katerina smiled in return. That was the attitude she needed to have: focus on her future, on her children.

But Zandra kept talking. "The difference is, Diamandis knows. He remembers. He won't speak of it. Not to me. Not to Lysias. He's made some vague comments about not being fully in charge in the days after, but mostly he keeps everything that happened to him, everything he felt and still feels, under a very protective armor."

Katerina was reminded of their night. The night they had conceived the twins, when he'd started this whole journey with a kiss. Because she had caught a glimpse of some of his feelings about his childhood tragedy. He had been brought to his knees by the possibility of Zandra being alive, of the woman Lysias had brought to Kalyva truly being his sister.

I do not know how to bear it if it is true, he had said. He voice had been rough. He'd clearly been holding on by a tiny thread. *If it is a lie, vengeance is the only answer.*

But Katerina had seen through his anger. She should have kept her observations to herself, but seeing him so close to breaking had stripped her of caution.

You don't think it's a lie.

He'd looked at her, pain so evident in his dark gaze, when usually he never let his emotions show.

No. I do not.

She'd crossed the room to him then, not knowing what else to do. She had firmly told herself it was a *friendly* hug.

And it had been. At first.

He had let her comfort him, and even with everything that happened, even knowing that she should wish it different in the here and now, she cherished those moments where he had shown her some piece of himself that he did not show anyone else.

"I don't think he will ever truly be at peace until he deals with it," Zandra said. "Until he tells someone."

Katerina did not disagree, but she understood what Zandra was getting at. She understood that *she* should be the one to press, because Zandra thought she was a wife to Diamandis like Zandra was a wife to Lysias. That theirs was a union with love at its core. "I think you might misunderstand our relationship, Princess." She tried to smile, as if to say it did not matter or that it was for the best.

Zandra studied her for much longer than Katerina felt was comfortable. Or necessary. As though she saw right through the gentle smile.

"He allows no one speak to him the way you do," Zandra said thoughtfully. "Except maybe me." She shrugged, but her sharp, assessing gaze did not match the careless gesture. "Perhaps *you* misunderstand your relationship."

And Katerina had no idea what to say to that.

None at all.

CHAPTER EIGHT

DIAMANDIS SAT THROUGH yet another tedious meeting, then moved to the next—this one about tomorrow's ceremony and reception. It would be an all-day affair intended to allow the citizens of Kalyva to feel part of the new royal family.

Family.

Every time they said this word, something inside of him tensed, until his shoulders ached and his head pounded.

He needed to collect Katerina before he headed into the next meeting, as they would be going over a few last-minute details she needed to know.

He could have sent his assistant—useless as the fool was. He could have asked one of his staff members who *was* competent. But there was something he'd been putting off.

The ring. It sat in his pocket like a hot poker, and he felt a searing pain every time he thought about it. There were other options of course, but...

It was what his mother would have expected. And yes, she was long gone and would never know the difference. Even if she were still here, she would not approve of the way he'd handled this marriage—or of all that had happened to make it a necessity. So, to worry about it seemed wholly pointless.

But for the past few days, during which Marias had repeatedly informed him that Katerina not wearing a ring was causing whispers, Diamandis had tried to convince himself that he could use any of the other family jewels as an engagement ring. He'd put different ones in his pocket with the express purpose of giving them to her.

And never once pulled the trigger because his idiotic conscience wouldn't let him.

His mother would have loved Katerina. Her strength and her poise. The way she was never afraid to stand up to him.

So he'd retrieved his mother's engagement ring. The one his father had designed especially for her.

It had put him in a foul mood—which had already been accomplished by Katerina breakfasting before him, taking lunch in her rooms, and basically avoiding him.

He wanted to believe it was because she didn't trust herself to keep her hands off him after her ridiculous decision to keep things professional, but he wasn't so conceited. He knew it was more than that.

But then again, he wasn't so humble as to think the heat between them had *nothing* to do with it.

He reached her rooms and opened the doors to the grand sitting room. She was seated at a table in front of a large, ornate mirror. She had two women with her whom he did not recognize, and Stelios, a royal aide who usually worked in event planning.

"Oh, hello, Diamandis," Katerina said casually as her assorted attendants curtsied and bowed as Katerina should also have done. "You'll have to forgive me for not hopping to my feet, I'm feeling quite large today," she said, as if reading the disapproval he'd attempted to keep off his face.

Before he could respond, she pointed to Stelios. "Stelios has just accepted the position as my assistant."

"A fine choice," Diamandis said, with a slight nod to Stelios. He would have preferred her to have *asked* permission rather than *made* such decisions, but a queen had to have some autonomy—or so his mother had always said.

Diamandis was just not used to sharing any of the power or control that came with his position.

"Would you all give us a moment of privacy?" he asked of the staff.

More curtsies, bows, quick murmurs of *Of course, Your Majesty* echoed through the room, and then the staff slipped away as if they'd never been there.

"I think I will be quite irritated if your assistant ends up being better than mine," Diamandis said in an effort to be pleasant so he could give her the ring before he was tempted to pick an argument out of bad temper.

"You should have chosen Stelios for yourself."

"I was a bit concerned that working so closely with his husband might distract him from the tasks at hand."

Katerina shrugged. Smugly, he thought. "It will be your loss for not trusting him and Christos."

She attempted to get out of the chair, but clearly had not been facetious earlier when she had said that she was struggling today.

He helped her to her feet, and then because his attraction to her was a magnet he had not yet learned how to fend off, did not drop her hands. He kept her there, close enough to catch the scent of her delicate perfume.

She did not quite meet his gaze as she stood very still, looking at a spot behind him on the wall. She did not attempt to wrench her hands free. She just stood there and waited.

He should give her the ring, but instead, he dropped her hands in irritation.

"I am almost ready," she said, turning to a little table and picking up a pair of earrings. She studied herself in the full-length mirror as she attached one.

She wore a simple, casual dress that she might have worn when she was his assistant—complete with sensible flat shoes that had to be for comfort rather than any kind of fashion statement. But the dress was the kind of soft, stretchy material that hugged the swell of her stomach.

He had to step back toward the door as he was afraid he would reach out and touch her, demand of her what she had already refused.

"The meeting about titles should be interesting, but it got me thinking that there are some gaps in my knowledge regarding the history of the Agonas reign."

"You can always utilize the family library or Zandra's tutor if there's something you wish to know."

"I don't think the tutor can help me with this subject," she said. She turned to the mirror and fastened her other earing. She studied her reflection, then turned very slowly to look at him with an expression he couldn't read. "What happened the night of the coup?"

The blood in his veins turned to ice. He didn't *mean* to take a step back, but found himself closer to the door than he had been all the same. He had to work very hard to make certain his voice was commanding and not...affected. "Why would you ask me this?"

"I am to be queen. I think I should have a slightly better understanding of the events than dry facts taught in history books. Even Zandra doesn't know what really happened, and she was there."

"The history books will tell you all there is to know." All anyone ever needed to know. He *wished* it were all he knew.

"The fact you won't speak of it makes me believe there *is* more to know."

He did not retreat any farther, did not allow himself to clasp his hands behind his back as he wished. He simply stood still and stared her down.

She did not blink. She didn't so much as nod her head in deference. There was a certain kind of warmth in her expression. It reminded him of the look in her eye that had led him down the dangerous path that had ultimately brought them to this moment.

She had shown him empathy, and he had forgotten his imperative control. He would not again.

"It does not matter what you believe, Katerina," he returned coldly. "It matters only what I say is fact—this will always be so. You may be the future queen, but my will supersedes yours."

Her mouth firmed, anger flashing in her eyes, but when she spoke, it was with her usual calm assistant's demeanor.

But she is your assistant no more.

"Even you cannot make your feelings facts, Diamandis. King, queen or commoner."

"You are both soon-to-be queen and commoner, and what you feel does not signify."

She smiled, but there was no warmth in it. All the warmth had drained out of her.

Because you wanted it to.

"Yes, you have made it quite clear that my feelings—that no one's feelings—matter. Here, there or anywhere. What we need to clarify, however, is that while you might see the role of queen as simply to push out the children you don't want, with no emotional connection whatsoever, *I* see it as a responsibility. And that requires *some* understanding of what happened during the most fraught time in our kingdom's history."

"How easily it has become *our*," he said, the seething anger he had to control forming something like a red haze in his vision. "You would *dare* speak to *me* of responsibility?"

"Yes. I would," she returned, as though his anger did not affect her in the least. "I know you fancy yourself the most responsible and important person in all the land, and better than everyone, but the fact of the matter is that the backbone of all that responsibility is your staff—of which I was once part. Of which I was once in charge."

Even in his anger he could not argue with her. She had been that, and more. So he chose his best weapon and defense: detached disapproval.

"We do not have time for you to pick a fight, Katerina. We have meetings and things to accomplish so that tomorrow goes off without a hitch. If you'd like to throw a childish tantrum, perhaps you can wait until our honeymoon."

"Oh, is there to be a honeymoon?" she returned acidly. "Even though I refuse to share your bed?"

"But of course. We must give the people the fairy tale they desire." He smiled at her, and knew the small, petty feeling of having won was not conducive to achieving his goals; knew that his temper was causing him to be…antagonistic.

But she had poked at old wounds, and he only knew how to strike—hard and fast—to keep them from swallowing him whole.

Katerina blamed herself for the fact that this had devolved into an argument when she'd only been trying to reach him beneath his armor. She knew how to handle him better than this, and she shouldn't have let Zandra's words fool her into thinking otherwise. She had known he would use his cool demeanor as defense against the question. She had known this would not be an easy topic to broach.

She had *known*.

And still she'd dived in headfirst as though this were the first time she had been faced with the challenge of Diamandis and his trauma. Hands off. No entry. The end.

They could give the kingdom a fairy tale, but it would never be true.

Because although Katerina might create her own little fairy tales in her imagination, Zandra was wrong. Diamandis did not care for her feelings or for her at all. She was a vessel and no more. Perhaps because he'd once respected and appreciated her work, she could be some kind of pseudo assistant, too, but that was all. Trying for more was as futile as trying to escape him had been.

"We should not be late for our meeting."

"No," he agreed, but he did not move to open the door. Instead, he moved toward her again. She tried very hard to remain still. Tried to harden her heart against him. Because his temper might poke at her own, but she was always weak enough in the aftermath to feel sorry for him and how little he seemed capable of dealing with his many issues.

"I wished to speak to you alone so I could give you your engagement band. It is an oversight that Marias has insisted I rectify before the public questions it." He pulled out a small box from his pocket, flipped open the lid and held it out to her.

She stared at the sparkling band. There were many encrusted jewels, but no large centerpiece as she might have expected a royal engagement ring to have. It also didn't look like any of the royal jewelry she was familiar with. "This isn't a piece I recognize."

"No. This was my mother's personal engagement band."

Katerina sucked in a sharp breath. This was…unexpected. It was the antithesis to the fight they'd just had. But he took her hand and slid the ring onto her finger. "It is what the people would expect," he said flatly.

He did not look at her, and Katerina knew him well enough to know that though he might sound flat, stiff or detached, he was working hard to perfect his mask of emotionless indifference.

What the people would expect.

Katerina wasn't sure she agreed with that. The *people* would expect fancy royal jewels—and this ring was of course beautiful and elegant and royal, but it wasn't one of the well-known pieces that centuries of royals had worn.

This was personal. His mother's *personal* engagement ring.

His mother, whom he'd lost so tragically. And Katerina knew, because of all the things he never said, that he must have loved his mother very much. So all her anger and frustration with him leaked out of her in one go.

He was getting his way, steamrolling her into this life she had not wanted. He was demanding and commanding and antagonistic.

And yet so many things she knew he didn't deal with were wrapped up in this marriage—memories and family. She had seen him fall apart over getting his sister back after years of seeing him only as a lonely, stoic figure. That had been a shock. *That* had been the moment she'd realized there was a beating heart underneath all that ice.

He preferred the ice, and he would fight tooth and nail to keep it. But when so much pain was underneath, how could she not understand that? How could she not empathize with him?

He still held her hand in his though the ring was long since settled on her finger. He stared at it, a very perplexed expression on his face she did not fully understand. It didn't appear as simple as regret, but she wondered if he did wish he could take it back now that it was on her finger.

"Are you sure this is the ring you wish me to have?" she asked gently.

He kept his gaze on the ring, then slowly released her hand. He stepped back, clasped his hands behind his back, and looked at her with vague detachment.

"My mother would have liked you. Very much."

The compliment had the strength to make tears threaten. Queen Agathe had been a beloved figure in Kalyva, so it would have been a compliment no matter what. But to have Diamandis say it to her meant something deeper. The heart she was trying so hard to protect felt bruised.

And ached for him. "Why?"

"You are practical and reasonable and kind. All things she was and which she valued."

"Diamandis…"

"Come, we are already late, and this is not a good look." He turned abruptly and opened the door. He held it open and did not look back at her as he waited for her to exit.

And Katerina had no words, no way to articulate all she felt, all she wanted for him and from him. So she said nothing, and walked out the door.

CHAPTER NINE

DIAMANDIS DREAMED OF his mother. It was an excruciating pain he hadn't suffered in years. One he thought he'd eradicated after that first year following her death, when she'd appeared in his dreams, just out of reach, every night.

He had learned to push his body and mind to the brink of exhaustion every day, and sleep had been mostly dreamless since.

Mostly.

It was not the best way to begin his wedding day, which would be a lengthy process that involved much smiling and bowing and performing for the people. It would at least be mentally exhausting in all the ways that would help him sleep tonight.

His wedding night.

He was getting married today. To Katerina. He would be a father in a few short months. Everything from this moment on was an irrevocable change, and he had no choice but to accept and handle them all.

He was the King of Kalyva. He had a kingdom to run and the Agonas legacy to protect. Everything else was secondary to duty. Everything else would be kept in its careful compartment.

He got out of bed and let the staff in with breakfast, messages, and all the accoutrements involved in dressing the king for his royal wedding. There would be the wedding, the procession, the royal dinner.

Then they could leave on their honeymoon. Diamandis did not let his mind drift to Katerina being there too. He pictured himself alone in the old, isolated castle on the other side of Kalyva. It would a period of respite that he rarely allowed himself.

And she would be with him, and for the aesthetics of it all, they would need to share a room.

Katerina would not like this. If she continued in her hands-off nonsense, neither would he.

But it would be done. *Likes* and *wants* did not signify, as per usual.

When Lysias arrived, dressed and pressed in a uniform befitting the husband of the princess, Diamandis excused his staff. He and Lysias could make the procession to the chapel alone. Diamandis needed some moments free of fluttering staff. He'd excuse Lysias as well if he could get away with it, but this was not custom. He would arrive at the chapel with his best man and the wedding would begin.

He only prayed that Lysias did not bring up anything significant. "I know you have said it is no great hardship, but I appreciate the swap all the same," Diamandis said, hoping to keep the conversation light.

"I'm certain I can find a way for you to pay me back," Lysias said, flashing his careless grin. Much like Zandra, the Lysias that Diamandis had been friends with as a boy, and the man he knew now, seemed like two different people.

Life had done that to Lysias, who, after the coup, had been labeled a traitor along with his parents. This had been the doing of Diamandis's cruel advisers—Diamandis being too useless with grief to make any of the necessary decisions.

Lysias's parents had been sentenced to death for aiding a coup, and Lysias exiled at the tender age of twelve.

It was a miracle in Diamandis's mind that Lysias had been able to forgive him. Though Diamandis had not given the orders himself, even when he'd begun to realize they had been wrong, his pride had kept him from reaching out to Lysias. He had been afraid that correcting the wrong would cause more upheaval.

And the princess had still been missing. He'd been certain that even if the Balaskas family was innocent, they knew something they wouldn't tell.

Until Lysias had brought Zandra back to him, and the fact that he'd saved the princess when he'd been a boy had come to light.

Diamandis had certainly not forgiven himself for the years of suffering he had brought upon his childhood friend. If he had been stronger, he would never have let his advisers make such knee-jerk decisions.

"I hope it is not the prospect of your bride causing this expression on your face, Diamandis. The people will not feel any measure of assurance that this is a love match when you are scowling so."

Diamandis blew out a breath as they walked the length of the great hall toward the chapel. It was quiet here since most of the action was to take place in the chapel or outside the entrance. As his bodyguard, Christos was nearby, though not visible, but that was about it.

Diamandis did not wish to speak of his thoughts, not when Lysias would no doubt take it as an invitation to have a conversation Diamandis did not want, so Diamandis was vague. "I was thinking more of the past than the future."

Lysias was quiet a moment—but only for a moment. "I hesitate to give you advice, knowing how violently you reacted to that when we were boys."

"*Boys* being the operative word."

"Have you changed so much, then? Or just learned to hide that nasty temper because you had to?"

Had to. And how. "There are many things I had to do."

"Yes. There were and there are. I have no knowledge of what it is to be king, but I do know something of what it is to be a husband and soon-to-be father."

Diamandis wanted to refute both labels. He did not want them. They were being thrust upon him because he had made mistakes. Been careless. They were his *punishment*, and he would take this as he had taken all the rest. It was his due.

When Diamandis said nothing, Lysias continued on. "I spent my formative and early adult years believing everyone I loved would either die or betray me, because that was the lesson my childhood taught me, or so I thought."

Diamandis didn't stiffen. He straightened his tie that did not need straightening as they stood waiting for their signal to enter the chapel. Diamandis wished it would hurry up.

"That is not living, though. Not really. We can let our pasts define us so much that we do not really live, or we can deal with what tragedies befall us and attempt to live in spite of them. I let my past be defined by its most tragic moment, instead of remembering all the good that also existed."

"You sound like your wife," Diamandis muttered, because he could find no other words. He had no arguments for this. Except the one he knew his old friend would argue with.

I do not deserve to "really" live like that.

"Yes, but I know something she does not, because she cannot remember it. I am glad for some of it, for her sake, but *I* remember your parents. I wish she could remember them, and I wish you would not forget them so. Even being the most powerful people in Kalyva, and dedicated to the throne and the Agonas legacy, they were, at heart, kind, loving people. They would not want their son to blindly commit himself to the throne and nothing else. They would want you to have what they had, and it seems to me you have a chance for that here…if you'd let go your preconceived notions of what you *have* to do, and focus on all you *could* do."

Diamandis tried not to think about what his parents would want for him. He ignored the echoes of his father's voice, offering advice about life. He focused on the crown and only the crown.

Because the crown was controllable. Family and love were not. He had learned this, locked in a dungeon, watching his father's soft spots end his life; listening to the screams of his mother, his brothers, and being unable to save them. Neither anger nor begging had made a difference.

His father had trusted a man he'd treated as a brother—and that man had let the discontented political faction inside the castle walls.

When you loved, you could not protect what was important.

When you loved, you failed. You did things that could never come to light.

So Diamandis did not speak and did not acknowledge Lysias's words in any way. He waited for the signal, and when it came, he moved forward without ever saying a word or even looking Lysias's way.

Because he *was* the throne. And nothing else.

Katerina was in a wedding dress adorned with lace and jewels and surely meant for the princess, but it was now hers. It had been altered to fit her growing belly and her shorter frame. But it was not hers, she knew this.

Not the wedding, the husband, nor the crown. She was an imposter.

And still, excitement fluttered in her chest. She was to say "I do" to King Diamandis Agonas and she shouldn't want to.

But she did.

A failing, certainly, but she was determined to be smart about it all the same. So she stood, ready and waiting for her cue, outside the grandiose doors of the royal chapel.

Alone.

Oh, not really alone. Attendants milled about. Some fussed with her dress, some with the flowers. But no one stood by her side ready to walk her down the aisle. Zandra would stand up with her, but because she was the princess, she was already in the chapel with her brother, awaiting Katerina's arrival.

So Katerina stood alone, looking at an artistic representation of an ancient Kalyvan wedding depicted on the giant doors that would soon open for her.

She had no father to walk her down the aisle, and she knew of no demand of an invite from her mother. She had no family. She definitely did not wish her mother or her father were present, but she couldn't help wishing for a friendly face. Someone to hold on to.

She smoothed her hands over her stomach. "I will always be a friendly face for you two," she whispered so the attendants didn't hear. Because she would always, *always* give her children everything she hadn't been given.

Someone behind her cleared his throat and Katerina looked over her shoulder to find Christos there.

"Your Highness." Christos gave a low bow. He straightened with a smile.

But he should be guarding Diamandis, not outside the chapel with her. "Shouldn't you be inside?"

He held out his arm. "Diamandis thought perhaps you would like a friendly face to walk with you down the aisle."

It was a kind gesture, but… "How did Diamandis know I would view you as a friendly face?" Christos was devoted to Diamandis and to the safety of the sovereign. Katerina had been friends with many of her coworkers when she was Diamandis's assistant, but Christos had been something of a father figure. Someone who felt *safe*. It was why she hadn't known who else to go to when she'd needed help escaping Kalyva months ago.

It was something *surely* Diamandis did not know, or Christos would not still be his bodyguard or driver.

"I'm afraid I confessed to helping you leave only a few days after you did. I could not stand the worry over being caught." He tucked her arm into his.

Katerina could not hide her utter shock. "And he didn't fire you?"

"I expected him to. I even offered my resignation. But he said if you were so desperate to leave, then it was the right thing to do to help. He was glad you had someone to turn to in a crisis."

Katerina couldn't make sense of that. "I do not understand him," she muttered.

"Perhaps he doesn't understand himself," Christos offered as the doors were opened—her signal to move forward. To say *I do* to Diamandis. To the kingdom of Kalyva.

She walked down the aisle, toward Diamandis. Her king. Her almost husband. Handsome in all his white and crisp royal finery, a perfect contrast to his dark features. Her heart stuttered, traitor that it was.

He'd given her his mother's engagement band. Had sent her a friendly face to walk her down the aisle as the entirety of the kingdom's eyes were on her.

He was a *good* man, underneath all those walls he'd built and the arrows he slung to protect them.

No, she did not think he understood himself—nor did he want to.

Christos bowed deeply to the king, then surrendered Katerina's arm to Diamandis. He took it, drawing her up to the altar. She felt his gaze move over her, the heat in it, carefully banked but there.

It would always be there. Could she resist it forever?

The bishop began the ceremony, but Katerina couldn't focus on the words. She watched Diamandis's face. And he didn't look away. He studied her as if he was having the same strange experience of feeling as if they were totally alone. As if they could still choose *not* to do this if they wanted.

This man frustrated her, angered her, and could be such an utter and total ass. But he'd given her more than she'd gotten from anyone else: kindness, respect, trust. He'd believed in her as his assistant, and now as his queen. He'd never once acted as though she wasn't up to the task.

Maybe he could never love her—or wouldn't allow himself to—but he had still been there for her in so many ways that no one in her life had ever been.

If anyone had gotten close enough, her mother had driven them away.

She still could. It was a chilling thought Katerina could not focus on here under the gaze of so many.

"I do," Diamandis said firmly, and this was Katerina's cue to pay attention. To respond to the bishop with the correct words so he could declare them husband and wife.

King and queen.

Forever.

And she didn't want to run away. The fear that had lived deep inside her when she'd found out she was pregnant was fully gone now. No matter what happened, he had promised himself to her. He would never break that promise. Maybe he could not be the husband or father she wanted him to be, but he would not abandon her.

He pulled her forward by the shoulders and pressed a very chaste kiss to her lips. Then he turned her to face the guests.

She was officially his queen. And this was not a punishment. It wasn't even a *job*. Here, surrounded by his family, his court, his people, she realized this was just life.

Her life.

Their life.

She would have to make the best of it.

CHAPTER TEN

THE PROCESSION AND dinner were interminable. This did not surprise Diamandis. He had little patience for grand events at the best of times, and this was not the best of times.

Katerina looked a vision. The white of her fanciful gown seemed to make the golden tones of her skin glow, and the sparkle of it all continued to catch his eye so that he seemed to be forever looking around the room for her when they were not side by side. She smiled at everyone she talked to. She ate and whispered and laughed with Zandra.

She looked happy.

And something deep inside ached to be a part of that happiness, even as he had to focus on anything else to keep the evidence of his arousal from announcing itself.

But every time he caught her eye, or turned to find her gaze on him, he saw something…different. As though she'd said "I do" and things had changed. She looked at him with…*something* in her gaze. A warmth that made him feel…

Like he was on a very dangerous precipice. One he could not allow himself to fall off.

When at last the dinner ended, and they could make their escape, he could not find Katerina at first. After asking far too many people if they'd seen her, he finally located her himself. She was huddled in a corner with Zandra and a second or third cousin on their mother's side. Zandra held a baby that must be Monika's, while Katerina stroked the baby's chubby cheek.

"It is time to leave, Your Highness," Diamandis said stiffly and awkwardly. He wanted to do so immediately, but instead found himself drawn into a conversation about his distant relative and her brood of children. Talk of solid foods and diapers seemed to delight Katerina, but he did not wish to hear any of it and finally extricated her from the conversation.

"The plane is waiting for us," he said, leading her away from the dwindling party. His staff would take care of everything else, while Zandra and Lysias made the remaining formal goodbyes.

"I would think the plane could wait for the king and queen if we so desire it," Katerina said, still with that look in her eye.

"But I do not desire it," he returned. As was custom—or was now expected because of his parents' wedding—they did not have to give a grand goodbye. They were allowed to sneak out, as lovebirds might.

He hurried his pace, eager to be away from baby talk and thoughts of lovebirds.

"In all the years I worked for you, I don't think you ever went to Anavolí," Katerina said conversationally. She was so relaxed. So calm. All the while wearing a complicated gown and being largely pregnant after a long, exhausting day she hadn't wanted in the first place.

She made no sense to him anymore. He'd always understood her as his assistant, but she'd changed the game. She seemed to have her own vision of what her new role was in his life and he didn't share it. Know it. Understand it.

And still she kept talking about Anavolí, the royal holiday castle.

"I would have thought it made-up if I had not had to handle the arrangements when your political allies wanted to use it," she continued.

"I have not been in quite some time. The demands of the

throne are significant. I'm rather loath to leave now, but the kingdom expects such displays of..."

"Romance?" she supplied.

He fought the impulse to look at her. "If you wish." He led her outside. Christos offered a nod as they emerged and he led them to the car. He drove them to the airport, then personally saw to all the security measures. He even sat with the pilot while Diamandis and Katerina took seats in the cabin.

She chattered away the whole flight. About the people she'd met for the first time today, or people she'd worked with who had given her gifts and kind words. This was not any Katerina he knew, and it left him feeling oddly imbalanced.

Because, again, she looked visibly happy. She was glowing with it. This was not the woman who'd refused him in her sad little apartment in Athens. It wasn't even the woman who'd calmly told him she wanted a business partnership.

This was a new Katerina, and he wanted to laugh along with her when she told a story about Marias hitting the champagne a little too hard and tumbling out of his chair, his toupee sliding off along with him.

It had been so long since he'd truly laughed and the impulse felt odd enough to enable him to resist. Instead, he looked out the window and watched as they began their descent to the western coast of Kalyva.

"Diamandis, why did you send Christos to walk me down the aisle?"

He did not break his gaze from the view outside the window. It was dark—this area of Kalyva was largely isolated and the royal family owned enough of the land to keep people from encroaching, so there were few lights aside from the necessary ones to land the plane.

He considered her question and tried to make his answer pragmatic. "You needed someone."

"But the plan was for me to walk by myself. What changed?"

He had seen the crowd, the long aisle, and the thought of her having to face it alone had twisted him up inside.

He could hardly tell her that. "Christos suggested it."

"That's not what he told me, Diamandis."

Diamandis shrugged. "It is what happened," he lied. Easily. That was the kind of man he was, after all. Built on a lie. A secret.

She said nothing more as the plane touched down, as they were ushered off and into the car that would drive them to the castle.

Anavolí was much smaller than the royal palace. This had been built almost a century ago for a princess who had been frail, and the king at the time had thought her own more private dwelling would lengthen her life.

It had, and she had even married and had children here and so it became a popular retreat for any royal needing a rest or change of scene.

His parents had brought them here as children in the summers to play in the ocean—no lessons, no protocol. Just life. And family.

He had been back a handful of times since they'd died—mostly to prove to himself that he was stronger than any memories could ever be. But he'd been younger then. More... steadfast.

These days he knew better than to tempt the fate of a happy memory.

The drive to the castle was short, and when Diamandis helped Katerina out of the car at Anavolí, she let out a little noise of pleasure.

"Oh, isn't it lovely in the dark?" A smile curved her lips. "It glows, and you can hear the surf. It reminds me of the beaches at home."

"You grew up in Seir, yes?" he asked, rather than look at the white structure glow in the welcoming lights. Rather than be inclined to picture the bright blue water lapping at the sand just behind the building.

He would see it all soon enough when the sun rose.

She looked at him as if surprised he remembered her origins, but of course he knew which town every member of his staff was from. Even if she was no longer his staff.

Your wife. Your queen.

"Yes. I cannot say I enjoyed my childhood there, but I love the beaches. I love to swim or at least I did when I was young."

Diamandis said nothing to this information as he led her inside the castle. He had a small staff here, ready and waiting, and they led him and his wife to their bedchamber.

"I'm afraid we will have to share a room to avoid speculation or gossip on our honeymoon."

Katerina drifted through the room, toward the open balcony that looked out over the sea. "It is of no matter," she said, quite philosophically for a woman who'd been insistent they not blur lines mere days ago.

"I cannot imagine why you don't make more use of this place, Diamandis," she said, taking a deep breath of salty sea air out on the balcony.

He knew better than to join her. Safer to stay inside and watch from afar. "I considered giving it to Zandra and Lysias as a wedding gift, but I think they both rather prefer the bustle of the city. Nevertheless, it will be a fine place for them to bring their children to for summer holidays."

She turned to face him. She was shadowed, except for a slim shaft of moonlight that cut across her face. "What about us?"

"What about us?"

"Will we not do the same?"

Diamandis chose his words carefully. "We may, though often the responsibilities of the crown weigh too heavy to get away. But you could bring the children, of course, any time you wish."

She turned back to the sea. "I suppose they will have to be born first."

A small silence stretched out between them. Diamandis found himself in the strange situation of not knowing how to fill it. But he needn't have worried, for Katerina did quickly.

Not with words, though. She reached behind her and began to pull the zipper of her dress down. "Can you help?" she asked.

"Perhaps you should step inside. I could call one of the maids—"

"No, no. Just pull the zipper down for me and I will handle everything." She stepped over the threshold and back into the main room. She turned her back to him, giving him no choice but to unzip her dress, revealing her beautiful back.

The scent of her wafted up around him, rich and floral. He stepped away and allowed her to deal with the remainder of the zipper herself. He reminded himself that she had been very clear.

"It is beautiful and should be saved for some historical thing or another. But it is very heavy and I'd like it off." The fabric slithered from her and fell to the floor with a soft *whoosh*.

Then she turned to face him, in an intricate piece of lacy lingerie that could only be meant to entice a man.

He wasn't the one who wanted to be hands-off, but…this was suspicious. "I thought you wished to remain business partners." He could not take his eyes off her—the flimsy lace, the glorious glow of her.

She nodded. "I did. I thought I could guard my heart if we did not muddle matters with a physical relationship."

He recoiled at the word *heart*, but this did not seem to stop her. It certainly did not stop his sex from jumping to life.

"But this is silly. This…compartmentalizing. Our life is our life, regardless." She removed the lace from her body to stand naked before him.

His perfect, beautiful queen.

He felt frozen, as though his very insides had detonated and he was merely a shell of the man he'd once been, with only one thought: *her*.

"I wish to be with you, my king," she said, sliding her hands up his chest and around his neck. "Here, on our wedding night. It belongs to us, after all. Not to Kalyva."

But she had said something about her heart, and this felt more dangerous. He should not allow it to happen. She had been right: business required a clear mind, and absolutely no muddying with desire.

No hearts. He *was* Kalyva. Nothing more.

Be strong. Harden your heart. Do what must be done, no matter how difficult. Resist feeling.

Resisting her would be power. It would be the smart move, and he should absolutely do it. But she was warmth and light, and she was his.

So he gave in.

His kiss was like the last time, and it singed through Katerina like the fire it was, but this was about more than lust, and she wanted to show him all she had to offer. She didn't want to put all her desire for him in one box, and all her other conflicting emotions for him in another. They were all one jumbled thing, in one box.

Tonight, she wanted to show him tenderness and care— all the things he did not want, and yet so desperately needed. Without fear. Without holding herself back.

She knew he'd sent Christos to walk her down the aisle. She knew this place meant something to him and that it hurt him to be back here. She wore his mother's ring, and she'd seen him through highs and lows.

She knew him. Good and bad.

She wanted it *all*. Making the best of everything as best she could.

So she soothed his savage hunger by rubbing her hands slowly up and down his back. By pulling her mouth from his and pressing soft, careful kisses to his cheeks. His jaw.

"What are you doing?" he rasped.

"Taking my time," she replied. She kissed along his collarbone as she unbuttoned his shirt, one by one, in a slow, careful rhythm. Unbutton. Kiss. Unbutton. Kiss. When his chest was revealed to her, she pressed herself to him, reveling in the warmth of him, in the hardness of his chest and the coarseness of his hair.

She traced her fingers over his skin, delving into ridges, smoothing over hard lines and strong muscles.

His hand curled around her neck, his thumb pressing her chin up so she had to look at him. There were storms in his dark eyes, and she wished she could be the lighthouse that led him safely to shore.

"Diamandis—" Words even she did not want to say threatened. She should be smarter than this, but...

"Do not speak," he said, the words coming out rough and pained, though she knew he thought he was being forceful and commanding. She knew he was trying to take some control of the situation because he felt like he did not have any.

Because he was afraid of what he felt happening between them—and maybe it wasn't the same as what she felt, but it was *something*. Even if he refused to acknowledge those feelings, that fear.

So she did not speak again. She nodded, and she gave herself over to him and what he wanted. While she allowed herself to feel it *all*.

His free hand slid over her shoulder, then cupped one breast, his thumb brushing over the already hardened nipple. She closed her eyes to lose herself in the sensation. She didn't want control. She didn't want to think. She only wanted to feel the pleasure move over her. She wanted to sigh and moan and groan without thought.

She wanted to give him all her responses unchecked. He bowed his head and sucked the other breast into his mouth, using his tongue to tease her until she was panting, begging, forgetting any thought she'd had of being slow and romantic.

There was too much need built up inside her. She tipped her head back, pleasure arrowing down from where he touched— licked. She pulsed with need and decided to give in to it. In to him. She decided to be the soft place for his ragged edges to land.

She gently raked her fingers through his hair while he made her shake with need. His mouth stayed on her breasts, but his hands slid down, finding the hot, needy core of her. It took nothing at all to have her exploding apart, his name on her lips.

He straightened, but she held on to him, forcing herself to open her eyes. She could tell he was trying to convince himself to step back, to put distance between them. So she led him to the bed before he could find his center of control. She pushed him onto the mattress, then straddled him, guiding the thick length of him inside her. Slow, slick, perfect. His eyes were like dark flames, his grip on her hips tight, as if she were the center of all he had.

She wanted to be.

So she moved slowly, teasing him as his eyes watched the place where they joined. He watched the long, slow slide. The slick, delicious friction.

Another peak washed over her, and she shuddered and lost all sense of rhythm, because there was too much. He was all-encompassing and she wanted to give in to all that he was.

His grip tightened, and he arched up into her, taking over. He was taking over, and she relished it. His gaze lifted to hers.

"You are mine," he growled. She knew he was lost in the moment. She knew he did not *want* her to be his.

But she was.

"Say it," he demanded, a king used to giving orders and having them obeyed.

She decided this was one order she always would. "I am yours, my king."

He took over, the pace wild as she shattered, over and over again. The crash of it all was bigger, stronger. It wracked through her, top to bottom, and when he roared out his release, she was limp, sated and happier than she'd ever been.

No matter how short-lived she knew it would be.

CHAPTER ELEVEN

DIAMANDIS STOOD ON the balcony watching the waves crash against the empty shore. The sun was just barely peeking above the watery horizon.

He had not slept.

She had done something to him. Scrambled up his insides so he had nothing safe and strong to hold on to. He could not fathom how. He only knew that it was all her fault.

I am yours, my king.

He hardened, here in the dim morning light, and knew if he went inside, she would take him. She had changed the game, and he felt powerless. And he had no idea how to get his power back.

Except…

There was always the terrible truth of what he'd done. The thing that no one knew.

Almost no one.

It would horrify her enough to keep her distance, surely. But could he risk the knowledge ever getting out? If it saved him this?

No, that would not go over well. He would simply have to be stronger. Compartmentalize better. He could play the role of dutiful husband and not feel anything. He would simply have to be careful. Besides, soon she would no doubt be too uncomfortable to share his bed. Then she would have the children and need time to recover.

He could keep himself apart, while giving her the image of a devoted husband. Because he *was* devoted, after a fashion. He did not want her miserable. She had previously been a kind of partner. Yes, by doing her job well, but also just by... being there. He'd even realized, after she'd left and he'd found himself with a strange emptiness in his chest, that he'd rather enjoyed her company.

And had missed it when she was no longer there.

For work-related things, of course, because what else could matter? What else was there beyond Kalyva? Nothing. So it had been a strange kind of freedom to be around someone who did not *need* him to behave a certain way. A perplexing pride had come from taking care of her in small ways, as she took care of him.

It could be that way again, if he was careful. Besides, she would be a wonderful mother, warm and giving. He dared not let himself think of her holding children—their children—in her arms lest he forget the real, important thing here: she would be a good enough mother that he would not need to be involved.

The needs of the kingdom came first.

There was *only* Kalyva. Not them.

If he could find a way to make her understand the necessary lines he had drawn, perhaps this could be that partnership she had wanted, that comforting companionship he'd lost when she'd left. And all without forgoing what they enjoyed in the bedroom together...

He scrubbed his hands over his face. Hadn't he learned anything about temptation and Katerina? About fooling himself?

He heard the soft sounds of movement and straightened. But Katerina was closer than he'd assumed, because before he could rearrange his expression to be suitably opaque, her hand slid up his back and she came to stand beside him.

"Good morning," she greeted, then yawned.

He did not allow himself to look at her. He could feel the satiny soft fabric of the flimsy nightgown she wore. It would be too much of a distraction when he was not yet on solid ground. "You should still be asleep."

"It seems you don't sleep at all."

She had her arms wrapped around his shoulder, leaning into him like she belonged there. "What is bothering you?" she asked, like this was a normal occurrence. Waking up together married. Sharing a conversation.

Knowing each other well enough to see through whatever masks they put on.

She had always seen through him far too well, but it hadn't seemed like such a threat when she was his assistant. It had seemed practical, as long as he did not give in to the attraction underneath it all.

And he hadn't, until Zandra had returned. Until everything had been upended. All these months later, he still hadn't rebuilt his defenses.

He was afraid that with Katerina by his side, he never would.

She gave him a little, encouraging squeeze. "You have carried the weight of everything since you were fourteen. *Fourteen*. No more than a boy."

"It was old enough to rule the country."

She tsked. "You were a *child*, regardless. Whether you want to accept that or not is no matter. You are a grown man now, and I don't know why you shouldn't share some of your burdens with your wife, who also happens to be the queen."

He had once shared his burdens, his grief, with all the men who had promised to help him, to support him. He had shared with the people his father had trusted, and so he had, too, by default. He'd believed everyone had his and Kalyva's best interests at heart, because he had been nothing but a black hole of grief.

And he had been taken advantage of. If he had not realized it when he did, his entire reign would have been a joke—and over long ago.

"Let us go to breakfast."

She sighed, but she did not argue. She let him go, though not before rising to her toes and brushing a kiss across his cheek. It was just a little gesture of affection, the kind he was forever telling Lysias and Zandra to do *in private*.

As though she were simply…ignoring everything he'd ever told her about what this marriage was to be. He followed her back into the room, that churning anger born of a feeling he would not acknowledge was beginning to brew.

"I do not know what you are trying to do, Katerina."

She pulled a robe on, then looked at him as if truly puzzled. "Do? I'm not trying to *do* anything, Diamandis. Except live my life and not torture myself with it." Then she studied him and smiled. "Oh, that's probably quite confusing for you." She crossed over to him and suddenly he didn't understand what was happening.

She was more like her old self, back when she'd been his assistant: constantly challenging him and forever unbothered by whatever his reaction might be. Quite happy with her own situation, regardless of what he thought.

And then she kissed him—another quick affectionate peck—while he stood, stock-still, trying to make sense of it.

"We have made our choices, Diamandis." She said this with her hands on his shoulders and a pleasant, content look on her face. "We are married. We are to become parents. For my children, I will move forward and accept what life throws at me. And I will make the best of all of it."

"And what brought on this sunny attitude?" he returned, sounding more strained and less dismissive than he had intended.

She seemed to think his question over. "You gave me your

mother's ring. You sent Christos to walk me down the aisle. I am pretending to believe my mother simply didn't care enough to show up for the wedding and cause a scene, but I have a sneaking suspicion you made sure that she could not attend and ruin it."

He stiffened because she was correct. The first night they'd returned to the castle after she'd told him about what a problem her mother was, he'd made certain to keep her far away from Katerina and the palace.

"That was not done for your benefit."

"Perhaps not. Perhaps none of it was, Diamandis. But regardless of all the reasons behind these things, you have been good and kind to me, even when I want to throttle you. That extends to when I was your assistant." Her expression sobered some, and that made something twist in his chest like pain. "I believe we can build a good life together, if you allow yourself to."

She said it with such certainty, as if her optimism could make it so. "You have clearly never had the hardships of life destroy everything, Katerina."

He thought she might take offense at that, or be hurt by it, but instead she just gazed up at him. *With pity.* She even patted his cheek like he was a poor, misguided child. "Oh, Diamandis. Life is hard, and tragedy unavoidable, but that hardly means you can't enjoy your life. In fact, I think it means you should enjoy it all the more when it is good."

"And this is good? A husband you did not want—a husband, in fact, you ran away from with the intent of keeping our children to yourself?"

His cold words had the desired effect. The warmth in her eyes cooled and she removed her hand from his cheek, but she did not step away. She did not break eye contact.

And it was in that moment he realized he'd expected her to. He'd expected her to step back, hurt and quiet, and withdraw. That was the reaction he'd wanted.

Instead, she slid her small hands over the swell of her stomach—a reminder, always, that she grew their children there. They were real, even if he could not hold them yet.

"Would you like me to apologize for the choices I made?" she asked, quite calmly, as if she would give such a thing if it was what he wanted.

He could not stop himself from scowling.

"I cannot. By leaving, I thought I was saving you, Diamandis. Not that I'm entirely selfless, just that… I did not want to be the reason you were conflicted or even more burdened than you already felt. Part of that was not wanting to deal with you in that state, but part was not wanting to see you, or to empathize with you in your suffering. I left because I could not fathom being the one to add to your burden when I had spent years trying to take some of it away."

He did not have words for this…this honesty. This…

She was lying. Tricking him. Trying to soften him for some… some reason.

Because for many years she *had* taken some of the burden off his shoulders, though he had never asked her to do it. She had always been there when he'd needed. She had been like his conscience, and she had reminded him that he was human and not a robot.

"And yes, some of the running away was brought on by the fact that I never wanted to be like my mother," she continued, the vulnerability she rarely exposed coming to the surface now. "She wanted to burden anyone she could. I don't know how many powerful men she tried to convince that I was their daughter."

This information shocked him enough to forget what he was trying to accomplish. "What do you mean?"

"Oh, she'd parade me in front of anyone she'd slept with, anyone she thought she could convince to accept paternity. She was certainly not choosy in her partners, either before I was born or after. Of course, she only ever tried to convince anyone who had money. Which leads me to believe my real father had none." She shook her head and cradled her belly with her arms, as though she would protect her children—*their* children—at any cost. He knew she would. "But I am not my mother. Of course I make mistakes, but I will love my children more than myself."

She kept using the word *love* as though it wasn't a weapon to be used against people. As though it was to be enjoyed, sought after. As though love protected when all it seemed to do in his life was destroy.

"So I am not claiming pure selflessness, Diamandis," she continued. "But I made that choice from a place of caring. For them. For you. And I made the decision to make the best of this situation out of that same feeling. First for them, and now for you. I will love the family we create in spite of you."

Then she smiled, and it was beautiful and open. As if none of that pain mattered. Because though they weren't born yet, she cradled their children in her arms. Their family. *Theirs.*

"Perhaps you could have breakfast brought up to the balcony while I get dressed. I'm starving." And with that she sailed off to the dressing rooms, leaving him wholly and utterly confused.

Katerina enjoyed her breakfast out on the patio overlooking the ocean below. She even enjoyed Diamandis's stifled discomfort. He didn't know what to do with her simply enjoying things—the *bougatsa* she couldn't seem to get enough of, the beautiful view of the lapping waves.

She knew he'd spent most of his adult life compartmentalizing. She'd done a lot of that work for him, but she was done. For the both of them. If he wanted to keep things separate from here on out, he'd have to do the work himself.

He watched her eat. At first, it was almost like he was

counting every bite, but then...well, he was watching her mouth. She licked a piece of flaky pastry from her lip.

His gaze grew intense, and a tingling warmth crept through her body. Last night had been beautiful. He would scoff at such a word, she knew, but it *had* been. It had made her feel like they really could...do this marriage thing. This family thing.

Oh, he'd throw more walls up, this she knew. It was what he was best at, but maybe she had enough resilience in her to break them all down. She thought about this as she finished her breakfast, sitting back in her chair and licking her lips once more. She watched his reaction very closely.

"We shall go for a swim," he said, somewhat abruptly.

"*We* shall?"

"You said you enjoyed swimming back in Seir."

"Yes." And she'd been determined to enjoy a swim here, but she hadn't expected him to voluntarily accompany her.

"I have obtained a swimsuit for you, and some sunscreen. We should go before the heat of the afternoon." He motioned at the bedroom behind them. "Everything is laid out for you."

She did wish to swim, and if he was going to join her, all the better. So she went back inside and found a beautiful maternity suit in a pretty shade of purple, a broad hat for the sun, and a cover-up, along with sandals. His staff had thought of everything.

When she rejoined him, he too was dressed for the beach. He said nothing, but his gaze raked over her. She tried very hard not to smile. There was something incredibly enjoyable and freeing about simply accepting that she wanted him. And he wanted her, even as she lumbered down to the beach.

A section had already been set up for them with chairs and umbrellas, a little container of waters, juices and snacks. Someone had thought of everything.

Katerina looked at her husband. He was gazing at the sea, an inscrutable expression on his face.

He had come here with his family as a child, and she imagined he was trying very hard not to remember that. She couldn't help but wonder if he *should* remember. Still, she let him have his moment and she stepped into the surf. The water was cool but nice as the sun was already beating down on them.

It was strange to be in the ocean again. It had been a long time—years really—and she'd never been pregnant before, so this was a first. Her balance was different, that was for sure, and still she waded out. She felt lighter, buoyant somehow. Like she had back in those old, almost carefree summers when she'd been able to escape her mother and swim out all her feelings in the surf.

She didn't know for how long she swam, only that it was the first bit of quiet and calm—both around her and inside of her—that she'd had in a very long time. It made space for all sorts of thoughts and feelings, all centered around the man who was now her husband.

Forever.

He might not have wanted a wife or children, but he was not a man who would turn his back on them now that he had them. This was it, and—

Strong hands clasped her at the waist. "You should not be out so far."

She eyed Diamandis as he took hold of her. His expression was stern, his grip strong. Water dripped from his short, dark hair. How he managed to still look like a king in swim shorts in the middle of an ocean was beyond her.

"I am a strong swimmer, Diamandis."

"I do not care. It is not safe. Particularly in your condition."

"You mean being pregnant with your children?"

His stern frown turned disapproving. "Yes," he said tightly. "And as you are my wife, and they are my children, I will ensure you are all safe."

She did not reply to this. She had never questioned whether she would be safe with Diamandis because she had always known she would be. Just as she knew, in this moment, that he saw a long-ago night when he'd lost so much. She didn't want him to have to remember that on this pretty day at the beach.

She changed the subject. "What else do you know about me?"

His gaze sharpened, as he was brought from the past to the present. "What do you mean?"

"You know where I grew up, and it made me realize I never really thought of the advantage you have. You would have run a background check on me. Talked to my references. You probably know things about me that even I don't. Otherwise I wouldn't have been cleared to work so closely with you."

"I know where you went to school, your degree, your grades. What scholarships you received, and how quickly you paid your loans back. I know your work history. Would you like me to recite it for you like some kind of test?"

She shook her head, amused at the impatient tone of his voice. He was humoring her and he wasn't happy about it. "What about things that wouldn't be found in an employee report?"

His gaze was all disapproval. "I do not understand this conversation, Katerina."

"I am simply curious. Should our union ever be called into question." She smiled, though this had nothing to do with anyone questioning him. "What would you tell people in order to prove that we have a marriage—?" She could not bring herself to add *born of love*. The words got lodged in her throat. "A *real* marriage."

"I would tell them I am the King of Kalyva and any *questions* could be considered treason punishable by jail time." The waves lapped around him, but he was steady, as if nothing, not even the ocean, could knock him over.

Katerina sighed heavily, even as she bobbed with the waves, the only thing keeping her in place his strong arms around her waist. "That would not be the right course of action."

"Then what would?"

"Perhaps digging to the depths of your acting abilities and pretending you might actually like me."

He scowled. "I do like you, Katerina. You would not have been my assistant for all those years if I did not."

"Because I am efficient."

"Because you are brilliant."

She had not expected that.

"I did not appreciate it back then because I did not know how badly the job could be done. You knew everything, handled everyone, and made my life easier with it."

She couldn't call it *impassioned* exactly, because he was clearly exasperated with her. Or exasperated with something. "I'm not sure any of that means more than efficient," she argued, simply because she liked the way his expression darkened even farther.

"Your favorite color is purple. You like those ridiculous tiny dogs like the ones Mrs. Markis has. You do not like olives."

She thought back to that odd first night back at the palace when he'd said he knew what she liked, and her dinner, a meal that that was traditionally served with olives, had not been. The *bougatsas* served at every breakfast since her return.

He had to have arranged in advance to get her a swimsuit for it to be here this morning. And the suit was purple—her favorite color.

Suddenly, this wasn't so enjoyable. It was weighty. It was meaningful.

"Does this answer your ridiculous question?"

It did. In more ways than he no doubt wanted it to. Because...these were all small things. Inconsequential things, really.

But they made up who she was and had no bearing on what she'd been to him as an assistant. If he'd absorbed this information...

Katerina did not really know what love was. She had never been loved. She didn't know who her father was and her mother was incapable of it. She had made friends, but it had never felt permanent. More like swimming through an ocean of people—she might stop and play, but she was never meant to remain in the water forever.

Diamandis had been loved as a child, by all accounts, but for so many years he'd spent his life with the weight of an entire kingdom on his shoulders, and no one to love him. So she did not think he knew either. She did not think he was cognizant of all these little pieces of her that he must have collected over years of her being his assistant—someone who should have mostly been beneath his notice.

"Come. You should not be in the sun much longer. You will get too warm."

"I like being warm." Or maybe she just wanted to stay in this moment where she thought, really thought, she might mean more to him than a capable assistant or accidental mother of his heirs.

"I read it isn't good for the babies."

"You read?"

"I do know how, Katerina," he said, so dryly she couldn't help but laugh.

But a heavy weight settled in with all that mirth as he led her back to the shore. Not a bad one, just an emotional one. He'd been reading about pregnancy, and it made his earlier comments about keeping his family safe that much more poignant.

Duty was at the center of all he was, this she knew, but it was not his duty to see to this all by *himself*. That was why he had a staff. The fact that he was here, the fact that he knew all those things about her was because...

He wanted to. Or couldn't help himself. Because he felt something deeper than duty.

They returned to the castle, and Katerina entered the shower feeling off-kilter.

You do not like olives. He'd said it forcefully, and she was quite certain she'd never mentioned it aloud before. It meant he had noticed that she always left olives on her plate when they were served to her.

He had to have noticed himself.

She'd always thought she was the only one who noticed anything.

She dressed for dinner, though she didn't feel particularly hungry. Instead she felt achy and unsteady, but she chalked this up to the emotional response to Diamandis somehow knowing her.

She did not need to verify that he could not have told her what Christos's favorite color was, or what Marias's food preferences were.

She walked out to the balcony where dinner was arranged. None of the dishes contained olives, though she knew Diamandis favored them and they were quite prevalent here.

At the center of the table was a bouquet. They were flowers from the wedding. On the day of, she hadn't thought much of them, but now she thought about how every year on her birthday he had presented her with a bouquet.

This was not unusual. Every member of staff received a token on their birthday. But that first birthday in the palace, he had presented her with a bouquet of hibiscus flowers.

"My favorite. How did you know?" In the moment, her words had been a joke—at least to her. She'd assumed he'd had some staff member call the florist and asked for whatever the florist thought or knew were her favorite.

But now she noticed that her bouquet contained hibiscus blooms. She looked up at him as he settled himself onto a chair.

"Who made the flower arrangements for the wedding?" she asked, failing to sound casual.

His eyebrow rose. "Beg pardon?"

"I was curious." She tried to smile, even though her heart pounded like she'd run a marathon. "Which staff member picked out the flowers for our wedding?"

"Portia ordered them, I believe. She sorted out most of the decor."

"But did she *choose* them?"

He frowned at her. "I suppose I made the final choice."

"Why?"

He shrugged, clearly finding her line of questioning bizarre. "No one else would do it."

"But why did you choose hibiscus?"

Diamandis's frown deepened. "I'm not sure I gave it much thought." He stared at the flowers, like… Like maybe he was realizing the same things *she* was realizing. All the things they'd paid attention to about each other without realizing why.

"They're my favorite," she said, with none of the humor she'd once used. This was a serious kind of confession. Almost as if it meant something…else.

He blinked. Once. An arrested kind of look swiftly flashed across his face before it was gone. "I'm sure Portia knew that."

But it wasn't Portia. It wasn't anyone else.

It was him. He knew about the olives, the flowers. He hadn't fired Christos because he'd been glad someone had taken care of her—no matter how furious he must have been at the way she'd left. He'd even gone so far as to have the man walk her down the aisle.

He *knew* her, and over the years he had cared for her in a hundred small ways, just as she had done the same for him. She'd seen everything she'd done as merely her job as his assistant—knowing how he took his coffee, making sure seating charts did not force him to sit next to those he found insufferable, buying him birthday presents she knew he would like.

He'd always displayed what she gave him somewhere in his office.

This was not simply *assistant* work, no matter how often she'd told herself it was.

"Are you going to sit?" Diamandis asked, eyeing her speculatively. "Did you spend too much time in the sun?"

"No, I'm fine," she said. She sat down on a chair and tried to breathe normally, but she was realizing too much at once for her to handle.

It didn't surprise her to discover that she might be in love with him. That thought had plagued her for years, but it was the reality of loving him, of being married to him, of actually thinking he might love her back.

He would never say the words. She knew this as certainly as she knew the color of his eyes. And still...she had to tell him. She had to tell him here, now, as all their years together seemed to knit together and create an overwhelmingly beautiful tableau of two people who cared about each other, even when they pretended they didn't.

"Diamandis."

He looked up from his plate, a patient look on his face. It would disappear. Everything would likely disappear when she said the words, and still she said them.

"I love you."

CHAPTER TWELVE

DIAMANDIS HELD HIMSELF very still. It reminded him, oddly and discordantly, of when he'd first heard those gunshots in the castle.

He was frozen.

Because everything would change from this moment on.

No. I will not let it.

"This is…unnecessary," he managed to say, perhaps more stiffly than he'd ever said anything in his life.

She laughed. He found that as incomprehensible as her words. "Katerina, this is quite—"

"Unnecessary. Yes, you said."

Love. She could not. She had convinced herself of this foolish notion because…because…she was impressed that her bouquet had contained flowers she liked.

My favorite. How did you know?

He still remembered that moment. It was years ago. She'd received her birthday flowers—a common token of appreciation he gave all staff who might enjoy such things—and she'd smiled so beautifully, so unguardedly.

My favorite. How did you know?

And he'd looked at the bouquet and made sure, every year, that she had her hibiscus blooms.

But that was simply…it was simply what his parents had taught him to do: take care of your staff and they will take care of you.

You're something like a family, his mother had once told them.

Diamandis pushed this thought away as far as it would go. "You've been in the sun too long." He imagined he sounded quite knowledgeable, certainly not as rusty as he felt.

There had to be some reason, some rationale. She couldn't really love him. This had come from absolutely nowhere and he was certainly not worthy of such a ridiculous emotion. Not from her. Not from anyone.

"So love is a delusion brought on by sunstroke?" she returned, still with a smile.

"It might as well be."

"Oh, Diamandis. Honestly! Do you really need to be so dramatic about it?"

"Dramatic?" Offense poked through whatever other feeling had gripped him. *Fear.* No. He had nothing to fear.

He was the king, and he'd already lost everything.

"Yes, dramatic. I love you. There's no need to try and discredit my feelings. They are mine. I tried to guard my heart—quite valiantly, if I do say so myself. But I could not, because my heart was already yours long before that night in your office." She moved to him and put her hand on his chest, looking up at him through inky lashes. "I love you, Diamandis. I know you will not reciprocate this feeling. I think you might even believe you're incapable of it."

Love. He had never anticipated this from her. Not today. Not ever. She was too practical. Too rational. She knew him too well.

He could not do this. He could not give in to her words. It would be weakness and could not possibly end well. This was the lesson of his life.

"You do not know me, Katerina." There was a darkness inside him that no one knew.

She shook her head. "I know you better than anyone, I think. And I love you. I'm not sure it was a choice, but it *was* my choice to say that to you. To accept it. To accept everything that has happened."

It was impossible. "You will not repeat this." Love was a weakness for people like him. And she did not know him. Not the way he knew her. She would never understand the dark pit inside of him.

"You do not get to command what I *say*, Diamandis. Or what I feel. If you wish to continue on as if you do not love me, that is *your* choice. But I have made mine."

"I am the king."

"And I am the queen. I will say it whenever I wish, but let us agree here and now—I do not require any response from you. These are my feelings, Diamandis. If they seem confrontational to you, that is your problem."

"I have no problems, *glyko mou*."

"Neither do I." She smiled sweetly at him, and he did not understand one second of this.

So he decided to ignore it. He ate his dinner, said nothing more of love, and when they were faced with their bed that evening, he gave in to his desires. Yet again.

He was not so arrogant as to promise himself he would not give in to her, time and time again. But his feelings? He would *never* give in to those.

They did not speak of the conversation for the next few days, and Katerina did not push it. She had said her piece—what more was there? Instead, she set about enjoying the rest of her honeymoon.

And it was truly a honeymoon. They swam every day. Diamandis liked to swim straight lines, clock his time. It was exercise for him. She preferred to splash him, sit in the shallow waves, dig her fingers and toes into the sand and watch the birds swoop down into the surf.

She could be practical and focused—it was what made her

a fantastic assistant. She enjoyed order, but she also enjoyed taking a break from it.

Diamandis should as well.

She could not allow herself to think she would get through his many walls. She could not believe a loving marriage was on the other side of this, but if she could get him to smile on occasion, if she could get his shoulders to relax when they were alone, would this be enough?

They ate lazy meals outside, the sun bronzing them both. He timed how long they spent in the sun, noticed how much water she drank, always so cognizant of her well-being. She knew that in his head it was about protecting his heirs.

She knew that in his heart, in a way he wouldn't acknowledge, it was about love.

If she did not drift too close to personal topics, or love, he would even laugh and converse with her and not retreat to a room on the excuse of *royal business* he could not specify.

So she did not push. She did not bring up those off-limit topics. She loved him in every way she could imagine—in their bedroom, on the balcony, at the beach. She let him have her in whatever ways he wished, given her ever-growing stomach.

Each day of that was harder than the last. The more she allowed herself to feel love, the harder it was to be met with endless stoicism, even though she knew it was the only response he'd ever give.

But she would endure it. Whatever it took. Because while he never said *I love you*, he also never said *I do not love you*.

One night, with the stars shining above them as they ate a cold meal on the grand patio that sloped down to the beach, soft music lilting through the air from the invisible speakers, she stood, held out her hand to him and said, "Dance with me, my king."

There were few things he refused when she called him *my king*. Still, there was a pause. That flash of distrust.

Because he did not trust her love, nor any casual showing of it. Passion he accepted, but gentleness he saw as the enemy. Her heart ached for what he must have suffered at such a formative age to make him so suspicious of a soft feeling.

But he rose and took her hand. He pulled her close as they swayed to the music, their bodies in perfect tune. He held one of her hands in his, the other slid down the curve of her spine. She knew what he wanted, but she couldn't help herself. She wanted something more first.

"I have been thinking about names," she informed him somewhat abruptly.

The hand on her back stopped its lazy trail downward. He did not drop her hand, but maybe that was because she held on so tight.

"There isn't much to think about. There is royal protocol to follow," he said stiffly.

"Yes, Zandra and I discussed the customs with her tutor. I am not opposed to the tradition exactly, but surely there's some wiggle room."

"I assure you, when it comes to the heir to the throne, there is no wiggle room," he returned in that supercilious way that tempted her into a smile. She should not find his arrogance amusing or attractive, she supposed, but what kind of king would he be if he did not have *some* degree of arrogance?

"The twins should have a name that *means* something. The tradition of naming them after grandparents seems foolish when naming them after your parents or siblings would be more meaningful."

"No," he said flatly, with icy coldness. He even took a step away from her, but she held on.

"Very well, but the custom includes the queen choosing one name from her own family for the fifth name, but there are no relations I'd particularly want our children to be named after.

And your royal names are so long. Perhaps we could just *skip* a fifth name."

"And have our children be singled out in the history books as the ones who did not get a full name?"

She huffed out an irritated breath. "Diamandis. Honestly. You cannot possibly think anyone would notice or care."

His gaze moved from the ocean to her, and he surveyed her as if she'd grown a second head. "They are the heirs to the Kalyva crown, Katerina. Every Kalyva citizen will notice *and* care."

She had not given it the consideration that he had, clearly. Even disagreeing with him, she was warmed by the thought he must have put into their children's names.

And she supposed she could hardly argue with his feelings on the matter. He was the royal one. He knew what kind of attention he would receive, and had always received, as heir. But… "They will still be children before they are heirs."

"You cannot separate the two things," he said, with a hint of ardentness that surprised her. "If you do…" But he didn't finish that sentence, just let it trail off into silence.

She got the impression his mind had traveled to something else. Some *time* else. He looked so troubled.

"If you do, what?" she asked gently, trying to bring him back to the present, since surely that emotional response meant he was lost in the maze of his past that he kept locked away.

"If you do not wish to choose a name from your family, simply choose one you like," he said, building back that formidable mask of his. "And if you insist on not doing that, we will have Zandra choose."

"Not you?"

His mouth firmed. He said nothing.

"You haven't even asked," she said softly, even though she'd meant to swallow down the words. The hurt.

"Asked what?"

She studied him. His gaze was on the dark ocean, even as they swayed to the music. Was he impossible to reach? "What sex the babies will be."

"I assumed the doctor would have told me if it was known." He did not look at her.

He did not step away from her.

She'd had no idea how hard it would be to exist in this place, where he neither reached out nor pulled away. Where she did all the work, and he was just...a statue.

"Do you not care to know?"

"Apparently you do not."

Katerina had considered whether she'd wanted to find out beforehand, but she liked the mystery of it. Now she studied Diamandis's face and wondered. "Would it make it feel more real to you? If you knew? If they had names already picked out?"

"I do not know what you mean. There is nothing to feel. They are real. They are why we are here."

He was being purposefully obtuse. Anger and irritation stirred within her, but that would not get her what she wanted.

What do you want? Because he has made it quite clear he will not love you.

She pushed that voice away. It sounded too much like her mother.

"You can feel one of their feet," she said, taking his hand and pressing it to where the baby's foot was lodged hard against her side. It was painful at times, but she reveled in tracing the shape of it, knowing it had to be an elbow or a foot. Perhaps a knee.

She wanted Diamandis to feel some connection to the lives inside of her. She needed in this moment to reach him in a way she hadn't yet.

He did not pull his hand away, though she felt his entire

body's resistance. But whoever in there was currently trying to kick his or her way out chose that moment to move.

Diamandis jerked in surprise, though he did not pull his hand away. "It moved."

"They do that. More and more."

He flattened his hand, moving with the roll of whatever body part was pushing against her. "It seems impossible," he murmured.

"Even though I can feel them in there, rolling about, it still seems impossible to me too."

She watched him and the emotions that moved over his face. She saw a kind of wonder that she felt so deeply herself it made her want to cry. She reached up and cupped his cheek with her hand. His gaze moved from her stomach to her eyes.

"They are real and they are ours," she murmured, needing to get that through to him. They were not heirs. Not problems to be solved. They were their *babies*. Maybe she could accept that he would never love her, if she could get him to love his children...

His hand stayed on her stomach, following the movement of whichever baby was snuggled up to her right side. When he pulled his hand away, she couldn't simply let him go. She reached out, pulled him close and pressed her mouth to his.

The kiss was soft, needy maybe. But not the sexual kind of need. It was the need a heart felt when it had been alone too long. When it had been unloved too long.

She knew. She had been both.

And so had he.

As if he read these thoughts, or felt that same connection, he broke away from her. He stepped away. "I cannot." He shook his head, turning his back to her. "I cannot do this with you any longer."

"Do what, Diamandis?"

He gripped the railing of the balcony, head bowed, as if the weight of it was too much to bear.

"We will return to the palace tomorrow," he said, his voice ragged. But he straightened and collected himself, put that mask back into place. "We will go back to the way you said you wanted it. A business partnership. Nothing more."

The pain was searing, but not just her own. That he would deny himself... That he could not allow himself any...moment of connection. She could drown in that pain, or she could see it for what it really was.

"You realize this only proves that you love me."

"I do not care what it proves, Katerina. This is how it must be."

"I will still love you, Diamandis." She tried to sound calm, but she was afraid it all came out sounding rather desperate. "You cannot push me away far enough to change that. It is not for you to change. I will love you. No matter what."

He did not look back at her, but she could see that his chin had come up as he released the railing. "We will both come to regret that," he said, then strode away, leaving her on the balcony.

Alone.

It was a painfully familiar feeling in Katerina's life.

CHAPTER THIRTEEN

THE FLIGHT BACK to Kalyva was quiet. Diamandis expected anger or some sort of reaction from Katerina, but she remained stoic.

Which was good. Stoicism was an excellent trait in a queen. She would need it in spades.

So why do you feel guilty? Again?

Diamandis scowled out of the window as the palace came into view through the clouds. He had done what he could stand. What was necessary.

He had felt the movement. A life growing inside of her. *Two* lives.

They will still be children before they are heirs.

He had been given that—a childhood. And he had not been prepared, not really, for all that had suddenly landed on his shoulders at fourteen. Though it was no fault of his parents, he could hardly allow the same thing to happen to his children.

The plane landed and Diamandis was sure this heavy, dark burden inside of him was simply relief at being back where he belonged. Where he could take care of his kingdom and get some distance from his wife.

Before they could even unbuckle their seat belts, Christos appeared.

"Your Majesty." He bowed to Diamandis, but his gaze darted to Katerina before he nodded toward the exit. "There are some…concerns about our arrival that I wish to speak to you about in private. Perhaps you and I can disembark first."

"And leave Katerina behind?"

There was something strange in his bodyguard's expression, something that put Diamandis on high alert. "All right." He stood, but so did Katerina.

"What is it you want to keep from me?" she demanded.

"Just a few details, Your Highness. No need to worry." Christos smiled at her. But she clearly didn't believe it any more than Diamandis did.

"Is something wrong?" Katerina asked, curling a protective arm around her belly.

Diamandis could still feel the baby move under his hands. *His* baby. Flesh and bone. But this was not the pressing matter.

"I assure you, Your Highness. This is simply...official palace business." Christos pointed Diamandis to the door, but Katerina grabbed onto his arm.

"I do not believe you, Christos. If there is something of importance going on, I should know about it. I am the queen. You can't just shut me out because it might be unsavory."

Diamandis should probably insist she obey, insist she do this *his* way and stay here while he and Christos had their private discussion, but he was tired and he wanted—*needed*—to be away from her.

You realize this only proves that you love me.

Maybe it did. Maybe he did. But that did not mean he had to give in to it. He simply had to get away, and letting Katerina have her way in this would make that happen more quickly.

"What is the issue, Christos?"

Christos straightened. "The queen's...mother has arrived at the palace. She has been..." Christos cleared his throat. "Difficult, at best, but the staff do not want to cause any sort of...dustup."

Diamandis was shocked. He had paid the woman a small fortune to keep her distance. It had been nothing to him to ensure Katerina's peace for the wedding. And now this woman dared show her face after taking what he had offered?

Irritation bubbled through him, but when he looked over at Katerina's pale face, something much darker threaded with irritation.

"Thank you, Christos, for the warning."

"She's quite adamant she won't leave without…" He simply trailed off.

"Without throwing a tantrum?" Katerina supplied coolly. "Yes, she's quite good at those. I'm sure it will be embarrassing." She turned her gaze to him, chin lifted, skin paler than he'd ever seen it. Her eyes seemed devoid of everything, including life. "I will handle this."

He was surprised at how her reaction lit a fiery fury within him. That anyone could have caused this reaction from her was beyond unacceptable. "No, *I* will handle this," he said firmly.

"She is my mother."

"Yes, and I am the king." He took her arm and nodded to Christos. "Have the staff move her to my office. We will be there shortly."

Christos bowed and left, and Diamandis led Katerina off the plane and into the car. She was silent as they made the short drive to the palace. When he helped her out and escorted her inside, he gave her hand a squeeze.

"You are exhausted and no doubt hungry. You will go to your rooms and rest. I will handle your mother."

"I know you think that because you stopped her from coming to the wedding you can handle her, but I assure you, Diamandis, you should not be alone with her. Trust me on this."

"How—"

"I don't need to know what you did to keep her away. I only know she would have been there to ruin things if someone had not interceded. I warned you about her, so it had to be you. But you simply cannot underestimate the damage she can cause."

"I am the king, Katerina. What can she do to me?"

But this was clearly no comfort. She shook her head. "I

will go with you. It is not up for discussion." And with this, she strode forward, even though he was supposed to lead her into his office.

But Katerina entered first, breeching protocol. A tall, willowy blonde stood up from the little settee. She adjusted her hat and turned to face them.

"Mother." Katerina greeted her with no inflection in her voice.

"There you are, Katerina." The woman wafted toward Katerina, arms outstretched. Diamandis watched in surprise as Katerina seemed to shrink in on herself. He'd never seen her look quite so...small.

She did not return her mother's hug, though she didn't fight it off either. She stood there stiffly, her green eyes oddly blank. He was not certain he'd ever seen her quite so disassociated from what was happening around her. It was a feeling, a coping mechanism he understood so well because...

He used it almost every day. And it was fine for him, *right* for him and his many sins, but he could not stand to see it in Katerina. He wished to whisk her away from this woman who would suck all the light right out of her.

Her own mother.

"Your Majesty," Ghavriella greeted, though she did not curtsy as she should have.

Diamandis said nothing in return. He needed to combat his temper before he dealt with this...contemptible creature.

"Is there a reason you're here, Mother?" Katerina said. There was no emotional response in her words, merely a kind of bland, detached politeness she'd often trotted out as his assistant when dealing with difficult people.

Including him.

That darkness deep inside twisted harder because no doubt he deserved it. He was no better than her mother.

You could be...

"I thought you both should know the truth, lest it come up at an…inopportune time. I don't suppose we could perhaps have this conversation over lunch?"

"I'm afraid that won't be possible today, Ms. Floros," Diamandis said before Katerina could respond. No matter what, he would not allow this woman to be under the palace roof any longer than necessary.

"Well, surely your wife's mother qualifies for a stay in the palace?"

"We will be quite happy to make arrangements for you." *But not in the palace* was left unsaid, but he could tell by the flash of temper in her green eyes—eyes that matched Katerina's—that she understood the slight.

"What truth did you wish us to know, Ms. Floros? I assure you, the throne will handle whatever it is with the necessary action."

"Action?" She let out a little laugh. "Well, good luck with that, I suppose. We can't all bag kings." Ghavriella sent Katerina a nasty little smile. "I guess you really *were* watching and learning, no matter what you said."

There was a flash in Katerina's gaze then, but it passed quickly. Banked. Hidden. Diamandis wished he could save her from whatever pathetic ploy this was, but she was determined to see it through. So he'd do what he could to hurry the woman along.

"I'm afraid Katerina and I have important business to attend to. Perhaps you'd like to share your information with Katerina's assistant, and we can go from there."

"I doubt Katerina wants her assistant to know who her biological father is," Ghavriella said, examining her nails.

He expected Katerina to have some reaction to that, but she seemed as detached and uninterested as ever.

"It *will* come out now, I fear. Better we control the narrative, don't you think?"

"You have claimed many men as my father over the years. Why should I believe it this time?" Katerina asked.

"Because it is a secret I have tried to keep by using those other men. No one wants their daughter's father to be a jailed traitor, after all."

Diamandis had been on the receiving end of many attempts at manipulation since he had been made king. In those early days, he had fallen for far too many. These days, he did not let them win.

But a cold dread coiled tightly within him. "Is this a generic traitor or...?"

"Thropos Palia."

Katerina thought maybe she'd heard that name before, but couldn't remember when or where. One look at Diamandis told her that *he* knew the name.

Katerina had been determined to be unaffected. It would just be another lie. Something to get under her skin—no, not even that. It would be something that would get Ghavriella the attention she so craved. From a powerful man.

The *most* powerful man.

She'd have to think about Katerina at all to care about getting under her skin.

"I mean, the king marrying the daughter of one of the men responsible for his parents' deaths is quite a story, don't you think?"

Katerina tried so very hard not to react outwardly. Her mother thrived on emotional reactions. But Katerina understood now where she'd heard that name.

Thropos Palia had been one of the ringleaders of the coup that had led to the murders of Diamandis's family.

"It sounds like you do not quite have your story straight, Ms. Floros. While Thropos was involved in the coup, he was hardly the ringleader," Diamandis said, calm as ever. "It also seems odd timing to bring this to my attention *now*."

Katerina was glad for him in this moment because she did not feel calm. She felt...too many things to name.

She turned slowly to her husband and tried to keep her tone very careful—anything to avoid giving her mother the reaction she wanted. Simply a truth. "It isn't true, Diamandis. No matter what she says, it's never true."

"I'm sure we could have it authenticated, Katerina. Thropos is still alive in some Grecian jail, is he not? A king such as yourself could get the necessary tests taken care of, and quickly, I assume."

Katerina whipped her gaze to her mother. It was a tactical mistake, but Ghavriella had never once, in all her many attempts at claiming paternity for her daughter, offered to have it authenticated. Usually when questions of validity came up, she wailed and threw massive tantrums.

Anything to get what she desired, which was always more about attention than money—though she quite enjoyed monetary payoffs as well.

"And for what reason would we have such a story authenticated?" Diamandis asked, raising a skeptical brow. "He is indeed in prison. Where he will stay. He has no claim over me or my wife, regardless. Pardon me if I do not say this tactfully, but it seems you are creating problems where there are none, Ms. Floros."

"But you are wrong." Ghavriella smiled. Coldly. "If you'll excuse me for saying so, Your Majesty. I told him. Many years ago. Back then he wanted nothing to do with her as she had nothing to offer. But now...well, now she has quite a bit to offer. Doesn't she?"

A heavy silence followed. Or Katerina assumed it was silence. Her heart thundered so hard inside of her chest it was a wonder the sound didn't fill up the room. A pain twisted inside of her, all the way down into her abdomen. She smoothed her hand over her stomach, trying to breathe through this.

She had warned him, hadn't she? Her mother ruined everything. Always. Even things that didn't need ruining.

Diamandis had already pushed her away. She was his queen in name only, and still her mother would take that little shred of what they'd shared and try to destroy it.

Diamandis took Katerina's hand in his, squeezing until she met his gaze. "It has been a long trip this morning. Go and rest." He brushed a kiss over her knuckles.

"She is lying." She had to be. But there was a small bubble of fear all the same. That this would be the time her mother didn't lie. This would hurt more than all the lies that had come before—and there had been many, many wounds before this one.

He nodded. "We will certainly get to the bottom of it." Then he gave her a reassuring smile and nodded to someone. She was ushered away by the staff, led upstairs to her rooms and fussed over.

One of her maids even tucked her into bed like she was a child. Only, her own mother had certainly never done such a thing in Katerina's memory. Her childhood had been about surviving Ghavriella's whims.

And now she was here to ruin everything, just like always.

But Diamandis had said he would handle it. That he would get to the bottom of it. No one in her life had ever offered those things, and she knew she was looking for heartache if she trusted it, but she was so exhausted. Everything hurt. She just wanted to cry herself to sleep.

So she did.

CHAPTER FOURTEEN

DIAMANDIS DEALT WITH Ghavriella in the same way he dealt with any scheming beggar. He smiled, he nodded politely, and then had her escorted to a private residence away from the palace where she would be waited on and watched while he decided what to do.

He wanted to check on Katerina, but that would have to wait. These allegations were serious. Diamandis did not think they were true—why not bring them up when he'd first approached her about staying away? But that didn't mean Ghavriella couldn't attempt to make them a problem, true or not.

Because what Katerina's mother clearly wanted was some kind of spectacle. Katerina had warned him of that herself.

So he met with Marias. He could not meet with the entire council over such a potentially dramatic situation, but his oldest adviser and a man who had counseled his father could surely be trusted to keep this information quiet and offer Diamandis appropriate advice on how to proceed.

He knew Diamandis's deepest secret, after all.

"This is a disaster, Diamandis," Marias said firmly in response. "You cannot be married to the daughter of a traitor."

Diamandis had expected disappointment and irritation. He had been prepared for these emotions he tried to avoid, but they were not his actions and he could not undo the simple facts.

"We do not know this as truth, and I am inclined to believe

it is deceit. However, we will verify if it's accurate. What I'm looking for is advice on how to deal with Ms. Floros."

Marias shook his head. "She is a disaster. You cannot be married to her."

Frustration welled up within Diamandis, but he shoved it away. "I *am* married to Katerina, regardless."

Marias said nothing, as if...

Diamandis laughed. Not kindly. "Are you suggesting I divorce her? Make my children bastards? Put such a black mark on the throne simply because a known liar and schemer wishes to make a splash? Do not answer those questions, because surely you cannot be so stupid."

Marias's eyes narrowed. "Be careful, my boy."

But the fact Marias could even *consider*... There was no *careful* to be had. "I am your king, not your boy, Marias. A man of your experience and steadfastness to the crown should know better than to overreact to a minor challenge. And anything that would change the fact that Katerina is my wife and the mother of my children is an overreaction."

Marias shook his head. "You are going to make mistakes because of this woman. You already are. Just like your father once did."

And we all know what happened to him.

Those words had always echoed in his head after a lecture, without Marias needing to say them. Because he had said them years ago, to great effect.

Diamandis could not fathom why this made him think of Katerina's reaction to her mother. The way she had tried so hard to be stoic but had been affected by the woman's manipulations all the same. She had endeavored to give no reaction, but in the end she had reacted in just the way Ghavriella wanted.

How could she not? They were very powerful manipulations.

For the first time, Diamandis considered Marias's words— not for how much he agreed with them or not, but for how much they were the appropriate thing to say to a fourteen-year-old who'd just lost his parents and siblings, regardless of his royal responsibilities.

Just like your father had become a curse, when his father had been nothing like Katerina's parents. His father had been good and noble and *kind*. More concerned about Diamandis the person than Diamandis the future king.

It had been wrong. Diamandis believed that… But Katerina's words were there. *They will still be children before they are heirs.* The feel of his child moving underneath his hand… Would being a cold, remote father really be better for those babies than being the father Diamandis had had?

Conflict brewed in his heart, like a great chasm widening down the center of him. He looked at the man he'd trusted for so long, desperate for a clearer answer. "What mistakes did my father make, Marias?"

"Excuse me?"

"I have been told, time and time again, since the day I became king that his death was his own doing. For trusting people, for caring for people. Maybe this is true, but I find I am of an age, about to become a father myself, that I require more information. When you all natter on about the mistakes my father made, which specific ones are you referring to?"

Marias sputtered. "He put his trust in all the wrong people."

"He put his trust in you. Are you the wrong people?"

Marias straightened himself, puffing out his chest. Anger flashed in his eyes. It was not the first time Diamandis had openly defied him. It would hardly be the last, but there was something about his anger in this moment that did not match the situation. That landed in Diamandis all wrong.

Before, Diamandis had only ever thought of himself. What he felt. What a failure he was to his father's memory, and how much he wished he could change the past.

When had that changed? When had he begun to look to

the future? When had he begun to look at his former self with some amount of separation—as if the boy he'd been was a different person to the man he'd become?

He had a very bad feeling that he knew the answer to that.

"Let us not worry ourselves about weakness. What we need now is strength, Your Majesty. That strength you were very good at until *she* came along."

She. As if Katerina were the problem. In fact, she was indeed proving to be a problem for Diamandis, but he did not like Marias taking the liberty of questioning the situation. Ever. He did not like any of the ways Marias was reacting today. In this strange new mindset, everything Marias said felt wrong. "What are you trying to hide by not answering a very simple question?"

"We have real problems, Your Majesty. Current, imperative problems to deal with. If the press catches wind of the identity of Ms. Floros's father—"

"She is no longer Ms. Floros. She is your queen, Marias. Should the press catch wind of it, then I will hold you personally responsible for the leak."

Marias snapped his mouth shut. He stood there, clearly at a complete and utter loss. Diamandis found he too was at a loss, because he did not know how to take counsel from this man now that he had all these new questions in his head.

"When you are ready to discuss the specifics of my father's weaknesses and mistakes, perhaps I will be ready to listen to your advice. As it stands now, I will act under my own counsel, and only my own counsel."

"As you did on the day of the coup?" Marias demanded.

Diamandis held himself very still. He never thought of that day, of that specific moment. He never thought of the secret only he and Marias knew.

But Marias liked to bring it up, didn't he? It was a form of manipulation, just like the ones Katerina's mother resorted to. Using the thing that hurt him to get the behavior Marias wanted.

You're overreacting. Marias has been a steadfast adviser who cares about the crown.

But Diamandis's father had cared about *him*.

"Perhaps, Marias. But I am no longer a boy of fourteen." *A boy.* He had been a boy. Katerina had said that, and he'd argued with her. He had been old enough to be a king, old enough to rule a country.

A child, she had said.

He found it hard to disagree with her, here in this moment. The adult that he was, making the choices that needed making for the woman he— For his queen.

"We are done here. If you cannot endeavor to find it within yourself to offer advice that protects the queen as well as the king, then perhaps it is time you resign."

Diamandis left Marias sputtering and arguing. There was too much to do, and yet… He wanted to discuss this with Katerina. He wanted to find out what *she* wanted to do. She had always given him sound advice as his assistant, and now as his queen.

It had been foolish to seek Marias's help in the first place. Marias's responsibility was to ensure the crown remained respected in the eyes of the people, not to consider Katerina's feelings.

If you are considering Katerina's feelings over what might happen to the crown, then Marias is probably right, and the results will be disastrous.

Just like your father.

It was that old curse he'd lived with as a weight on his shoulders, loving his father all the same. Marias being incapable or unwilling to point out one clear mistake had left Diamandis on shaky ground.

What was his father's mistake? Was it trusting his brother-in-law? Was it ignoring his council advisers? Was it loving his wife? His children? What was this grand mistake? Diamandis needed to know so he could avoid it.

He could not figure out what was happening inside of him, what was shifting. Why was he now questioning things he'd previously always seen as fact? In all his years as king, he had never once allowed himself to look back with compassion at the fourteen-year-old who had made mistakes that had ended people's lives.

But there was something wholly life-altering about Katerina wanting to share his burdens. Something...absolving about her loving him. How had she separated the boy he had been from the man he was now with a simple word on a balcony at Anavolí?

Seeing her with her mother, seeing the way she had changed into someone else entirely had thrown him. No, not someone else. A child. A child who had never been loved or protected. A child whom everyone had failed.

He wanted to reach across time and fix that for her, but he could not. If there was anything in this off-kilter moment he knew for sure, it was that you could not erase or fix the past. He could only fix this moment.

When he strode into Katerina's set of rooms, Stelios and one of Katerina's maids were cleaning up a tea service and whispering about something.

They both stopped immediately, curtsied and bowed. In the silence, Diamandis could hear the sounds of muffled sobs.

"The queen has requested some time alone, Your Majesty," Stelios said firmly.

Diamandis could hear her crying all the way out here, and she wanted to be alone? No. "You are both dismissed," he said, already across the room and pushing open the door.

Katerina was curled up on the bed, though she pushed herself into a sitting position when he entered. Her face was red, her eyes puffy, and her hair a mess.

"Please, Diamandis, leave me be," she said, her voice scratchy.

But it reminded him of a moment he'd long since forgotten, when he'd been small—so small his brothers had not yet been born. He had snuck into his parents' room at night after bedtime. He could not remember why all these years later, because what he'd stumbled onto had stopped him cold.

His mother had been sitting on the edge of the bed, crying into her hands. His father had gone to sit next to her, pulling her into his chest, holding her, whispering soothing words to her.

He'd been so shaken by his mother's tears that he'd crept back to his room, crawled into bed and forgotten whatever it was he'd wanted her for.

His mother had been crying, and it had shaken his world. There was so much that little boy had not known or understood, and there was all the pain and heartache that was yet to come. He did not like to think of himself as a boy. He had no trouble blaming the obnoxious teenager he had been, but not that scared little boy.

It was harder to blame the boy for all of life's cruelties.

All these years later, he didn't know what his mother had been upset about, and there was no one to ask. But maybe the point wasn't *what* she'd been upset about. The point was that her husband had sat down next to her and comforted her.

So Diamandis did what his father had done.

And look what happened to him.

He had been murdered in cold blood. But that was no personal failing. How had Diamandis spent all these years believing it was? Was Marias to blame? Himself? Something or someone else?

He did not know. He only knew he could not let his wife cry all by herself.

He crossed to the bed and sat next to Katerina, gathering her up into his arms. He didn't say anything—there was nothing to be said.

He just held her.

Katerina tried to get a hold of herself. Surely she could manage that so they could focus on the problem at hand and solve it.

But Diamandis had pulled her into the warmth of him. He held her there, stroking her hair. He didn't tell her not to cry.

He simply held her.

Which made her cry harder, but she didn't mind so much. Not here in this comforting cocoon. It was a kind of release to cry, but it was so much better to say all that had been bottled up inside of her with nowhere to go for so long.

"I wish I didn't have a father. Or a mother. I'd rather be an orphan. Which probably is very insensitive of me. I know how much you loved your parents and wish they were here."

"I did. I do. But my loss does not mean you should have to love the parents you were given."

"When we got married, and she wasn't there, I allowed myself to think I was finally free. I will never be free of her. As long as she can use me as a pawn, she will." Katerina forced herself to look at him, though her eyes were puffy and her head ached. She must look a fright, but she met his gaze because he had to understand. "And now you. She will never stop, Diamandis. No matter how many times you beat her at her own game. As long as she thinks she might get some scrap of attention from a powerful man, she will make your life hell."

He studied her intently for a very long time, no doubt cataloging all the stupid ways she'd fallen apart. But he stroked her hair one more time and wiped tears off her face with his own hands, oh so gently.

"I am the king of Kalyva. No one can make my life hell without my permission, *glyko mou*."

Well, that must be nice, she wanted to say. But she just rested her head on his shoulder. She was all cried out. Exhausted. But she knew from experience that now it was all out, she would be able to think about the situation rationally and clearly.

She would find the best option for moving forward. She would somehow save Diamandis from her mother's manipulations. She had to, for his sake. For her children's sake.

"Do not worry. I will gather myself and figure out a way to deal with her." She lifted her head and tried to pull away, but he did not let her go. He studied her.

"It is a weak threat at best. If there is a story here, it will be a blip. Even if it is true, you did not grow up with the man. One could hardly connect your life to his. But I do not think it is true, my queen."

"The truth won't matter if she has her way, Diamandis. Zandra did not grow up in the palace, yet we welcomed her home—and rightfully so. She is the princess, and she deserved to return home. But people did not care who she was or whom she had been raised by. They cared that she was your father's daughter."

"It is not the same."

"It will be, for some people."

"I do not care about some people. One cannot be universally loved. Even Zandra has her detractors. This is not the goal. The goal is to ensure that the nasty words are pointless and do not turn into violent dissent against us as a family. I do not believe something like this can cause the kind of uproar your mother would no doubt like."

"Maybe not, but she'll only keep trying."

"Your mother is a cruel, selfish woman."

She had heard this all her life. Maybe not in those words, but so many people had tried to impress upon her that while her mother was quite awful, it wasn't Katerina's responsibility to bear. Cut her mother out, let it all go.

She wished she could. She wished she knew how. Diamandis would expect her to be that strong, and she could not be. Still, she forced herself to nod and smile. "Yes, I know. I shouldn't let her get to me."

But Diamandis's mouth firmed in confusion. "Of course she gets to you. She has betrayed you, time and time again. This is not so easy to forgive and forget. Not from anyone, but especially not from a mother."

He spoke from experience, she could hear it in the conviction of his words. He would not speak like this if he had not been betrayed by someone close to him, which made little sense considering his family had been murdered and he let few others close.

"Who betrayed you?"

He sucked in a breath and let it out slowly as he looked away. "I have betrayed many."

She didn't think that was true, but even if it was… "Not me, Diamandis. Never me."

His eyes searched her face, and she held very still. She wanted this to be the moment he gave in. She wanted it to be the moment he understood what they could have if he'd only let his past go.

But she also knew, based on her reaction to her mother, that she had not let her own past go. So who was she to hope the same for him when his past was all the more traumatic?

"Why do you always seek to absolve me, Katerina? Even before, when you were my assistant. I am an arrogant, inflexible ogre, but you have always insisted I am better than I really am."

"You are a bit of an ogre," she agreed, chuckling when he glared at her. "And underneath all those quirks, I suppose, is a man who guards a soft heart because of a tragedy that marks him still. I absolve you because I know where these behaviors come from, and I know you could do better if you could realize that those past mistakes don't define you. I love the man you are, Diamandis, regardless of those things you think make your heart black."

"There are things I have done that you do not know about, that no amount of love can absolve."

She knew this. She knew that there were things, things from the night of the coup, that he held on to. Secrets he wished to take to the grave. Secrets that it would change him to confess. "Tell me," she whispered, desperate to be the one who got through to him.

But whatever moment she thought they might have dissolved before her eyes. His gaze went very blank. He brushed a kiss over her forehead, but there was no real warmth to it. Maybe kindness, but not love.

He gently pressed her into the pillow as he stood. "Rest, my queen. I will handle everything with your mother."

No one had ever said these words to her before. She looked at him, wishing it were that easy. Wishing she could believe him. Wishing…

He had comforted her. He had held her while she cried. When she thought he would have turned away or scolded her for such a foolish emotional outburst.

He'd absolved her too.

And if they could give each other that, maybe there was hope for them even in the shadow of her mother's accusations.

But only if Diamandis put down his heavy burdens, and that seemed even less likely than getting rid of her mother for good.

CHAPTER FIFTEEN

DIAMANDIS IGNORED MESSAGES from Marias over the next few days. Though most of them were apologetic, Diamandis had no time to decide how he felt about his adviser. About the things changing inside of him.

He had only one concern: to find a way to keep Ghavriella Floros away from Katerina for the rest of her days, regardless of the veracity of her claims.

So he consulted a man he knew could outmaneuver an operator like Ghavriella and was relieved when not two days later Lysias came to him with answers.

"It pays to have a billionaire for a brother-in-law," Lysias said, not waiting for Diamandis's ever-missing assistant to announce him.

Diamandis looked up from his desk as Lysias sauntered in. Though Lysias was irreverent and obnoxious within the palace walls, he could be counted on to act with decorum in public, and Diamandis was learning to accept this.

Slowly.

"I should hope so," Diamandis returned, which caused Lysias to chuckle as he lowered himself onto the chair opposite Diamandis's desk.

"Ghavriella and I have a friend in common—your former royal doctor."

Diamandis scowled. The former royal doctor had been prepared to falsify Zandra's DNA results for Lysias and had consequently been relieved of his position.

"It appears they both met with Thropos in the prison in Athens *after* the wedding. I leaned on the good doctor a bit and he admitted Ghavriella was attempting to forge your wife's paternity—something Thropos was willing to be in on, hoping it might gain him some measure of clemency."

Something dark and hot welled up inside Diamandis. It was an old feeling of betrayal he often tried to squelch with ice lest it get...out of hand. His hand curled in a fist as he tried to manage his temper. "Did she really think she'd get away with this?"

"I don't see why not. It's not so difficult, particularly if the person you're doing it to doesn't know what you're up to. I had once planned to forge Zandra's paternity. I would most certainly have gotten away with it."

"You say that with such ease, as if you don't feel guilty in the least."

Lysias shrugged as if the betrayal he'd almost enacted mattered not at all. "I don't."

Diamandis would never understand the man who had once been as close as a brother and was now his actual brother-in-law. "Why not?"

"Well, for starters, I didn't go through with it. If I held myself accountable for everything I thought about doing or almost did, I would be depressed all the time. Oh, is that your problem?"

Diamandis spared Lysias a cool look, but the man only smiled wider. It had eased some of the anger inside of him though. The scheming woman had been caught in time to do no further damage to Katerina.

This time.

"She wished to cause a ruckus. No doubt she will try again."

"Yes, but if she's attempting to forge records, it's likely she knows who the father is and wants no one to know. I know you have men on her, but I can put one of mine on her for the foreseeable future as well, should she seek to find a new target when she realizes this one will not work."

Diamandis nodded. It was something, and while he could keep one of his own men on the case, Lysias tended to have a staff that was a little bit more…rough around the edges. Which was exactly what he needed.

But this made him think of the doctor, of Marias's questionable loyalties, the councilmembers he'd had to dismiss—all the men who'd used him in the past under the guise of caring for the Kalyvan crown.

"Am I such a bad judge of character?" Diamandis muttered, not having meant to say it out loud. But the past few months had been a constantly humbling exercise in sifting through all the staff members he thought had been on his side purely because they had been on his father's.

"You are in a difficult position, Diamandis. People have used the memory of your parents for their own ends, including myself. Anyone who truly knows you doesn't blame you for this."

"Perhaps *someone* should blame me."

"I think you do that enough all on your own."

Diamandis had had quite enough of Lysias. He nodded to the door in dismissal. "Thank you. This will indeed protect the Agonas legacy." Diamandis considered it a dismissal, but Lysias continued to sit there, studying him.

"You wish to protect your *wife*, not your legacy."

"She is the queen of that legacy."

"Hmm."

Diamandis stood. He needed no more of Lysias's poking. He had the information he needed and he would use it to protect his legacy, which just happened to include Katerina. "That will be all, Lysias."

"Unfortunately, there is one more thing I'd like to discuss with you as a member of the council. Marias isn't happy."

"And I am not happy with Marias, so I suppose that makes us even."

"He's been spending an inordinate amount of time sucking up to Zandra these past two days, and in ways that make me realize previous overtures since her return might not have been quite so genuine. He claims his reasons are lost time and wishing to see his beloved king's children supported and happy, but there is something I do not trust about the man."

"You yourself told me Marias was not one of the people who would have voted against me."

"Yes, but only because there was no one to replace you. Now that Zandra is confirmed to be the princess, it feels... questionable. Especially considering he doesn't approve of Katerina."

"He doesn't approve of *you*."

"But he does approve of my bank account."

Diamandis shook his head. He already had his own doubts about Marias, but how could the man he'd trusted for so long be working against him? "Marias was like a father to me. I would not have succeeded without him."

"But did he step into that role because he wished to support you, because he loved you like a son, or because it gave *him* power?"

Diamandis could only stand there in silence. His own suspicions had been drowned out by his feelings. By his loyalty to Marias. He had talked himself out of those very questions without ever answering them.

But Lysias voicing them...

"I am an outsider, of course. I have no idea what happened that night aside from what little I saw on my end of it. It is Zandra's belief that you are the only one who fully knows what happened."

No, not only him. Marias and him. The secret keepers. *For the good of the kingdom. If anyone found out...*

Lysias did not take Diamandis's silence as a hint to leave. He just kept at it. "But Marias's words and attempt to ingratiate himself with my wife make me wonder if that is true."

Diamandis's head whipped up to glare at Lysias. "What do you mean?"

Lysias stood. "I don't have details or evidence or information. I have vague suspicions. Just keep in mind, Diamandis, that secrets have more power than the truth ever will. And it has taken some time, and some doing, and your sister's love, to get to a point where I have forgiven you for the role you played in my parents' murder. Because you were a boy who had been traumatized, and the adults who should have cared for you instead used the tragedy to seize power."

Everyone kept talking about how much of a boy he'd been, but the kingdom had expected him to become king. He had been expected to rule. How could everyone now decide he'd been *just a boy*?

"I got rid of everyone who had a hand in the aftermath. Anyone who voted for your parents to be executed without sufficient evidence. No one involved is still in my employ."

"Are you so certain?" Lysias asked gently.

Gentle enough it felt like a dagger. Because no, he was no longer certain. He just was too torn up to do anything about it. And what kind of king did that make him?

Just like your father. Who will die this time?

"As I said, I do not have any proof, but I could get it," Lysias said carefully. "With your permission."

"And without it?"

"I would not stick my nose into it. As long as there seems to be no danger to my wife. It is not my goal to upend your life, to discover if Marias is an enemy, unless you want answers."

Diamandis tried to keep his breathing even, tried to work

through all that roiled through him. He didn't want to poke into it. He wanted to tell Lysias to forget all this foolishness. Marias had been good, had gotten him this far. Secrets weren't powerful. They were *necessary*.

But it was as if Katerina were here beside him because he knew what her advice would be. What she would tell him to do.

She had never trusted Marias.

"You have my permission."

Katerina had spent some time after her mother's appearance wallowing. It turned out that wallowing as a queen was quite nice. People waited on you. You didn't need to get out of bed in order to eat your weight in cookies. If you said you didn't want to do anything, you didn't have to do anything except sit in a cocoon of blankets and pillows and feel sorry for yourself.

But she couldn't indulge herself for long. She was too used to *doing*. Restlessness pushed her out of bed and in search of work. Stelios was far too competent an assistant to leave her much to do, so she'd cornered Tomás and commandeered some of *his* assignments.

She didn't think Diamandis would approve, exactly, but he had made himself scarce after her emotional breakdown and who could blame him? She'd likely be able to do some work to help out Tomás without Diamandis ever—

"Your Highness? The king," one of her maids said at the door.

Well, *that* figured.

Diamandis strode into the little sitting room where she'd been doing her work. He frowned at the tablet in front of her. "What are you working on?"

"Well, I needed to occupy my mind with something, and Tomás left your appointment log in such a mess that I took it upon myself to fix it."

"You are not my assistant any longer," he said, though not as disapprovingly as she might have expected.

She turned in the chair and gave him an arch look. "I am better than Tomás."

"A tree would be better than Tomás."

Katerina shook her head, trying not to smile. "Why do you keep him around?"

"I have not had time to hire a new assistant. No one compares to you, Katerina."

His words shouldn't please her as much as they did. "I could still handle *some* of my old duties. Obviously it wouldn't do for the queen to answer phones or deal with dry cleaning, but I could handle some things. I could certainly attempt to train the young man."

"Soon you will have enough to handle," he said, nodding toward her stomach.

She looked down at it, placing her hand over the bump. "Yes, I suppose." She rubbed at the little twinge she felt there, and then looked at her husband. "I haven't seen much of you."

He sighed. "I tasked Lysias with tracking your mother's activities to see if she's been up to anything, and it appears Lysias discovered that she was attempting to forge a test that would prove you were Thropos's daughter, but it is not true."

Katerina did not move. It wasn't a surprise exactly. She'd been trying to accept it so she could handle it if it turned out to be true, but it was just another of her mother's cruel ploys. "I see."

"It seems she has been planning this since the wedding. The traitor is not your father, Katerina. She cannot cause harm to you in this way."

Katerina looked blankly at the wall behind him. She wished this were a relief. "She will keep trying."

He moved, then surprised her by kneeling before her and taking her hand in his. "And we will keep proving her wrong," he said, as seriously as any vow. "Lysias has put a man on her. We will watch her until her end days to ensure she has no power to harm us."

She blew out a breath, surprised at how shaky it was. She kept thinking she knew how to deal with this, but… He was the epitome of a mixed signal. And she knew that this was because he *was* a mixed signal. Inside, he was fighting a raging battle between what he truly was and what he thought he should be.

But no one had ever taken care of things for her before, and she did not know how to pretend that didn't matter. So she leaned forward and pressed her mouth to his. Just gratitude.

And love. "Thank you."

She expected him to withdraw. Comforting her was one thing, born of his innate need to solve a problem. But this moment was more than simple comfort.

She sat on the chair and he kneeled on the floor, which put them nearly at the same height. They were so close that their noses practically touched and he studied her as if she were a puzzling mystery when she knew she was not.

The true puzzle lay inside of him. And instead of putting it together, he kept pushing the pieces farther and farther away from each other.

He laid his lips on hers once more, gently. Not as if she were fragile, but…sacred. And he kissed her just like that, until she was shaking and blinking back tears.

"I thought you wanted to keep your distance," she murmured against his mouth, because while she might not resist in this moment, she could hardly ignore the fact that he'd been so quick to run away before.

"I suppose neither of us is very good at sticking to our guns when it comes to each other."

She wanted to smile, but it was different. He wanted her in his bed. She… "But I love you, Diamandis."

He did not pull away. There was something…different about

him. She wished she could believe he was changing, but she wanted him to so desperately that she was afraid it was only wishful thinking on her part.

"You do not know me, Katerina," he said, so very seriously.

Which was absurd. "I worked as closely with you as anyone for years. I know who you are, Diamandis." Just as he knew her, whether he'd ever admit that to himself or not.

"But not what I have done."

He sounded so tortured, so burdened. She laid her palm against his cheek. "Then tell me. Don't walk away. Don't push it away. Tell me, Diamandis. It will change nothing."

CHAPTER SIXTEEN

DIAMANDIS'S HEART FELT as if it were trying to escape his chest. It beat hard and painfully, and it was difficult to breathe.

He wanted to tell her. He wanted to lay his sins at her feet. She was always absolving him, so why not for this too?

Please, for this too.

Lysias's words about secrets having more power than the truth rattled around inside of him. *Power.* Had everything always been about power while he'd just been trying to survive?

If he told her, she would know the secret that Marias had told him no one could ever know. But maybe if she knew it, she would stop asking more of him. Maybe *she* would keep her distance since he could not.

Maybe she would finally understand why he could not be the husband and father she clearly wanted him to be.

Maybe she will love you anyway.

This, he knew, was the most insidious thought of all, because he wanted it so desperately to be true. But he was kneeling in front of her like some kind of supplicant. Carefully, he rose. "I do not mind you doing some of Tomás's work if it pleases you," he said.

Had he really expected that to work? He didn't know, but she was on her feet, gripping his hands so he couldn't retreat farther without yanking away.

"Tell me what you have done," she said earnestly. "Tell me what you think is so horrible that I could not love you. Prove to me that you are a man who does not deserve love and happiness, Diamandis, because I will never believe it if you do not disabuse me of the notion that you are a *good* man. *I* have only ever seen the good."

She looked like such a *warrior*. Like she would take on armies, pregnant and furious. Beautiful and fierce.

He could not deny in his heart that he loved her, and likely had for a long time. He had tried—valiantly, he liked to think—to escape it. But the feeling was there. It was a poison he could not eradicate. A poison that would likely kill them both.

Love always did.

So he would have to kill the love. Even if it meant unearthing his darkest secret that he swore he would never tell a soul.

"I have committed murder."

Katerina did not gasp. She did not drop his hands and step away. She simply looked at him as though he'd said *I can fly*.

"Dearest, what on earth do you mean?"

Dearest. When he should be dear to no one.

"You and Zandra have been telling me over and over that I was *just a boy* when I became king. That I was a victim to the circumstances, though I lived and everyone I loved died or disappeared."

"Yes," Katerina agreed. "Because that is the truth. Just because you weren't murdered doesn't mean you weren't traumatized."

"And what about those who cause trauma?"

"Diamandis—"

"I murdered my uncle. Should I be excused for that too, simply because I was fourteen?"

And still she did not step away. "If the history books are true, he is the one who killed your mother."

"Vengeance, then. Vengeance is the excuse?" he demanded harshly, because she was not reacting as she should. She kept seeking to excuse him, when there was no excuse.

Marias had told him that there was no excuse. That it was an evil thing he had done. That he should have handled it better. That as king, he was not worthy, but he would have to lead anyway. Marias would show him the way.

Maybe not in those exact words, but that was the message Diamandis had received, and he did not know how to go back and view it any differently.

Katerina inhaled and then led him over to a bench where they could both sit. She drew him down next to her, never letting go of his hands. "Tell me what happened. The whole night. Let it go, Diamandis."

He withdrew his hands from her, though he did not get up and leave like he should. "I can never let it go."

"Just tell me," she insisted. "Walk me through it. Maybe I'll find a way to hate you yet."

He scowled at her because she was treating this...all wrong. She didn't think she would despise him, but she would. She had to. Marias had said...

He did not know if it was strength or weakness to confess all, but it would solve the problem of Katerina. He was sure of it. She would keep her distance and then things could go back...

He did not know what they could go back to, but he also did not know how to resist her any longer, so he would have to give her the tools to hate him. *Please hate me.*

"My parents were shot—"

"No, Diamandis. The whole thing. From the beginning."

The beginning. He did not wish to remember or relive the beginning. That it was a day like any other. That his mother had talked excitedly at breakfast about going to Anavolí the following morning. That he had sulked because he felt he was too old and mature to splash about the beach with the children.

He did not tell Katerina those details. Could not bring himself to voice them. Achilleas and Rafail kicking each other under the table. Zandra whining about not liking eggs, and his father grinning at his mother while telling Zandra that they were very special eggs. Magical eggs.

And then any magic had died hours later.

He had been silent too long, but Katerina did not push him. She sat there, shoulder to shoulder with him, waiting patiently.

"If there was any tension beforehand, I did not know it." That was the beginning. That to him it had been a day like any other. "Zandra had been put to bed, and Achilleas and Rafail were supposed to be asleep, but had been sneaking into each other's rooms. I often did any extra studying at this time, so I was in my room. One of my father's guards and one council-man came in unannounced. They said there was some cause for alarm, and I was to go with them. I wanted to gather my brothers and sister, but they assured me they already had men on it."

He had believed them. He hadn't had a doubt in his mind that they were telling the truth. He had followed, like a lamb to sacrifice, but not slaughter.

That had been for everyone else.

"We heard gunshots before we got to the basement, but they said I would be meeting my parents and the children down there. Everything would be fine."

He could still remember how afraid he had been, because he'd been so certain he was being led to join his family in a place of safety where they already were.

"When we arrived downstairs, no one was there. No one would explain. They just told me I was safe and locked me in a room." He still remembered the dark. The soft echo of gun-shots he could only barely make out. The feeling of not know-ing what was going on, or where his family was.

Left alone and in the dark.

Katerina slid her arm over his back, rubbing from side to side. "I suppose they were trying to protect you."

"I thought so. It was Marias who found me, who let me out. He cautioned me to stay where I was, not wade into the chaos, but he could not tell me where my family was. I had to find them."

Then you must take this. To protect yourself. Diamandis had not questioned why Marias was carrying a gun. He'd questioned nothing because he'd only wanted to find his brothers and sister. For some reason, in that moment, he'd been so certain his father would be fine. He was strong and invincible, and Diamandis was like him, so he would go and save his siblings like their father was no doubt saving his mother.

But he'd only found death and blood in the boys' room and nothing in Zandra's. "The boys were already dead."

Katerina rested her head on his shoulder and said nothing. In the silence it felt like the only option was to go on. To see it through. To tell Katerina what he'd never told anyone.

"Zandra appeared to be missing, so I set out to search for her. I thought maybe she was with my parents, so I doubled back to their rooms. I heard..." It haunted his dreams. His waking hours. His everything. "I heard my mother crying. Sobbing. Begging."

Bang.

Then nothing. Just what had felt like an endless moment during which Diamandis had not been able to move. Maybe if he had...

"A man all in black, carrying a large gun, stepped out of my mother's room. He turned the gun toward me, but... I shot him first." Sometimes, in his memory, it didn't make sense. The man had paused, giving Diamandis the opportunity to best him. "I shot him."

"He was going to shoot you," Katerina said.

Sometimes I wish he had.

"I left him to die."

"What were you supposed to do?"

He stood abruptly and paced away. "You do not understand." She didn't. She couldn't. If it had been anyone else, perhaps...

But Katerina was so calm. "No, I do not understand. I cannot imagine what it must be like to be forced to take a life, but you *were* forced. No one would have blamed you for this. Why would you turn this into a secret?"

But he could see Marias's face as he'd pulled back the mask of the gunman. The shock. The horror. It hadn't been just anyone.

It had been Diamandis's uncle.

Everyone will blame you for this, Diamandis. They will think their king is a murderer. This will not do. Your father never would have done something like this. He was weak, but you...

"It was my uncle. My mother's brother. I killed my own uncle."

"That does not change the circumstances around it, Diamandis. You defended yourself against a man who was going to kill you. Who killed your parents and was part of the group that killed your brothers. I'm sure that was... Of course you would feel guilt, confusion. I understand your feelings at having been forced to do such a thing, but I cannot understand why you would blame yourself for this?"

This must be our secret, Diamandis. For the good of Kalyva. For your father's name and legacy.

"Marias..." He hadn't been able to find the words. The memory seemed to have changed on him, turning Marias— his savior, the man who'd led him away and told him what to do when he'd been lost—into a villain.

Katerina's expression immediately changed. "Do not tell me that old fool had something to do with this. Oh, *that* would make sense. The ridiculous hold he has over you!"

"He has no hold over me. He did not lock me in that basement room. He let me out. You do not understand. I later learned, *from* Marias, that a few council members used the coup for their own gains. They could have stopped it, but instead my uncle gave the violent mob the means to invade the palace thinking he'd have some sway over me. Those council members who'd claimed they'd saved me, who placed the blame on Lysias and his parents, they didn't want the monarchy to be overthrown, but they wanted someone they could control. A boy. Me."

"I'm sure they did, but who says Marias didn't want to as well?"

Diamandis looked down at Katerina blindly. "But he didn't work with them. He worked *against* them. He helped me get rid of those who sought to grab power, who blamed staff for their own defections."

"Which gave him the highest place on your council and cleared out any rivals he might have among your advisers. It won him not just your trust, but your devotion. You *owed* him. He kept your secret and convinced you it was a secret no one would understand, when I think it is something that anyone would understand. Who benefits from it being a secret, Diamandis?"

"The kingdom," he said, because that had always been the answer he'd been fed. The answer he'd felt. He wasn't worthy because...

Katerina rose and crossed over to him. Her eyes were wet but her words were strong. "Think, Diamandis. Think beyond the scared, frightened boy you were, to the reality of the situation. No one would have blamed you for killing any man in self-defense, let alone the one who killed your parents. Regardless of who he was to you."

"I don't..." But he'd been having doubts about Marias, hadn't he? Could it be that the man he'd trusted was as bad as those early political graspers?

But he had killed a man. He had been too weak with grief to see through the machinations of his father's men.

Men, when you were a boy.

Are you still a boy? Are you too weak now?

He looked at Katerina, who had never led him wrong in all her years in his service, and now was his queen. Who'd never put her own needs or wants above his. He trusted her more than anyone. She understood his responsibility to the kingdom, and his father's memory. She had always been correct about things, even when he hadn't wanted her to be.

Because she was a marvel. A wonder. Beautiful and strong. *His.*

But if he loved her, then history would repeat itself. He would make concessions for her, more than he'd already made. And someone would sneak into the cracks, as his uncle had.

For a moment, he could see the pools of blood in his brothers' room, but instead of the boys, it was Katerina's lifeless body he saw. The image was fictional, but if he gave in to this, it could become real.

"Perhaps you are not wrong," he said—or tried to, but his throat was closed so tight it was hard to push out the words. "Perhaps my oldest confidant is in fact a traitor to me and the crown."

He could not trust a feeling, could he? Not when it came to anyone.

"Thank you for this clarifying discussion," he said stiffly.

Confusion chased over her face and she reached out for him. "Diamandis…"

He sidestepped her arms and began to back away toward the door. "I think you are quite right about many things."

She continued to follow him as he backed away. "I'm glad, but—"

"Marias will be dealt with swiftly as my concerns about his loyalties have been growing lately. What you've shed light on makes it clear we cannot move forward with him in my employ."

"I think that's the right course of action, but—"

"It will be a messy political business and I will be very busy. I think it's best if you return to Anavolí, with the medical team of course. Perhaps Zandra would like to join you."

Confusion was being replaced with frustration, and a little flash of anger. "I have been by your side while you've dealt with many a political mess, Diamandis. I will hardly run away now just because I am your wife or because I am pregnant."

"Politics is no longer your duty, nor is standing by my side. Your duty is to birth our children. Best if it's done away from the political storm, I think."

"Birth...? You want me to spend *months* at Anavolí without you? Have our children over there while you remain here?"

"It would be best. If I do not see you before you leave, I bid you farewell." He gave her a stiff bow.

"Diamandis, you cannot honestly—"

But her words abruptly halted because he had walked away. And never looked back.

CHAPTER SEVENTEEN

KATERINA HAD FELT many things in this palace, but confusion to this degree was new. She had *no* idea what had just happened. What Diamandis was thinking. What was behind this decision.

She was angry, yes, but she could not begin to fathom what had happened during that conversation. She had expected him to be angry and upset. She would not be surprised by self-blame or recriminations, because the men who should have protected him had manipulated him instead. They had brainwashed him into this warped vision of himself.

And still, under all that, he was a good man. No doubt forged by the parents who had loved him, and each other, so very much.

Her heart ached for Diamandis, that they had been ripped from him so cruelly. All because of a throne. All because of men and their greed for power. So many different attempts at getting what they wanted through manipulation and violence and cruelty.

Katerina rubbed the side of her stomach. The twinges had been getting more frequent, but the nurse had assured her that as long as they were not consistent, or more painful, everything was fine.

Go to Anavolí. Alone. What was he thinking? That she would *abandon* him?

But she was so tired. The pregnancy was taking a toll, and if there was going to be upheaval, then maybe…

No. She couldn't leave him. He wanted it, so she couldn't do it. She finished her work on Diamandis's appointments, ignored another uncomfortable twinge, and then asked Stelios to have a lunch brought up.

When he announced its arrival, he also announced Zandra.

"The princess has requested to eat with you, if you are up for it."

"Of course."

Zandra entered ahead of the staff with a rolling tray of food. She plopped down into a seat near Katerina. "I have heard that Diamandis wishes to send us away."

Katerina smiled at the blunt way Zandra put it, though she didn't feel particularly smiley about it.

"That is his current grand plan."

"Are you going to go along with it?" Zandra thanked the staff members once they had lunch set up, then dismissed every single one of them. Katerina waited for everyone to leave before she answered Zandra's question.

"I don't want to go, no."

"Lysias is not too keen on letting me out of his sight this far along," Zandra said, running her hand over her belly with a fond smile. "And I am not eager to leave him either, though I do want to go to Anavolí. I think I might remember it. But seeing it in person would clarify it for me. Perhaps we should all go there once Marias is dealt with."

It sounded so nice. The four of them—the family—taking a vacation together. Katerina had never imagined such a thing. And her children would have a cousin their age. They would have a true family. A kind, loving family.

What about their father?

She knew it was foolish to wish for a man to change, but surely when he saw them…

But he'd confessed everything to her, everything he thought was shameful about himself, and left. Coldly. He wanted to send her away. Anytime he felt something, he put distance between them.

It would likely be the same with the children. Perhaps worse, if familial memories made being with them even more distressing and emotional.

"Aren't you hungry?" Zandra asked when Katerina had still not made herself a plate.

Katerina shook her head. "No. The babies have been quite active in there and it doesn't do much for my appetite."

"You must keep your strength up though." She put her own plate aside and bustled around the cart making a new plate. She handed it to Katerina. "I will not leave until you've eaten at least half."

Katerina had to swallow down the lump in her throat. It was such a strange thing to be so looked after, so taken care of. Diamandis had comforted her after her mother's cruelty, and now Zandra, pregnant herself, was fussing after her and making plans for future family vacations together.

"Zandra, do you understand your brother?"

"Oh, not at all," Zandra replied emphatically. "He's a complete and utter mystery. I think Lysias is able to shed some light for me sometimes, but the man makes no sense." Zandra took a big bite of her slice of cheese. "Except, to me, it is clear Diamandis loves you very much and has for some time."

"*Is* that clear?"

"Perhaps not to you. But… I know he loves me, no matter how annoying he finds me. So I can recognize it in him, even if he can't. I can see the way he looks at you, talks to you, treats you. There is a kind of…fear in it."

If she had said anything else, anything about love or joy or sweetness, Katerina would have scoffed. But it *was* fear she saw in him, so how could she argue with Zandra? "Every time I think I have made some progress, he only pushes me farther away. I am getting tired of it. Perhaps I should accept that he only has push inside of him. Maybe…" Her throat closed and a lump formed there, but she managed to speak on. "Maybe I should go to Anavolí. Give him some space. He can deal with all this and…" Katerina trailed off because she felt so tired. So wrung-out. Maybe space *was* the only option.

"Well, it would give him time to miss you, maybe."

"You're very supportive, Princess. I don't know how to express how much I appreciate it." She rubbed her stomach, where that same old pain was lodged. Maybe one of the babies was kicking a nerve.

"Are you all right?" Zandra asked.

"Just one of my twinges."

"Twinges?"

"A little pain, here and there. Nothing consistent. Nothing to worry about." Still, this one wasn't going away quite so quickly.

"I don't have any twinges. And you're quite pale."

"Well, you only have one in there."

"Katerina, you should consult your doctor before we make any more plans to leave, don't you think?"

"We? I thought Lysias would not want to be separated from you."

"He won't, but I'm hardly letting you go by yourself. You need a friend. Lysias will stay here and talk some sense into my stubborn brother, and I will go with you. We'll take a little break for a few days and come back next week and sort everything through. Doesn't that sound good?"

"I would not count on anyone getting through to your stubborn brother if I cannot."

Zandra smiled at that. "You have always been the best at getting through to him, that is true. But maybe a little distance, a little missing you is just the ticket. Now, you stay right here. I'll have someone fetch your doctor and then we'll begin making plans, all right?"

Katerina nodded, overwhelmed by Zandra's kindness and warmth. "You don't have to go with me, really, Zandra. I appreciate—"

"I won't hear any more about it," she said, heading for the door. "We're sisters."

Sisters. Katerina had a sister. A family.

Finally.

Diamandis spent his morning going through historical records he'd never before allowed himself to consult. He got the full picture of who Marias had been to his father.

And who he had not been.

Then, he planned. At first, he did this alone, and then, in a moment he would have once called weakness, he consulted Lysias.

"I think giving him his full retirement is too kind," Lysias said, brooding, which was rather unlike his usually irreverent brother-in-law.

"We will call it insurance over a kindness." Diamandis knew he should feel *something*, but mostly he felt numb.

The man he'd trusted was a grasping traitor. Not so overtly that he could be sent to jail, but just insidious enough to make it clear he had never been on Diamandis's side.

Ever.

A staff member announced Marias's arrival.

"Would you like me to stay?" Lysias asked. Diamandis saw it for what it was: a kind, supportive gesture between friends. Family.

When they'd been boys together, they had been close friends. Like brothers. It had taken nothing at all for Diamandis's advisers to convince him that Lysias was a traitor to the crown, deserving of any bad thing that happened to him.

"I have not been a good friend to you."

"I think the same could be said about me. Even if my attempt at revenge did reunite you with your sister, I assure you it was purely accidental."

But it did not feel like an accident. It felt like a second chance. "I would like this to change."

"Well, Diamandis, we aren't just friends anymore. We are brothers."

Brothers.

Diamandis nodded. "I appreciate the offer to stay, but I feel as though this is something I'd rather do on my own. Perhaps…perhaps we should have a family dinner tonight. The four of us."

Lysias bowed. "Gladly, Your Majesty."

And he only sounded a *little* mocking as he said it. He took his leave and Diamandis gave the signal for Marias to be sent in.

Marias entered Diamandis's office with a stiff body and an inscrutable expression.

"Have a seat, Marias," Diamandis instructed, taking his own seat behind his desk. He looked down at the older man and began. "I have a few questions to ask you to determine how we should move forward at this current juncture in our working relationship."

"Very well."

"I have taken many things you said at face value over the years, Marias. I have trusted your guidance, your discretion, and your dedication to the crown."

"Yes, and you did not question it at all until you let your feelings for a woman cloud your reasoning."

Diamandis raised an eyebrow but did not let his temper take over. "Perhaps," he agreed equitably. "I'd like to discuss the coup with you."

Marias's mouth firmed. "As you wish."

"If you could go back and change anything, would you? Before, during, after?"

Marias's eyebrows drew together in confusion. "I would do whatever it took to steer your father toward an action that would have saved his life."

"Like what?"

"What do you mean?"

"What specific action would you have advised him of that you feel would have saved his life?"

Marias blinked. "Why, not trusting your uncle, of course."

"And why didn't you advise him of this in the time leading up to the coup?"

"I did. Your father did not listen because your mother begged him to give her brother a place on the council."

Diamandis would once have believed this. He looked down at the notes he'd taken as he'd gone over records. "Unfortunately, I have gone back over the council logs from the months leading up to the coup and there is, in fact, not one word spoken against my uncle by you, or anyone else." Love had not poisoned his father, not by any stretch of the imagination. "No evidence anywhere of you counseling my father to listen to his brain, not his heart."

Marias huffed and fidgeted in his chair. "They were private conversations."

"There is no evidence of any meetings you would have had with my father privately. You were merely an alternate at this time, an associate council member who spent more time in administration than in one-to-one face time with the king. Is this not true?"

Marias seethed and said nothing. Diamandis, on the other hand, felt nothing but ice all the way through.

"It makes sense why you might have wanted to ascend those ranks. Why you thought, with someone else on the throne, you might have a better chance at a higher position."

"You have let your little *wife* poison your mind."

Even then, Diamandis's temper did not jump, because of course this was not true. There were many things his feelings for Katerina might have affected, but this was not one of them. "Katerina has always been most reasonable, most levelheaded. I can see why this would be difficult to see as she has never cared for you, but she never let that sway her. I cannot say the same for you. Quite an emotional response for a man so determined I should have none."

"I do not know what it is you wish to accomplish, or what the queen or your brother-in-law wish to accomplish, but if you let these...these...*schemers* have some influence over you—"

"Neither Katerina nor Lysias has done anything but support me these past few weeks. *Me*, yes. Not the crown."

"You *are* the crown."

"I have endeavored to be, it is true. I thought I had to be that and nothing else, and perhaps I should be. But when I was fourteen, I was a boy. My parents and brothers were murdered, my sister lost to the chaos. And you, you saw an opportunity to twist and turn the whims of fate to give yourself power over me." His temper was licking at the edges of his words, but still he sat and watched Marias turn an impressive shade of purple.

"I have advised you in leading the kingdom well. I helped you oust those who blamed the wrong people, the people who sought to control you. I did what I saw fit, and I will not apologize for it."

The biggest issue was that Diamandis believed him. Marias had done what he saw fit. However, that did not make it right. "Maybe you did. But it was wrong, and it was cruel. To use my shame against me, my fear against me, my *grief* against me, all so you could determine how I would act." Diamandis looked at the portrait of his father beyond Marias's head. "I have endeavored to be a stronger king than my father, but in doing so I have made many mistakes. Including keeping everyone so far away that many were ready to vote against me just months ago."

"Not I, Your Majesty. I have always supported you."

"Because you have control over me. But no longer." Diamandis met the man's gaze. He iced the temper away and spoke calmly and clearly. "You are relieved of your position."

"You cannot fire me. I am an elected member of the council."

"You will resign."

"I will not," Marais said, punching a fist on the arm of the chair.

His temper, his panic, only aided in Diamandis keeping his calm. "You will if you wish to keep your retirement pension from the crown. You will retire, and you will leave. Otherwise, I will present what I have to the council in a bid to cancel every last benefit, honor and recompense you've received." He offered Marias a bland smile. "Do I make myself clear?"

"You will live to regret this."

"Maybe. There is always a chance of that. But I assure you, you will regret more if you should ever try to undercut my position, if you continue to make Zandra uncomfortable and my brother-in-law suspicious, if I ever hear you having said an unkind word about my wife. I will make sure you lose it all. Whether that's tomorrow or twenty years from now."

"This emotion, this insanity, it will be your end, Diamandis. Just like your father."

For so many years it had been the weapon used against him, but Katerina had given him armor for it. She had heard all the horrible things he'd been taught to believe would ruin him and loved him anyway. Absolved him, like always.

Just as his parents had always done, and no doubt would have continued to do if they had lived. They would not like the man he'd become—cold and remote and dedicated only to the crown.

But they would love him. And in that love, there was always hope. Hope that he could change, could be better.

Diamandis looked from his father's portrait to Marias's angry face. "Perhaps it will be my end, but I have finally realized I would rather live like my father for a short while, than live like the man I've been until I am elderly." He rose. "You are dismissed, Marias. Unless you'd like to throw a fit at the next council meeting and lose everything. It is up to you."

Marias sat for long past what was proper. "Your king is on his feet, Marias."

Slowly, with a face turning an ever-darkening shade of purple, Marias got to his feet. "You will regret this, and I will live out my retirement laughing at your misfortune."

"Very well." Diamandis smiled at Marias. "Do not forget to bow to your king, Marias."

The man scowled but bowed stiffly, then stalked out of the room. Diamandis knew he would have to keep an eye on the man, but the threat of losing his retirement payout was a large one. He would be bitter about this, but Diamandis did not think danger would befall them from his actions.

Marias simply wasn't brave enough to do anything in the light. Or to do it to a man rather than a boy.

Diamandis breathed in, surprised to find he felt...lighter. There was an odd sadness to the whole thing, because he had spent so long trusting Marias, but there was also something freeing in learning. Growing. Changing.

Loving.

Because he loved his wife. His sister. His brother-in-law. The family they had scrabbled together out of the ashes of tragedy. And if that meant an end to him ruling Kalyva...

So be it.

He would go to Katerina now. He would tell her he loved her. He would ask her to stay. He would endeavor to be the man his father had been. Not only a king, but a man behind the crown as well. He would change. With her help, he could. She believed in him, and wasn't she always right?

Brighter than he'd felt in decades, he skirted his desk and strode for the door, but before he reached it, it burst open and Zandra ran in.

His heart turned to ice.

"Diamandis! It's Katerina." Zandra's face was pale, and she reached out for him. "You must come at once."

CHAPTER EIGHTEEN

KATERINA HAD NEVER known such pain. Such fear. The twinges had quickly become something more, far more by the time the doctor arrived.

Still, the doctor spoke calmly as she insisted Katerina lie down and get comfortable while she checked her out. She murmured some things to a nurse who hurried out.

"Are the babies okay?" Katerina asked, worry clogging her throat and making the words hard to push out.

"We're going to get some instruments that will allow us to monitor them, but right now they're fine. It looks like you might be going into labor. Early labor is quite common with multiples," she said matter-of-factly.

"It's too early."

"It is early, but not necessarily too early. We will do what we can to stop the labor and go from there." The doctor patted her hand reassuringly. "You have the best team to help you, Your Highness. Your job right now is to rest and try to relax. I believe the princess has gone to find your husband."

Diamandis. She wanted him here. To hold her hand. To hold *her* as he had after her breakdown over her mother. But...

She knew what this would do. Any hint of loss would push him farther into his shell. He would see it as his own failure, no matter how idiotically stupid that was. "No. Please, I don't think... I don't want him in here."

The doctor was clearly perplexed by this, but she nodded.

"Very well. I'll go and tell your assistant. You just lie here. Just breathe, all right?"

Katerina nodded and tried to do what the doctor said. Breathe in. Breathe out. Put the pain somewhere else. Put the worry *anywhere* else. There was pain and it was scary. All of this was scary.

She wanted someone, and if she let Diamandis in on any of it, what would be left? A tear slid down her cheek, though she would have thought herself stronger than that.

The doctor returned. "If you do not want your husband in here with you, is there someone else? Someone you can talk to in order to keep your mind off things?"

A bubble of panic welled up inside of her. *Alone. Always alone.* But that wasn't true because Zandra had said she'd go to Anavolí with her. "Princess Zandra, if she can. If she isn't busy. I..."

The doctor nodded and made a motion to a maid who quickly disappeared.

Another wave of pain swamped Katerina, and she felt something was wrong. Just wrong. Like something was leaking out of her. Like the pain was stealing her ability to breathe.

"Something's wrong," she managed to rasp. It was all wrong.

The doctor's expression got very grim. "Katerina, I need you to stay with me. I need you to fight."

There was a grayness swimming around her vision. Fight. She knew how to fight. She'd always had to fight. But this was too much. Too much pain and too much weakness. A blackness was creeping over her.

She heard her name. She heard instructions, but she stopped feeling any of the pain. She was going somewhere else.

And in the blackness, all she wanted was her husband. He had promised he would take care of things, hadn't he?

But even the king could not take care of this.

* * *

Diamandis ran through the palace, shoving his way into Katerina's rooms only to be met with Stelios and a maid blocking his way.

"Move."

Stelios shook his head. "The doctor has said the queen does not wish to see you at the moment."

It might have hurt, but he didn't feel it because fear was clawing through him. Zandra was not one to exaggerate and she had said that Katerina was not well.

"You cannot ban me from my wife's side. I am the king."

But Stelios did not budge and looked ready to fight him if he pressed. "The doctor was quite clear."

Diamandis was ready to take on such a fight, but a great commotion arose around them, both from inside the bedroom and outside the sitting room. Doors flew open and medics with a stretcher rushed forward while a nurse came out from Katerina's bedroom.

It was chaos.

And in the confusion of the chaos, Diamandis ran forward into Katerina's bedroom. The doctor shouted orders from Katerina's bedside.

Her hands were bloody, and Katerina was still—too still—and pale.

Gone.

The blood was a visceral reminder of a past he'd worked so hard to forget. But he'd foreseen this, had he not?

Katerina and blood.

This is what love did.

"Your Majesty," the doctor said once she had instructed the medics. "I have called emergency services to transport the queen to the hospital." Katerina was moved to a stretcher. Lifeless.

"She is…dead?"

"No," the doctor said, following the medics carrying Katerina away from him.

Blood. Blood. Blood.

"Meet us at the hospital, Your Majesty. We are working hard to save all three lives. I will explain everything once she is stable."

Then they were gone. And he was in a room alone with bloody sheets.

Until his sister ran in. She was breathing heavily, her arm curled around her own rounded stomach. She should not have run. Lysias was not far behind her. Diamandis stared at both of them, neither quite making sense in the context of everything.

Blood.

"What has happened?" Zandra asked. He barely felt the hand clutching his arm. "Diamandis?"

"I have sentenced them to death."

"What?"

"Come, Diamandis," Lysias said firmly, taking his other arm. "Let us go to the hospital and wait for an update."

He did not remember anything from that moment on. It was all a blur and suddenly he was in some sterile, private waiting room of a hospital. Life and death did not care if you were royalty. Tragedy did not care if you had already seen your fill.

Lysias and Zandra took turns at his side, reassuring him that things would be fine. That the longer it took, the better prognosis there must be. If she was dead, he would know.

But they were wrong. He knew this in his soul. Even when the doctor explained that Katerina had gone into early labor. That there were complications, but they were working to deal with them.

He was not allowed to see her, so he knew.

She was dead. He was certain of it. They were all dead because he had loved them. Because he had wanted to make it all real.

And this was his payment for such foolishness.

Zandra sat next to him after the doctor left and took her hand in his. She squeezed. "Have faith, brother," she said.

"There is no faith. They are dead. It is my fault. I loved them. I have sentenced them to death."

Zandra did not move away, but he could tell she didn't understand. Couldn't. She thought he was overwrought, and he was, but Zandra could never fully understand.

"You sentenced them to death…by loving them?" she repeated. A question.

"Yes." A curse.

She was silent for a few moments, though she did not let his hand go. "Do you really think you have such power?" she asked incredulously. "Your emotions control *science*? The human body?"

He sighed heavily. "Fate, Zandra. Fate controls everything. And mine is death."

She scoffed. She *scoffed* at him! Here in the middle of yet another bloody tragedy. "We make our own fate, Diamandis, or I would have been dead in a ditch long ago. But I fought. I survived the unthinkable. It was so bad I don't even remember it, nor do I want to. And I am here, back where I rightfully belong, because I do not care about fate, and neither should you. You are the king of Kalyva."

He shook his head. She couldn't understand. "Our father…" But he could not say the words. The words Marias had programmed into him long ago. Emotion. Connection. The enemy. The beginning of an end.

And why might he have wanted to isolate you from any kind of love?

He swallowed against his tight throat. Could he really believe that when the loss of everything he'd wanted to love was so evident?

Zandra uncurled his fist, and then she put a picture in his

hands. It was an old snapshot of their parents. Not a royal portrait, but one of the more casual family snapshots. Not in their royal finery, but two regular people smiling at the camera.

His mother was pregnant. With him.

"I have been carrying this with me, trying to remember them. Sometimes I think maybe I do. A word. A flash. But I guess I'll never know for sure it is them."

He tried to pull his hand away, but Zandra pressed the picture more firmly into his palm.

"Not so long ago, I looked at their portrait in your office and asked them to show you love. Maybe it's a silly thing to believe, but they brought you Katerina. Your babies. And nothing you do or don't do will change the outcome of what happens in this hospital. But you are the only one who can choose faith, love and future, Diamandis. Not fate. Not tragedy. *You*."

He said nothing. What was there to say? His parents were dead, even as they looked back at him from this picture.

Zandra brushed a kiss across his cheek. "Lysias and I are going to go in search of food. We will be back soon."

She was lying. They could have any staff member bring them whatever food they wished. She was giving him a moment alone.

With this picture of his parents.

He stared at it, no matter how his mind screamed at him to put it away. To put this all away. To freeze himself out once again.

But his heart ached for them. For the love and support they'd given him in their too-short lives. Zandra had said she'd looked at a portrait and asked for something. She'd asked for love for him, which was foolish. Silly indeed.

But he had certainly been given it. Katerina had been steadfast in her love. Never pulling it back. Never questioning it. Katerina believed in love, in him.

Just as his parents had.

He stared at their long-gone faces.

"Not a day has gone by where I have not missed you," he heard himself say, as if he were outside his body, watching some other person talk to a picture of dead people.

"I do not know who to beg, or to which deity I should supplicate myself. I only know you and your love. Please, please... I need her. I need *them*. If I am to be punished for loving, punish *me*." He pressed his forehead to the picture.

He heard the door open, but did not look up, assuming it was Zandra and Lysias. But someone cleared their throat.

When he looked up, it was the doctor. He leaped to his feet.

"You have two sons, Your Majesty. They are both healthy, needing only moderate interventions." She smiled at him.

He could not take this information in. Not yet. "The queen?"

"She is still fighting. You may come and meet the babies."

"I wish to see Katerina."

The doctor nodded. "Once she is stable." And she led him out of the room, down a maze of hallways, to a room with little plastic cribs. There were two nurses who curtsied upon his entrance.

The doctor guided him over to two little enclosures. "Baby A is five pounds, five ounces," the doctor said, pointing to the infant on the left. "Baby B is four pounds, eight ounces, and we're monitoring him to make sure everything is going well. But they're both healthy, Your Majesty. Very well developed for being early."

Diamandis could only nod. They were so small, wriggling and moving about, one with his eyes open—a dark, inky blue. The other with his eyes closed as the wrap of blankets he was swathed in wriggled.

"In regard to names, are the royal customs to be followed?" a nurse asked.

He looked down at the two babies. Sons. *His sons.* So tiny.

So helpless. With little shocks of dark hair. And Katerina was not here to see them. To love them.

Love.

"No," he said, surprising even himself. He had been given twins. Just like his brothers. Names that deserved long, happy lives.

"This is Rafail Youkilis Lysias Agonas," he said, as the newborn scrunched up his tiny face. Diamandis looked down at the one still being monitored. "This is Achilleas Alexander Balaskas Agonas."

"I will make sure it is noted right away," the nurse said, scurrying off.

"Would you like to hold them?" another nurse asked.

He would. Every cell of his body ached to hold his children, but he needed their mother with him.

"I need to see my wife. The babies should be with their mother."

The doctor nodded solemnly. "The queen will be under for a while longer yet. Once she wakes, we will have a better idea of her prognosis. But she is strong, Your Majesty. And we will do all we can for her. You can go and see her now, and we will bring the babies in when we can."

Diamandis nodded. "Very well. Take me to her."

More hallways, bright and white. Curtsies as he passed. Whispers. But nothing mattered. Only Katerina.

He was ushered into a private suite and there she was on a bed, in the midst of a cold hospital room. Pale. Lifeless. So many monitors hooked up to her beeping and flashing, but he could see the rise and fall of her chest.

Breathing, alive. Not blood. Not death. Alive. If she breathed, there was hope. Zandra had told him to have faith. After seeing his children, he felt compelled to have all the faith in the world. Just for them.

"She will be asleep for a while yet, Your Majesty. The

nurses will check periodically. You are welcome to stay as long as you like. We will work on getting the babies moved in here as soon as it is possible."

Diamandis nodded and waited for her to leave before he crossed to the bed. He knelt down next to it on the hard floor and took Katerina's limp hand.

He did not waste time, because time was always fleeting.

"I love you. My queen, my heart. If… I will be everything you need, I promise. A husband. A father. I will love you all more than life itself, but you must come back to me."

Please, he said silently, thinking of the picture of his parents in his pocket, *bring her back to me*.

CHAPTER NINETEEN

KATERINA COULD NOT quite make sense of where she was or what had happened. Something beeped obnoxiously. She felt... fuzzy and heavy and out of sorts. She could not remember where she was.

Had she made it to Anavolí? Was she ill? The babies... The babies...

But then she heard a cry. A baby's cry. And she forced her eyes to open.

The room was dim, and it hurt. Moving at all felt wrong, but there in a corner was a man. Not just any man.

Diamandis, tall and regal but looking exhausted, held a small bundle of blue in his arms. The room spun a little around him and she had to close her eyes, but when she managed to reopen them he was still there. With a baby.

Her baby. *Their* baby. She looked around wildly until her eyes dropped to the two hospital bassinets. Two. *Two.*

"Diamandis..." But her voice didn't come out as more than a rasp.

His eyes flicked to hers immediately and he crossed to her. His gaze tracked over her. "You are awake."

"Are they okay?"

"Yes. We have two sons, Katerina, and they are doing just fine despite the early entrance." He tilted the child in his arms so she could see his precious face. Dark blue eyes, tiny, tiny nose. A shock of black hair. Hers. Here. Alive.

But she was in this bed. She was…all wrong, and Diamandis looked at her as if she would disappear simply by the looking. "Am I going to die?"

He lowered himself into a chair that was positioned next to the bed. He adjusted the baby into a one-arm hold. He took her hand with his now free one. "No, *glyko mou*. I am the king and I will simply not allow it. You will be quite well and we will go home soon. Together."

She swallowed against so many things. Bits and pieces came back to her.

I will love you all more than life itself, but you must come back to me. Surely she had dreamed such passionate words? Surely it was all a dream?

"*We* will go home together?"

"Yes, I'm afraid I will not allow you to be out of my sight for quite some time." As if to prove it, his gaze tracked over her face. Then he blinked and forced his mouth to curve.

"You will be happy to know I have broken royal tradition, per your request. You told me they should have names that mean something. So I have named them after my brothers. And they only have four names, for why shouldn't history wonder why our children are so special that they will break tradition?"

She searched his face. Something had changed. She could feel it, and yet…

"You will have to wait to hold them, I'm afraid," he continued. "But it is a good enough reason to get strong, is it not?"

"Diamandis…"

"Achilleas is asleep, but he is off all the machines. I will bring him over when he wakes. But they are both fine, strapping young princes."

"Diamandis…"

She didn't know what she wanted to say, but something in his whole being simply crumpled. He lifted her hand to his mouth and pressed a kiss there, pure anguish in his gaze.

"I thought I had lost you. I could not bear the thought," he said roughly.

Her husband. Her sons. Her life and her heart. Everything was fine, and she would get better. She would make sure of it. "Everything will be all right."

He nodded and kissed her palm once more. "Katerina, I love you. I thought this was a curse. I thought I had doomed you, but Zandra reminded me that while I might be king, I do not have that kind of power."

Katerina had hoped to hear those words someday, but had mostly convinced herself they would not come, even if she knew he felt such things. Even if she thought she could get through to him. She wanted to reach out and touch him, touch her son. *Rafail*. But she couldn't seem to move in the ways she wanted.

"I suppose I had to visit with death to get this kind of confession," she said, struggling to shift in the bed.

He shook his head, his expression pained. "Because I am a fool. But I will... I will endeavor to forgive myself for the mistakes I have made, because they were made with an honest heart, if nothing else. I will endeavor to make no more, but I suppose this is life. We make mistakes. But I will never mistake this simple fact again. I love you. I want you by my side. I want to be your family, to raise our children as my parents raised theirs. Our children will know love and faith and...everything we wish them to. Together."

Tears tracked over her cheeks, but her husband wiped them away. Love and faith. Together. The family she had known they could be, if only she could get past his walls.

And now here they were. Not perfect, because she *had* nearly died, but this was life. Never perfect, but beautiful nonetheless.

Diamandis pressed a kiss to her forehead, and when Achilleas awoke, he brought the boy over so she could see him. So she could see both of her beautiful sons, in their handsome father's arms.

She had been alone so long, and now she had a family. One made of love and hope. She was proud to be the queen of Kalyva, and she was good at it. But nothing in her life would ever match the joy of loving her husband, and the pure perfection of being a mother.

A month later, finally healed and strong, Katerina requested something of her husband he almost refused to give.

"I cannot allow it, Katerina." He even glared at her.

But she sat in the chair, feeding the insatiable Achilleas, who had grown faster than anyone expected. Diamandis held Rafail, pacing, as was often the only way to get the energetic boy to sleep.

"I will see my mother, Diamandis. If you will not bring her here, I will go to her."

"Over my dead body."

Which was how, a week later, she was seated in a receiving room while Christos ushered her mother into the room. Diamandis stood behind Katerina's chair, and the boys were in another room in the care of Zandra and Lysias.

"I thought I was to meet my grandchildren."

"I made it very clear you would not be, Mother."

Ghavriella sniffed. "Then I do not understand why I am here after being treated so rudely the last time."

"You mean when you came here to lie about the paternity of your daughter," Diamandis said coolly.

Ghavriella rolled her eyes. "Honestly."

But she could clearly come up with no retort.

"I asked you to come here today, because as much as I would love for you to be a part of my children's lives, some things are going to have to change. I will not let your toxic behavior touch my children."

"Yes, I know. Such a terrible mother! So *toxic*. Feeding you, clothing you, getting you to school and back. How very *dare* I?"

Diamandis made a noise, but Katerina held up her hand. She had expected this behavior. She and Diamandis had both begun to see a family therapist to deal with their issues. They were acting today on her advice, and the driving need Katerina had felt to stand up for herself. To draw this line in the sand.

To be the adult in the situation. She did not expect the same of her mother, but she wanted to behave in a way that made herself proud.

"When you are ready to truly build a relationship with us, to join us in family therapy—"

Ghavriella made a sound of shocked outrage.

"—I will be happy to attempt to mend fences. But this is my line in the sand. You will play no part in my children's lives without this step. No matter how you scheme."

"Utterly ridiculous! I'm sure everything is all my fault. Well, I don't need you or your royal children, Katerina. I am doing just fine on my own."

Katerina did not react. She nodded at her mother. "Very well. But understand this—I will protect them from everything. I do not know why you could not do the same for me, but I understand now, truly, how very much not my fault that was." Which was why she had truly needed this moment. She had not expected her mother to change, but she had needed to bring that realization full circle.

"You have married a king and you whine at me about protection?"

Katerina kept her bland smile intact, then nodded at Christos, a signal they had agreed upon. "That is all, Mother. I hope someday you can find it within yourself to change."

Christos offered Ghavriella his arm. She looked at it, then at Katerina, then at Diamandis. She whirled away and stomped out of the room without an escort. Christos bowed to them, then followed her out, no doubt to make sure she actually left.

Katerina let out a long, slow breath. She did not feel good, but she felt settled. She had made her choices, made them clear, and shut the door without locking it forever. She had little hope her mother would change, but she would always allow for the possibility.

And she would never let her mother turn her into a small child again. Her sons and her husband had given her a strength she had not known she possessed. She would protect them from everything.

That was what today had been about. Proving that knowledge to herself. No one, not even her mother, could ever turn her into someone she did not want to be again.

She rose and Diamandis held out his arm. She took it and they silently exited the room.

"You seem content," Diamandis murmured as they walked down the hall to where their babies were. He held her arm as they walked, a thoughtless gesture these days, but that was what made it all the more beautiful.

"I am." She smiled up at him. "Sometimes you need to make a stand and create boundaries for yourself." She paused, reached up and fitted her hand to his cheek. "And you can because there are so many people who love you standing behind you."

He pressed his mouth to hers. "Always, my queen."

EPILOGUE

DIAMANDIS WATCHED HIS wife chase after their sons in the sand on the beaches of the castle at Anavolí. His childhood best friend carried his niece on his shoulders while Zandra, heavily pregnant yet again, looked on laughing at Rafail's and Achilleas's toddling antics. Here at Anavolí, where Diamandis and Zandra had once done the same as children while their parents watched.

His family. His love. His heart.

He still had the picture of his parents that Zandra had given him in the hospital two years ago. He showed it to the boys often, so they would know the grandparents they'd never gotten to meet and the uncles they had been named after. He even spoke of them with Zandra, to the point where she felt like she did remember more than she had before.

He no longer let that old grieving love be a curse. He considered it part of all that love he was so lucky to have, every day.

Lysias handed his daughter over to Zandra and began to chase the boys so Katerina could take a break. She walked over to where Diamandis stood.

"It's a shame we have to head back tomorrow," she said when she approached. "But it will be good to get back into a routine. The boys will be feral if we do not."

"I do not mind them feral."

His wife censured him with a sideways look. "Of course *you* do not," she said, making him chuckle.

She sighed, watching their boys, joy lighting her face. "You know, the doctor is quite certain it would be safe to try for more." She slid her arm around his waist and leaned into him.

He kissed her temple. "Whatever you wish, my queen."

And he would find a way, for all his years, to give her—to give their entire family—exactly that.

* * * * *

COMING SOON!

We really hope you enjoyed reading this book. If you're looking for more romance be sure to head to the shops when new books are available on

Thursday 20th July

To see which titles are coming soon, please visit

millsandboon.co.uk/nextmonth

MILLS & BOON

MILLS & BOON®

Coming next month

THE MAID MARRIED TO THE BILLIONAIRE
Lynne Graham

"You took me by surprise… You shocked me," she muttered unevenly, struggling to catch her breath. She was thoroughly unnerved by the sensations that had shimmied up through her taut body and then down again to a place that had ignited with a burst of warmth, mortifying her to the very bone.

Enzo released his breath on a measured hiss. "Relax. For a moment, I was tempted. But nothing is going to happen unless you want it to. I'm attracted to you. I know I shouldn't be but I'm not perfect. In fact, it seems I'm all too human. But you are completely safe with me, *piccolo mio*."

"Maybe I don't need to be safe…with you," Skye said uncertainly. "You make me feel things I didn't expect to feel. You make me curious. I know, like you said, I shouldn't be in these circumstances. But the truth is, I am and I'm attracted too."

"So…" Enzo breathed a touch raggedly. "What do you want to do about this?"

"We—we could try a kiss…just *one*," she stressed.

Continue reading
THE MAID MARRIED TO THE BILLIONAIRE
Lynne Graham

Available next month
www.millsandboon.co.uk

LET'S TALK
Romance

For exclusive extracts, competitions and special offers, find us online:

f MillsandBoon

🐦 @MillsandBoon

📷 @MillsandBoonUK

♪ @MillsandBoonUK

Get in touch on 01413 063 232

MILLS & BOON

THE HEART OF ROMANCE

A ROMANCE FOR EVERY READER

MODERN

Prepare to be swept off your feet by sophisticated, sexy and seductive heroes, in some of the world's most glamourous and romantic locations, where power and passion collide.

HISTORICAL

Escape with historical heroes from time gone by. Whether your passion is for wicked Regency Rakes, muscled Vikings or rugged Highlanders, awaken the romance of the past.

MEDICAL

Set your pulse racing with dedicated, delectable doctors in the high-pressure world of medicine, where emotions run high and passion, comfort and love are the best medicine.

True Love

Celebrate true love with tender stories of heartfelt romance, from the rush of falling in love to the joy a new baby can bring, and a focus on the emotional heart of a relationship.

Desire

Indulge in secrets and scandal, intense drama and sizzling hot action with heroes who have it all: wealth, status, good looks…everything but the right woman.

HEROES

The excitement of a gripping thriller, with intense romance at its heart. Resourceful, true-to-life women and strong, fearless men face danger and desire - a killer combination!

To see which titles are coming soon, please visit

millsandboon.co.uk/nextmonth

JOIN US ON SOCIAL MEDIA!

Stay up to date with our latest releases, author news and gossip, special offers and discounts, and all the behind-the-scenes action from Mills & Boon...

 @millsandboon

 @millsandboonuk

 facebook.com/millsandboon

 @millsandboonuk

It might just be true love...